TO HELL WITH Bad Decisions

A HELLION HARLOT NOVEL

WRITTEN & ILLUSTRATED BY
NIKKITA BELL

Cover, interior artwork, and graphic illustrations by Nikkita Bell.

Nightwish – Disco Script Retro Font by Fortune Co, commercial license.

Line Editing by Megan at Thorns & Roses Co.

Copy editing by Alexa at The Fiction Fix.

Proofreading by The Cauldron Author Services & The Moody Scribe

ISBN: Paperback - 979-8-9919244-3-6

ISBN: Hardcover - 979-8-9919244-4-3

First Edition, December 2025.

Published by Nikkita Bell and Scorpion Script Press.

www.nikkitabell.com

THE HELLION HARLOT COLLECTION

BY NIKKITA BELL

#1, THE BOMBSHELL DEVIL'S ADVOCATE

An October Winters Novel

———

#2, TO HELL WITH BAD DECISIONS

A Reagan Valentine Novel

For those who know their worth and refuse to settle for less—take up space, demand what you're owed, and remind the world exactly who you are.

To my uncle, the man who taught me what real music is: thank you for inspiring a playlist for the ages. May your spirit continue to rock and roll all night and party every day.

And to the red-haired Demoness who pulled the Bombshell out of the darkness: I can't imagine existing in a world where you don't. This book is for you.

Happy birthday.

TO HELL WITH *Bad Decisions*

TRACK LIST

SCAN TO LISTEN TO THE PLAYLIST HERE!

Please be advised that this is a dark adult novel and may include themes that are disturbing to some readers.

I created this series to provide a fresh perspective on villainy, featuring bad gals you can't help but root for. It is important to remember that **this book is told from the perspective of a demon**, a creature who should not be held accountable to the same moral standards as a human. While I invite you to explore these darker sides, the health, safety, and mental and emotional well-being of my readers is of utmost importance to me. Please make sure to read through this list of trigger warnings to help you make an informed decision before delving into this universe.

While this story centers on the main couple, both characters have romantic and/or sexual encounters with other people, including past relationships and present explorations that may occur separately or together.

WARNINGS: Adult language, sexual content (18+ only), depictions and references of death/murder/loss of loved ones, religious/Satanic references, religious trauma, light body horror/demonic transformations, descriptive gore and violence, knifeplay, threesome, voyeurism, substance use, coercion and manipulation, alcohol consumption, historical references to misogyny, homophobia, and bigotry.

DEMONIC HIERARCHY

OF THE HELLION HARLOT SERIES

THE KING OF DEMONS

LUCIFER MORNINGSTAR / SATAN / THE DEVIL

THE THIRTEEN PRIME EVILS

HEAD DEMONS CREATED BY THE DEVIL WHO HAVE DOMINION OVER HUMANS AND SUPERNATURALS CREATURES.

DEMON OF CHAOS

DEMON OF DEBAUCHERY (CURRENTLY INHABITING LOS ANGELES, CA)

DEMON OF DECEPTION (CURRENTLY INHABITING LAS VEGAS, NV)

DEMON OF DESTRUCTION

DEMON OF DOMINATION

DEMON OF DOUBT

DEMON OF ENVY

DEMON OF GREED (CURRENTLY INHABITING MANHATTAN, NY)

DEMON OF MISFORTUNE

DEMONS OF NIGHTMARES AND FEAR (TWO-HEADED TWINS)

DEMON OF PESTILENCE (LOCATION UNKNOWN)

DEMON OF VENGEANCE

DEMON OF VIOLENCE

UNDERLINGS

HIGH-LEVEL DEMONS

MID-LEVEL DEMONS

LOWER-LEVEL DEMONS

HELLSPAWN

FOR MORE INFORMATION ON THE PRIMES, PLEASE TURN TO PG 407 FOR THE GLOSSARY

Side A
CHERRY PIE MIX
A

TRACK ONE
Looks That Kill
BAD DECISIONS
EAT YOUR HEART OUT, MR. NEPHILIM.

TRACK ONE

LOOKS THAT KILL

Hollywood burns with the rage of the bombshell who set it ablaze, and I couldn't be prouder of the bitch. The city's a train wreck and, in true silver screen fashion, the longer you look, the more macabre it gets. I, of course, have the best view of all: from the darkest depths of my crumbling strip club, where I tally broken dreams one dollar bill at a time.

Neon and hellfire paint my office in a glow that could rival a sunset, casting harsh shadows across my desk. Outside, sirens scream from every corner while the stench of burned flesh and charred wood choke the air. The smoke can be seen for miles, and it's enough to send every goblin and ghoul scurrying home after their night of trick-or-treating. Then, there are the rubberneckers, Devil love 'em—the pathetic few who would fight each other bloody just to get the money shot of a tragedy.

My office chair creaks as I reach for the cheap blinds,

more flimsy garbage with gaps than plastic. A neon 'Bad Decisions' sign flickers against grimy brick walls across the alley—yet another reminder my strip club is a sinking ship held together by duct tape and wishful thinking. I yearn to drown out the noise, the cacophony of madness that wages war beyond these paper-thin walls. If demons could get migraines, I'd have worn out every neurologist in Hell decades ago.

Fuck, I lost count. Let's try this again…

Fifteen…sixteen…sev—huh. A two-dollar bill. Haven't seen one of these in a century. Raking through tonight's pathetic excuse for tips, I recount each crinkled dollar bill until my eyes blur. The sum never changes. Dismal. Disappointing. A succubus can't even keep a strip club afloat in a city drowning in sin. Somewhere, Lucifer's laughing his ass off—if he can tear himself away from his witch's cunt long enough to notice.

I know what went down in Hollywood tonight. Hell, I had a hand in its success. A thousand-year-old witch walked through fire and bested the Devil himself for a shot at another millennium. Meanwhile, I'm stuck counting singles in my personal, neon-soaked purgatory. Dirty deeds don't come cheap in this city, and a demon's got to pay rent.

The familiar, bass-heavy rhythm of '80s hair metal crashes through my office as the door swings open. Indigo—my *only* dancer with a lick of death-defying sense—leans against the frame, pale as moonlight and twice as cold.

"Reagan." Her sweet, melodic voice bleeds into the music.

I offer her a small smile. "What is it, Indy?"

She props a hip against my doorframe, tattooed arms crossing over her bare chest. "Sterling ran out without paying. Again. Said I couldn't get him up."

"Fuck's sake," I mutter under my breath. "That limp-dick, shit for brains bastard hasn't been able to get a stiffy since the eighties. I'll handle him."

Indigo flashes me a sharp-fanged grin as I rise from my desk and close the space between us. I brush a lock of purple-blue hair out of her face; I can't fight the frown weighing down my features. She's paler than usual, even for a vampire.

"You eating enough, Indy?"

She shrugs. "Slim pickings lately."

"Mmm." I tap my claws against my lips. "I'll fix you right up. Hang tight."

Her eyes, that strange mix of stormy gray and violet, sparkle. "You're always so good to us."

"There aren't many of you left, and now that the Devil's Second has checked out and thrown away the key, I'm running shorter than ever. Keep yourself alive, doll. You're the only one here with a brain in that dead skull of yours."

I leave my prized employee behind as I prowl through my crumbling strip club. My latex platform boots clunk and thud against the faded mauve carpet, countless stains crunching beneath every step. I catch

Charlie's glowing eyes—my bartender and most trusted ally. I silently urge him to keep an eye out for any trouble. Business has been regrettably slow ever since Tober drove those Violence demons away, and Devil damn me, I'm still conflicted over it all—they *may* have cost me a few of my girls over the years, but their patronage kept the lights on. Talk about being stuck between a rock and a hard place.

Cold air tickles my cheeks as I exit the club, and the stench of smoke practically slaps me in the face. I run my fingers over my prickling skin, channeling my human glamour. My veins, once gleaming orange like magma, disappear along with the glow of my amber eyes. In seconds, my crimson skin fades to pale, peppered with freckles. To any innocent bystander, I'm just a redheaded temptress clad in latex and a corset, ready to lure men into my bed. No one would ever guess I was a hellish creature with direct ties to the Devil himself. Distant, but direct nonetheless.

The world is different through the eyes of a Debauchery demon. Where humans see colors and shapes, we see...*more.* And *far* worse. We know what damns every soul, what desires—dark or innocent—haunt their minds, and sometimes, we even uncover their best-kept secrets. Demons do more than just see. We feel. We manipulate. We *feed.*

There's one now, a simple human creature down on his luck, scraping for one more quarter to shove into the payphone. *Just one more minute,* he thinks—he begs.

Then, there's another, not too far down the road. She clings to her beeper as she roams the dimly lit street, awaiting that special message—the one her boss sends her when he's up for a fuck. Her thoughts are like a bad record scratching on a loop.

Maybe he'll leave his wife tonight. He said he would. He said I was worth it.

Her desperation is as palpable as it is pathetic, of course. But who am I to judge a potential meal?

And speaking of meals, there's mine right now: Mr. Sterling, a sad excuse for a middle-aged man who is all ego and no balls. He jaywalks across the street in his drunken state, staggering toward the Roosevelt Hotel, equal parts sexually frustrated and embarrassed. His thoughts are as loud as the Boulevard at this hour and twice as ludicrous. He actually thinks he can score himself a 'real' woman for the night, one who can cure his impotence. Bless his artery-clogged heart.

I ignore the predatory eyes of tourists and locals watching me as I rush to the hotel. It's a night and day difference compared to my joint, with its newly restored neon sign burning bright red and freshly-painted white concrete glittering in the moonlight. If Cherry could give me an extra buck to keep up with the structural integrity of my damn motel and strip club, maybe we'd stand a chance in this town. Maybe that's the allure, though: the dirt, the grime, the darkness that pulls you in.

Sterling wanders through the Roosevelt like a lost puppy, scanning for the bar. Irrational fear poisons his thoughts, terrified Indigo may have followed him here. He's right to worry, of course...but it isn't a petite, purple-haired vampire who tracked him. It's a five-foot-eight-inch succubus dressed in black and armed with a seething distaste for egotistical bastards.

I take my seat at the bar shortly after my prey, minding my business while he nervously chats up the tender. "Taking a load off after a long day on set," he says with an air of self-importance. "Working on that new superhero film—you know, the one with the fancy red suit."

My, oh, my—he lies like a Persian rug. Cherry's goons at Paramount shelved that production months ago. Besides, everyone in the biz knows you never talk shop off the lot.

Sterling's gaze lingers on the drink menu for far too long; not out of indecision, but for fear of next month's credit card bill. With a quick gulp, he slides the menu over to the bartender and orders a Long Island. Funny— for a man who claims to be so high on Hollywood's food chain, he sure has cheap taste.

I wave the bartender down. "I'll have what he's having," I drawl in long, drawn-out syllables and effort-less Southern charm. I lay the accent on thick, upping my voice an octave or two from its lower, strait-laced tone. Best to put all those acting lessons to good use.

It certainly gets my victim's attention.

If you looked up the word 'dumbfounded' in Merriam-Webster's dictionary, you'd find a mediocre shot of Mr. Sterling's grubby mug. I knew he wouldn't recognize me. A man so self-absorbed and driven by his measly chode (or lack thereof) would never remember a woman like me. Nevertheless, he owes me money, and I'm not about to let my ego get in the way of my livelihood.

Sterling's eyes rake over my body like an animal starved, lingering where my corset cinches my waist impossibly thin. His thoughts flood my mind, an endless loop of all the revolting ways he wishes he could have me, wondering if the carpet matches the drapes—a question I *never* tire of, given my naturally red tresses.

"Beggin' your pardon, sir, but I couldn't help but eavesdrop." I flutter my lashes with practiced precision. "You must be some sort of big shot producer—maybe a director? I sure do love movies. I even bought this outfit to try to fit in—you LA folk are always so fashion-forward. I hopped on the first Greyhound from Savannah just so I could see the stars!"

Hell on wheels, I'm laying it on thick. Bullshit pours out of me like a busted water fountain, a show that would make the Demon of Deception himself kneel at my feet. And Sterling? Oh, he laps it all up like a dog in a drought.

That's when the pathetic fool starts to chat me up, spewing horse dung about Academy Award nominations and brilliant screenplays gathering dust in studio vaults. He bores me to tears with his lies, but my expression remains awestruck and smitten. If anyone deserves the Oscar tonight, it's me—a century of practice makes for one hell of a performance.

My charade continues as I laugh at his stupid jokes, lean in a little too close, and touch his knee playfully. It's the perfect formula, each gesture deviously calculated. I'm so close to sinking my claws into him, I can practically taste sweet victory. But from the edge of my vision, something bright and shiny captures my attention.

A handsome young man stumbles into the lobby, looking all disheveled, wounded, and helpless. His thoughts are loud in my head despite his distance, scratching like a broken record—thoughts of self-doubt, self-loathing, and a whole lot of—wait. Is that—? No. It couldn't be.

A demon hunter? Here? *Now*? They should be a couple blocks away, trying to rid the world of October Winters. I try not to let my gaze linger on him, but there's something about his aura that leaves me curious, if not a little disturbed. I've had my fair share of Nephilim encounters, thanks to my witchy little bombshell. They're all the same: half-human, half-angel super soldiers with stark-white auras, determined postures, and some sort of God complex that makes them prone to irrational decisions.

This one, however... His aura isn't stark—it's erratic. It's like a flickering light bulb, dimming and brightening but never staying lit, a reminder that his glow's about to run out. Then, there's that posture; his shoulders are tensed so high, I wonder if there's any neck at all. If only he'd just loosen up a bit, I could see if he has that tattoo on his neck, the one Tober once mentioned acts like a divine alert system whenever a demon is near...

Good thing my human glamour has proven effective against them. I'm in no mood to deal with the recent Nephilim epidemic, especially not when I have a task at hand.

My breath catches in my chest when his eyes finally meet mine, almost as if he knew I was staring. The haunted look is a dead ringer for those who frequent my establishments. Tortured. Conflicted. Longing. It's almost...tempting.

Pull yourself together, Valentine. You've got enough on your plate, and you know better than to mess with a demon hunter. You *also* know better than to stick around this close to one.

"You got anywhere to be tonight?" I flit my attention back to Mr. Sterling, leaning in closer and running my fingers over his. "I'm stayin' at the motel a couple blocks down. It's gettin' late, and I don't feel particularly safe on these streets. Care to walk me home?"

My painfully fake words are heavy with implication, triggering a physical response from him. I can practically feel the heat rolling off his body.

He offers me his hand, taking the bait quicker than I expected. Before I know it, we're making our way out of the hotel and straight toward my little spiderweb.

The trek from the Roosevelt to Bad Decisions is a short one, barely three blocks down the Boulevard, but it feels impossibly long with a tipsy Mr. Sterling clinging to my arm. He slurs his words, spilling anecdote after anecdote, making himself out to be this big Hollywood hotshot bursting with more dollar bills than he knows what to do with. His lies would fool the average gal, but not me, not when he's stumbled into my bar week after week without so much as two pennies to rub together. I should throw him to Deception's snakes after I'm through with him—he'd make one hell of a meal.

We finally turn the corner on La Brea and face the rotting façade of my motel. It's then a discordant frequency hits my nerves and leaves a sour taste in my mouth, both of which are not my own, but my victim's. His emotions invade my mind, body, and soul as his anxiety grows.

I try to cull the beast before it takes over.

"Why don't you come on up? Let me repay you for your kindness."

He hesitates for a moment, irrational fears crippling his thoughts as he eyes the motel. *Too close to the strip club*, he worries. *That purple-haired gal could catch me.*

That's when I step a little closer. I grasp for the magic deep within me, abilities that grant me the power of Persuasion, and run a single finger down Sterling's grubby cheek. A little red line forms on his skin, invisible to humans but very prominent to someone like me. It's a special little mark we Debauchery demons love to refer to as a Kiss—the act of claiming a victim to feed from. All at once, my magic calms him, and his woes roll off his shoulders.

I lead my victim up pebbled stairs and down the neon-washed walkway to my favorite room—666. I pull the old, rickety key and plastic tag from my bust, tracing the faded Starlight Motel lettering worn smooth on one side, the Devil's numbers etched deep on the other.

The lock yields with a satisfying click, and I guide Mr. Sterling over the threshold once I get the damn door open. I'm pleased to see October left the place spotless— well, as spotless as a forty-something-year-old relic can be. The tobacco-stained wallpaper and water-damaged ceiling add to its charm. Ugh.

"Couldn't get a room anywhere else, baby?" Irritation crawls up my spine at the sound—*baby.* How I loathe pet names. I have a name, and it's one I'm quite proud of. Alas, it would be wasted on this low life. Instead, I simply smile at him.

"California's a lot more expensive than where I'm from, darlin'." I lay my twang on thick. "This is the best I could do."

I take the cheap jacket from his shoulders, toss it on a dresser that's seen better days, and rub my hands over his back. The fool sighs and turns to putty in my grasp, moaning something or other about how badly he needs this tonight. I lightly push him onto the bed and pull the studded belt from my hips, playfully running it along the mattress. Sterling's eyes glisten with equal parts fear and excitement, widening when I straddle him and crash my lips to his.

His body convulses beneath me, a pathetic mess of clammy hands and strangled moans as I draw his sexual essence through our kiss. It flows into me like liquid fire—not just energy, but life itself, awakening an ancient hunger I've neglected for longer than I care to admit.

If I'm not careful, my control will slip. The glamour that paints me human will fade and reveal what truly lies beneath my skin. But *fuck*, the power is intoxicating. There's nothing I love more than to suck a man dry.

"My, you're a dirty one, aren't you?" he chortles as I link my belt around the bed frame and secure his wrists tightly. "What'd they teach you in Alabama?"

Savannah, idiot. And they taught me how to spot a fool like you from a mile away.

But I won't waste any more time—not when I've got tips to count and a vampire to feed.

I reach for Sterling's lap as my thighs clench around his hips, my fingers finding exactly what I expected—the world's softest disappointment despite his mental arousal. It's a win-win for me; I get all the benefits of feeding on him without the snag of having to do the actual deed. I couldn't have planned it better myself.

Embarrassment washes over him like an icy storm. His brows knit as he struggles against the belt rendering him powerless against me, and I can tell he wants to run, just like he did with Indy. But here's a promise written in lipstick and sin: Mr. Sterling will never run out on me or my girls ever again.

"Oh, honey," I coo as I glance at his sad excuse for a manhood. "Looks like the key's in the ignition but the engine's dead. What a shame. Good thing I've got something that'll fix you right up."

A little "Wait, where are you going?" echoes off the walls as I saunter over to the nightstand and grab an old phone—its once-white sheen now aged yellow—and nestle it between my shoulder and ear. Sterling's panicked breaths tickle me pink as I press the speed dial code into the clunky receiver. After two prompt rings, Charlie's deep, monotone timbre greets me on the other line.

"Charlie? Mind sending Indy over to room 666 at The Starlight? Let her know her eleven o'clock is ready for her."

"I-Indy?" Sterling stutters, his voice cracking. "Who's that?" Beads of sweat roll down his already-damp forehead, and I can practically see him piecing the puzzle together. He isn't stupid enough to forget Indigo's name. No, he knows *exactly* who she is.

I don't dignify his question with an answer. That would play out the charade longer than needed, and Indy will be at the door in seconds, thanks to her vampire speed. Time to switch gears. I run my fingers over my skin, shedding my human glamour. My spiral horns jut out from my skull, and I use my red tail to groom any flyaway hairs that tangled in the process.

Sterling's eyes widen in disbelief, as if he's witnessing the impossible instead of another Hollywood parlor trick.

"Hard times in this city lately." My voice returns to its natural tone. "Why, these days, it's nearly impossible to honor the 'customer's always right' code when you're strapped for a nickel—especially when said customer is a cheapskate who comes in, week after week, squeezing a free show out of one of my best girls, on *my* dime, and then has the nerve to blame his sad case of limp dick on her. It's bad for business, Mr. Sterling."

Knock, knock, knock. Right on cue.

I saunter toward the door, unlocking the deadbolt as Sterling's labored breaths grow heavier. His begging and pleading are like nonsense to my ears. I open the door to reveal my little vampire, who, even in five-inch heels, barely reaches my chin. I marvel at those violet-gray eyes and thousand-dollar smile.

Sterling reaches for his last lifeline. "Look—I'll pay. I'll pay double. Just let me go."

"Oh, you'll pay. But Indigo doesn't just want your money. Her payment runs more red than green."

The fear in his eyes flashes brighter than any Hollywood marquee. The thud of his heart grows heavier, faster, drowning out the sirens and music outside. Indigo snarls at her dinner, and the unmistakable 'click' when she reveals her fangs sends a thrill through me. My work here is done.

"He's all yours, doll face. Take as much as you need.

But do me a tiny favor, will you? Leave a little leftover. We'll want to keep him alive enough to spread the word about our...payment policy."

Sterling's screams drown out the egregious melody of tearing flesh and splattering blood. The door snicks shut as I exit, making my way back toward Bad Decisions. The incessant buzzing of my establishment's larger-than-life neon sign irks my sensitive ears, another reminder that the electric bill is due and I'm still in the negative. The little symbol carved into the threshold of the entrance catches my eye—two little heart-like circles connected by a stem.

Cherries, the symbol of the Demon of Debauchery himself. An emblem that seems to haunt me wherever I go. They're everywhere in this city if you know where to look—his ingenious way of marking his territory. Hell, it's even branded onto my skin, just proof I too am some sort of precious possession in his eyes.

Another night, another job well done. As I'm about to walk into the club and resume the mundane, my attention snaps to a familiar disturbance, that same erratic, flashing aura from the Roosevelt. The demon hunter.

Oh, Hell. The fool followed me here. He lurks in the shadows across the street, inconspicuous as ever, like a lion watching a lamb. Poised. Hungry. Ready. It's a shame his emotions betray him. There's fear there, cold and crippling beneath the surface. And the anger? It's almost as thick as the smog choking this city on a summer night.

A glint of metal catches the light as he closes in—something ancient and lethal. His white-knuckle grip holds fast, heartbeat thundering so loud, I almost mistake it for my own, and his breath comes in shallow bursts. I know a threat when I see one, and this one's lunging at me, knife in hand, a holy prayer on his lips and a mission from God burning in his eyes.

Control is a fleeting concept, one I can barely grasp with my red-painted claws. Being Hell-Bound to one of the Devil's Thirteen Sons leaves little room for free will; I'm lucky if I get a whisper of choice in my servitude. I may not have much, but what I *do* have—what I'll protect with every fiber of my being—are my girls. My club. *My* territory.

Eat your heart out, Mr. Nephilim; my webs are woven with bad decisions, and this is the last one you'll ever make.

TRACK TWO
Live Wire
REAGAN, IT'S A DEMON HUNTER!

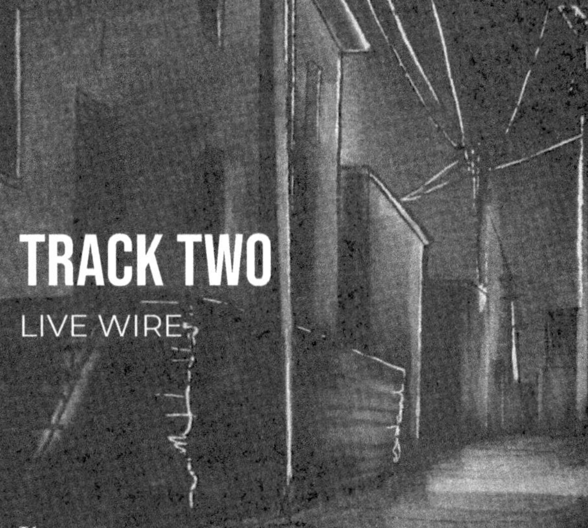

TRACK TWO

LIVE WIRE

I'm not afraid of demon hunters.

I'm not afraid of their holy sparks and sharp knives, not afraid their divine magic could crack open the Earth and send me straight to where my kind comes from—or worse: annihilate me from existence. I'm not even afraid of the one right in front of me: a tall, peculiar specimen with salt-and-pepper hair despite his youthful features and mournful eyes that look like they've seen the Devil himself.

What I *am* afraid of is what he'll do to my girls.

Dodging the Nephilim's dagger with dancer-like grace, I slip underneath his arm. My red-arrowed tail wraps around his ankle with viperine precision, tugging hard and forcing him to his knees. He's a clumsy fella, too tall for his frame and about as coordinated as a baby giraffe fresh from the womb. This won't take long.

His face collides with the ground, a sickening thud echoing against the concrete as I retreat into the shadows. I charge toward the back entrance of the club, just down the alley connecting The Starlight to Bad Decisions. Black and white images flash through my head like a roll of film, quickly bleeding red as I assume the worst.

His Holy Light burning Charlie alive. His dagger sliding into Indigo's undead heart. The ancient prayers that would crumble my building and leave nothing but a pile of ash in his wake.

I can't let him in. I have to lure him away.

But where? I can't stray too far, not in my demon form. There are humans everywhere; them witnessing a demon-angel face off would be a disaster. The Demon of Deception will already have his cleanup crew working overtime at Hollywood Forever, and I'd rather die than owe those sleazeballs a favor.

No. I do this alone, on my terms.

The Nephilim isn't far behind now. His footsteps grow louder, despite my efforts. Grunt after grunt, he hurls warbling bursts of magic my way, something reminiscent of miniature explosions of hot-white light, so blinding, I can almost feel the latex catsuit melting into my skin. Try as he might, he misses every single shot. One blast takes out a fire hydrant, covering us both in water. Another fires a hole into a parked car, sounding the alarm. A third hits a garbage bin and sets last week's trash ablaze. The irony doesn't escape me: this entire situation is a dumpster fire, a complete and utter shit show suited for another Hollywood blockbuster. Seems like the Holy Order of the Nephilim will slip a demon hunter license to just about anyone these days. This sorry excuse for a foe is anything but a threat, and I'm tired of him making a mess of my turf.

When I've finally lured the amateur farther away from the club, I slow my pace just enough to fool him into thinking he's gaining ground. I spin around slowly, deliberately, facing him with a menacing, sharp-toothed grin. He skids to a halt, blessed dagger thrumming in one hand while jagged, erratic, white-gold sparks fall from the other. His magic crackles and pops like a live wire touching water. The acrid stench of burnt rubber hits my nostrils, and bile rises into my throat.

Hatred flashes in his eyes as he stares me down, but that's not all that bleeds through—something raw and broken tightens in my chest. It builds, layer upon layer, like a tempest in my ribcage, emotion twisting inside me like a living thing. A bramble of discord suffocates my conscience as irrational thoughts take over.

First, it's confusion, spreading through my mind like spilled ink. *Why can't I get it right? Why can't I think straight?* It's quickly replaced with a wave of fear, but what am I afraid of? I know how to bring this monster to his knees with the wave of my hand. Then comes the sorrow, an ache so dull, I press my hand to my chest to soothe the pain.

But there is no pain.

There's only emotional static. Desperation. Hopelessness. And it grows louder and louder with every passing moment. It's like being caught in someone else's nightmare with no escape.

That's when it hits me: these feelings aren't mine.

They're his, this broken, damaged Nephilim whose inner demons will destroy him before he has a chance to destroy me.

"What did you do with that girl and the man she was with?" the Nephilim's voice cuts through the night air.

He's a handsome fella, with a baby face that would make mortal women weak in the knees. Under better circumstances, where we weren't two creatures sworn to destroy each other, I too might have felt a tingle. But no man is worth dying over, even if he *is* an angel.

There's a sort of breathy, smooth texture to his voice, one I don't expect from someone so tortured beneath the surface. That's all his heroism is—surface level. The constant resonance of his emotions betray the altruism of his tone and the hatred in his eyes. The audacity is almost charming—the fool is trying to deceive the very creature designed to read, manipulate, and feast on human emotions.

"Bold of you to assume I did anything at all. I'm just a hard-working business owner. I pay no attention to who comes and goes from my establishments." The words pour from my mouth like liquid velvet, just as smooth and innocent as earlier with Mr. Sterling.

"They went in, you came out, and there were screams." He steps closer to me, gripping that stupid dagger tighter. "You killed them."

"Sounds to me like you failed to do your job, angel boy."

Before he can manage a retort, I reach deep into the well of power pooling in my chest. It's unlike the flashy abilities the Demons of Violence, Chaos, and Domination gift their Underlings. No, mine are far more devious. It starts as a warm pulse beneath my sternum and spreads through my glowing veins like liquid starlight. In an instant, a shimmering gold mist releases from my veins and snakes its way toward the demon hunter.

He swats at the barely visible mist, fighting it as if it were a swarm of bees, but it overpowers him, swirling over his skin like a lover's caress.

And then, it hits him.

I watch his green eyes turn black as his pupils swallow his irises. His rigid stance loosens, as if his entire body sighs in relief…before it starts to convulse.

My magic typically works like the finest psychedelics, slowly turning one's mind against them and then placing them somewhere neither on this plane nor the next. For some, the effects are euphoric bliss. For others, catatonic surrender.

I'd hoped my Nephilim hunter would crumble into either state, but dread crawls up my spine as I realize the horrifying truth: I've never tried manipulating a half-angel before.

This outcome is catastrophic, terrifyingly so.

He claws at his skin as an addict would, fingers raking red lines into his neck as he struggles to pull at the neckline of his hoodie. He's desperate for relief, for escape from the dark influence plaguing his mind. His thoughts scream into my consciousness louder than before:

Make it stop—get out, get out, GET OUT! Burning—everything's burning, help me, please—hot, too hot, make it STOP, STOP, STOP—

The psychic assault feels so real, even I can feel the itch in my skin. My magic has backfired superbly, driving my victim into madness rather than relief. It has created this never-ending loop driving us both mad. I need to get out.

I stumble backward, my platform stilettos catching in the cracks of the asphalt beneath my feet. The hunter collapses to the ground, grunting and writhing like an animal in pain, but I can't tell whose pain is worse. All I know is that I need distance. I need to *run—*

Just as I turn to flee, something impossibly hot sears across my hip.

I cry out, floundering as blessed iron tears through latex and skin. My hand immediately flies to the fresh wound, but I quickly jerk it back when I find the wound is sizzling. *Hot. Burning. Everything's burning.*

The holy dagger falls at my feet with an echoing clang, surrounded by the ebony ichor of my demonic blood. Panic builds, suffocating me as the pain continues to grow. The heat from the wound continues to scorch my skin, and I look down to see it's barely a scratch—but fuck me, if it doesn't feel like it's cut me in half.

The demon hunter's agonized roars reduce to a whisper as I make my escape. I take a sharp left around a corner and struggle to catch my breath. I'm soaked to the core, water and blood dripping from my latex bodysuit. I curse my choice in attire in the heat of the moment. I need to get out of this fucking thing. I need to push through the pain. I *need* to get back to Bad Decisions.

I quietly slip into my club through the back entrance so as not to alarm the staff. They have enough chaos to deal with tonight—this mess is mine and mine alone. One hand pressed against my bleeding hip, I navigate the narrow hallway to my office, shouldering past stacks of inventory and dodging the perpetual clutter I never seem to have time to organize.

My office is exactly as I left it: a disaster zone of scattered books, overflowing filing cabinets, and never-ending paperwork. I kick my old leather chair aside with my good leg and tear through my desk drawers with increasing desperation. Papers flutter to the floor as I ransack the desk, searching for that damn key. The pain is still so hot, so distracting; I can feel my heart pulse throughout my entire body, like I'm fighting an infection.

Then, I see it—a flash of gold half-buried under a stack of invoices. My hands shake as I snatch up the safe key, and I steady myself against the desk as a wave of nausea hits. Blood seeps through my fingers, staining my outfit a deeper black.

A thin, piercing whistle starts ringing in my ears like a tea kettle, and soon, the blaring music from beyond my office walls begins to dull. Fuck. Fuck, fuck, *fuck*. This thing is going to kill me, and it's no bigger than a kitten scratch. This is *not* the way I'm going to die.

The safe clicks open on my third attempt. I dig past hundreds of crystal necklaces, protective charms, and healing herbs until my fingers close around what I need—a small vial of Indigo's blood, dark as midnight and twice as precious.

"Thank you, Indy." My words come out in a shaky whisper as I pull the cork free with my teeth.

The vampire blood hits the wound like cool water on flushed skin. The relief is immediate but incomplete—the bleeding stops, the fire dims to a manageable burn, but the underlying corruption of blessed magic still aches beneath my skin.

It'll have to do. For now.

Heavy, distorted guitar riffs thunder from the main room as my hearing sharpens back to normal, but the familiar chaos of my club is quickly overshadowed by something else—an eerie resonance thrumming from deep within the safe. The sound vibrates through the metal like a tuning fork striking bone.

Strange. The safe never made *that* noise before.

I shift aside more relics, crystals, and bottles,

following the sound until my fingers brush against something that makes my skin crawl.

A particular black tourmaline crystal necklace lies coiled on the bottom shelf—the very same necklace I'd collected from October Winters three days ago.

The crystal's surface glimmers just as erratically as Mr. Nephilim's aura did, flashing on and off in no specific rhythm. My curiosity is stunted by a sonic boom erupting from somewhere in my club. The windows shudder, and a thin crack sprouts up on one of the walls. For a moment, I fear we're in for another one of Destruction's untimely California earthquakes, but this isn't demonic. No, it's the exact opposite.

And then, I hear them.

The screams of my girls.

Jasmine's banshee wail cuts through the walls before choking off mid-shriek—like someone severed her vocal cords. Stasia's hooved feet thunder across the dance floor in frantic, uneven beats. And beneath it all, Indigo's voice cracks as she cries out for Charlie, raw with terror I've never heard from her before.

The crystal pulses against my palm, hot as fresh blood.

What the fuck is going down in my house?

My wound has dulled to a manageable throb as I clasp the necklace around my neck and tuck it into my halter top. I navigate through the chaos of my office toward the door, but before I can reach the handle, it flies open. Indigo stumbles inside, her cold, pale hands reaching for me. Black, demonic blood spatters across her skin like freckles, streaked with the tears from her stormy gray eyes.

"Reagan, it's a demon hunter," she gasps, words tumbling out between ragged breaths. "He killed Jazzi. Oh God, there's so much blood everywhere. I can't—and he's got Charlie cornered by the main stage. Reagan, if he kills Charlie—"

"Hey." I catch her cheeks between my palms and force her wild eyes to meet mine. "Indy, listen to me. He's not going to kill Charlie. I'll never let that happen."

Indigo searches my face for something, anything—reassurance, hope, a miracle…something tangible to hang on to. But all I have is my word, and we both have to believe it's enough. "Get yourself into the dungeon downstairs, lock the doors, and stay there until I come for you, understand? Don't open the door for anyone else. Indy, do you understand?"

She nods furiously and chokes out another sob before disappearing back through the doorway with vampiric speed.

So, the Nephilim managed to drag his sorry ass inside after all. My breath catches in my chest when I realize I've somehow manifested my greatest fears, but rage follows shortly after. It resonates with my pulsing, glowing veins, doubling down as I clench my jaw. He may have taken Jasmine's life, but there is no way I'll let him have Bad Decisions.

Readjusting the torn latex clinging to my skin, I roll my shoulders and exhale deeply. Time to face the music.

The main floor is an absolute battlefield, ridden with demonic blood and shattered debris. Broken glass cracks beneath my feet, and I almost slip on all the spilled alcohol covering the linoleum dance floor. Charlie brawls with the hunter, who thrusts his holy blade at the demon's torso. But my clever bartender is too quick; Charlie dodges to the side and grabs the Nephilim's wrist and shoulder, yanking him forward and slamming him into the bar top with a thunderous crack. I urge myself forward to interrupt their battle, but I nearly trip over a corpse.

A headless corpse. Jasmine.

I stifle the tears welling in my eyes as I find her severed head just feet away, thankfully covered by her long, tangled hair. She never could tame that mane of hers…

Oh, what I'd do for October Winters and her firepower right about now.

Grunts echo in the club as I stare at Jasmine. A flash of light reflects against the wooden floors, and my head snaps up. The Nephilim managed to overpower Charlie with a blast of Holy Light, forcing my demon to the floor, groaning as the light sears his skin. My breath catches. The horrors are real—and for once, the Demon of Fear isn't responsible.

The hunter turns to face me, and I force a sadistic smile.

"Going after my bartender, Sparky? You sure know how to make a gal jealous."

He sneers, lips curling in disgust as he saunters toward me.

There are rumors about what happens to a demon when it's killed. Some say they can be reconstituted. Others say they just get sent back to their Prime's realm. I don't know what awaits me if I meet my end by a Nephilim's blade, but I can promise this: whether I'm scattered across dimensions or chained in some infernal limbo, I'll claw my way back just to make this mother-fucker's life a living nightmare.

The hunter is just a few feet away from me now, eyeing me like a predator. I cock my hip outward, folding my arms over my chest, almost beckoning him with my sardonic stance. The crystal continues to hum between my latex and skin, vibrating as he draws closer.

I half expect him to give me some sort of heroic speech and put me out of my misery with a stab in the chest. But before he can, time seems to freeze for a moment. There's nothing—no speech, no stabbing, not even a prayer.

Instead, the dagger slips from his fingers onto the floor.

Those eyes—those impossibly green eyes that burned with such hatred seconds before—soften into something far more human. His tense features crumble as despair washes over his face, and trembling fingers reach for the silver cross at his throat. He stumbles backward as if struck in the chest, staring at something beyond me only he can see.

"Declan," he whispers, the name breaking on his lips. "No. No, no, no…"

Declan?

The name strikes a chord, jogging memories from just days before. There's no way this is a coincidence. He couldn't be referring to that dirty rat October's been toying with…

I peer into the hunter's mind for a moment. Although his thoughts are as erratic as the sparks flying from his fingers, one thing is for certain: one of his own has just been killed.

The pieces slam together with sickening clarity. The black tourmaline crystal nearly sears my skin, and I pull it from my breast. Both it and the grief-stricken Nephilim before me flash with the same, off-beat aura.

You've got to be fucking kidding me.

This salt-and-pepper-haired Nephilim who dared lay hands on me and mine…is Declan Lovejoy's apprentice.

Before I can process the weight of this revelation, the hunter disappears into wisps of Holy Light, leaving nothing but the echo of his anguished whisper.

And here I stand, in the wreckage of my sanctuary, blood on the floor and walls, tables and chairs over-turned, liquor bottles shattered, with the lingering stench of fear and death. But it's not the battle that will haunt me for days to come—it's the look in his eyes. The pure, devastating loss. The kind that tears apart any soul, human, demonic, or divine.

He felt it when it happened. Somewhere deep in whatever bond connects mentor and apprentice, he knew the exact moment Declan Lovejoy's heart stopped beating.

I'll be double-damned. The bombshell actually fucking did it.

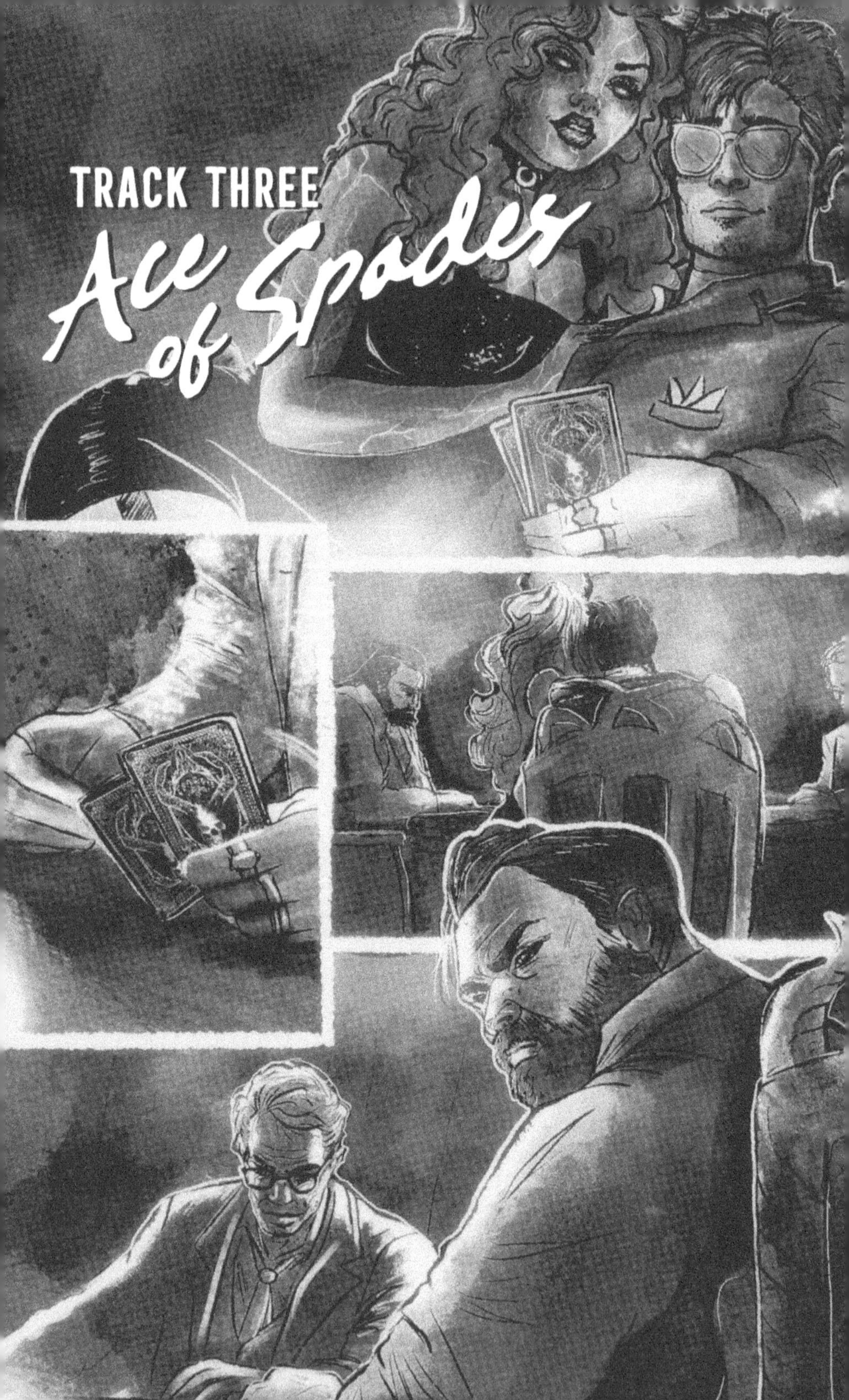

TRACK THREE
Ace of Spades

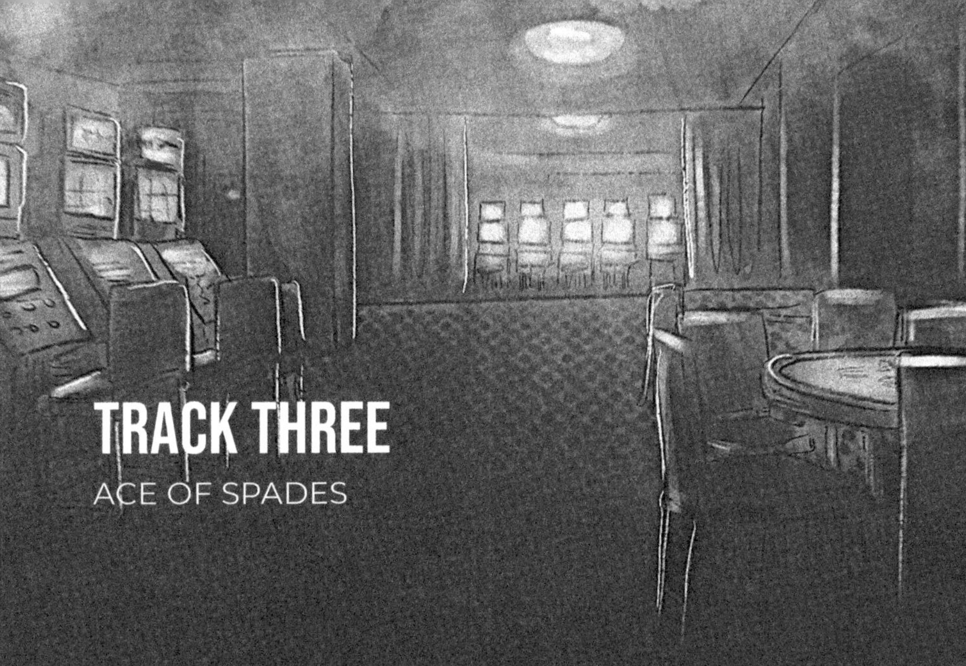

TRACK THREE
ACE OF SPADES

Heartbeats. Heavy breathing. Static from the broken speakers.

That's all I can focus on as I survey the scene. I don't have time to worry about my throbbing feet, the weakness in my knees, or the ache in my heart upon seeing Jasmine's mangled body. Instead, I look to Charlie. Charlie, who, despite his half-human nature, couldn't possibly look more demonic right now.

What the fuck was that? His voice invades my mind in a growl unlike one I've ever heard from him. Charlie's always had a quiet charm, a stoicism I've always attributed to his character. But right now, his inner thoughts are anything but subdued.

I don't have the strength to speak, so I Tap into his mind to respond.

Just another pretty boy with a death wish. I imagine the

quiver of my inner voice betrays the nonchalance I'm trying to project.

Charlie bolts toward the dungeon door without a backward glance, leaving me alone with the wreckage of my club. With a heavy sigh, I drag myself to the office and retrieve the caddy of cleaning supplies I keep stocked for these kinds of disasters. I catch my reflection in the full-length mirror at the corner of the room, and I nearly jump at the sight.

I'm a mess. A beautiful fucking mess. My signature red waves have devolved into a rat's nest, my bodysuit still dripping with a cocktail of fire hydrant water and blood—mine and Indigo's—but it's the fresh wound cutting across my hip that stops me cold, a permanent reminder of how close I came to losing everything.

I hover my fingers over my tangled hair, letting the magic flow through me. Within seconds, the matted mess transforms into smooth, voluminous waves that cascade over my shoulders. I kick off my heels and begin peeling away the latex from my skin, the familiar squeaking and popping sending an oddly comforting rush through me as the material releases its grip. A hiss escapes me when the material brushes against my fresh wound. Studying the cut, I notice it slashes through the black widow tattoo inked onto my hip. Tender skin replaces the wound, but I know the blade's magic will long outlast the scar.

I slip into a sheer robe left hanging on the back of the door, the black fabric doing little to preserve my modesty. I imagine this would be someone's sick and twisted wet dream: a scantily clad, busty redhead mopping up blood and discarding dead bodies. My more depraved clientele would take out a second mortgage for a show like this. Note to self: invest in a camcorder and a dot com.

The night takes another delightful turn as an other-worldly heat spreads through my core. That distinctive aroma fills the air—cloying sweetness cut with something sharp and tart—and my ears prick at the sound of a voice I know all too well. Melodic, aristocratic, and insufferably smug.

Marvelous. Just marvelous. As if I didn't have enough unwelcome visitors tonight. I should start charging extra for the inconvenience.

Crimson smoke billows and clears, revealing the Prime himself—short but commanding, every inch of his outfit is designed to offend the very concept of subtlety. He's perfectly groomed, from his pristine hair to his bedazzled shoes, sporting those signature yellow shades and an outfit so gaudy, it practically blinds me. My beloved boss, the Demon of Debauchery himself, has graced me with his presence. Must be my lucky night.

"Reagan Valentine." My name rolls off Cherry's devious tongue in his haughty English accent. Those two words alone promise nothing but bullshit. His dark, demented eyes drink me in before he steps closer. "You're looking positively murderous this evening."

I flip my hair over my shoulders and loosen my robe while my narrowed eyes find his. "You would too if you'd spent the past six days dealing with handsy Violence Underlings, demon hunters who missed the concept of an invitation, and a boss who portals into your office unannounced."

He flashes me one of those grins, that toothy, effortless one that makes both men and women grow weak in the knees. It never fails to grind my gears. "Darling, I should be the *highlight* of that list." Cherry leans against my desk, his sequined black jacket glimmering under the city lights peeking through my window. He watches intently as I spruce up my curls and sigh at the reflection in my office mirror.

"What do you want?" I ask, my voice hard and unwavering.

"What—I can't simply visit one of my establishments?"

"Not without an ulterior motive."

"Reagan, you wound me."

There's that signature line of his, one I hear him use on countless of my demonic 'siblings'. He gracefully hops up to sit on my desk, leaning on one arm and studying the black-painted nails of his other hand. His nonchalance thrills me, truly, and I make it known with another sigh.

"I'll ask again: what do you want?"

"Always so serious," he coos. "You know, I've always found you to be dreadfully rigid for a Debauchery demon. Too structured. But you're efficient. Fiercely loyal. And drop dead gorgeous."

I spin to face him, dipping my chin and tilting my head with a narrowed stare. If he doesn't get on with it soon, I'll lose it. Finally, he sighs with a roll of his eyes.

"Ugh, you're no fun. Alright. I want you to be my date to a poker game this evening."

Poker game? As if I don't have more pressing matters. I rest a hand on my hip while gesturing with the other. "Can it wait until *after* I've cleaned up my club?"

"Get one of your girls to take care of all that. This is important. And when I ask something of you, you damn well better get your priorities straightened out."

Any hint of mischief and playfulness disappears from his tone, and it almost feels like the walls are shaking again. His eyes flash black behind his yellow-tinted glasses, and microscopic gold cracks crawl from his hairline down to his cheeks. That otherworldly heat assaults me again, like an unrelenting grip holding me back, reminding me of my place. *He*'s the one in charge. How could I forget?

When I bow my head in submission, Cherry chuckles. "Splendid, darling. No need for a human glamour— you'll be among *family* tonight. Now, hop to it and slip into something demonic. We're headed for Sin City."

I've never been to Las Vegas.

Sacrilege, I know, especially for a Debauchery demon. You'd think I'd have traded one hellhole for another by now, set up shop where my business would not only be affordable but legal and thriving. I could be swimming in cash and looking fabulous while doing it.

But that wasn't part of the deal I made all those years ago.

No. I just *had* to set my heart on California.

At least it's nice, weather-wise—I'd take the temperate climate over Nevada's scorching heat any day. If I wanted fire and brimstone, I would have stayed in Hell.

Cherry's arm slides around my waist as we navigate the casino's garish, navy blue carpet. Cigarette smoke and heavy cologne assault my nostrils while slot machines trill their mechanical songs above the racket of desperate gamblers. It's enough to make me want to rip my ears off. Worse, a familiar dread crawls up my spine as I scan the crowd—my red skin, twisting horns, pointed tail, and glowing veins would cause panic among humans, Halloween or not.

Then, I look closer at the faces around us, and relief floods me in an icy rush.

Demons, every last one of them. Not a single human in sight. How perfectly convenient.

I barely had time to process the last few hours, let alone choose the right outfit for the occasion. 'Family' only means one thing in Cherry's vocabulary, and, judging by the location of this alleged poker game, the truth was painfully clear: We were meeting with the King of Las Vegas tonight. The Demon of Deception.

"This some kind of demons-only casino?" I ask.

"Only the biggest and best in town," Cherry caws, extending his arms and nearly smacking me in the face with that absurd cane of his. "The Hellrider is Vegas' only haven for our kind, mostly known for housing demonic dealings and many a kerfuffle. Completely invisible to humans, mind you. Dessie's got the entire place tapped with Cleaners. Honestly, it could use a facelift." Cherry lets out a disgusted groan. "So tasteless. No imagination. No sense of style whatsoever."

"I imagine you think you could do better?"

"Imagine? Darling, I *know* I could do better. Just look at what I've done with Los Angeles."

"Los Angeles is nothing but a cesspool of desperate fools and the vultures smart enough to prey on them." The words sting on my tongue; they're a borrowed sentiment, one that never fails to remind me of my luckless past and sordid present. Regardless, they couldn't be more true. "It's the perfect place for Deception and his rabble. We, on the other hand, could do so much more with Vegas."

"Right you are." Cherry taps my abdomen with the end of his infernal cane. "Unfortunately, Dessie and I have a complicated history with our seats of power. It all started a century ago, you see. He set his eyes on Hollywood, and I, Vegas. So, naturally, we each seized what the other desired most—purely out of spite, mind you. I snatched up his precious Hollywood while he claimed my Vegas, each of us determined to deny the other their heart's desire. Sure, we barter Underlings occasionally or set up contracts and agreements, but I've come to learn something rather valuable after all these years ruling sunny California. While Vegas may have been my original obsession, Hollywood proves far better suited to Debauchery's particular brand of excess. All that glitter, all those beautiful people destroying themselves for fame? Why, it was practically made for me. Wouldn't you say so, love?"

The thought never occurred to me.

On the surface, Debauchery and Deception are opposites in every way that matters—appearance, personality, tact. But beneath one's theatrics and the other's calculated brilliance operates the same fundamental wavelength, one of cunning and ruthlessness. It's no wonder Lucifer didn't merge them into a single entity the way he did Nightmares and Fear. Cherry's precious ego would riot at the very suggestion, trampling any hope of demonic convenience.

No, separation served them well, two predators circling the same territory and perpetually trying to outwit each other.

We finally reach an unassuming elevator guarded by two Watchers—the Demon of Domination's goons. They loom in their demonic forms: tall, muscular creatures with glowing amber eyes, cramped faces, and hands built for crushing skulls. The moment they spot Cherry, one presses a thick finger to the 'up' button. Within seconds, we're ushered inside.

The dark and gloomy penthouse floor greets us, a single spotlight cutting through the center of the room. I stay close behind Cherry as he leads me forward into the pool of light.

A massive round table dominates the dimly lit room, one that would make King Arthur jealous. Three Gothic, throne-like chairs surround it, their high backs carved with intricate Hellspeak inscriptions. There's an ethereal light pulsing from the center of the table, and as I move closer, I can make out at least two dozen glowing spheres casting dancing shadows across the green felt.

Soul orbs like the ones October harvested from that movie theater a few days ago.

Well, isn't that charming? This isn't some friendly game of cards—it's demonic Texas Hold'em, and the stakes are actual human souls.

"Fashionably late, as always," comes a gravelly Brooklyn drawl as we enter the room. There's another player at the table, one whose very essence drips as green as the dollar bills he so desperately craves. And that's when I remember poker can't be played with just two.

The Demon of Greed—the third player—sits beside the Demon of Deception. A three-piece suit crafted from the finest materials money can buy is draped over his massive figure. Those small, calculating eyes narrow as we approach, tracking our every movement. Cherry slides into his chair with a fluid grace, looking at me as he pats his lap. *Have a seat, darling,* his voice purrs directly into my mind. I do, though I add a performance of my own, sliding across his lap and molding my body to his slight frame like some kind of lovesick groupie. This is how he demands his succubi behave in public— devoted, adoring, completely under his spell. In this moment, I'm not one of his employees; I'm a trophy who worships at his altar.

"Traffic was horrendous. You know how it is in LA— and on Halloween, no less? Dreadful." Cherry waves his hand dismissively then grips my waist. I lean into him more.

Greed sneers at the whole spectacle, though I'm not sure if he's more disgusted by our twitterpated display or the garbage Cherry's spewing. Knowing Greed, it's likely both.

I've met the Demon of Greed a handful of times in my tenure as a Debauchery demon. He's a hateful, venomous creature often wound up by the competition needlessly fashioned by his twelve other brothers.

And then, there's Deception, one I've heard too much about but never witnessed firsthand. He's nothing like I imagined. His human glamour presents as tall and lanky, with prominent cheekbones and a sharp, defined jawline. Thick-rimmed glasses frame his face, magnifying brown eyes seeming to catalog every secret in the room. A perpetual smirk plays at his lips, the expression of someone who knows exactly what cards everyone else is holding. His long, bony fingers drum against the green tablecloth in a calculated rhythm. He doesn't acknowledge my existence, reserving his attention entirely for his brothers.

"Love what you've done with the place, Dessie." Cherry's feigned adulation drips with condescension despite his saccharine smile. "One might even forget it used to be a dump in the seventies."

"Don't bullshit a bullshitter." Deception chuckles, fingers still drumming a calculated rhythm. "What was that you said downstairs? Tasteless, no imagination, and —what was the third?"

"No sense of style," Greed adds.

"That was it." Deception slaps his hand against the poker table, the sharp crack nearly making me jump. "Mind if we deal you in, brother?"

"By all means." Cherry tightens his hold on me. A demonic dealer—some lesser demon with trembling hands and a sweat-slicked brow—deals two cards face down to each Prime. I glance at Cherry's hand, catching a glimpse of what looks like a weak draw, maybe a potential flush.

"Pretty little thing you've got there." Deception finally nods in my direction, his tone suggesting I'm nothing more than an expensive accessory. "Thought you'd bring the brunette this time. I sure do love looking at her."

"This one's just as stunning," Cherry promises.

"I love me some redheads." Greed regards me with a sickeningly twisted grin. He turns his attention to the table, pushing forward several soul orbs. "Twenty souls from Wall Street."

Deception's foxlike smirk widens as he waves his hand, telekinetically adding a handful of glowing orbs to the pot. "I see your twenty and raise another fifteen, fresh from juvie."

"Teenagers, Dessie? How delicious," Cherry scolds with mock disapproval. "Didn't think you'd stoop to the twins' level."

"Yeah, well, somebody's got to now that they're ah… caput, as it were."

The casual mention doesn't escape me. The banishment of Nightmares and Fear had sent shockwaves through the Underworld, leaving the remaining Primes not only restless but genuinely fearful—or so I'd heard.

Cherry calls both bets, sighing dramatically. "On that note, I need a favor. Think you've got some Cleaners to spare to cover up a mess in Hollywood?"

"Oh Hell, that snafu over at Hollywood Forever? It's all over the news. Looks like Daddy's, ah…" He adjusts his glasses on his nose. "…*little protégé* finally decided to emerge out of whatever shadowy corner she's been lurking in to reclaim her spot at the top, hasn't she?"

"Guess you did a shitty job at taking care of her last year," Greed grunts as he lights a cigar. "You're lucky she didn't send your scaly ass to Hell like she did the twins."

"Now, now, none of that. My boys and I did a bang-up job on her. There was no sign of her for a whole year. It was—and I mean this quite literally—pure bliss."

Deception has a serious case of verbal diarrhea, which I care very little for. I start tuning out their mindless chatter, just another demonic pissing contest between brothers that could bore the dead back to life. The game drags on with predictable monotony: Greed, cocky as ever, throwing souls around by the dozen; Deception matching every bet with that insufferable smirk; and Cherry sitting there like a sphinx, content to watch his brothers tear each other apart.

When my boredom finally peaks, I survey the room with fresh eyes. The collective glow of the growing soul orbs illuminates more of our surroundings, revealing the shapes of countless demons lurking in the shadows, some twisted into their monstrous forms, others maintaining their human glamour. It's a regular supernatural convention, low-level shapeshifters I vaguely recognize huddled in one corner while a trio of vampires presses themselves against the far wall, avoiding the light entirely. Fear drips from their pores like a demonic waterfall, and I can't help but wonder: why are they here? And why are they so afraid?

I've lost count of the hours in this windowless room. With each hand dealt, the pot swells larger, the ethereal glow of countless soul orbs merging into one massive beacon, bathing the entire room in sickly light. As the stakes climb higher and the war between Deception and Greed intensifies, so does Greed's reckless abandon.

Deception is a genius when it comes to games, a puppet master who feeds off watching his victims squirm, or so the stories went. Once again, he proves himself the perfect counterpoint to Cherry's theatrical flair. In many ways, I wonder if I would have thrived better under his thrall. But there's no use fantasizing about alternate realities.

My Prime sits uncharacteristically silent through the entire game, quiet enough to make my own brow drip with sweat, just like the trembling dealers and the Underlings in the shadows.

Finally, after what feels like hours, he speaks up.

"I hear you've been shacking up with pigs, brother," Cherry quips, melting into his make-shift throne. Cards dance between his fingers as he eyes the Demon of Deception. "What's it like on the Las Vegas police force these days? What do they call you? Officer Do-Good? Now that would be adorably ironic."

Greed snorts. "Hilarious. You come up with that one all by yourself? Or did you suck it out of one of your has-been celebrity comics?"

"Ah, ah, ah—no need for hostility here." Deception's voice remains velvet-smooth while his lip curls into something predatory. "Besides, I'm hurt you'd assume I'd pick something so…boring. My lies require a sense of style, you understand? A certain, ah…what's that word you like to use? *Panache?*"

"Right, because an alias like 'Kevin' is a *much* better option."

"As if 'Cherry' is any better?" He flashes my Prime a sardonic grin.

The dynamic between the three brothers is tumultuous at best. Where Debauchery and Deception match each other in cunning, Greed eagerly skulks, hungry for recognition he so desperately covets. But beneath their obsessive competition and colorful insults is a kind of begrudging respect. Each brother, for all his authority, remains totally and completely useless without his siblings. These three need each other—of that, I have no doubt.

And that's what makes them the deadliest of all the Thirteen.

Cherry's fingers rake through my hair with practiced indifference, like a child absentmindedly toying with his favorite doll. This casual possessiveness—so typical of him—grounds me as the tension in the air grows so thick, I could choke, but his touch never falters. Within each rhythmic stroke lies a silent promise: I am his, and I always will be.

"I'll add my succubus to the pot."

I jerk upright, heat flushing through my skin. My ears burn with anticipation. His statement hangs between all of us, loaded with implication. He isn't actually referring to *me*, is he? Deception and Greed's eyes flick my direction, both sets of eyebrows knitting in interest.

"You've got thousands of those. What's so special about this one?" Greed leans back in his chair and folds his arms over his chest.

"Other than her assets," Deception adds, cracking a sickening smirk while his expression turns hungry.

Cherry's fingers continue to play with my red curls. "This one's not your run-of-the-mill Underling. She's very close to The Devil's Second. *Deliciously* so. One might even say…attached to her."

Deception's chuckle practically shakes the room, and the growing intrigue in Greed's eyes has my stomach in knots. Cherry continues, "We all need to be in Daddy's good graces right now. Everyone knows the quickest way to his heart is through his mousy little witch. Seeing as one of you ran her out of Vegas a year ago and the other refuses to give her a loan, I'd say neither of you is her favorite at the moment. I, on the other hand, spoon-fed her success tonight. I've already got a leg up on both of you. You own my succubus, you win over October Winters, you gain the favor of our father. Win-win-win."

The shock barely has time to process. It's a bluff. It *has* to be. Though if it were, Lord knows Deception would sniff the lie out faster than a bloodhound. I hold on tight to my composure, forcing myself to lean into Cherry's touch and fight my instinct to pull away. "Trust me," he had said earlier, as if placing trust in a Prime wasn't already a death wish. Still, Cherry and I have danced for the better part of a century, and I know when to follow his lead.

I flash his brothers a gentle, seductive smile while unlatching the collar around my neck. Leather and metal thud against hardwood as I toss it on the table, adding to the pot. All Cherry needs is one more Diamond. He better fucking have one.

"All in." Greed shoves his remaining souls forward. "Throwing in a clan of vampires too—old money."

Deception, looking uncertain for the first time tonight, folds his cards.

Cherry grins wickedly. "I call."

Greed flips his hand, a shit-eating grin plastered across his face. "Straight to the Ace. Eat that, you smarmy fucks."

I strain to catch a glimpse of Cherry's cards, but he clutches them to his chest. *Come on, Cherry,* I send him a telepathic blast. *Don't you dare fuck me over.*

My heart hammers against my ribs. The implications crash over me—what would it mean to serve under Greed? My entire existence could pivot on five fucking cards.

But no matter how this plays out, I'll keep my chin up. I'll survive whatever comes next, and when the dust settles, Cherry will get exactly what he deserves.

The Demon of Debauchery lazily flips his cards, and the entire room seems to still.

"A flush always beats a straight, darling."

"You little shit," Greed growls, rocketing to his feet and nearly overturning the poker table. "You fucking cheated. You both always fucking cheat!"

"Same time next year then?" Deception looks all too pleased with himself for someone who just lost a handful of Underlings and souls. Who am I kidding—of all the

Primes, Deception's well never runs dry. He'll recoup his losses the second he walks onto the casino floor. Greed grunts in response, kicking his chair toward the table like the petulant child he is. Cherry, on the other hand, erupts in prideful giggles, slapping his knees as he rises and pulls me close. I recoil at his touch, desperate to shove him away and demand explanations before he even thinks about laying hands on me. But he leans in, undeterred.

"You didn't think I'd let them have you, did you, darling?" His voice drips honey against my ear. "You're mine and mine alone."

The sentiment doesn't excuse his deceit, but it *does* calm my frigid nerves.

"You're forgetting something, brother," Cherry calls out to Deception, who towers well over six-feet as he buttons his simple suit jacket. "The main prize."

Greed sneers and storms off into the darkness while Deception flashes a grin that could rival the Cheshire Cat's.

"Come on out, Thane." Deception's voice echoes behind us. I spin around instinctively, searching as my curiosity piques. Who the Hell is Thane?

A figure emerges from the shadows, a handsome older man with silver hair and perfectly sculpted features, carrying the weight of the world on his shoulders. He's not just old; he's weathered. The bags under his eyes harbor secrets and exhaustion I can't even begin to fathom. He's in a simple black turtleneck, with a dark gray coat slung across his delicate shoulders. When his eyes meet mine for a split second, I'm frozen in place. Glacial blue. Haunting. Piercing. I can't place him— human? Halfling? Something else entirely?

Before I can get a read on his aura, Cherry gently shoves me aside and stalks toward the man. Despite his short stature, he *still* radiates dominance beside the taller, older stranger.

"Hello, my lovely. Oh, how I've missed you." Cherry slides his cane up the man's arm. Shockwaves ripple through me as I watch my Prime channel the man's essence into the black tourmaline pommel of his cane. Twisted black and white mist emerges from Thane, and Cherry steps back when the siphon is complete.

Then, he presses his lips to the man's thin mouth and devours the rest of his essence through a kiss.

What in the *actual fuck* have I been roped into?

When they pull apart, Thane nearly topples over. Cherry catches him with ease then flashes me a triumphant grin.

"Come on, darlings. Time to return to the City of Angels."

TRACK FOUR
Cherry Pie
LET'S PLAY A LITTLE GAME... OF CORRUPTION.
WHO WOULD YOU LIKE ME TO CORRUPT?
A DEMON HUNTER.

TRACK FOUR

CHERRY PIE

We arrive back at Bad Decisions in a huff of red smoke. Charlie's head jerks up, his grip tightening on the broom handle, while Indigo snaps her dustpan shut with a sharp clatter. They're both in their after-hours attire—Indy drowns in an oversized band t-shirt, the black lace trim of her panties just visible beneath the frayed hem, and Charlie sports a loose flannel and dark jeans that hug him perfectly. The casual clothes signal what I already know: dawn is creeping closer, and Bad Decisions has officially closed its doors for another night.

Good. We could all use a fucking break.

"Place looks as good as new." Cherry lays the flattery on thick, all honeyed words and falsities. The club's a far cry from 'new,' despite Indy and Charlie's best efforts. "Come, Reagan. We have much to discuss."

I lock eyes with my two most-trusted allies, offering them silent approval and a curt nod that tells them to make themselves scarce. They know better than to linger when Cherry's around. But then there's the matter of Mr. Silver Fox, this unexpected, uninvited guest whose presence, despite all the emptiness in my club, somehow fills every corner with unspoken tension.

Can you hear me? My gaze flits to Charlie, projecting my thoughts into his mind.

Loud and clear, comes his raspy, echoed response.

Good. Watch over the old man. He's one of Cherry's. And make sure Indy makes it downstairs soon. Sun's coming up.

I got her, he whispers back.

Mind-Tapping is just another one of those nifty tricks we Debauchery demons share. It doesn't quite work across Broodlines—believe me, Indigo and I have spent months trying to break the barriers, to no avail—but it sure does come in handy with Charlie.

Their voices fade into the background as I lead Cherry into my office for what seems like the thousandth time. All's quiet now that the patrons have left and the music's shut off, the rancid stench of burning bodies seeming to have subsided. All that remains now is my incorrigible boss and the millions of questions circling in my head.

"Pardon my French, but what the actual fuck was all that, Cherry?" I slam the door shut and plant a hand on my cocked hip as he makes himself comfortable on my desk.

"That, my little crimson cupcake, was demonic politics at its very finest."

"Clearly," I muse. "Well, you didn't drag me to Vegas and back just to ruffle my feathers and waste my time, so what was the point?"

"I've got a little business proposition for you, my love. If you find yourself with free time, that is."

As if a failing business and demonic turf wars don't drain me enough.

A weary sigh threatens to escape me. Still, something in his tone makes my pulse quicken. I cross my arms tightly against my chest and tilt my chin for him to continue.

"You saw what happened tonight. The state of the Underworld as of late has been"—his lips curl into something between a smile and a grimace—"*rocky*, to say the least. The demonic pecking order is in shambles after what our mutual blonde friend did to Nightmares and Fear." He steps closer, voice dropping an octave. "Banishment is a relatively new concept. Though, as we both know all too well, nothing stays buried in Hell for long. Regardless, my brothers and I, well…we've grown a bit restless."

Ha. Not the word I would use. Given my experience with the Big Thirteen, I know better. 'Restless' barely scratches the surface—they're terrified, and Fear isn't even around to reap the benefits. My eyes narrow, skepticism ever-growing. "I couldn't tell."

He continues, "Boundaries aren't just being overstepped, they're being *demolished*. Every Prime and their Broodline are only out for themselves, and the alliances I *do* have are barely hanging on by a thread. Power plays are afoot, and I need to protect my assets."

"Says the Prime who was so willing to give one up not twenty minutes ago."

"How many times must I repeat myself? I never had any intention of giving you up. It was a bluff—one neither Deception nor Greed cared to call, even with my bait."

"Bait," I bite, the word stinging my tongue. "That's what I am? Collateral for October Winters' favor?"

"Oh, darling," he coos. "Your human side is showing."

And just like that, the heat of my frustration turns to ice in my veins. My breath catches as I wait for him to reach out, to twist a lock of my hair around his finger or let his gaze drift to the cleavage revealed by my new top…but he maintains his distance. The confidence in his stance never wavers—not even a flicker of hesitation.

"I always enjoy you halflings. Watching those last dregs of humanity cling to the surface brings me more pleasure than a happy ending at a massage parlor. Pity that yours is more like a parasite, never failing to sink its claws in deep."

Resentment circles within me, white-hot and blinding. Every reminder of my humanity, of this *parasite*, as he so lovingly calls it, hammers home the truth: I am not a true demon in his eyes. I'm Turned. A halfling. A bargaining chip in his sordid games against his brothers, forever measuring short against the creatures he's Sired.

Fuck my humanity. I wish I could be rid of it.

I make the move Cherry hesitates to take, stepping deliberately forward. In my five-inch heels, I physically tower over him, yet his power radiates, making me feel small. Still, I press on, kicking his knees apart with practiced confidence and settling myself between his legs. "You sure do love the sound of your own voice, don't you, boss?"

"I do, yes."

"Well, as much as my parasite and I are simply itching for another one of your lessons in halflings and humanities, would you kindly mind getting to the point of this conversation?"

Cherry's eyes narrow for a fraction of a second before his demeanor shifts. There's a glimmer of genuine fascination there laced with something…darker. Admiration. Pride. His gaze lingers on my lips for a moment before he rubs his hands together slowly. Deliberately. "There's my little demoness. How I love that mouth of yours."

I flash him a playful smirk, hoping it will mask the discord of emotions twisting inside of me.

"Fine then. I've got a prized possession of sorts—one I happened to bring home from the poker game tonight. A little slice of Heaven that Greed, Deception, and I share. I need you to watch over him for me."

My eyebrow arches dangerously high. "'Him?' Not that older gentleman we brought back with us…"

"The very same."

Warning bells clang through my mind, first at Cherry's peculiar choice of words and then at his uncharacteristic transparency. "What's so special about him?"

"He's a delectable morsel. What of it?" Cherry's casual tone doesn't match the predatory gleam in his eyes.

The pieces slot together with sickening clarity. "You've got to be kidding. You want me to babysit one of your sex slaves?"

He tsks. "Such an ugly word. Get with the times, love. They're referred to as 'subs' these days."

"Since when?"

"Since the Demon of Debauchery—the *brilliant* Prime who coined the term—deemed it so."

I roll my eyes. "For how long?"

"For as long as I need."

I turn away deliberately, crimson curls cascading over my shoulder as I stalk the perimeter of my office. The sheer audacity of his request settles like ash on my tongue, bitter and thick. Babysitting a plaything as if I'm still some desperate Underling searching for scraps of approval. Those days are long behind me. I'd sooner waltz into the Debauchery realm of Hell and host afternoon tea with Hellspawn before I'd run a fool's errand for Cherry.

"I'm not doing this for free," I say, my voice firm, commanding.

Cherry's shoulders rise and fall with nonchalance. "Name your price."

The words hit me like a slap. I didn't expect it to be

that easy, not when he constantly reminds me I work for him, not the other way around. How many sleepless nights have I spent rehearsing this moment? How many times have I stood before my mirror, staring into my own glowing demonic eyes, and demanded what I'm owed with the conviction of someone who'd never get the chance?

Too many to count.

But here I am. And here goes nothing.

"I've been running Bad Decisions and The Starlight for nearly forty years now, and that's forty years too long," I begin, toying with the rhinestones embedded into his lapel. "The place is in shambles and clubs are a dying business, even in Southern California—especially with this whole internet thing blowing up. Why leave your house to get your rocks off when you can lock your-self in a room with some dial-up and a bottle of lube?"

Cherry huffs, flashing me an all-too-pleased-with-himself grin. "One of my best ideas."

"The point is, strip joints have lost their charm, and I'm not making enough to keep both places afloat. Also, for one reason or another, my house always seems to be the perfect battleground for demon hunters and entitled Underlings. You don't give me the proper security to protect my staff, and girls are getting harder to come by." Finally, my voice rises with years of suppressed frustra-tion. "Still, I've given you everything you've ever asked of me. Souls, bodies, essences—I never ask questions, and I'm not about to make a habit of asking them now.

But what I will do, what I *should* have done years ago, is demand what I'm owed."

He lifts his head in my direction, expression as unreadable as a wet newspaper. "And what is that?"

"Beverly Hills."

"Beverly Hills?"

"I'm a high-level demon in a low-end job, and my days are numbered," I explain, leaning over him as I place my hands firmly on either side of him on the desk. "I want out. And I want to take Indy, Charlie, and whatever's left of my team with me. We deserve better than Hollywood's gutter, Cherry. I want a place where I can get studio executives and A-listers to fall at my knees. I want to be where the *real* power is, the kind that bleeds money, corruption, and all the dark little things that make it taste sweeter. I could give you so much more."

The proposition weighs heavily on Cherry's mind for a moment. The hollows of his cheeks deepen as his lips purse, those dark eyes narrowing to calculated slits behind tinted lenses. *Come on, Cherry. Take* my *bait.*

When he finally slides the sunglasses from his face, I know we've entered dangerous territory.

"You're right, Reagan. You *could* give me so much more," he murmurs, his response turning my blood cold. That's when he finally reaches out, dragging one finger up my arm before twisting it through my curls with practiced intimacy.

My stomach drops. He's going to refuse me.

"Your proposition is…tempting," he continues, voice

deceptively soft. "I mean, you've definitely sold me on it, but it's dreadfully convoluted." His finger tightens ever so slightly in my hair. "It *should* be as easy as snapping my fingers, whisking you off to the west side, draping you in Dolce, and letting you loose among the elite. But it won't be that easy."

He releases my curl, allowing it to bounce back. "You see, love, there are politics far beyond your understanding. Just imagine how it would look to promote a Turned demon over one of my Sired? Oh, how the hierarchy would have my head."

And there it is again, the age-old conundrum: Sired vs. Turned. Pure-brood vs. halfling.

"Of course, they'd be less inclined to make a mess of things if you proved your worth."

I lean in closer, fighting the urge to dig my claws into the desk. Instead, I match his coquettish tone. "Haven't I spent enough time proving my worth?"

"Oh, you have, darling. To *me*. But what of my Sired?"

I dip my chin, batting my thick lashes at him, and run my hands up his chest. "Since when does their opinion outweigh yours?"

"I told you, love. It's just politics," he says with a dismissive wave before capturing my hand in his. His lips brush against my knuckles, leaving a ghost-like trail of heat—another one of his intimacy tactics designed to soften the blow. "I'd hate to give you what you want and watch you fall victim to yet another demonic turf war.

Violence's Underlings were a hassle, but your own Broodline?" He shakes his head, still holding my hand captive. "We need to be a united front, now more than ever."

"What are you suggesting?"

His lips curl into a predatory grin against my fingers. "Let's play a little game…of corruption. You said it best yourself—the real power lies there. And what are we if not the mere definition of corruption?"

My eyes narrow as the implications sink in. Cherry's games are legendary, elaborate webs that ensnare both hapless mortals and cocky supernaturals alike. We've turned corruption into an art form in this city, feeding off the power flowing from every tempted soul. The rush never gets old. But if this game grants me my greatest desires? I'll bite.

"Who would you like me to corrupt?"

Cherry's smile grows, all teeth and sadism. "A demon hunter."

A demon hunter, the biggest enemy known to demonkind—and he wants me to fucking corrupt one. My first instinct screams at me to fire back, to unload my laundry list of questions, demand contingency plans, craft an entire fool-proof strategy that wouldn't end with a halo choking me into an early grave. I look out the window behind Cherry, marveling at the burning sun peeking over the horizon. I think back to the little blonde witch who showed this city what she was made of, the one who, despite all the impossible odds stacked against her, lived by a simple philosophy: show up, party hard, and peace out.

We could all learn a little something from October Winters.

Sometimes, diving in headfirst without a plan is exactly the kind of chaos this world needs.

Temptation pulls at me, igniting a flame that's remained dormant for longer than I'd like to admit. The morbidity of the mundane has truly left me a shell of my former self, the woman—no, *demon*—who enjoys toying with others and bringing men to their knees. It's my nature. Inherent. Inescapable. And I'm tired of letting the parasite win.

"I'll take care of your pet for as long as you need. I'll even play your little game. But promise me, Cherry—promise me Beverly Hills."

"Corrupt a demon hunter, and you'll get Beverly Hills."

Cherry extends his hand, and I watch the magma-like veins bloom beneath his human glamour—delicate as spiderwebs, deadly as poison. When our hands clasp, I can feel the world hold its breath. His eyes ignite behind his shades, twin amber flames matching the fire behind mine. In that moment, something fundamental shifts the fabric of reality. Power surges between us, and I feel the invisible chains of our pact lock into place.

The deal is sealed. There's no going back now.

I have to corrupt a demon hunter.

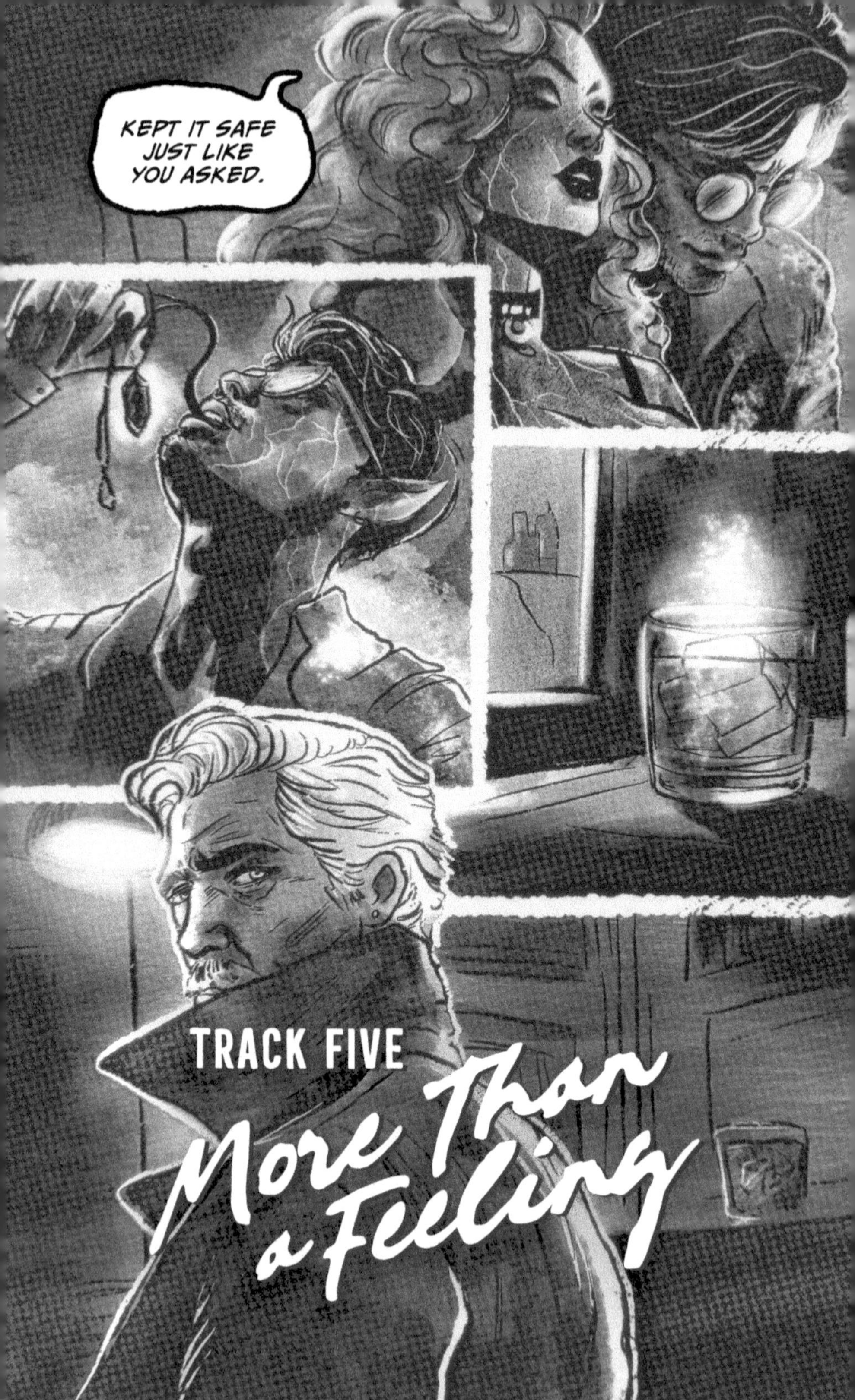

KEPT IT SAFE
JUST LIKE
YOU ASKED.
TRACK FIVE
More Than a Feeling

TRACK FIVE
MORE THAN A FEELING

Cherry always loved his games. We've played them together for years—collecting specific types of girls for the club, preying on innocent college freshmen, manipulating licentious husbands. Standard debauchery.

But this game…

This game feels different.

I'm not even sure if it's a game anymore, or if it's simply the means to my end. One thing's for certain: Cherry never sends an Underling on an errand if it isn't worth it. He may be an enigma wrapped in theatrics, but he always protects his own.

A trait he passed to me, horns and all.

"Reagan, my love." Cherry interrupts my thoughts with a snap of his fingers. "There is one other thing I'd ask of you tonight."

My gaze narrows in contempt at his fingers, a threat burning on my tongue, but I know better. I can't test the limits of our relationship, not when I have a job—multiple jobs—hanging in the balance. Instead, my posture takes on a more sensual flavor, one I know he'll respond to positively.

"How may I serve you?" I purr, sidling close to him.

"Oh, how deliciously thoughtful of you," he purrs back, hooded eyes gleaming gold behind his lenses. "But I'm hungry for something else entirely, something you possess that, regrettably, isn't your beautiful body." His fingers toy with the straps of my dress. "Bring me the crystal."

My eyes instinctively flit to my safe, which houses hundreds of black tourmaline necklaces. Without a word, I retrieve the brass key and unlock it, revealing my stash. There are too many to count, innumerable crystals filled with the sexual essence of my victims I keep locked away for when the hunger strikes. Demons don't eat, not in the conventional way. We survive off the essence of our prey, whether that be straight from the source or through these nifty little crystals that act as a to-go box of leftovers.

Some demons, particularly high-level ones, store more than just snacks in their safes. Some crystals contain essences far more potent and valuable than any mortal's.

The crystal Cherry wants is the same one I held hours earlier: the black tourmaline necklace containing the sexual essences of two sinful Nephilim.

"Kept it safe like you asked," I say, running my fingers over the ridges of the crystal. Its flickering glow is dimmer now, almost nonexistent. I dangle the necklace by its chain in front of Cherry, watching his eyes dart back and forth as it swings under the fluorescent lights. There's a hunger in those eyes, always shielded behind colorful lenses that match his elaborate outfits. Tonight, though, his eyes seem darker, more demented, more famished than ever.

"Excellent," he mutters in a voice so low, it sends a shiver up my spine. He takes the necklace by its chain, cautious and deliberate with every movement. "It's a shame one of the hunters perished tonight. How very lucky of us to have captured a bit of him before he met his end."

"Luckily October had him wrapped around her finger," I remind him.

"In more ways than one," he says suggestively, tilting his head as he studies the crystal. His voice shifts to something softer, something barely there. Captivated. Enthralled. "Did you know Nephilim essence is a delicacy rarer than salvation in Hell, Reagan?"

I nod slowly, my own attention fixed on the swaying pendant. Something inside pulls at me, a power so great and so tempting, even someone as disciplined as I can feel a twinge of hunger.

Cherry brings the crystal to his lips, releasing a ragged breath that fractures into a guttural moan. A tangled helix of black and white mist pours from the crystal, writhing in the air like serpents as they invade my Prime's nostrils and mouth, slipping beneath his sunglasses to penetrate his eyes. His moan deepens into something obscene, almost orgasmic, as if he's tasting divinity itself. His body trembles, knees buckling as the essence floods him.

"Sublime." His voice drips with euphoria, echoing in discordant harmonies like the true monster he is. Spider-web-like gold veins creep up his skin as the pale tone of his human form flushes deep crimson, similar to mine. It isn't until his dark, twisted horns begin peeking out of his skull that I realize something…

One taste of Nephilim essence is enough to rip the glamour off any demon, even a Prime.

"I'd almost forgotten the taste of a young one," Cherry purrs, drawing his now razor-sharp claws to his lips. His forked tongue flicks between them, savoring each metaphoric droplet like precious wine. My stomach burns with jealousy, and I can't decide which I covet more—his lethal grace or the feast I'm denied.

The tension breaks as pleasure ripples through his frame, shuddering away his demonic features like frost melting in sunlight. His human glamour emerges beneath—flawless, as always. Cherry adjusts his rhinestone-studded jacket with a flourish, flicking invisible dust from his shoulders. Such theatrics should be cringe-worthy, yet on him, it's perfectly, *terribly* right.

"Here you go, darling," he says in his glamoured voice, dangling the black tourmaline necklace in front of me.

My brows reach sky high. "There's still more left in there."

"Indeed, there is."

I struggle to pick up what he's putting down, to understand the mischief behind his words or that playful gleam in his eye. He simply lets the crystal hang in space.

So, I warily take it from him.

"Hang on to that one," Cherry says with a delicious grin. "You never know when it will come in handy."

A primal urge takes over, and without a second thought, I bring the dark crystal to my lips. Temptation tugs at my insides for the first time since my transformation, and for a fleeting moment, I remember what it feels like to be human.

"Ah, ah, ah, my little cherry pie. That is not yours to consume." My boss breaks the memory quicker than it started. Of fucking course, it wasn't for me. Hell forbid I should have any semblance of payment or pleasure for my own.

My indignation is palpable. "Then what, pray tell, am I meant to do with it?"

His twisted smile reaches those beautiful, demented eyes. "Play our game, of course."

It's in this moment of silence between our intentions that something lethal is born, some kind of understanding, a shared ambition. Pure debauchery.

My Prime mutters about meeting me in the main showroom as he preens at his reflection in my full-length mirror before walking out of my office. His heeled boots and cane echo across the floor of the main room, followed by his boisterous pandering to my employees—or what's left of them.

I'm left alone with nothing but the black tourmaline crystal in my hands. It's lighter now, harboring the essence of one Nephilim rather than two, the essence of that irksome apprentice.

Suddenly, it hums again, just like it did earlier. This time, it's low, like white noise one could easily miss during the club's working hours. I'm reminded of how the pendant pulsed erratically when the source of its magic stood mere feet away, how it glowed brighter, grew hotter as he approached me.

And that's when it hits me: I may have a head start in his little game after all.

When I finally return to the showroom, I find it spotless, cleansed of the earlier carnage but also void of colorful lights and false pretenses. The main floor loses all its mystery and allure the moment the lights flick on. Harsh fluorescence exposes every ugly truth. Water-damage stains the ceilings yellow and brown, blisters of paint peel like diseased skin, and patches of mold form an excellent breeding ground for bacteria. The dance floor's linoleum has faded to a sickly beige, cratering where countless stilettos scraped away its luster.

And my poor velvet booths. I was so proud the day I rescued them from that abandoned diner during the '60s, even prouder when I re-upholstered them myself with deep-red velour. Now, they're barely a shell of what they once were, dust-ridden, crusty, and dry after years of spilled alcohol, reeking of stale cigarette smoke and cheap cologne from my patrons.

Bad Decisions was meant to live in shadow, where the only light that mattered would dance across bare skin and liquor bottles.

I find Cherry minding his own business—a miracle, really—looking more radiant after his little meal. He straightens when he spots me and glances at his wristwatch.

"Goodness, where has the time gone? I haven't even formally introduced you to your new house guest!" He links his arm with mine and eagerly escorts me from the main stage to the bar.

Tucked within the furthest corner of Bad Decisions sits that lonely stranger, the painfully handsome silver fox.

"Reagan, I'd love for you to meet your charge for the foreseeable future—Vincent Thane...my pet."

Pet. What an unfortunate life sentence for a human.

Folding my arms over my chest, I study the older man, dressed in head-to-toe black with a woolen gray coat tailored perfectly to his broad frame. I try to place his age somewhere between 65 and 70, watching the wrinkles around his eyes deepen as he offers me a soft smile.

My lips curl in return with a sardonic grin. "Charmed."

"Now, you two play nice. Daddy's got work to do. I'll be checking in." My skin crawls at my Prime's choice of words. When the Demon of Debauchery finally vanishes in a swirl of crimson mist, I feel a weight lift off my shoulders—until I remember he's left me alone with his…pet.

The rickety stool scrapes against the withered linoleum as I drag it away from the bar and sit down. "Vincent, huh?"

"You must be Reagan." His voice is like aged whiskey, smooth and warm. It sends a shiver up my spine.

"Must I be?" I tease, leaning my body into the bar.

My observant instincts take over as I start cataloging the minute details of this silver fox. His hair is neatly groomed, with a close-shaved undercut, longer at the top, side-swept to the left in a perfectly low pompadour held together by pomade. His scent reeks of expensive bergamot and sandalwood—Gaultier, no doubt— enhancing his luxurious aura. And his clothes? Expertly tailored. I even catch the glint of silver around his turtleneck, a perfect little accessory to complete his posh look. There's a gentleness about him, a quiet elegance that feels understated yet commands attention all the same. I would expect nothing less from a pet of Cherry's.

That's exactly what he is. A well-maintained, well-groomed pet.

I motion for Charlie to whip our guest up a welcoming beverage, sending a precautionary message through our Mind-Tapping ability. "Welcome to my neon purgatory," I start flatly, avoiding the elder's gaze. "I'd apologize for the third-rate accommodations, but it's the best I've got, and you'll just have to get used to it."

He gives me a pained grin, something between a wince and a chuckle. "I've lived under far worse circumstances. Your club is charming."

'Charming' is the last word I'd use to describe Bad Decisions, but his flattery is a welcome balm after the night I've had.

I watch from the corner of my eye as Charlie slips a bit of his influence into the amber liquid, two smoky tendrils of demonic magic slipping through his fingers and mixing into the beverage with ease. Charlie's not just an expert mixologist; he's a unique breed of incubus. While Debauchery demons of our variety typically manipulate victims through our bodies and pheromones, some like to take a more creative approach. Charlie manipulates emotions through vessels, beverages being his specialty—impressive for a creature so low on the demonic hierarchy.

He places the glass on the bar top and slides it over to the older man, who raises his hand in protest.

"I won't be needing that," he says, his low voice carrying the ghost of an accent I can't quite place. He politely pushes the glass across the table toward me. The fluorescent light above catches in the amber liquid like lightning and quickly reveals my own reflection, where the glowing, lava-like magic flows beneath the cracks in my skin.

I blink in shock at my new guest, gaze flitting to my trusted bartender, whose thick, dark brow rises so high, it gets lost beneath his bandana and backwards ball cap.

Before we can Tap into each other's thoughts, the Silver Fox speaks.

"I don't blame you for your skepticism. I'm a stranger, after all, dropped on your doorstep like an abandoned infant you're just expected to care for without so much as a note or an explanation. There's something you can't pin about me—maybe it's the calmness in my voice, or how, despite my seemingly human nature, my demeanor could not remain more phlegmatic. Or maybe what you're truly puzzled by is my aura. I imagine it's quite dark these days. I haven't had a chance to look." He glances at Charlie's concoction once more, huffing out a laugh. "You don't need to test me with demonic truth serums disguised as alcohol. While I'm sure your low-level incubus is quite talented, I've indulged in enough of those over the years to know honesty is the best policy, and the best way to win over a skeptic is to divulge your own secrets first."

In all my time on this plane, I've rarely felt the

painful sting of a metaphorical slap to the face. But his words catch me completely off guard, leaving me wondering what sort of mess Cherry has dragged me into.

Truth is, I hadn't taken the time to read his aura, but now that he's mentioned it, I couldn't be more curious… and undoubtedly bemused.

It's a low, pulsing light shadowed by swirls of darkness, not unlike the young demon hunter from earlier. Before I can speak, Vincent continues.

"I understand our mutual acquaintance has set you on a dangerous quest," Vincent speaks slowly, intentionally, his fingers clasped together in a polite fold. "Corrupting a demon hunter. Not an easy task, especially if you haven't a clue where to start."

I tilt my head at him, marveling at his calculated gestures. How did he know about the deal? Does he possess some inhuman hearing abilities? Did he snoop around while Cherry and I had our meeting in my office? I let it slide, the intrigue of his statement reeling me in.

"What do you know about corruption, Silver Fox?"

"Is that my name now?"

"It is to me."

"Corruption isn't as daunting as it seems. It should come easily to someone like you." His gentle smile flickers, there and gone in an instant. Something in his tone, that melancholy ballad of dark secrets and timeless grace, pulls me forward, and I find myself leaning in closer.

"It starts slow at first. There's the hint of temptation, that primal urge that pulls them toward the forbidden fruit despite their better judgment. They remind themselves of their virtue, of their higher calling, of that pious indoctrination that runs on a loop in that soft, helpless little brain…

"But all it takes is a taste, a drop of sweet nectar that sets the nerves ablaze and delivers a moment of relief and satisfaction. It's never enough, is it? Such is the nature of seduction.

"Then comes the itch. The hazy thoughts. Blurred lines. The obsession that creeps up their spine like rampant vines twisting and tangling their reality…until it's all they can think about. 'What's one more taste?' It's a simple question, after all. Innocent. Fair. One that tears down those intricately built walls. For a moment, they fight the urge. Their heart swells with pride over their self-restraint. For a moment, they believe—actually believe—they're above it all. That the demons would never win. But here's the thing about darkness: once they've had a taste…they always come back begging for more."

The man reeks of Shakespeare and Poe—a morbid blend of poetic prose and dark humor. He speaks as if he's plucked from a different century, his haunted eyes never meeting mine, even after his monologue.

"Speaking from experience, are you?" I ask, tilting my head.

He simply flashes me a small, wistful smile. He's

quite the looker, even with the little wrinkles that etch decades of unrest into his skin. When he looks up at me, time stands still. Something about those piercing, glacial-blue eyes cuts through me with immaculate precision, and I can't ignore the pressure coiling up my spine as I fight to look away. He doesn't just look at me. He sees *through* me, unraveling every pretense, every calculated motion, all without uttering a single word. Who is this man? And why does Cherry find him so special?

His fingers tug on the hem of his turtleneck, revealing skin so sun damaged, I almost miss the faded symbol inked across his jugular. My eyes narrow as I struggle to decipher the design but quickly widen as a realization hits me like a brick.

I know that mark. It's the same one I've seen more times than I care to admit—an eight-pointed star hidden beneath a monstrous demonic skull.

Well, I'll be double-damned.

Vincent Thane is a motherfucking demon hunter.

TRACK SIX
Livin' on a Prayer
YOU PROBABLY DON'T BELIEVE ME. PROBABLY THINK I'M CRAZY.
NO. I DO. I BELIEVE YOU.
I WOULDN'T. MONSTERS AREN'T REAL.

TRACK SIX
LIVIN' ON A PRAYER

Charlie's ocean-blues lock onto mine across the bar. I shoot to my feet, claws curling inward, ready to strike at a moment's notice. Silver Fox offers me another gentle smile and raises his hands in surrender.

"Easy there, Miss Reagan," he says. "I am no threat to you. My powers haven't worked in decades, and I am fresh out of holy blades."

My fingers uncurl, though my mind stays razor-sharp. "How the hell does a demon hunter become a Prime's pet? That's…well, it's not just impossible, it goes against everything—divinity, demonology, all of it. Every single rule."

"Oh, it's very possible, I assure you. It's a crime punishable by something far worse than death."

"What's worse than death?"

"To a demon hunter? Being cast out from the very

Order that raised you, trained you, and molded your entire existence."

My eyes narrow. "You were excommunicated? They actually do that?"

"They do much more than that," he says, his voice carrying decades of bitterness. "Once your soul is tainted by evil—even a drop—you're damaged goods. Broken. Worthless. No use to anyone once your purity is compromised." He pauses, studying the beverage he refused. "But that's a story for another time, preferably over drinks not laced with incubus influence."

I think back to Declan Lovejoy, a hunter whose soul was undoubtedly tainted, but he remained in the Order's good graces. How did that one slip through the cracks?

"Can I get you something else, Vincent?" I ask.

"I wouldn't mind a place to rest my head for a bit. Been a long night, after all."

"My motel's all yours. Follow me."

I escort the older man out of the club and toward the motel, where my remaining human employees drape themselves over the balconies for a morning cigarette. The sun finally crests the horizon, casting a golden glow over Hollywood Boulevard. I squint into the distance— no more smoke, no more sirens, just a hushed blanket over sleeping streets that will soon stir to life, welcoming the endless parade of tourists and locals.

I lead him up the stairs in comfortable silence, heading to the second level towards the room right next door to 666. He'll be safe here, away from the riffraff.

Once he's settled into the room, I waste no time. "Listen here, Silver Fox. I've had one Hell of a night, and I'm fresh out of patience. Since you're so eager to spill your secrets, and I'm graciously providing you shelter while Cherry runs off doing Devil-knows-what, let's make this interesting. I'm going to ask you some very direct questions, and you're going to give me very direct answers. No more of this cryptic Shakespearean bullshit. Are we clear?"

Something shifts in his expression—a glint of recognition I know all too well. Respect for someone who doesn't play games. Irony is, I'm currently in the middle of the greatest game of all.

"Crystal. And I couldn't agree more. Besides, you don't strike me as the type to know much about my kind," he starts, and I immediately shut him down.

"You'd be surprised how many of 'your kind' I've dealt with in the past few days. I've already got my sights set on one."

"Do you?" he asks, running his fingers over the bed frame, nightstand, and walls. "Tell me about him."

The familiar knot of caution twists in my gut, that little voice questioning whether I should trust this man, this walking contradiction who must have done something unforgivable to get himself banished by his own people. But I already made my decision, and I wasn't going to turn my back on it.

"He's young," I start.

"He probably isn't. We age very slowly."

"No, this one definitely is. And his aura was very… erratic, like a flickering lightbulb. And I don't know what that means." I lean forward slightly. "Have you ever experienced it?"

"Interesting," Silver Fox—Vincent—muses, stroking his chin. "Erratic, you say? Was it white?"

"White enough. Hints of gray."

"His soul has been compromised. I can't say how— that can be done in several ways." He pauses thoughtfully. "But that will work to your advantage. It means he will be more susceptible to corruption. If you *can* find him, he may be your best bet to complete Cherry's task."

Skepticism grips my insides, still perplexed at how he knew such intimate information about our deal. "That was my next question. Where does a demon hunter go when they aren't actively hunting?"

"The answer varies—some have temporary homes, others return to headquarters."

"Headquarters? Where?"

"Varies," he replies in a maddeningly vague tone.

"Vincent." I glare daggers in warning.

He simply smiles. "What else do you know about him?"

I consider the question, sifting through the details from our brief encounter. There's the black tourmaline necklace, the one that glows and flickers just like his aura, especially when he's nearby. But I don't have time to waltz around Los Angeles playing treasure hunter with a glorified mood ring.

"He was involved in a mass killing last night not too far from here. Lost his mentor in the process."

I expect Vincent to tense at the mention of a fallen brother, but apparently, he's too far removed from his past to give a damn.

"Well then, you have the perfect spot to start: the scene of the crime."

"Wouldn't he be foolish to return?"

"It wouldn't be foolish at all—not to him. His first instinct will be to retrieve the body. Demon hunters, they…" He pauses, choosing his words carefully. "Let's just say they have very particular ways of honoring their dead, especially if they fall at the hands of a demon."

That's just the problem; I don't actually know how Lovejoy died. In my mind, October killed him. But I know her, and while their twisted history never made a lick of sense to me, I can't make any assumptions. For all I know, she may not have laid a finger on him.

Wishful thinking is all I have to go on.

Still, Silver Fox has a point. If I want answers, to find this Nephilim before Cherry grows tired of waiting, there's only one place to start.

Hollywood Forever Cemetery. Where the dead don't always stay buried.

I've always wanted to be an actress. It's what brought me to Hollywood all those years ago, expensive valise in hand and stars in my eyes, ready to make it big, along with a beautiful collar wrapped around my neck, forever marking me as one of Debauchery's little dolls.

I stand before my vanity mirror in a fresh outfit, pieces borrowed from Indigo's trunk. Channeling glamour magic through my fingertips, I trace over my features, shifting minute details of my appearance. Mr. Nephilim had already seen my usual disguise: a simple human version of what I looked like before my transformation. Same features, minus the crimson skin, glowing cracked veins, and various demonic extremities.

For this performance, I need something slightly different.

I start with my nose, defining it more sharply, adding piercings, two in each nostril, one at the septum. Then, my eyes, switching them from my natural hazel-green to ocean-blue, as tumultuous as the waves of the Pacific. I trace my fingers along my jawline, softening the defined edges into gentler curves.

Finally, I step back to admire my handiwork.

Torn fishnets. Disheveled, fire-engine red hair. Smudged makeup. A little extra powder from my eyeshadow to mimic soot.

Looking at my reflection, one could easily forget the truth of my nature.

Hollywood Forever isn't far, just a couple of traffic lights down the street. I'm grateful for my high-tops;

heels would've made this trek absolute hell. As the sun shines behind the palm tree-riddled horizon, I slip through the cemetery gates. Disappointment washes over me as I survey the scene: far to the left, where they hold movie nights, a massive stage is being dismantled by construction workers. Electricians sort through tangles of wire while others break down what must have been audience barricades.

But there's no sign of carnage. No fire damage. No battle remnants whatsoever.

I think back to Cherry's comment just hours ago in Vegas, something about Deception sending Cleaners to scrub away the supernatural mess October left behind.

The morbidly curious part of me had wanted to see the bodies, the remains of whatever undead she'd raised, some glimpse of scorched earth and chaos.

Instead, there's nothing. Not a single goddamn trace.

A fucking shame.

The crystal necklace burns hotter against my skin as I venture deeper into the cemetery. I pass countless graves of Hollywood elite—actors, producers, legends who left their mark and achieved immortality through cinema. Toward the west end sits a mausoleum surrounded by a tranquil pond. Geese honk aggressively at ducks, and tiny turtles bask in the fading November sunlight.

When I finally reach the mausoleum, my necklace has started searing against my chest. I unhook the chain and study the crystal—the inner glow flickers faster now, more erratically.

Bingo.

I slip inside, silent as death itself. Sticking to the shadows, I move carefully past aisles of walled crypts until I hear something that stops me cold: soft sniffles and the wavering voice of a man. He's speaking in a language I can't quite place, though it sounds familiar. Latin, maybe?

"Corpus fratris invocamus. Corpus fratris invocamus. Corpus fratris invocamus."

His voice is utterly shattered, the words tumbling out in whispers. With each repetition, hope drains from his tone until only raw desperation remains. Small sobs cut his chanting, staggered breaths echoing off the cold stone walls.

That's when I see him.

A broken Nephilim on his knees before an elegant stained-glass window, praying. Begging. Hoping for salvation.

He looks—dare I say it—hauntingly beautiful in this light. Morning sun filters through the colored glass, painting reds and blues across his features while his salt-and-pepper hair catches the light like a halo. For a moment, I forget what he did last night. I forget that he tried to kill me, that he murdered Jazzi. The pure rage in his eyes, hatred that could move mountains—none of that exists here. Right now, he's simply a broken angel, another lost soul desperate for saving.

Time to begin my performance.

I deliberately stumble over my own feet, gasping

loud enough to shatter the sacred silence. His head snaps around instantly, misty green eyes locking on to mine. I curse under my breath and bolt, forcing him to give into the chase.

"Wait!" he calls out, his footsteps echoing closer. I sprint across the mausoleum toward the central hall that divides the crypts, spotting an ornate sarcophagus in the atrium. I duck behind it and force myself to pant heavily, loud enough for him to hear my ragged breathing.

The crystal is burning a hole in my pocket now. He's so close, I can almost see his erratic aura flickering along the walls. Finally, he finds me.

"It's alright—I'm not going to hurt you."

A lie. A beautiful lie. His voice does little to convince me, and I watch the quarrel behind his gaze—grief at war with duty, a ravenous storm calming at the sight of a damsel in distress. There's a warmth in those troubled eyes, an ingrained compassion unlike anything I've ever witnessed firsthand. When he crouches down to meet me at eye-level, his movements are careful, deliberate, as if he's worried his own darkness may betray and devour us both. His extended hand trembles slightly, but that smile…oh, that sweet smile almost makes me forget how lethal he truly is. It's like a lifeline, one he's desperate for me to grab hold of. Little does he know, he's the one who's drowning. "What are you doing here? Are you alright?"

"Were you at the show?" I sob out, avoiding his hand.

"Yes." His quiet response echoes off the marble walls. "How'd you get in here?"

With a small shrug, I concoct the perfect lie. "My friends and I snuck in between sets to get a couple hits in before that new band came on—ya know, the one with the female lead. By the time they started, we were so fuckin' high, we didn't even want to go back out there. We had our own little sanctuary here. Just a couple of misfits trying to feel...*something*. But then, we heard screaming. The music was still playing, but their screams were louder. My friends went to investigate...and they never came back."

He nods slowly. "Did you see what happened?"

"I can still smell the burning bodies. That's what it had to be, right? The flames were so close, so hot, it's like they were right next to me. I tried to look outside—" I pause for dramatic effect, taking in a breathy inhale. "All I could see were...bodies. Dead bodies. Bones barely held together by rotting flesh. They were eating the pit, like monsters right out of the movies." My gaze flits to his and back at my feet, and I tuck a spare lock of hair behind my ear. "This is stupid. You probably don't believe me or think I'm crazy. I was so fucking high—"

"No," he interrupts, inching closer. "No. I do believe you."

"I wouldn't." I look up at him again, forcing tears to fall. "Monsters aren't real."

His thoughts unfold as my magic reaches deep into his mind. Even through my carefully crafted charade of torn clothing and a mess of dark makeup, he sees something others would not: someone broken but beautiful. He marvels over the mascara streaking my cheeks, how they make my glassy blue eyes appear ethereal in the golden glow of the sunrise shining through the stained-glass windows. I watch him fight the urge to reach for me, to tangle his fingers in my red hair and offer the kind of comfort he desperately craves for himself. The muscles in his arms twitch, yearning yet resisting. He's hungry, *so hungry* for connection, to know another who has suffered the same devastation and loss. *Maybe,* he thinks, *we could heal each other.*

A foolish, innocent wish. I'm not the antidote he so desperately craves. I'm the poison.

"What's your name?" He settles beside me on the stone floor. The heat of his body is enough to swallow the cold whole. I can see it now, that tattoo on his neck—the Nephilim mark. I see how it burns his skin, warning him of danger nearby, but his thoughts pay it no mind. Right here, right now, the threat of the Underworld is meaningless, and all that matters to him is the beautifully broken redhead he yearns to put back together.

"Jasmine." It's the first name I can think of—the name of the banshee he killed at my club, whose severed head and milky white eyes still haunt me. Her name weighs heavy on my tongue, something that isn't mine and I have no right to. I shouldn't soil her memory with my twisted manipulation, but the damage is done, and I've already stained her name with a dark purpose.

"Jeremy." His own name feels like a confession on his lips.

We sit in silence for what feels like hours. The sound of our steady breaths fill the mausoleum, but all I can hear are his thoughts running on a loop. Our hands are inches apart, resting on the marble, and for a moment, I consider reaching for him.

But what happens when an angel and demon touch? Would either of us burst into flames? Would he discover my truth? Unveil the glamour I've so perfectly cast?

Cherry's bargain demands far more than a simple touch. If I'm going to corrupt him, I'll need to get much closer than this.

My muscles tense as I take a sharp breath and take his hand…

And the world doesn't end. No flames, no revelation, no divine retribution, just his hand in mine, warm and achingly human.

"I'm so sorry," he all but whispers. Then, the words start falling out, rushed and panicked. "I'm sorry I couldn't save your friends. There were just too many of them, and she was *so* strong…and then, she did something to my mentor. I heard him in my head—he told me to kill her. I knew he was speaking to me. Now, I can't hear him anymore, and I've searched this entire cemetery three times over for his body, and—"

There it is; the moment I've been hoping for. His grief becomes a weapon in my hands, his desperate need for connection betrays the oldest rule in the book: *Never reveal the truth to humans. Always come up with a convenient lie.*

He doesn't even realize what he's done, of course. I couldn't have planned it better myself.

"'She?'" I look up at him through tear-soaked lashes. "W-what are you talking about?"

His lips open and close repeatedly, as if his brain is short-circuiting, struggling to find the perfect cover-up for this untimely outburst.

Finally, he sighs and leans his head against the marble sarcophagus. "Now who's the crazy one?"

I offer him a gentle smile. "Guess we're just a bunch of fuck ups, huh?"

"You could say that." He returns the gesture.

I fight the urge growing inside me, the dangerous pull toward the innocence in his voice, the genuine kindness. Does he have any idea what I really am? Can he feel it in his hunter's mark?

I slip into his mind again, testing the limits of my charade. The static has quieted, the storm calmer than when I first encountered it. There's raw pain there, sorrow deep enough to move a statue to tears. He blames himself for what happened to his mentor, desperately wanting to find the body and perform the proper cleansing rituals.

But underneath all that grief, there's something else—comfort. I watch him studying my features through his memories, marveling at my eyes, which he compares to the California sky, and my hair, which reminds him of the stunning stained glass just aisles away. He sees me as a masterpiece, a work of art to be treasured.

If only he knew what kind of monster hid behind the canvas.

I break the silence. "Is it safe out there?"

"Eerily clean," he says as he nods grimly.

"Jesus," I breathe out. "I need to get out of here, need to wash the horrors off me." I force uncertainty into my voice. "I don't live too far away… Would you—I mean, you don't have to—" I duck my head, brushing unruly curls behind my ear with practiced shyness.

His grip on my hand tightens. "Let me walk you home. As consolation for…everything."

Everything? Is that his idea of an apology for the mess he made of my club, for killing Jazzi? I swallow my rage and focus on the job. I've got a role to play.

I pull us both to our feet, craning my neck to meet his eyes as he towers over me. I hate how beautiful he looks in this light, how much it hurts to stare into the face of someone who wanted me dead just hours ago.

But I have to do this. Cherry didn't ask me to corrupt a Nephilim for fun. There's an ulterior motive buried in this game.

And I'm going to dig it up.

TRACK SEVEN
Pour Some Sugar on Me

TRACK SEVEN
POUR SOME SUGAR ON ME

Charlie keeps a studio apartment on the corner of Fountain and La Brea, just a few blocks from Bad Decisions and safely tucked away from the main tourist chaos. It's a modest space on the eighth floor of an old building, right above a convenience store. It's just big enough for the incubus and whatever conquest he's entertaining. He occasionally lets me borrow it for my own needs when the club feels too public and the motel too clinical.

There's a spare key hidden beneath a potted lavender plant by the door. The fragrance reminds me of Indigo—my little vampire with eyes that sometimes mirror that same soft purple. I smile to myself as I crouch to retrieve the key, letting Jeremy and myself inside.

"Live here alone?" Jeremy asks as he studies the barely decorated apartment.

"It's temporary," I assure him. "My job's always on the go—never know where I'm gonna end up next."

"I can relate. What do you do?"

"I work in radio. Hop around when it suits me. Yourself?"

"Uh…" He pauses, searching for the right words. "Security consulting."

"Security consulting," I chuckle. What a convenient—albeit brilliant—way to cover up the truth. I gesture toward the neatly made queen bed, one that's definitely seen its share of action. "Make yourself comfortable."

Without hesitation, I start unhooking my jean shorts and shimmy them down my legs. Jeremy jolts backward, immediately spinning around to shield his vision.

"What's wrong?" I ask with feigned innocence. "Never seen a girl in her underwear before?"

He breathes out a throaty laugh. "I'd prefer to give you your privacy."

"How chivalrous," I drawl sarcastically, peeling the fishnets off. Impatience gnaws at me; he should be looking, should be falling into the trap I've laid. This was supposed to be the moment I hooked him, as if the trauma bonding at the cemetery wasn't hook enough. After all, he *did* walk me home and come inside. He could have left the moment we reached the door.

But he didn't.

Which tells me he's curious enough to stay. And curiosity, in my experience, is a gateway to corruption.

I've never been one to charge headfirst into trouble

without a strategy. As much as I'd love to live life reck-lessly, it's not in my nature. Guidelines and contingencies are my bread and butter, with effective results as the main course.

However, Jeremy's chivalry is an precarious variable in the equation.

Time to kick this into high gear.

I slip every last article of clothing off me, positioning myself just so my reflection catches in one of the many floor-length mirrors next to Charlie's bed. We Debauchery demons are a vain bunch, and there's no doubt the place is covered in mirrors so he can enjoy every view of his partners—for that, I am grateful.

Jeremy's eyes find my body through the mirror, lingering far too long on my exposed parts. He thinks I can't tell, thinks I'm too preoccupied, but I know.

That's when I slip into a hot, steaming shower without closing the bathroom door and carry on our conversation.

"I'm in desperate need of a drink after last night," I start. "Wanna join me?"

"This early in the day?" His voice cracks as he draws closer for me to hear.

"Hell yeah," I laugh while soaping up. "It's never too early to drink the trauma away."

"I-I'm not much of a drinker." The hesitance in his voice, coupled with the weight of his gaze, makes his nervousness palpable. The hot steam coating the mirrors obstructs his view of my body, water running down the opaque shower curtain. *This is safe,* he thinks to himself. *I'm not really looking.*

"You're over 21, right?" I ask, poking my head out from behind the curtain to note his prematurely gray hair. He nods. "And you're not a drinker? We've gotta fix that. I know a great place. You local to LA?"

"Afraid not."

"Small town?"

"Something like that."

I yank the shower curtain away, catching him by surprise. Instead of turning around again or shutting his eyes like the sweet little thing he is, he stares, frozen in place.

Sometimes, a little banter is all it takes to catch a man off guard.

And there's the primal itch, I think, practically hearing Silver Fox's monologue.

I choose not to chastise him, not to tease with the usual, "Take a picture; it'll last longer." I don't want to shame him into looking away. I want him to look harder. Drink me in. Map out every inch of this glamoured body so when he does eventually break, he will know which parts to explore first.

I wring out my freshly washed curls into the drain and exit the shower slowly, feeling every drop of water slide over my skin. I shake out my head, and the cold ringlets plaster to my back as I take a step closer to him. His already rigid posture straightens even more when I finally approach him. Our eyes lock, neither of us looking away. From this angle, this close, I can drink in the beauty of his gaze—sea-green like the Malibu coastline, where sunlight transforms the waves from emerald to gray. There's a curious ring of amber around his pupils, which dilate with every heartbeat. They're striking, mesmerizing, almost as intense as Vincent's glacial blues. For a moment, I have to look away.

The chaos in his mind is so loud, I can practically hear it without even reading his thoughts. There's so much turmoil between desire and guilt, it makes me want to reach out and quiet the storm.

The itch. The hazy thoughts. The blurred lines.

Finally, I break the silence.

"Can you get me a towel?" I gesture toward the simple black towel hanging from a hook on the door behind him.

He scrambles for it then, hands trembling as he extends it toward me, those darling green eyes darting away faster than I can blink. Tension hangs thick between us as we both fall silent. His mind continues to spill its secrets to me, and for once, I'm grateful to be a Debauchery demon. Imagine trying to corrupt the incorruptible without any supernatural influence?

I would have lost this game before it even started.

An hour later, we find ourselves strolling side by side down Hollywood Boulevard, following the Walk of Fame stars. I casually point out the legends, actors from my younger days who were among the first to earn their mark on this famous street. He pays them no mind, nodding absentmindedly and offering the occasional, "Cool," or "Nice."

Devil help me, he couldn't be more typically male if he tried.

We approach a local dive, and I quickly scan the doorways for Cherry's insignia but find nothing. I'd be safer in a demon-owned establishment, but that could also mean disaster if Jeremy went in guns blazing—or, in his case, holy daggers flying—and risked exposing our world to humans.

"This is the place—it's fucking stellar. They're the only ones who ever play the good stuff these days." I note his rigid posture, the way he draws his bottom lip between his teeth and eyes the establishment warily. "What's the matter? Never been to a bar before?"

"It's a little loud, isn't it?"

"It's a sports bar cranking '80s hair metal on a Sunday afternoon *and* LA's playing against San Jose. I'd be disappointed if it wasn't loud."

"I guess I'm just used to quiet nights in with books."

I reach for his hand, fingers intertwining as I tug him toward the entrance. "Come on. You're going to love it."

For so early in the day, the place is surprisingly packed.

Neon beer signs cast the bar in green and blue hues, reflecting off countless bottles on the bar top, some empty, some freshly opened. The bartender, a grizzled man with arms full of tattoos, slides drink after drink to his patrons with ease, cheering with the crowd as LA scores yet another goal on the thick television screens. Hard rock pours from the speakers while pool balls crack in the back corner and a handful of patrons shoot darts at a target. The entire place reeks of sex, alcohol, dirt, and grime.

This is pure, unadulterated Dive Bar Heaven. But to Jeremy, it looks like we stepped into one of the Thirteen Realms of Hell.

I push through the crowd of patrons and wave down the bartender. In one, smooth motion, I order two of his nastiest, strongest shots and knock mine back the moment the glass hits my palm. The liquor burns down my throat like liquid fire, and I let out a triumphant "Woo!" before sliding Jeremy his glass.

"What's in this?" He holds it up to the dim neon light, squinting suspiciously.

"Does it matter?" I giggle, pressing closer to him with practiced flirtation, my hand finding his arm. "Whatever's in it will help us forget the rest of the world exists. No fires. No accidents. Just you and me."

He considers my offer for a moment, and anticipation crackles within me. Finally, he lifts a hand in polite protest.

So drinks aren't the way to his heart. Good thing I

have plenty of other tricks up my sleeve. I shrug, downing his shot as well.

The energy in the room shifts as the opening chords of a new song crackle through the speakers. My eyes light up, and I gasp, a grin spreading across my face.

"I love this song!" I shout over the thundering guitar riffs and pounding drums that pull me to my feet. I grab his hands, dragging him into the center of the room with me. My hips immediately find the rhythm, swaying to the driving beat as I throw my arms up and let the music consume me. The sound transports me back to the '80s, when classic rock and heavy metal coursed through my veins.

I sing along with the anthemic chorus, eyes closed, letting my hips move with deliberate sensuality— putting on a show for my unwitting audience. When I grip his shirt and pull him closer, aligning our bodies, I feel his sharp intake of breath. His eyes widen at the contact, but the desire radiating from him is unmistakable. The air grows thick with unspoken hunger, charged by the dangerous attraction building with every touch, every step I lead him toward the darkness.

"You remind me of someone," he shouts over the music as my hand trails down his rigid chest.

"Know a lot of redheads?" I smirk and grip the hem of his cotton shirt, lifting it ever so slightly to find that sweet spot, that delicious little treat right under the navel where taut muscles and veins pop like an arrow, begging me to go lower. I lightly brush my fingertips against his skin.

The broken little angel hesitates at first then huffs out a breath. "Not many. Maybe one. She wasn't as…friendly as you."

"You think I'm friendly?" I tease, my voice lowering while I lean closer into his face.

There's a war raging in his mind between what he desperately wants, what I'm so freely offering him, and the iron-clad rules drilled into him: *Demon hunters cannot take lovers. We cannot compromise our destiny. It's forbidden.*

What a miserable, soul-crushing existence. No wonder he's so wound up.

I spin around, pressing my back against his chest, letting my body mold to his. I reach behind me, finding his hands and guiding them to my hips as I continue moving to the rhythm. "Relax a little, Jeremy. Losing yourself in something beautiful after facing the grim reaper might be just what the doctor ordered."

He swallows hard. *I want to,* his mind practically screams when I slip inside his thoughts. *God help me, I want to, but I can't.*

I push the envelope further. Releasing myself from his grasp, I spin around to face him, dancing for him alone. Behind my back, I let my glamour slip just enough to reveal the crimson skin and cracked golden veins of my true form, slowly releasing my pheromones into the air to find an unsuspecting target…

Which, unfortunately, doesn't go according to plan.

Within moments, a patron approaches: an older man with a bandana wrapped around his head and a leather vest covering his bulky frame. His grubby hands find my waist and pull me close. He reeks of alcohol, cigarettes, and exhaust fumes.

A biker. Lovely.

"Been watching you from across the room," he grunts. "This little boy not giving you what you need?"

I glance over at Jeremy, whose entire demeanor shifts. A new emotion radiates from him—something raw and primal that I never expected from someone I'd just met, let alone a Nephilim who's been denied the sins of the flesh.

My unwelcome dance partner pulls me flush against him, pressing his arousal into my lower back. "You just need a man who knows how to handle a woman like you."

"Is *that* what I need?" I echo, deliberately pulling away to show my disgust. I need Jeremy to believe I don't want this stranger's attention. I need him to act on that jealousy burning in his chest. Time to get this show on the road.

The man pulls me back, spinning me around to face him. "C'mon, baby. Let me rock your world and show you what a real man can do."

That's when everything changes.

It happens faster than lightning—Jeremy shoves me aside and his fist connects with the biker's face with bone-crushing force. The sound echoes through the bar like a gunshot.

And damn, is it a beautiful sight.

But that's not where it ends. The asshole stumbles over a bar stool, crashing to the floor while Jeremy towers over him, foot poised to drive into his ribs. Within seconds, the biker's entire crew converges on us, fists clenched and ready to pummel my Nephilim companion.

My, my. What has come over my righteous little victim? It's as if the Demon of Violence himself has him possessed.

While the biker crew closes in on him, a glimmer of silver catches my eye near the floor. A pair of keys lies just feet from the fallen biker, and a sly grin spreads across my face. As he writhes in pain, his bloody nose painting crimson streaks across the hardwood, I casually bend down to swipe the keys and slip them into my back pocket.

Meanwhile, Jeremy stands in the center of the bar, facing six men head-on. I half expect Holy Light to burst from his hands as this newfound rage consumes him, but instead, he's pure, primal combat—dodging punches, landing brutal kicks, practically roaring with animalistic fury.

Something tugs at me from deep inside, warmth spreading through my entire body. This side of him is absolutely delicious, almost painfully so. A sudden hunger overcomes me—Hell, what I wouldn't give to channel this rage into something more carnal, something debauched.

The darkness has already taken root, revealed by that telltale gray flicker in his aura. I can't help but smile. If there's anything that blonde bombshell taught me, it's that even the holiest souls have a dark side just waiting to be unleashed.

After Jeremy's taken down every last member, I slip through the remaining crowd and grab his hand. "Come on—we need to go!"

He spots the bartender heading our way and tightens his grip, leading me toward the back exit and out into an alley lined with parked motorcycles.

"Jeremy, what the hell was that?" I gasp, fighting back delighted laughter. "You practically fucked up that entire crew!"

"He disrespected you." He shrugs, chest still heaving as he catches his breath.

"So, you punched him in the face?"

"I didn't want him touching you like that."

Oh. How perfect.

A handful of people pour out of the bar then, searching for Jeremy and me. When one spots us in the alley, he shouts back indoors for the gang.

Shit.

My eyes flit toward the motorcycles, and another delightful idea comes to mind. I use my abilities to sniff out which one belongs to the asshole who got handsy with me and reach into my back pocket while approaching the Harley.

"Get on!" I toss him a spare helmet and snap mine into place.

"We can't take this. It's not ours!" he hisses, eyes darting around for witnesses.

"Sure we can." I dangle the keys inches from his face. "Lifted these off the dickhead who got handsy with me. Now he gets to walk home with that bloody nose you gave him."

"Jasmine, I don't—"

The biker from the bar kicks the door open, mumbling to his friends about how he wants to give the kid a swift punch in the gut. Jeremy's eyes widen as the man's bellow reverberates through the alley. He throws one leg over the bike and settles behind me, gripping the sides of the bike like he's bracing for impact.

I smirk as I flip down my visor. "You'll fly right off if you don't hang on to something more substantial." I reach back to grab his hands, guiding them to my hips. "Hold on tight, handsome."

I turn the key and pull in the clutch. The motorcycle roars to life when I hit the starter. The asshole sprints toward us, yelling obscenities while pressing a dishrag to his bloodied nose. I twist the throttle, and we lurch forward, tires squealing on asphalt as we tear away into the sun blazing over Mount Hollywood.

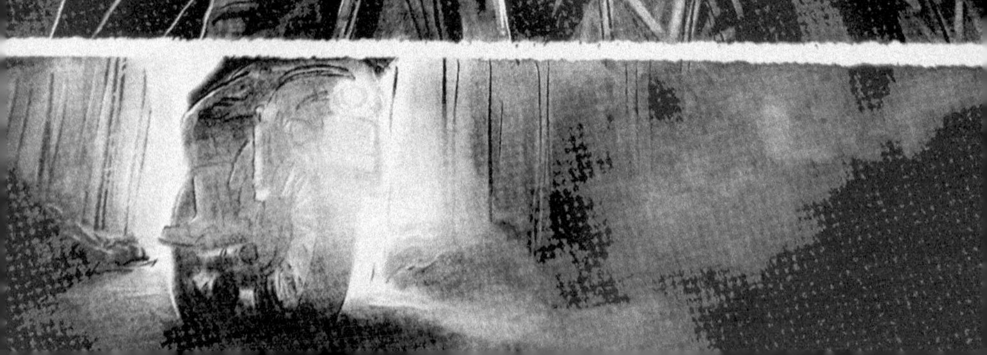

TRACK EIGHT
Dirty Deeds
Done Dirt Cheap

TRACK EIGHT

DIRTY DEEDS
DONE DIRT CHEAP

Wind whips through my hair and pounds against my body in relentless waves. The Harley's engine growls beneath us, vibrations rising through the frame into my chest while exhaust fumes sting my nostrils. Behind us, three—maybe four—other bikes gain ground as we weave through typical LA gridlock. Tires screech as I wrench us into a sharp left, diving into an alley to shake our pursuers.

The thrill of the chase floods me with more euphoria than any victim's essence ever could. And the terror radiating from Jeremy pressed against my back? I salivate at the thought.

His arms tighten around my waist, clinging to me for dear life.

"You got anything you can throw at them? A knife, lighter—anything?" I shout over the engine noise.

"You want me to throw a knife at them? That's so dangerous!" His voice rises in horror.

"You're kidding me, right? You just beat the crap out of most of them! We need to shake them off our tail before we're biker dinner!"

"I don't—" He hesitates, and I feel one of his hands leave my waist. "I have an idea. Just keep your eyes on the road, okay?"

My eyebrow arches with curiosity as I do exactly that, focusing on the street ahead while wondering what he's planning.

As expected, his mind is a chaos of erratic thoughts—grappling with his morality, convincing himself using his powers is necessary to protect me from 'violent hooligans.' Hooligans—really, kid? His logic is beautifully flawed, riddled with the early stages of corruption already taking root.

Here we are: two outlaws committing grand theft auto and plotting to harm our pursuers, all in the name of chivalry.

I couldn't have orchestrated it better myself.

I nearly jump in my seat when a thunderous explosion erupts behind us, blinding light flashing in the side mirrors. The acrid stench of burning trash hits me instantly, and I struggle not to retch. Heat radiates against my back as I whip around to assess the damage. A jagged crack of light has split the asphalt, cutting straight through the alley toward the biker gang and igniting a row of dumpsters in roaring flames.

"What the fuck did you just do?" I ask, an incredulous laugh lacing my words.

"Don't worry about it—just keep going!"

The dumpster fire continues to rage behind us, leaving nothing but freedom on the horizon.

Our quick pursuit turns into a leisurely drive along the Sunset Strip, where most of Cherry's establishments stand proudly, fresh coats of paint and new LED signs replacing the old, mercury-filled neon. I take us further west of the city, where pristine tree-lined streets and expertly manicured lawns come into view. Run-down boutiques are replaced with crystal-clean storefronts adorning expensive brand names. Then, naturally, there are the gargantuan homes, each with luxury cars parked in its arched driveway.

Beverly Hills. A city that's just one corrupted Nephilim away from becoming my new reality.

"Do you know where you're going?" Jeremy finally breaks the silence of our drive.

"Of course I do." I turn my head to flash him a playful wink through the helmet visor. "I know Beverly Hills like I know my own body."

For once, I'm not lying.

I've spent too many years dreaming of this place, of what it means to be a high-level Debauchery demon operating in the upper echelons of a diamond-studded city. Status is everything in the demonic hierarchy, even across Broodlines. It's one thing to be high-level— granted powers and abilities beyond the average lesser or mid-grade demon—but it's entirely different to be accepted by the Sired as one of their own.

No amount of raw power will earn me the respect I deserve. I need to prove to the Sired that I belong among them. I intend to be the first human-turned-demon Underling to infiltrate their inner circle.

All I needed was to finish breaking this already-fractured demon hunter.

It's around 4 PM when the Harley's fuel gauge shows we're down to a quarter tank. I've taken us as far up into the canyon as possible before it descends into the Valley, where nothing but the sprawling Los Angeles skyline stretches before us, bathed in the golden light of late afternoon. We've parked on a street lined with billion-dollar estates that have hosted countless Hollywood parties. I recognize one from a gathering I attended with Cherry in the late '90s and smile to myself as I remove my helmet and swing off the motorcycle.

Jeremy stretches, taking in the sprawling skyline and mesmerizing view. "Where are we?"

"Mulholland Drive," I say. "Home to the stars, legendary parties, and more than a few adult film sets."

His eyebrows shoot up. "You're kidding."

"Do I look like I'm kidding?"

He shrugs, turning back to study the vista. "It's just so beautiful up here. Peaceful. Unassuming."

"Isn't that always the way?" I move to stand beside him. "The most unassuming places are the ones hiding the darkest secrets." I turn to face him. "You look like you may have a few of your own."

He scratches the back of his neck, fingers toying with his prematurely gray hair. Finally, he mutters, "You have no idea."

On the contrary, I have plenty.

I jog up the concrete path toward the party house, a four-story behemoth built in that sleek, modern style I haven't been able to stomach since the turn of the century. If memory serves, there should be a small cherry insignia hidden in plain sight, marking this as a safe haven for those of my Broodline. I search the entryway, pushing aside massive planters and overgrown foliage until I find what I'm looking for.

There—there it is: two small circles connected by a curved stem, carved discretely into the wooden window frame.

I push open the door with ease, and Jeremy's footsteps quicken behind me. "What are you doing—? This is breaking and entering!"

I flash him a playful grin. "It isn't if the door's unlocked. C'mon, let's check it out."

We slip into the house unseen—just two outlaws looking for sanctuary. The place is opulently pristine, not a speck of dust marring any surface. Cold marble floors stretch beneath our feet while sleek modern furniture dominates rooms that feel more like showrooms than a home. It's soulless at best but brimming with potential. I could transform this sterile monument into something magnificent.

Soon, I might get the chance.

I discover a wall lined with rows upon rows of CDs, cassettes, and vinyl records. At the CD tower, I sift through hundreds of albums spanning every genre—pop, rock, R&B, country, the works—eagerly hunting for the '80s section. I grab my favorites: Mötley Crüe, AC/DC, Ozzy. Removing each disc from its case, I watch the rainbow fractals dance across the iridescent surface before threading the center holes onto my fingers like expensive rings.

I locate the stereo system and press the eject button, revealing a 5-disc changer that can cycle through multiple albums automatically.

"Love these sound systems," I say, loading the discs. "Being able to shuffle between CDs without having to manually record everything onto mixtapes. Pure genius."

"You really love music, huh?" Jeremy observes, keeping his hands clenched at his sides, as if touching anything would leave evidence of our break-in.

"How could you not? Music fuels the soul; helps you escape. I'm sure you feel the same about your books."

He smiles sheepishly. "My books are more academic."

Music pours from the elaborate stereo system wired throughout the house, bass and drums crystal clear through the speakers. It's lightyears better than the duct-taped piece of shit held together by prayers and spite at my club. I find the bar cleverly disguised as a simple marble tabletop near the balcony and immediately rifle through the remnants. The demons who last called this place home were gracious enough to leave behind an impressive liquor collection—whether leftovers or stockpiled for the next party, I couldn't care less. I grab one of the priciest bottles, already opened, and take a generous swig.

Thank Hell that alcohol doesn't affect demons. This stuff could strip paint off a Ferrari.

I settle onto the edge of the couch, crossing my legs deliberately. "Tell me more about yourself, Jeremy."

I extend the bottle toward him again, and just like earlier, he gives me that same polite shake of the head, hand raised in gentle refusal. He remains silent and still.

I attempt to pry more out of him. "You mentioned something earlier about a mentor."

Darkness washes over him then, his grief so thick, I can almost taste it. Visions flood his mind of that mentor—Declan Lovejoy, devastatingly handsome and completely insufferable. Jeremy's memories shimmer with quiet moments: Declan helping him research ancient tomes, teaching hand-to-hand combat, beaming with pride at his achievements...and then, there are the other moments. The tender ones.

"You'll learn soon enough, lad."

"As long as I'm here, I'll protect you."

"I'm proud to call you my apprentice."

Stolen moments woven between years of hunting monsters, saving innocents, and serving their holy cause. All Jeremy has left now is the ghost of a charming smile, warm brown eyes, and that deep, soothing voice that once made him feel safe.

Well, I'll be damned.

Jeremy was in love with his mentor.

Now *that* was an unexpected twist.

"People tend to remember the best parts of those they've lost." His voice drops to barely above a whisper, trying to hide the pain I can feel radiating from him. "The last thing I ever said to him was…not great."

Another memory surfaces: Jeremy's crushing disappointment at Lovejoy's actions, days of pent-up frustration over his choice of lover—that mousy blonde witch with more secrets than redeemable qualities—and finally, the flash of raw anger in his mentor's eyes when he dared to push back...

"This will be the last time you question my methods."

The words echo endlessly in his mind, and the longer I listen, the more they ache. I know that feeling all too well—when the person you love, the one you've put on a pedestal, the one you'd do *anything* to please, looks at you with nothing but disappointment. Or worse—indifference.

"But he's gone now. Missing, in a sense."

"Missing?" I ask.

"I couldn't find the body. I, uh…" He swallows hard as he sits beside me. "Everyone deserves a proper burial. Can't bury what you can't find. I should have never left him in that damn cemetery with that damn woman." His jaw clenches so tight, I'm surprised his teeth don't crack. "I wish I could forget everything. I wish I could flip a switch and make it all disappear—bury it deep with all of the other shitty choices I've made."

I glance down at the brown bottle in my hand, heavy notes of aged whiskey drifting from the open neck. Once more, I extend it toward him. "Sounds like you need this more than I do."

Jeremy breathes out a defeated sigh, eyes fixated on my fingers gripping the bottle. Finally, he grabs it from me and takes a long swig…

And nearly chokes it all out.

"Easy there, handsome," I say, rubbing his back as the amber liquid spurts across the leather couches. "You've got to ease into it. Here, watch."

I grip the bottle by the neck and bring it to my lips, drinking slowly and deliberately. The whiskey burns as it slides down my throat, and I savor every drop. When I lower the bottle, I catch the lingering moisture on my lips with my tongue, just a casual gesture that somehow holds his attention longer than it should. Meeting his eyes, I offer him a soft smile along with the bottle.

"Where have you been all this time, Jasmine?" he asks in a voice so low, so full of wonder, it makes my heart skip a beat.

"Lost in a city of angels, waiting to find the right

one." The sentiment lies thick, but it brings a genuine smile to his face.

We spend hours lost in conversation, the bottle of whiskey emptying as the sun sinks lower on the horizon. His inhibitions loosen with every sip, and he finally begins revealing glimpses of who he really is beneath that rigid exterior; someone who's actually, dare I say it, *charming*. I lean into his warmth with casual ease, toying with his fingers flirtatiously, almost absently, and can't help but smile when he responds in kind.

It's simple. Sweet.

I've forgotten he killed the real Jasmine. I've forgotten which side he's supposed to be on, that his entire existence revolves around destroying me and everything I am. Right now, he isn't the Nephilim demon hunter with a sacred mission. He's just Jeremy—a heartbreaking contradiction with silver hair framing boyish features who gets lost in books and knows nothing about the world beyond them.

It's not the way I imagined it would go—this game. I didn't expect heartfelt moments of conversation and revelation. I expected debauchery, pure and simple. Perhaps it was time to take this game a step further…and I knew exactly where to go.

"You know, I might have a friend who can help us find the body—er, your mentor," I lie smoothly.

His entire expression lights up like Christmas morning. "Really?"

"You bet. He's really good at tracking things down. Might be part bloodhound."

"Will you take me to him? Please, Jasmine. I'll do anything."

Sweet Hell, those words couldn't sound more perfect, considering what I have planned for him.

"Of course." I flash him a coy smile, running my fingers down his arm. "But we'll both need to change first. Where I'm taking you requires a certain...sense of style you regrettably don't possess."

TRACK NINE
Hells Bells

WHAT'S THE MATTER, DARLING? NEVER MET A PHENOMENAL WOMAN EMPOWERED BY HER SEXUALITY?

TRACK NINE

HELLS BELLS

The clock strikes ten, and the bells rattle through my bones.

There aren't many churches left in this part of Los Angeles—none with actual God-fearing folk, anyway. This old pile of stone and stained glass is about as holy as a dolled-up charlatan on Easter Sunday, a mockery of the very institution it represents.

The demons took over after the big earthquake in '94 —all part of Destruction's scheme to tear open a portal between worlds. I still don't know how the old fuck did it. Now every time Los Angeles quakes, more demons slip through the cracks, but humans are too busy running around like decapitated chickens to notice. Thank the Devil for that.

"What is this?" Jeremy stops in his tracks as he studies the church.

"You of all people should know what this is." I flash

him a smile, nodding at the silver cross round his neck as we stand before the white behemoth pulsing with dance music. "C'mon. This will be fun."

Heavy double doors sway open to reveal an arcade of marble bathed in flashing red lights. This cathedral, once a house of worship, is now a demon's playground, filled to the brim with hundreds of souls twisting and writhing against each other to intoxicating beats. They move as a single entity, bodies flowing in perfect unison, and I wonder if their dance is choreographed. Each gesture ripples in tune with liquid precision—hands raised to the air, one-two-steps, synchronized turns…almost as if they're spelled.

In fact, I *know* they're spelled. Hell, I can taste the dark magic permeating the air, feeding off their lust. Somewhere in this cathedral, a high-level Debauchery demon lurks, siphoning the sinful energy of every lecherous soul. Pity it isn't me.

"Something's not right," Jeremy shouts over the music as he struggles to keep up with me through the crowd.

"It's fucking amazing, isn't it?" My voice feigns innocence. His expression is a twisted mix of wince and grimace while his neck cranes to study the rave-goers. His thoughts are laid bare for me, spinning like a hamster on a wheel as he tries to decipher the source of the unmistakable magic cast upon the dancing mob. I have to pull him out of it. I *have* to break his walls.

"Oh, come on, Jeremy. You act like you've never been to one of these before."

Because he hasn't. Sweet, innocent Jeremy has never once surrounded himself by anything other than his pious Nephilim brethren and their crusade against my kin. Poor thing has probably never even kissed a girl before. His virginity, while baffling and a terrible shame, will be his greatest downfall when facing his demons.

"I'm usually working." He chooses his words carefully.

"Working," I repeat with a soft chuckle. Goodness, he and I couldn't be more similar. "We both know you could use a night off to…unwind." My wrists link around his neck, dangling off his shoulders as I coax him to join me in a dance. "Betcha 'security consulting' can get a little stagnant after a while, hm?"

There's a playfulness in my tone, and it's heavy with implication. I can only hope he's hungry for another taste.

"I thought we were here to find your friend," he reminds me, his expression unamused. "That he'd be able to help me find my mentor."

I peer into his eyes through thick, mascara-coated lashes and flash him a crimson smirk. "I did say that, didn't I?" I chuckle. "Oh, Jeremy, lighten up a bit more, will ya? We both survived some gnarly shit and lived to tell the tale. Take a night off. Celebrate. Dance with me."

He's hesitant. *Fuck*, is he hesitant. The thick concrete

walls he's worked so hard to build stand steadfast against my charm; it's enough to have me vexed, but I won't give up. Not yet. Not when I'm so close to my prize.

My hands drop from his neck and slip to his palms, guiding them to my waist. A jolt of electricity shoots through me as his fingers brush the bare skin of my hips, just above my leather skirt. The hesitation in his eyes, the way his lips part just slightly—it's enough to feed my growing hunger.

This is the moment I choose to forget everything else. Forget he killed Jasmine. Forget he tried to destroy my business. That his very existence is the antithesis of my own. Tonight, under strobing lights and among the damned, we are simply two survivors desperate to forget.

We move slowly in unison, not quite synchronized with the bodies around us but enough to create our rhythm. My fingers trace his jaw, feeling the hint of a five o'clock shadow breaking through the surface. His breath catches beneath my touch, and I watch his eyes dart from my lips to my eyes and back again. Sliding my hands down his chest, I feel his muscles taut beneath the buttoned shirt. He's lithe and lean, the ideal height, and for the love of all that is unholy, I know I shouldn't want him. Crave him. Wonder what his lips taste like, if his essence would invigorate me as it did Cherry, how his fingers would feel tangled in my hair and pulling at my scalp…

My hunger will be satisfied soon. It *has* to.

After all, my future depends on it.

A slow, throbbing bass line pulses around us. Jeremy's once-racing thoughts have settled to a leisurely hum as he loses himself in the intoxicating music. Relief and triumph surge through me as his fingers dig into my skin, instinctively pulling me closer until the space between us vanishes. When I lean into him, my body molds perfectly against his.

That's when I feel it—and *fuck*, do I feel it, his hardening length pressed into me, lining up perfectly with my groin, two damned puzzle pieces practically made for each other.

Our lips are inches away now. So wrong. So deliciously, temptingly wrong. But I have to know what Heaven tastes like.

I pull him closer by the neck and channel my demonic magic. *Just a taste…*

But the spell around us suddenly breaks. The crowd roars to life and bodies slam between us, yanking him from my grasp. We stumble slightly apart as the ravers awaken from their trance and erupt in thunderous applause, turning to face a disturbance at the altar.

Apt timing. As fucking always.

I should have known this crowd wasn't Kissed by any ordinary high-level demon, not at this size and certainly not this publicly. No, these humans were under the influence of something far more powerful—and far more deadly.

"Hello, my little hellions."

There he stands, the perfect Casanova—my boss, draped in another getup that costs more than my yearly rent. Rave lights dance across his oversized sunglasses, a kaleidoscope of worship pulsing to the beat while he extends his arms like some unholy messiah. And oh, how they scream for him.

Humans, demons, they all bow to the Demon of Debauchery. The living, breathing embodiment of sin itself. But Cherry's more than just another Prime, especially in this city. In Los Angeles, he's the one who wears the fucking crown. Humans are none the wiser, naturally. To them, he's just another socialite, a dazzling celebrity they can't help but fawn over.

Jeremy's posture tugs my attention back to him. Even in my best heels, I would still find myself looking up at him. He studies the altar, those delicate sea-foam eyes drinking in the sight of my master. But there isn't hatred in his stare, not like I'd imagine. There's something else. Something darker. The very same thing oozes out of every damned creature in this cathedral.

Desire.

I can practically feel it on the tip of my tongue.

"He's beautiful, isn't he?" I drag my hands up his back, grazing my dull human nails ever so gently over the fabric of his shirt. Oh, how I'd love to sink my claws into his flesh…

His breath hitches at my touch, and those little muscles in his jaw twitch in the most satisfying way before he swallows hard. I press against him, my fingers digging into his shoulders. Fuck me, he's tense. And scorching hot. His aura is a mix of confusion, arousal, and self-loathing—a cocktail I'd give anything to devour.

Perhaps I could.

Just one little taste…

My attention snaps to that familiar tug—Cherry. Our eyes lock in that silent, sinful way they always do, and the crowd seems to part for him like the Red Sea. He's gripping that fancy obsidian staff of his, the one embellished with a black crystal at its pommel. As he saunters over, he flashes a spine-tingling, predatory grin that would make a gator think twice. Time seems to slow. The music fades to a dull rhythmic thud until all I can hear is the clunk of his heels, the tap of his cane, the pounding of poor little Jeremy's conflicted heart.

Thump…thump…*thump-thump.*

As Cherry slinks closer, that mark on Jeremy's neck flares like a hot coal, snapping him right out of his little trance, and those veins crawling from his shoulders to his jaw go rigid. 'Tober tried explaining the nuances of that peculiar tattoo—some sort of divine security system that burns any time a demon or Prime gets too close. It still beats me how the damn thing actually works—it's clearly flawed, considering how easily I've been able to trick it. Jeremy steps in front of me in a flash, shielding me against Cherry's approach like I'm some sort of damsel who can't handle herself. The poor fool. He has no idea what secrets lie beneath such a perfectly woven glamour.

My hand tenderly meets Jeremy's shoulder, gently pushing him aside to make way for my master. Cherry's eyes glint beneath his rose-tinted shades, a devilish smirk carving shadows into his hollow cheeks. As I step into his waiting arms, the rhinestones embedded into his blazer press cool against my feverish skin. My body melts into his while his fingers cinch around my waist with a subtle squeeze, his breath warm against my ear as he leans in.

"My darling cherry pie," he murmurs. Hell knows cheesy nicknames grate against my very soul, yet a reluctant, melodic chuckle escapes my chest as I maintain the charade. This game of temptation is one I fully intend to keep playing until I win.

I have one too many tricks up my sleeve, and the stakes grow deviously higher as I press my lips to the Demon of Debauchery's.

Cherry's grip on my waist tightens as he pulls me flush against him. His tongue snakes into my mouth, gently caressing mine as we share a moment so rare, I can't help but get lost within him. He tastes as sweet as I remember—rich like Bavarian chocolate and smoother than a drizzle of honey. What more could I expect from the embodiment of sin itself? But then, there's a hint of something else—something just as exquisite and jarring as the groan rumbling in his chest—that pulls me out of the charade.

It's the fervent, ravenous energy oozing from Jeremy's body.

And fuck me, it is absolutely *mouthwatering*.

"Who's your friend, darling?" Cherry purrs as he pulls me closer. I throw a smirk over my shoulder, locking eyes with the demon hunter.

"This is Jeremy." I reach out for him. His eyes flit to my beckoning hand then back at my mysterious master. "I'd love for you to get to know him."

Cherry's grin grows impossibly wide. "Well then. Perhaps we should all find some place more…private. Have ourselves a little chat."

The air between us thickens as I beckon the Nephilim once more.

Finally, Jeremy slides his hand into mine.

None of us speak as we ascend the velvet-lined staircase to the choir loft. Cherry leads our unholy procession through the darkness, bass thrumming through bone and sinew. Our collective silence screams with Jeremy's aura, excitement, fear, and hunger swirling together in a toxic cocktail.

And beneath it all, shame.

The darling fool. His mind churns with fantasy and sin, completely blind to the gargantuan pipe organ looming above us. He's utterly entranced by Cherry's effortless magnetism.

The Prime peers over the balcony at his masterpiece below. "Glorious, isn't it?" His voice cuts through the darkness. "Intoxicated. Every single one of them." He pauses, savoring the sight. "Oh, how I adore these parties."

"You're brilliant at throwing them." I saunter closer, draping myself against him like I always do for an audience. "He's the brains behind every Hollywood A-list event. Everyone who matters knows his name."

I capture Cherry's lips, drawing a rumbling hum from his chest. A silver-ringed finger tangles in my hair —one of our more intimate performances—as we both turn to face Jeremy.

"I-I didn't know you had a boyfriend."

Our smiles mirror each other, predatory and knowing. Cherry's voice drips honey and poison. "Oh, you sweet thing. I don't do labels—they're so terribly convoluted and unnecessary. Imagine keeping this goddess to myself?" His eyes rake over Jeremy. "It simply wouldn't be fair…especially to her. I've always preferred giving a woman the freedom to make her own choices when it comes to her body."

The statement couldn't be farther from the truth, if one only cared to dig deep enough. But in this moment, demonic hierarchies don't exist; only we do.

That's when Cherry nods over at our handsome young friend. It's a simple movement, one that can easily be taken as an innocent gesture, but I know differently.

He's giving *me* the reins.

He's allowing *me* to be in charge. To pull the strings. Put on a show.

This isn't just Cherry's game. It's mine.

The mere implication intoxicates me.

And so, I begin my little show.

It starts with a simple unzipping of my leather skirt. The chains dangling from the sides jingle as the garment hits the floor, and my fingers fumble with the clasp of my spike-studded halter top. In seconds, I'm stripped down to a black, lacy thong, staring deep into the eyes of an innocent but tainted Nephilim.

Cherry chuckles at the sight of Jeremy's awestruck face. "What's the matter, darling? Never met a phenomenal woman empowered by her sexuality?"

The praise, whether genuine or forced for the sake of our charade, spreads through my chest like liquid sunlight. If I were in my demonic form, my veins would pulse and flicker with prideful fire. I savor the feeling, letting it fuel my performance, before I lock eyes with Jeremy and remove the final scrap of fabric concealing my body.

And there it is. That *look*. The one every succubus craves under the gaze of her prey.

Desperation. Longing. Unfiltered reverence.

His aura, now a faded shade of gray, reaches out for me of its own volition. Desperate tendrils stretch across the space between us, filling me with a primal, natural energy I've never felt the likes of before. Cherry flashes me a torturous smile, one laced with a hint of jealousy and longing of his own. He wants what every Prime wants, what is so freely given to me in this moment—the sexual essence of this conflicted, innocent soul.

But Cherry knows better, and we need to be careful, especially with a demon hunter who could send us to our Maker in a flash of Holy Light.

We both know better than to use our influence on such a fragile, pious creature. What would be the point when the goal is true corruption? Our powers would only cheat us of the real prize. Besides, the challenge of winning him over naturally, of watching him choose his damnation? Now *that* makes the game infinitely more delicious.

An enchanting array of colors bathes us in a living, breathing work of art, from the strobing rave to the moonlight pouring in from the intricate stained-glass window behind us. The radiance only adds to the atmosphere permeating the loft. The music shifts then, as if on cue, dropping to a hypnotic, bass-heavy beat that creeps from my toes to my fingers like velvet smoke. It only fuels the fire building within me and ignites a delicious idea.

"You're welcome to stick around, Jeremy. I always enjoy an audience," Cherry purrs, leaning nonchalantly against the grand pipe organ, stroking the pommel of his cane and watching as I saunter toward him. When I reach Cherry, I focus on a new task—unbuttoning his pants. Jeremy's hitched breaths may be lost in the music, but they roar in my ears. His mind scrambles like static, struggling to remember why he even agreed to come with me tonight.

"M-maybe I should…should…"

His inability to focus is a prize in itself. His eyes lock on my hands as I swiftly pull Cherry's trousers to mid-thigh. The Demon of Debauchery isn't one for full nudity, as I've learned over the last century. He's a busy man—one who visits establishment after establishment, event after event—and can't be bothered with mundane activities like dressing after sex.

I spin around on my heel, situating myself above Cherry's lap, and reach for his cock. Finally, after a day of weaving my web around an innocent man, I crumble the last of those steadfast walls his Holy Order worked so hard to build.

"There you go," Cherry groans as he enters me inch by inch. Several rows of metal tickle my insides as he delves deeper, one hand placed firmly on my hip while the other cups my breast. He rolls my nipple between his fingers, tugging lightly on the little bar that pierces my sensitive skin before toying with the delicate chain connecting one piercing to the other. The pain is glorious, a welcome distraction as my hips circle on his, dancing for the sweet man watching us.

I know this isn't his first time. The crystal thrumming with power against my skin is proof of that. October sowed the seed and opened his pure little heart to a world of darkness and pleasure; for that, I am grateful. She made my job an ounce easier.

Jeremy watches us with a hunger unlike anything I've witnessed since my human days. There's almost a sense of wonder—which only makes the situation that much more depraved—coupled with morbid curiosity. His eyes remained fixed on where Cherry's body meets mine, and I can practically see the fascination etched in his features at the sight of his first Jacob's ladder, or even my little piercing. Debauchery demons—especially their Sire—are known for their body jewelry, and I'm pleased to see the demon hunter's energy only grows the longer he stares.

Cherry moves painfully slowly inside me, in and out, out and in, and I, in turn, writhe against his thick cock in deliberate, circular motions that mirror the rhythm of the music filling our cores. He keeps one hand steady at my hip while the other slips between my legs, parting my lips to play with the glistening silver ball piercing my clit. The demon gently, teasingly, *expertly* drives me closer to the edge. My chest flushes so red, I almost forget I'm not in my demonic form.

Finally, my eyes lock with Jeremy's, soldered by pure lust. Despite the hundreds of souls downstairs and the Prime inside me, it feels like we're the only two people in the world. The connection is so raw and deep, I don't even have a chance to marvel at how beautiful he looks under this light—so tortured, so curious. There's something intimate about being watched that feels so close yet somehow painfully distant, and the lines of right and wrong continue to blur. I've always been wrong. I don't just want to be watched. I want *more*.

I beckon him closer with the curl of my finger.

To my utter surprise and inexplicable pleasure, the Nephilim gives in.

At long last, his wall begins to crack, and I yearn to smash it to bits.

The poor thing doesn't even know what to do with his hands. He reaches for my arms, then my waist, and hesitates just beneath the swell of my breasts—it's all too sweet. I take his trembling hands in mine and guide them to my nipples, encouraging him to feel the cool metal bars piercing them. But then, his fingers meet Cherry's, and he jolts back with a hiss.

Panic flares through me and turns my body cold. My instincts urge me to stop, to prepare for the sudden shift in our plans, and dig my fingers into Cherry's thigh in warning. This is it. This is when it all goes to shit, when this not-so-little Nephilim brings an entire church down, and along with it, my Broodline.

But destruction never comes.

Not even the slightest hint of it.

Instead, Jeremy's fingers meet Cherry's again. There's another hiss through his teeth, a pain he's clearly fighting as their skin meets, but it's fleeting, almost as if the mere touch of a Prime does…nothing. To either of them.

And then, his gaze flits to mine again.

Those beautiful, innocent green eyes.

As if asking for...permission. As if I'm the one in charge. As if the man—the *Prime*—behind me isn't one of the deadliest creatures in this world.

The power makes me dizzy with possibility.

My fingers dance along the nape of his neck, tugging at the silver-gray hair now damp with sweat. I urge him forward, to taste fruit so righteously kept from him.

Only to have him completely avoid my lips and crash his against Cherry's.

I half expect the entire world to light on fire.

Hell, I even expect the church roof to crack open and reveal the wrath of God. But then I remember Cherry is an expert when it comes to Nephilim. Silver Fox is living proof of that.

Jeremy's clothes are warm and damp with sweat as his body presses into mine, and finally, his hands settle at my waist. He grinds himself against my abdomen, and the stiffness in his jeans adds an extra layer of friction that drives me even closer to the edge. All the while, he continues to kiss Cherry, firmly, hungrily, and so very sure of himself. Jealousy bubbles within me, and I grab Jeremy's jaw to force them apart. Hooded green eyes meet mine, so drunk with lust that I could drown in them. I know that look. The adoration. The pure, unmistakable awe that creeps up your spine and spreads through your skin like warmth, unlike anything you've ever felt.

"Divine," Cherry mutters behind me. "Absolutely divine."

Divine is *exactly* what this is.

Landing the woman of your dreams might satisfy most men, but to be caught between her and Cherry—the raw embodiment of sin, whose mere existence transcends human desire? Baby boy shouldn't just count his lucky stars; he should thank the God he thinks made them.

The air tightens around us as we're faced with an impossible question—what now? How far does this go? And what does this mean for our game?

I need to take it a step further.

I stand at full height, feeling Cherry's pierced cock slip out of me, one row of metal at a time. With expert swiftness, I rearrange our chessboard, turning and bending at the waist. Jeremy and Cherry switch places, the younger leaning against the organ keys while the other situates himself behind me. Cherry's silver-ringed fingers grasp my hips as he pushes into me once more, and my eyes never leave Jeremy's. I dig deep into his mind in the moment, searching every crevice for a hint of hesitation or displeasure, only to find none. Absolutely none. But there's one thing he repeats over and over: *touch me.*

My fingers reach for his belt, unbuckling it and removing it from his pants like a cracking whip. Those beautiful green eyes never leave mine as I swiftly unzip his pants and tug them below his hips to pool at his ankles. Finally, his hard, neglected cock springs to life, taut against his abdomen.

A primitive hunger fills me, lingering in my core as Cherry's thrusts meet the rhythm of the music around us. Jeremy is a sight to behold; longer than I imagined, deliciously thick. My cunt clenches around Cherry's cock, gripping him as my insatiable hunger continues to grow. I'm eager to have the angel, just as eager as he is to have me.

I lean in, my tongue tracing the length of him, moaning at the contact. My eyes flutter shut for a moment while I tease him, never quite taking him in fully but never pulling away. He's a writhing mess beneath me, hips bucking into my hand, desperate for my lips, desperate to take it further. His fingers finally rake through my hair, pulling the thick, unruly waves out of my face to gather behind my head. Our gazes finally meet, and fuck—*fuck*—he's a mess. A desperate, simpering mess.

I take him into my mouth one delicious inch at a time. A pained gasp catches in his chest before he melts beneath me. All at once, the little virgin becomes putty in my hands, at the mercy of a succubus and her Prime.

My tongue continues to swirl along his cock as my head bobs up and down. I quickly feel his tension building, his pounding heart ringing loud in my ears as his thoughts beg for this moment to last forever. His fistful of my hair is rigid now, and he almost unintentionally attempts to guide me at a faster pace, but this is *my* show. *My* rules. And this delicious little virgin will not ruin the game this early.

I pull off him in an instant, my fingers gripping around the base of him and stroking with a steady rhythm. My other hand grips his chin as I meet him at eye level whilst Cherry remains buried deep inside of me.

"Not yet."

"W-what do you mean?"

"I mean,"—my nails dig into his chin—"not. *Yet.*"

But despite my steely tone, despite the command, Jeremy comes undone with a final, shuddering gasp.

If this were any other patron, I'd simply kick him to the ground, humiliate him, and demand he finish me off. Hell, there's a part of me that desperately wants to. Instead, I simply smile at him and lean in, my arm resting against the pipe organ. I open my mouth to speak…

But then, something peculiar catches my eye.

Milky-white drops run down my wrist, glittering like diamonds under the rave lights. Normally, I'd marvel at Nephilim biology—how they're beacons of sparkles and radiance in every aspect. But there's no wonder, no intrigue as Jeremy's essence burns my skin.

It starts as a crack at my wrist, a fracture in my perfectly calculated design. Crimson bleeds through like spilled wine over parchment, covering the façade of my glamoured skin. It isn't blood, no—demons don't bleed red. It's my natural skin color. The amber veins follow, pulsing with hellish light as they travel from wrist to shoulder, soon covering me whole. I try to clamp down, to get a hold of the transformation before it has a chance to take over, but it dissolves like sugar in water. Scorching heat builds in my skull, and two jutting horns emerge from underneath my hair. Behind me, something unfurls and lashes: my arrowed tail, freed from its prison.

This can't be happening—not this soon. Not here. Not now.

My stomach plummets as my demonic shadow towers over Jeremy's horrified expression.

My human glamour has failed—and there's nowhere left to hide.

TRACK TEN
Poison

TRACK TEN

MY HEART POUNDS LIKE WAR DRUMS IN MY CHEST, drowning out the dance music filling the church. I scramble for my clothes, attempting to shield my body while frantically searching for my Prime.

Where the fuck is Cherry?

The devastation on Jeremy's face is enough to rip my chest open, but I can't let it. Right here, right now, all that matters is protecting Cherry from a demon hunter.

I've heard the stories whispered across Broodlines, how effortlessly the Nephilim can destroy us, how even Primes can fall to their power. According to legend, once a Prime is 'killed,' they're reconstituted—reborn with a new face, no memories, and a clean slate to govern their domain of sin. It's not something I can risk, not when Cherry's fate is tied to mine.

But after what just happened...is our deal even still intact? Is Jeremy's soul corrupted enough to satisfy Cherry's hunger? Or have I failed so spectacularly, I'm about to discover firsthand what happens when an Underling meets her end?

Jeremy stands frozen where I left him—pants still unzipped and hanging low on his hips, hands braced against the church organ as his chest heaves with what looks like utter devastation. It takes him a long moment to process what he's seeing: my true demonic form, revealed through my own catastrophic lapse in judgment.

Finally, I spot Cherry in my peripheral vision, making his way toward the staircase. As I sprint toward him, a blinding flash erupts from the balcony. Jeremy's Holy Light blazes to life, intent on sending me straight to Hell. I grab one of the organ chairs and hurl it in his direction, hoping to knock him off balance and buy myself a few precious seconds to get the fuck out of here.

I'm a mess of ragged breaths and disheveled clothes and hair when I finally reach my Prime. "Cherry!" I call out to him. "What the fuck just happened back there?"

His boisterous laugh booms along with the bass below us. "Oh darling, don't tell me you didn't know a Nephilim's Holy Cumshot is essentially a demonic glamour-breaker. Tsk. Sometimes I forget how painfully young you are."

I ignore the quip and rush to his side to check his clothes for any untimely surprises. "Are you alright? Did any get on you?"

"All clear, love." He grins as he zips up his leather

pants, seeming impossibly calm, despite everything. "Though you should probably clean yourself up before he catches up to you."

"I need to get you out of here first." My words are a harsh whisper as I shove his cane and jacket towards him.

He chuckles, not embracing the urgency of the matter. "Always the fiercely loyal guard dog, aren't you, Reagan?" He never fails to tempt me with his backhanded flattery, but time is of the essence.

"*Come on*, Cherry—" I bite through gritted teeth. "He won't stay down for long. You need to get out of here before he realizes what you really are."

"He knows *exactly* what I am and fell right into our trap without hesitation."

I blink at the statement. "But now he knows what I am—"

"Did you really think you'd masquerade as a human the entire time? Half of the fun in corruption comes when they figure you out and indulge in you despite it. Come on, darling. You're a *demon*. Act like one."

The words cut deep, and a different kind of fire sears my veins now. Embarrassment. Shame. And Cherry notices. He pauses after buckling his belt and shoots me a smile so small, I almost miss it. "By the way, you've done well, Reagan. And in record time too. This one has potential. Deliver him to me once his soul turns black. Which, judging by that aura of his, won't take much longer." He fastens the last button on his shirt and tosses the rhinestone-studded jacket over his shoulder. "As always, it's been an absolute pleasure being inside you." With one final wave of his manicured fingers, Cherry disappears into the shadows, descending the stairs.

Leaving me alone with a demon hunter whose innocence dangles by a quickly disintegrating thread.

"You…you're that demon. The one from the motel." The words are quiet, hollow, echoing from deep within a rattled, broken heart. "It was you the whole time."

He stands at the top of the staircase, staring me down like a spider would a fly, and all at once, our roles have reversed. I'd be a fool not to notice the hurt in his eyes. His thoughts crash into me in jagged waves: betrayal, self-loathing, fragments of memory replaying on an endless loop, every word we spoke, every tender moment.

His mind jumps, erratic. *God, I kissed a demon. Two demons. And she touched me—was one of them a Prime? Wrong. So wrong. Why did I want him? How could I be so careless?* The thoughts spiral faster, over and over. *Demon hunters can't take lovers. I broke one of our sacred rules. I broke—*

I back away slowly, ready to bolt as he becomes a prisoner to his own thoughts. But my movement breaks his reverie, and he sprints down the stairs. I rush to the main floor of the church, where hundreds of humans thrash against the music. Cold sweat drips down my back despite the impossible heat permeating the church. I slam against bodies, my muscles trembling and frustration building in my throat as I desperately try to claw my way out of the crowd. The primal instinct to shield my demonic form overwhelms any thought of the pursuit behind me, or the fact that I'm a half-naked demoness sprinting through a horde of spelled humans.

They pay no mind, dancing the night away to their hearts' content. They're oblivious to the crimson-skinned demon weaving desperately through their midst, fleeing the Nephilim who hunts her. My heart hammers against my ribs, breath coming in sharp, shallow bursts as panic claws at my chest.

I need to escape this church. I need to lose Jeremy.

Before he catches me and destroys me.

My head snaps back to find Jeremy cutting through the sea of humans like a blade. I know he can see me—*focus on the horns, don't lose the horns*—and my hands fly desperately to the twisting obsidian jutting from my skull. Panic makes my fingers clumsy as I try to channel my glamour magic, but it's like grasping at smoke.

Nothing. The magic just won't fucking work.

Damn him and his glamour-breaking…never mind.

I finally reach the heavy oak doors and slip through them into the night air. The stolen motorcycle sits exactly where I left it, key tucked in the helmet. I don't waste time with protection, instead straddling the seat and slamming my boot against the starter pedal. The engine roars to life. I'm seconds from freedom—

Suddenly, I'm yanked backward.

My body slams into the cold asphalt, skin scraping

against concrete. The Harley crashes down, its weight pinning my legs to the ground. Before I can even process what happened, Jeremy's shadow falls over me. He drops to straddle my chest, his full weight pressing me into the pavement. One hand closes around my throat while the other rises, holy blade gleaming in the streetlight.

This is it. This is how I die.

But something shifts between us.

For him, it's deep, inexplicable yearning.

For me, it's desperate hunger.

He relishes having me at his mercy, the hunter finally cornering his prey. There's something in his eyes I've never seen before, a desire that has nothing to do with justice or duty. This moment awakens something dark within him, something that thrills at having complete control over the demon who deceived him. And despite everything—the lies, the betrayal, my demonic form laid bare—he still wants me. Still craves me. Still aches to give in to his darkest desires.

He tries to mask it with anger, to focus on the betrayal he should be feeling, but it's all a performance, a carefully constructed façade to convince himself he should hate me.

How can I fear a creature who has me pinned with a blade to my throat, yet trembles with want?

Jeremy's eyes narrow above me, pupils blown wide, practically consuming the green of his irises. The hand gripping my throat loosens, and his fingers drift down to graze my jugular, then traces the cracks of glowing amber that spiderweb across my chest. I writhe beneath him, desperate to free my trapped legs from under the bike, to get this Nephilim off me. The amber veins pulse under his touch, and I consider the unthinkable: releasing pheromones through the cracks in my skin, hoping to send him into a frenzy that might get him off my body.

But he's too strong.

He presses the flat of the blessed dagger against my skin, and I hiss as Holy Metal sears demonic flesh. The blade burns something fierce, but he doesn't push deeper. Not yet.

He lowers his face until we're breathing the same air, so close, I can see the gold flecks in his dilated pupils and feel the heat radiating from his skin.

"You like this, don't you?" he murmurs.

The blade is white hot against me—vibrating, searing, in a way that almost feels...pleasurable. His gaze continues to rake over my skin, noting my pulsing jugular and the sizzling of my crimson skin. Those green eyes narrow in scrutiny. "You sick creature."

A throaty, almost pained chuckle rumbles in my chest. "That's rich coming from you, Sparky. You don't see me judging your kinks. And we both know how deep *your* voyeuristic streak runs." The blade bites deeper into my neck, but I force the words out anyway. "Why don't you just kill me, Jeremy? Why don't you cut my head off like you did to my banshee?" I meet his gaze, letting venom drip from every word. "Get your revenge on the 'sick creature' who played you like the perverted little fool you are."

I know I shouldn't goad my killer. I know better than to flirt with death. But the road to Hell is paved with bad decisions, and I'm already halfway there.

I seal my fate with one final gambit: by crashing my lips against his and unleashing every toxic pheromone I possess.

All it takes is a second, a single taste.

La petite mort in its truest sense.

Jeremy jolts backward as my venom floods his system. He stays perched above me but begins to sputter, foam gathering at the corners of his mouth. He hurls obscenities through gritted teeth, thrashing against the poison coursing through his veins. But then, something catches us both off guard.

"Roache?"

A new voice.

A new presence.

And it sends cold, unyielding dread through us both.

The voice cuts through the tension between us, freezing Jeremy. His eyes widen in recognition as he drops the blade from my chest and turns to face our intruder.

"Reili…Keller," Jeremy breathes.

"Roache, where have you been? We've been searching for you since last night."

Pinned beneath him, I crane my neck to glimpse the

newcomers—two figures with stark white auras blazing so brilliantly, they nearly blind me. Dark tattoos snake across their necks, marking their sacred purpose.

Demon hunters.

I'm trapped, three against one.

"Roache, what in God's name—" The Nephilim called Reili stops mid-sentence, venom dripping from his voice as he takes in my demonic form. His expression twists with disgust, hateful eyes, and a permanent scowl. "Step away from the creature. *Now.*"

"Reili, look at his aura," the second hunter, Keller—a woman—whispers urgently. "It's gray. Grayer than it was last night at the cemetery. He's been corrupted. I told you there was something wrong—just like with Lovejoy. We should have cleansed their souls before it was too late."

I watch Reili's face shift from disbelief to cold authority. "Roache, explain yourself."

"It's not what it looks like." Jeremy pushes himself upward, keeping a knee planted firmly on my chest while fighting my venom. I struggle to breathe as my tail whips out instinctively, wrapping around his leg. He only presses down harder. "I-I was investigating. She was leading me to Declan."

What a beautiful little liar. The corruption takes root perfectly as he spins convenient lies to save himself. I can't resist twisting the knife. "My, my. Look who's discovered the fine art of bullshitting. You're a natural, sweetheart."

"Silence, beast." Reili's voice is ice as he hurls a sphere of Holy Light our way. It grazes my arm, and I shriek, the searing heat burning my skin as I thrash against Jeremy's hold.

"Lovejoy's dead," Reili states flatly. "His body was destroyed in the fire."

"But I heard him." Jeremy's voice cracks with desperation. "He didn't die in those flames—his soul is trapped somewhere. Please, we have to find him. We have to save—"

"Why chase ghosts when your own soul clearly needs salvation?" Keller snaps, cutting him off. "Your corruption runs deep, Jeremy, and it's beyond repair. No amount of cleansing can help you now."

"Keller, no. I didn't—"

"Your words say one thing, but your soul says another," Reili spits. "You've allowed yourself to become tainted, Roache. Keller saw it in both of you, but we chose our mission first. It's a pity Lovejoy perished before we could do what we had to—what we need to do to you now. You're in direct violation of the Sacred Pact. You're…" His voice trails off, a somber tone in his last few words.

"Compromised," Keller finishes. "Damaged."

The two hunters stand side by side, clasping hands while their free hands rise toward Jeremy in perfect synchronization. Together, they begin chanting in what sounds like ancient Latin, and a pure white light begins surging from their veins into their outstretched palms.

"Reili, Keller! Wait, please! You can't do this—"

But it's too late.

The brilliant light slams into Jeremy like a divine battering ram, hurling us both back against a nearby stone wall. I hear the sickening crack of bone—mine or Jeremy's, I can't tell—before warm black blood begins trickling from my ears. Everything blurs into a nightmarish haze of bodies, screams, and holy fire.

I force my trembling limbs to move, dragging myself into the shadows to escape. My glowing veins and blazing eyes make me a beacon in the darkness, so I desperately try to channel my glamour to appear human again. But my powers flicker, drained by the holy assault —my body needs time to heal.

Instead of trying to run, I collapse behind a thick hedge, pressing myself against the earth as my supernatural healing slowly begins to work its magic. I can hear them from here, see them through the leaves: two demon hunters towering above Jeremy's trembling body.

Reili speaks, voice firm despite the hints of despair in his tone. "Jeremy Roache, by the authority vested in me by the Holy Order of the Nephilim, I hereby strip you of your sacred duty. Your corrupted soul will rot alongside the damned when you finally stand before the Devil. May he show you the same mercy you've shown your vows—none at all."

It's as if the world stops as another flash of Light erupts from their hands, striking Jeremy's neck. His agonized scream dies in his throat as a sharp ringing floods my ears like broken glass. He clutches desperately at his neck where that tattoo brands his skin with righteousness. I watch helplessly as tears stream down his face, his fingers blistering from the searing heat as the mark fades to a ghostly shadow on his skin.

The Nephilim sigil dissolves before my eyes, vanishing along with divine purpose.

He'll remember this night for the rest of his life—the night he lost everything outside a desecrated church in West Hollywood.

Like a wounded bird, he crumples to the ground. Wingless. Hopeless. Utterly broken.

And without a word, the other Nephilim disappear into the night.

My strength eventually returns. I emerge from the shadows, wincing as the lingering pain from Holy Light and steel still burns against my skin, even as my body continues to mend itself. I need to leave soon—get back to Bad Decisions and drink from Indigo to fully heal.

But first, I need to cast one last line into the water before I walk away.

"Looks like you're on your own now, Jeremy." My voice carries a hint of dark amusement, but the words cut straight to the truth. He looks up at me, eyes brimming with tears and body trembling like a broken thing. "I know what it's like to be betrayed by the people you trusted most. To become worthless in their eyes. To be cast aside and left to rot." I crouch to his level, seeing my demonic form reflected in his glassy, devastated gaze.

"When you need somewhere to go—and believe me, you will—you'll always have a place at Bad Decisions."

Inviting another ex-demon hunter into my world is possibly the stupidest thing I could do. In fact, it might be the worst decision I'll ever make.

But beneath the eternal war between good and evil raging inside him, beneath his desperate need for acceptance and his crushing guilt, I see something else—the young man with silver hair and sea-green eyes whose heart has been shattered beyond repair by the ones he trusted the most.

Beautifully broken. Perfectly corrupted. And mine to deliver to my Prime.

TRACK ELEVEN
Sharp Dressed Man

TRACK ELEVEN

SHARP DRESSED MAN

1911

Savannah, Georgia

BROWN, RED, AND ORANGE LEAVES CRUNCH BENEATH OUR traveling convoy of wagons. The wooden doors barely cling to their hinges, and cool air seeps through the cracks, offering swift relief from an otherwise stuffy, overcrowded caravan.

There are at least ten of us packed into the wagon, stacks of trunks threatening to topple with every bump in the rutted road. I sit atop mine—a crocodile-skin trunk with freshly polished brass hardware, legs conveniently covering the embroidered initials M.B. from the prying eyes of my traveling companions. Not that they actually care to look; each girl is so absorbed in her last-minute touch-ups and primping before we reach our destination, they don't give me a second glance.

I pick at my freshly manicured nails, hands folded in my lap as my heart pounds against my ribcage. I try to silence the questions racing through my mind: has my father noticed I'm even gone yet? Has mother sent the maids to my chamber to turn down my bed for the night, only for them to discover half my belongings are missing? Will they even care to find me?

Of course they would. I was John Blythe's most prized possession, his magnum opus.

I was also the key to solidifying our family fortune.

He'd send his best men to track me down—of that, I'm certain. I glance out the small window of the wagon, noting the change in scenery, the different houses lining the streets as our convoy continues its journey.

Good, we've almost reached the next parish. Soon, we'll be crossing state lines, and I'll be further from my father and one step closer to freedom.

Le Bijoux Follies weren't your typical traveling troupe emerging from the city's demimonde. They—*we* —were a perfectly procured group of artistes. Courtesans, dancers, singers, even actresses who could give the commercial district's vaudeville acts a run for their money. Word was, they'd crossed the Atlantic to seduce American high society and teach our bland, provincial elite the true art of showmanship.

All led by one classic, timeless beauty who dazzled every theater from Paris to New Orleans: Valentina Rose.

She moved with the sort of grace you see in a cat's gait

—languid and effortless, her muscles flowing like liquid. She never had a hair out of place, as if each strand were curled to perfection then brushed into dark, silky waves that cascaded down her back. The rouge on her cheeks was always just enough, and her full lips carried a perpetual smirk that assured me she was always a step ahead.

Her skin is as soft as rose petals when her fingertips brush against my shoulder. I'm shaken from my trance as her tawny eyes search mine.

"Lost in thought again, my love?"

There's a hint of an Italian accent lacing her words, those little inflections that never fail to remind me she isn't from around here. I flash her a small, albeit nervous, smile.

"Nervous about my debut," I confess. "I've only ever danced in front of you and the other girls."

"You've been a dancer since you could walk—you're no stranger to performing. You're a natural. Think of cabaret as ballet with less clothing and a hungrier audience."

Cabaret was terribly different from ballet; I want to tell her, but something tells me she already knows—knows my woes, the fears dashing like racehorses in my head.

Demons can read minds, after all.

"I need you to be magnificent for me tonight, my beauty," she says, plucking a final stray feather from my bodice. "You'll be meeting a very special someone."

"Is it him?" I ask, trying to mask the excitement creeping into my voice.

"It is," she offers me a reassuring smile. "Now remember, the travel from California is quite the journey, so make it worth his while. We'll discuss the terms of our arrangement—should he find you worthy."

"Do you think he will?" My eyes must be as wide as saucers—probably even larger thanks to those makeup tricks I've learned to make them appear bigger than they really are.

"Anyone willing to offer their soul in exchange for fame and fortune is deemed worthy in his eyes, especially someone as beautiful and talented as you."

A slow flush creeps up my neck and into my cheeks at the compliment. She traces my face with her thumb, running a finger under my chin. I instinctively lean into her touch, desperately craving more of her attention— more words, more promises, more affection.

I'd heard whispers around polite society about the Follies, how they masquerade as performers but carry secrets deeper and darker than the depths of the bayou. Some said they were witches; others claimed they were the Devil's harlots, sent to us straight from Hell to drag the damned and depraved down where they belong.

In the eyes of many, it was all nonsense. Jealous gossip from bitter older women who were past their prime.

Little did they know, their suspicions were accurate.

I'd always been a peculiar girl. I never liked polite

society, absolutely *hated* cotillion, and would rather drown in alligator-infested waters than become a carbon copy of my mother. Curiosity got the better of me a few months ago when I sought out the Follies, hoping to find something more, a way to escape the world I was born into but never meant for.

That's when I found Valentina.

A woman who swept me off my feet and promised me freedom with a glimmer in her light brown eyes and a candy-red smile.

I look at her now, marveling at her smooth, flawless tan skin and the curves from her carefully cinched, stiff corset. A garter secures her intricate black lace stockings beneath a sheer black robe with feathered hems. She looks nothing like the creature I glimpsed that one night a few months back, when we explored the darkest corners of Savannah.

When she revealed her true self.

She had been straight out of one of Father's biblical texts, the ones with terrifying illustrations of the Devil's servants—a being with bat-like wings, curved horns, sharp features, and gray, cracked skin that resembled the gargoyles guarding churches. Those magnificent horns curved into an almost heart-like shape, mesmerizing in their terrible beauty. She was like a work of art, consuming the souls of her victims in front of me, an unsuspecting, innocent debutante.

I should have been terrified. I should have fled.

Instead, I was drawn closer.

And I fell completely under her spell.

A blur of black fur races between our clothing trunks, pulling me out of my reverie. One of the dancers, Amethyst, calls out, "You still draggin' around that mangy old cat, Tina?" The creature leaps onto the tallest trunk, repeatedly grooming and gnawing at itself as if it were plagued with fleas. Valentina reaches for the cat, scratching behind its ear with a chuckle.

"I've grown rather attached to him. There's something charming about a demon-possessed cat who doesn't know any better."

"I don't know who to feel worse for: the demon or the cat," comes the lilting voice of Emerald, or Emmie, one of the French performers.

"I can assure you, the cat is none the wiser. Felines are prone to demonic possession. Just be grateful no one has to pick up *your* litter. What a sad existence."

I smile at the thought, still somewhat perplexed by the inner workings of demonhood. Valentina promised my questions would be answered tonight, that the elusive gentleman from California could offer the deal of a lifetime in exchange for my soul.

I've always been warned to stay away from charlatans with honeyed words and beguiling smiles. But I willingly walked into a demon's den, and there's no turning back now.

We enter through the servants' quarters when we finally reach our destination—a gargantuan estate at least double the size of my family home, with countless carriages and gleaming new motor cars lined up out front.

It feels strange walking into an opulent setting as a performer hidden in the shadows. I'd grown accustomed to being escorted through the grand entrance with a gentleman caller on my arm.

The host of tonight's soirée is an affluent businessman with more money than sense. He's invited fifty of his gentleman friends—married men, widowers, and eligible bachelors alike—to indulge in a night of debauchery. For the right price, they can buy more than just a dance from a Follie. My father would shudder at the thought; he's far too much of a puritan for such devious proclivities.

I overhear servants scurrying through the labyrinth of this stunning Gothic mansion, chattering about how Mr. Kenneth's birthday needs to go off without a hitch, how exciting it will be to have live entertainment for the night, and hoping they might catch a glimpse of the show.

It only sets my nerves on edge more.

"One day, I'll own a home like this," Valentina sighs as she studies the mansion. "But instead of catering to the insatiable, deplorable appetites of men, I'll create a place where they get what they *truly* deserve."

I can't help but watch Valentina as she moves with such purpose and confidence. Attempting to mimic her posture, I straighten with the same conviction and poise she carries so effortlessly, my red bodice catching the subtle light in the study as the other girls and I prepare for our first performance of the night.

I give my ginger tresses a quick primp, tighten the straps on my heels, pick up my oversized feather fan, and follow the others toward the main party. But Valentina stops me dead in my tracks, squeezing my wrist gently.

"Not so fast, my beauty. He'll see you now."

Ice fills my veins. "Now? But the show—"

"The Gems will start the first few numbers, and you and I will go on last. Really give those old men a show."

The soft click of a closing door captures my attention. An unexpected warmth fills the room as I realize Valentina and I are no longer alone in the study. A sweet, yet tart aroma hits my senses, and I subconsciously lick my lips, my tongue suddenly thick in my mouth. I turn to face a stranger who nearly takes my breath away.

It's him. It has to be. The gentleman from California.

"My, my," he purrs as his gaze travels over me then shifts to Valentina for a moment. "You mentioned she looked good in red, but I didn't expect *this*. Ruby, is it?"

I nod at his mention of my stage name, the name Valentina gave me when I joined the Follies not even a month ago. I feel inexplicably small under his gaze, yet I can't help but be drawn in by his magnetic presence, desperate for his approval. This goes beyond my simple desire to escape my family's clutches. It's something deeper, more primal. Almost...infernal.

There's something deceptively unassuming about his

short stature, given the authority he commands. Confidence flows from him in an endless stream I long to drink from. He's dressed to the absolute nines in the most lavish clothing: a shimmering gold pin secures a crisp white bow tie against his collar, and an ivory swallowtail sits perfectly over his silk-lined, maroon waistcoat. An ornate golden pocket watch glimmers in the gaslight, matching the same peculiar glint in his spectacles with their red-tinted lenses.

But it's not his outfit that continues to pull me toward him. Perhaps it was the mischief in his smile, or the cunning in his voice, that low, seductive purr I'd give anything to hear over and over. Every nerve in my body stands on end, but I can't let it show. Tonight, I need to be perfect for him, just as Valentina said.

I couldn't bear to face my lover's disappointment and the rejection of her boss all in one night.

"You know who I am, don't you, darling?" He circles me like a wolf would its prey—hungry, salivating.

"You're Mr. Cherry, the proprietor of Les Bijoux Follies. Valentina's manager."

The dark-haired demoness retreats to the shadows of the study, watching us with a knowing smile.

"That's not all I am," Cherry says as he continues his saunter. "I'm in the business of making dreams come true, my darling. Why don't you share yours with me?"

I swallow hard and lick my lips again. "I want to leave Savannah. I want to go to California and become an actress. I want to sing and dance and hear people cheer for me."

"Is that all you want?" The question hangs heavy in the air. My first instinct is to say 'yes,' but when I catch a glimpse of his eyes—endless voids that suddenly glow red behind his spectacles—I nearly jump back. I remember Mr. Cherry is a demon, just like Valentina. He can read me better than anyone.

"I want to love freely." My words are barely above a whisper. I glance over at Valentina, whose beautifully full lips curl into a knowing smile. "I want to be free of the shackles of polite society, far away from the righteous and hateful."

Mr. Cherry nods when he finally stops in front of me. "Valentina tells me you would give your soul for this dream."

I attempt to swallow the lump in my dry throat. "I would, sir."

"Such a steep price to pay for something so easily attainable. I'll make this a little simpler for you, my darling. You can keep your soul, but I *will* require payment to make this dream come true."

"Anything," I blurt out. "I'll do anything."

Mr. Cherry's dangerous grin sends a shiver down my spine. He grips his walking cane, tapping it against the floor in an excited notion, and speaks. "You must deliver me a corrupted soul."

"H-how do I do that?" I ask as a wave of dread rushes over me.

His grin spreads. "Why, the easiest way is to kill, of course. I'm sure you know plenty of corrupt men—and women. Take your pick. Kill for me. Bring me their soul, and I will give you everything you've ever dreamed of. I'll make it even simpler for you and give you a year."

I've never even considered killing anyone before. Never had it in me. But if this was the price of freedom, if it'll take me thousands of miles from my family, and put my name in lights with Valentina by my side… I'll pay.

"What happens if I…" The words trail off into silence. I can't bear to speak to them, can't bear to know.

"Fail to deliver a soul? Well, then you'll forfeit yours. A fair trade, really—after all, I *am* making this painfully easy for you. What do you say, Ruby? Do we have a deal?"

He offers me his silver-ringed hand. My heart constricts and my mind races; where do I find the right person to kill? *How* do I kill them? Will I have what it takes to make good on this deal? And if I don't, what will that mean for my soul?

I shatter the negative thoughts and remember who I am: a strong, intelligent woman who's far too good for this town.

Without another thought, I take the gentleman's hand and seal my future with a shake.

"Splendid," Mr. Cherry exclaims, spinning around to take his leave. "I look forward to your performance tonight, Miss Ruby. Now, go out there and kill it."

The air seems to suck out of the room the moment Mr. Cherry exits. The urge to vomit overcomes me, and I gasp out a sob. Valentina rushes to my side, catching me as my legs threaten to give out beneath me.

"You're alright, my beauty. You did so well." Her voice—that honeyed, low purr—sends a rush of warmth through me.

"Valentina, what did I just do?" I ask her, my breath coming in shallow bursts. "How am I supposed to kill someone? Who would deserve it?"

"Think of it this way, lover: a corrupted soul ends up with the Devil one way or another. You're just delivering them sooner." Her logic is seductively twisted, framing murder as expediting the inevitable. The moment her hand finds my cheek and she stares into my soul with those enchanting brown eyes, I believe her.

"We'll work through this together, but first, your debut. I'll be right beside you the entire time." She pulls me into a tender, heart-stopping kiss, tangling her fingers in my wild ginger curls. I melt into her touch, savoring the softness of her lips, wishing this moment could last forever. Every inch of her feels like a warm embrace—a reassuring promise that no matter what decisions I've made, I will be safe. I *will* prevail.

"Just like we practiced," she whispers against my lips when she finally pulls away, running her thumb over my chin.

Valentina hands me my feathered fans and shoots me a wink. Together, we exit the study and navigate the labyrinth of hallways until we reach the entrance to the ballroom, where the Follies are putting on their provocative show.

The mahogany doors swing open, and we meet the heady stench of cigar smoke and anticipation. The ballroom has been transformed into an intimate theater, with low, warm lighting and countless plush couches scattered throughout. The piano man's composition shifts as Valentina and I enter the room, arms wrapped around each other's waists while our feathered fans—hers black, mine red—cover our scantily clad forms. The gentlemen lean forward in their seats, some adjusting their bow ties, others taking generous gulps of their beverages. All of them stare at us like we're pieces of meat to devour. For a moment, I feel as small as I did under the scrutiny of Mr. Cherry.

But then, I steal a glance at Valentina.

She drinks up their attention, commanding the room with her dazzling, red-painted smile, and sighs with satisfaction as she takes a deep breath, drawing in their essence. In this room filled with corrupt men, Valentina is the most dangerous predator. Little do they know, they will be her meal.

When we reach the center of the room, I catch a glimpse of Mr. Cherry near the front row, his eyes drinking me in hungrily behind those narrow, red-tinted glasses. His subtle wink reminds me this is only the beginning—my wildest dreams are finally within reach.

I mirror Valentina's grin when we begin our dance.

But my heart drops to my stomach when I meet a familiar gaze in the crowd, hazel-green eyes an exact match for mine.

Right in the middle of the room, at a round table surrounded by licentious men fawning over Valentina's Follies, sits John Blythe.

My father.

TELL ME WHAT I'M UP AGAINST SO I CAN PROTECT YOU. ALL OF YOU.
TRACK TWELVE
Shot in the Dark
JUST BE CAREFUL WITH HIM, WILL YA? DON'T LET HIM IN ON ANY SECRETS.

TRACK TWELVE

SHOT IN THE DARK

It's been two weeks since Cherry and I made the deal, and I'm about as close to my promotion as I am to touching the moon. The now-dark black tourmaline necklace lies in an antique pewter box, stripped of the light I'd grown accustomed to over those few short days. The crystal is just another reminder my brilliant plan, however flawed, failed, putting me back at square one: Nephilim-less and out of ideas. The closest thing I've got to a corrupted demon hunter is the old Silver Fox shacking up at my motel, and he's as used as day-old biscuits.

I almost had him—that green-eyed, tortured angel. His excommunication should have sent him straight into my arms, but, as always, reality's proven to be a cruel, sadistic bitch. I find myself glancing at the necklace peri-odically, hoping it would light up the way it did when its host was near.

But the necklace hasn't so much as flickered, not for almost two weeks. Not since he discovered what I am.

It's eerily quiet in the club this evening, and it's enough to send a rush of fear through my body. The regulars are MIA, and there isn't a hint of movement upstairs from any of my employees. For all I know, there's some new supernatural threat gripping the world by the balls, and I'm none the wiser, tucked away in my dungeon boudoir. My analog clock marks 10 o'clock, and I sigh with relief.

Break time.

Indigo typically takes her break on the second level of The Starlight, where the balcony curves left into a shadowy corner. She'll lean against the metal railing there, hidden from the flickering neon glow, content to observe the restless swarm of tourists and locals surging along Hollywood Boulevard.

"I just like to people-watch," she always says in that sweet, innocent little voice of hers, batting those false lashes and flashing her signature purple-painted smile.

Occasionally, Charlie joins her there for a smoke, mirroring her pose against the railing as they stretch their fifteen-minute breaks into hour-long conversations. Naturally, Indigo does all the talking—spinning grand tales of her life back in New York, how it all seemed so dull compared to the glitz and glam of Los Angeles. Even from downstairs, I can hear Charlie's thoughts as he marvels at her little quirks: the way her silver-gray eyes sparkle when she talks about classic horror films, how her voice climbs higher with excitement when she gushes about hunting through cemeteries because, "It's just so Hollywood."

It's those mundane moments, tucked away within the chaos of our tumultuous demonic lives, that keep me grounded. The constants. The reliability of it all. I find myself oddly comforted—and, I'll admit, a little baffled—by how someone could *genuinely* enjoy working a job like ours.

It only makes me more determined to protect what we have here. These dark, gritty lives carved from our little corner of Hollywood, feeding on humans as demons do and savoring every second of it. Together.

But something's a little different tonight. Indigo isn't at The Starlight. Charlie isn't with her. In fact, neither of them are anywhere to be found.

I try to distract myself, sitting at my vanity, crimson hair wound tight in rollers while I apply the perfect shade of dark lipstick. Gold-cracked veins glimmer and shine beneath the black boudoir robe resting effortlessly on my shoulders. The feathered hem of its sleeves tickle my skin as I perfect my cupid's bow. As convenient as my glamour magic is, nothing beats the pleasure of releasing a flawless, wavy curl from its roller, or the precision of drawing on a flawless cat-eye. It takes me back to different times—simpler times, when life was short and death was imminent. Life isn't that much different now, of course. Death is still imminent, but now, I know prayers and good deeds won't land me a ticket upstairs. No. Where I'm going is *much* warmer.

"Reagan," a sweet, melodic voice speaks from behind me, but the reflection in my vanity only shows myself. I jolt in my seat, panic spiking through my nerves as I spin around to find a little purple-haired vampire hovering in the doorway of my dungeon boudoir.

"You trying to give me a heart attack, Indy? Why aren't you on break?"

Indigo enters and throws herself onto my bed, the black crushed velvet sheets crinkling beneath her petite frame. She looks nothing like the terrifying creature she truly is—just a girl with big, doe-like eyes and outrageously bright makeup, ankles crossed and swinging in the air.

"Thought I'd spend it with you." Her effortless charm never fails to tug at my heart, and I can't help but notice little details about her tonight. Her cheeks are pinker than usual—is that from the new makeup I bought her, or has she *actually* had a decent meal for once?—hair swept up in a loose, messy bun instead of those sleek-straight tresses that usually cascade past her chest, shirt just a smidge too big for her small frame, which I could have sworn I'd seen Charlie wearing just a few days ago.

"Your roots are coming in, Indy," I tease with a knowing smirk.

"You know how it is—undead hair grows *ridiculously* fast. Nice little perk Greed threw in when he made us vampires. 'Everything in excess,' and all that. So, uh… got time to give me a touch-up?"

"If only. In times like this, I wish you were a Debauchery demon. Then you could snap your fingers and change your hair color instead of staining all my furniture blue."

She chuckles in that sweet, coy little way that never fails to bring a smile to my lips. "This place could use a little more blue and purple now and again."

Spinning in my seat to face the vanity mirror, I continue my little ritual. I can practically feel the vampire's violet-gray eyes remain fixed on me as I reach for a razor-sharp knife from my drawer, placing the cool metal at a diagonal against my eye and tracing the blade's edge with liquid liner.

"There are way better ways to do that, you know. I'm happy to teach you."

I can't help but flash her a smirk as I draw the perfect cat-eye. "Does my knife fetish make you uncomfortable, Indy?"

She lets out a soft laugh. "*My* fetishes would tickle you pink."

"I believe it." I throw her a wink.

The temperature in the room seems to drop as Indigo's demeanor shifts. Sweetness fades from her expression, replaced by something nervous and tense. "Reagan, jokes aside…can we talk?"

"Of course." I set down my eyeliner, turning to face her fully. I attempt to quiet my suddenly erratic heartbeat, knowing she can probably hear it hammering against my ribs.

"It's about the old guy—the one staying with us. How much do you actually know about him?"

"Why?" The word escapes before I can stop it, sharp with instinctive worry. I hate that I can't even muster the courtesy of an honest answer before jumping to defense.

"Cherry won him in a poker game, didn't he?"

"He did."

She sucks in her bottom lip, sitting up in my bed and wringing her hands in her lap. "I've met him before, at the annual poker game a few years ago when Greed traded me to Cherry. I was just a chip, of course. But that old guy? *He* was the jackpot."

It never occurred to me that Indigo came into my service the same way I was almost traded over to Deception and Greed. She was merely brought to my doorstep one day by Cherry during another one of his 'Hello darling, I've got you a present' drop-ins. The idea of being so dispensable, so replaceable in the eyes of your Sire is a dark feeling, enough to make you question your loyalties. Cherry framed it that he procured Indigo for me, that a vampire was just as exotic as a banshee or a siren or a succubus. That adding her to the menu would bring in a ton of business. In truth, it did; Indigo has always been a head turner at Bad Decisions, though I'll never know whether that's because of her striking violet-blue hair, her deceptively innocent look, or her supernaturally quick dance moves.

"You worried about him?" I meet the vampire's eyes directly, searching for any tells.

She shrugs, her gaze sliding away from mine. There it is.

"Indy, come on. If you know something, tell me what I'm up against so I can protect you. All of you."

"Just be careful with him, will ya? Don't let him in on any secrets. He's a corrupted demon hunter—those are the worst. More untrustworthy than any human. If he was willing to turn on the Big Guy, he'll turn on just about anyone."

The girl's right, and the realization hits me like a slap in the face. I'd been so focused on the game, I completely overlooked the ex-predator lurking under my roof. Vincent Thane—quiet, tortured Vincent, who kept to the shadows and spoke in careful, calculated whispers. A harmless, broken soul pawned by three of the greatest evils known to mankind.

Corrupted hunters don't just lose their way: they choose it, and this one made the deliberate decision to betray everything he ever stood for.

The truth is, I know absolutely nothing about him. If he's half as dangerous as Indigo suggests, I would be a fool to let that go on for much longer.

"Who taught you to do it like that anyway?" Indigo asks, interrupting my thoughts. She nods toward my knife and eyeliner. I flash her a sad smile as I run my thumb over the hilt of the blade. The ridges of an ornate rose surrounded by brambles of thorns trigger memories

I hold close to my heart. One day, I'll tell Indigo about Valentina—but not today.

My thoughts shatter as Charlie's voice Taps into my mind from upstairs.

Reagan, we've got a situation. You're going to want to come up.

What is it? I Tap back, rising to my feet and securing the belt of my robe around my waist. *Human? Demon?*

And that's when it catches my eye—the black tourmaline necklace, flashing erratically.

Worse. It's that Nephilim.

TRACK THIRTEEN
Rebel Yell

TRACK THIRTEEN

REBEL YELL

GOOSEBUMPS PRICKLE ACROSS MY SKIN AS A WAVE OF DREAD crashes through me. My first instinct is to rush upstairs and personally handle whatever threat awaits, but I force myself to recall the calmness in Charlie's mental voice when he reached out. The steady flow of his baritone carried confusion and wariness, but no panic, no distress.

I slip on a pair of black satin kitten heels adorned with marabou feathers, cinch the sash of my robe tighter around my waist, and run my fingers through my hair. Before leaving my boudoir, I turn to Indigo with a warning.

"Stay put, Indy. Don't come upstairs until it's safe."

"You know I can take care of myself, Reagan." Her voice is firm but still threaded with that familiar sweetness. I flash her a smile.

"I know you can, but I'd never forgive myself if you ended up like Jasmine. Please…stay."

Indigo nods, falling back into my bed with a grunt and staring at the ceiling as I take my leave.

The club sits in unnatural silence, broken only by the harsh buzzing of fluorescent lights overhead. Charlie looms at the bar, his demonic form partially unleashed. Massive horns spiral from his skull like gnarled branches, twisted into antler-like curves. His claws—black as night and obscenely sharp—curl inward, ready to attack. Though I can't see his eyes from this distance, I know they're blazing their signature black and red.

"I told you, I just want to speak to the owner," comes the innocent, near-strained voice of Jeremy Roache.

As I step closer to my bartender, the Nephilim comes into view, but to my surprise, he bears no resemblance to the sweet angel I'd met just weeks ago.

No. This is someone completely different.

A black t-shirt and teal flannel hang loose from his heavy shoulders, both a size too large for his diminished frame. His salt-and-pepper hair—that unnatural gray betraying his young age—is a disheveled mess, falling into his eyes from every direction. His once-healthy tan has faded to a sickly pallor, blue-green veins standing out like dark rivers along his forearms. He clutches his side, back hunched, lips parted as he fights for each breath.

He's inches from death's door, and I can't figure out why.

"Well, well." I stand firm next to Charlie, wrapping my arms over my chest. "What have we here?"

"I didn't know where else to go," he admits, digging his hands into his pockets before losing his balance and gripping the bar top for support. "Something's wrong with me."

"Have a seat over there," I murmur, nodding toward the crescent-shaped leather booths near the main stage. "Charlie here will get you something that'll fix you right up."

I catch Charlie's eye, motioning toward the bar. Time for him to do what he does best: craft the perfect beverage for a lonely, agonized soul. The bartender is behind his station in seconds, pulling a highball glass and cocktail shaker from the shelf.

Confession Draught? He Taps, his fingers beginning to twist and curl as dark magic gathers around them.

Make it strong, I respond.

I watch as my trusted bartender channels his powers of manipulation into the mixed beverage. The mixture glows green for mere seconds before fading to a natural amber. Confession draughts are Charlie's specialty—the perfect concoction to get patrons spilling their darkest secrets and deepest desires. They're also excellent for weeding out the serious threats from the mildly annoying ones.

My heels thud into the carpet as I deliver the Nephilim his drink.

"What's that?" Jeremy asks innocently, peering into the glass.

"Not poison," I jest with a sigh and slide into the booth across from him. "Trust me—it'll take the edge off."

He takes a whiff of the drink, his eyebrows relaxing when he realizes I might be telling the truth. After a tentative first sip, he swallows hard, wincing as the alcohol burns down his throat. He's not used to liquor—I learned that quickly during my corruption campaign—but he takes another sip, then another, and soon, he's gulping the draught like it's the Fountain of Youth itself.

Color returns to his face then, flushing his hollow cheeks with warmth. His breathing steadies, his posture relaxing, as if he's lifted the world's heaviest weight from his shoulders. He's calmer now, inhibitions lowered, though his body still carries traces of the inexplicable illness that clearly plagues him.

"Who are you? What's your name?" I ask him, though I know it quite well. It's a precaution used when someone's freshly under the influence of Charlie's confession draughts.

"Jeremy Roache," he answers without a second thought, and a sheepish smile creeps upon his features. "I'm a Nephilim. But you already knew that."

"Where have you been since I last saw you?" I ask, watching as he takes another gulp out of Charlie's concoction.

"I don't remember much of the past week or so. It's all...blurry. Some days, I can't tell what's real and what isn't. But what I can tell you is that it's been quiet. Eerily quiet. No more voices. No more missions. Just silence. Do you know what that's like? To be completely alone?" He stares straight into my eyes then. A red ring circles his irises, and the skin under his eyes looks even darker in this light. "Who am I kidding—you're a succubus. You're never alone."

There's a tug at the corner of my lips, one I try to suppress. I take comfort in the fact that even in his tortured state, he can still find room for humor. It's different from what I'm used to, based on our brief but intimate encounters.

"Why haven't you left Los Angeles? Don't you have a home—a family?"

His laugh is bitter, hollow. "Demon hunters don't have permanent homes. We're always on the go, always chasing the next lead, the next monster." He runs a hand through his prematurely gray hair, and I catch the slightest tremor in his fingers. "As for family, well…I never knew my mother. The Order took me in the minute I came out of her. And Dad? He's up there" —he tilts his head skyward—"doing angel stuff. Probably looking down right now, wondering why he ever bothered knocking up a human in the first place."

There it is again, that sheepish smile, the dark, self-deprecating humor that splits a grin across my face. I don't mean to laugh—I truly don't—but I can't help it. There's just something dangerously attractive about a man who can crack a joke while his world is falling apart, especially one who started out as a pious, self-righteous demon hunter.

This broken, cynical version of Jeremy is *far* more tolerable.

"Can I tell you something?" he asks, toying with his empty glass. I nod, watching as he leans forward, shoulders slouched, voice dropping to barely above a whisper. "Remember when I told you about my mentor? The one who went missing?" I nod again. "You probably already knew he was a demon hunter too. He's gone now. Dead. Poof. You know, I bet he's probably up there right now, blabbing away in that English accent, sounding way smarter than he ever actually was." His head sinks into his hands as he bites back a laugh. "God, I can't believe I just said that."

Now I *really* like this version of him. Anyone who can take shots at Declan Lovejoy has earned serious points in my book.

"Anyway," Jeremy continues, dragging his finger around the rim of his glass. "I heard him say something before he died; kind of like a mental blast thing we hunters can do. I think it was meant for me. He told me to kill October Winters."

My jaw tightens at the mention of her name.

"You know her, don't you? She was staying at your motel a few weeks ago."

I shrug, feigning indifference. "I don't pay attention

to my guests. Their money clears, my bills are paid, and that's all I care about."

"She's the Devil's Second—whatever that means. You know what's really pathetic? There isn't even a full paragraph about her in all the Order texts. For someone supposedly so powerful, she can't even earn a single page."

My eyes narrow at him. "Maybe that's because she's done a bang-up job keeping her identity secret from sanctimonious half-breeds like you, Sparky."

He lets out a soft chuckle, his smile going slack, and for a moment, I swear I feel warmth bloom in my chest. "I deserved that."

I study him for a moment, drinking in every detail. His head hangs heavy, as if his neck can hardly bear the weight of the turmoil consuming his mind. When I peer into his thoughts, I find a cacophonous mix of memories he'd never dare voice aloud—how he can't stop thinking about the moments we shared when I posed as a human. The mausoleum. Our little motorcycle chase. The church rave. Oh, how that one plays on a loop in his head.

He can't stop thinking about how alive he felt dancing with me. How Cherry's lips tasted like *actual* cherries. How my mouth made his body do unspeakable things.

He's trying desperately to reconcile Jasmine—my human alias—with the demon sitting before him now. He recognizes the crimson hair, the full lips, the curves of my body. But he can't see past the horns jutting from my skull. The tail that moves like a fifth limb of its own volition. The glowing cracks whittled into my skin like molten scars. The black and amber eyes that mark me as the monster I truly am.

But there's something else lurking in that troubled mind; an ulterior motive, teetering on the edge of spilling out. So, I beat him to the punch.

"What do you want from me, Jeremy? Why did you come here, other than having no other place to turn?"

Jeremy sucks in a breath and holds it for a moment, as if calculating the perfect response. Finally, after moments of silence, he speaks:

"I need you to help me kill October Winters."

The kid's got balls, I'll give him that. I raise my eyebrow, expression otherwise sharp and still. "And why would I help you do that?"

He blinks at me as if *I'm* the crazy one, as if the answer couldn't be more obvious. "Isn't she a threat to you? To the Prime you serve? Shouldn't a demon be Lucifer's right hand, not a witch?"

"Interesting logic you've got there: teaming up with a demon to kill a witch who serves the Devil himself. What exactly do you think would happen to me if Lucifer found out I helped a Nephilim assassinate his right hand, hm?"

"I don't care," he states flatly, his face completely expressionless, and for a moment, I regret having Charlie make him that draught. "Killing her will get me back in the Order's good graces."

Now it's my turn to stare at him in disbelief. "Have you ever actually killed someone before?"

He ponders for a moment then shrugs. "I've banished a Prime."

I roll my eyes. "I'll ask again: have you ever *killed* someone before?"

"No."

My voice turns to steel as I fight the indignation clawing at my insides. "Then you wouldn't know about the kind of darkness it takes to end a life. Witches are not like demons—they don't come with unholy fail safes and fine print. They're not inherently tied to a Prime against their will. You fight because it's your God-given right. She fights because she has no God. She's got enough darkness in her to murder for sport and laugh while her flames swallow innocents whole. You have no idea what it takes to kill her. She *will* outlive you, and she will *always* win."

"She's the villain." His green eyes glare daggers into mine. "She needs to pay for what she's done."

"She will always be a villain to you. We all will. I won't help you kill her, Jeremy, but I will show you kindness when your own Order refuses to."

His eyes soften for a moment, misty with tears threatening to spill. "W-what do you mean?"

"You need a place to stay? You've got it. You want to know what's happening to you? Why your powers are on the fritz? Why your aura's about as stable as lamplight during a storm? I can help with that too." I lean back, letting my words sink in before delivering the killing blow. "But don't you dare walk into my house and try to manipulate me into signing my own death warrant. You think I'm just some power-hungry Underling you can sweet-talk into betraying the Devil? Think again, Sparky. October Winters isn't just a witch—she's *the* witch. Cross her, and you won't just die. You will be erased, just like your mentor. So you can either drop your little vendetta at the door or get the Hell out of my club."

The words taste bitter even as I speak them, my own hypocrisy louder than the guilt pounding in my chest. As I study his body language, the sudden worry etching in his features, those pretty green eyes widening with horror and full of tears, I realize something: corruption has already taken root inside him and begun to flourish.

A real Nephilim would never manipulate a woman— demon or not—into an early grave. He wouldn't have come to her domain seeking sanctuary. He would have killed her without mercy, like he tried to the night we first met, or allowed his thirst for justice to fuel his crusade.

A real Nephilim would also never team up with his enemy to get ahead.

But he wasn't thinking like an angel with a higher purpose. Not anymore.

He was beginning to think like a demon.

"You'll let me stay here?" he asks in a voice so low, so full of disbelief, that I almost miss it.

I rise to my feet, giving him a full shot of my body through my sheer robe. His eyes linger for a moment but meet mine when I cross my arms over my chest. "As long as you keep your hands off my employees and my patrons? Sure. Consider yourself a permanent special guest."

I step closer, bending to meet him at eye level, my face just inches from his. The scent of his desperation mingles with arousal and fear. Just how I prefer my victims. My tail flicks with barely-contained energy as it catches his chin in its grasp and tugs him in.

"But mark my words, Sparky. I've got an entire dungeon full of medieval torture devices I've been *itching* to try on someone new, and I won't hesitate to make your life a living Hell if you step out of line. Have I made myself clear?"

Jeremy swallows hard and nods, and I let my tail trace along his jawline before pulling away. "Wonderful. Now, come with me—I'll introduce you to your new roommate. He's silver-haired, devastatingly handsome, and just as damaged as you. It'll be like looking in a mirror."

I can feel the weight of his stare as I sway toward the exit, his thoughts practically screaming as he scrambles to his feet behind me.

"Wait—you never told me your name. Your real name."

I simply smile as dark energy crackles along my fingertips, my sheer robe melting away like smoke to reveal the gleaming latex clinging to my demonic form like a second skin.

"You know demons never give out their real names, Mr. Nephilim. But you can call me Reagan. Reagan Valentine."

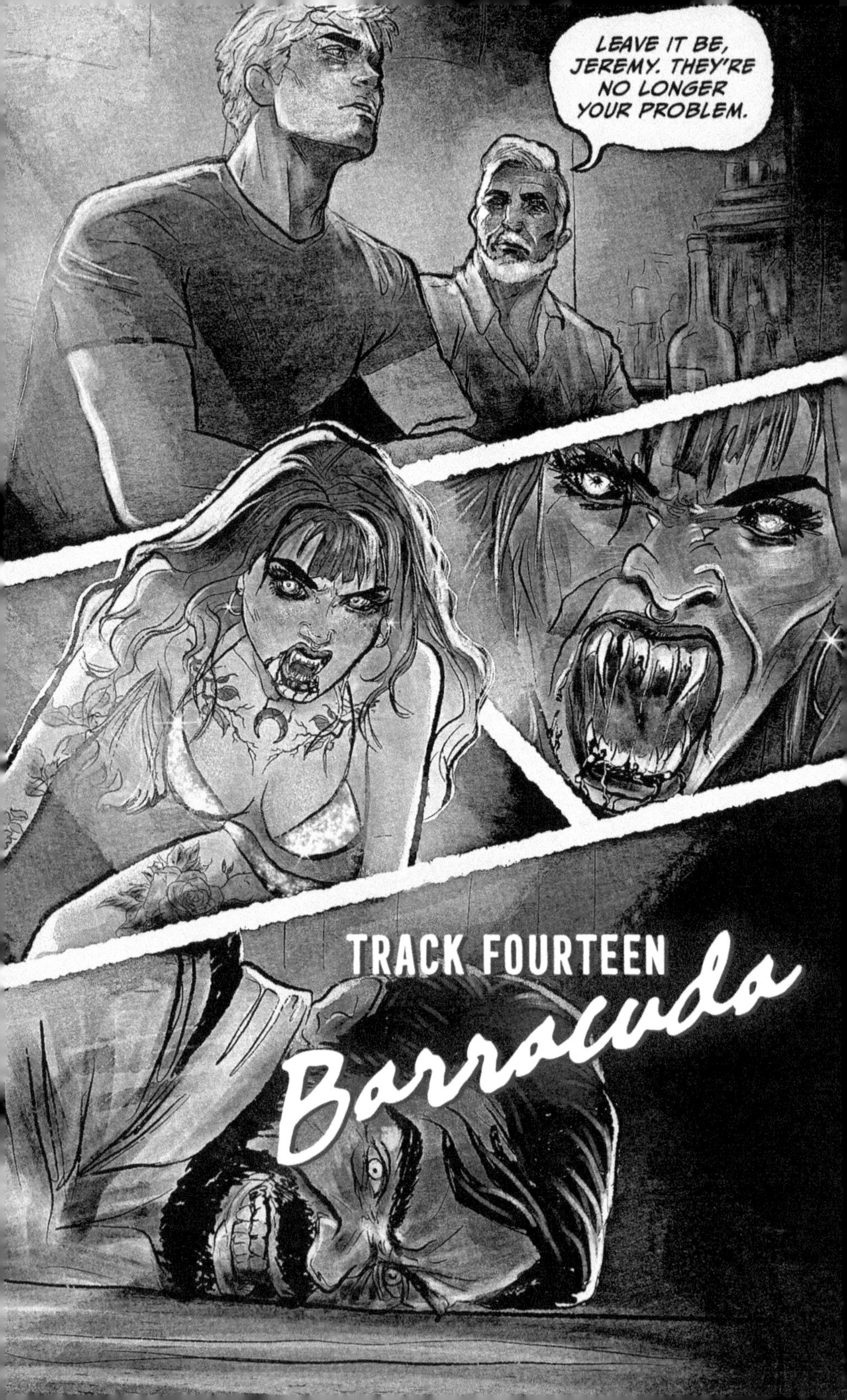

LEAVE IT BE, JEREMY. THEY'RE NO LONGER YOUR PROBLEM.
TRACK FOURTEEN
Barracuda

TRACK FOURTEEN

BARRACUDA

Of all nights, right in the middle of November, on a fucking Wednesday, an insufferable band of women decided to host a bachelorette party at Bad Decisions. They had their pick of venues—upscale cabaret shows, '70s-themed go-go clubs—but no. They chose the seediest joint on the boulevard.

And I'm at their beck and call.

There's a certain standard of expectation when one comes to my club. You won't get fancy hors d'oeuvres—you're lucky if you get a cold slice of pizza—and you might walk away with an inexplicable rash on your ass if you don't put down a seat cover. But I can assure you, the entertainment's sinful and the drinks are straight from Hell.

The bride-to-be is a middle-aged bimbo on her second or third marriage, judging by the thick tan line on her ring finger. She's a sex-crazed, self-absorbed broad stuck in the '80s, complete with shoulder pads that rival her cotton candy fluffed hair. And her friends? Don't get me started.

Indigo's center stage tonight in that sparkly getup she reserves for important guests—the one in which, when the light hits just right, she glitters as brightly as the disco ball spinning above her.

Charlie's the busiest he's been in months, crafting cocktails by the dozens, but he still steals the occasional glance at my best girl. I catch his eye, shooting him a quick little telepathic reminder: *Give their drinks an extra boost, will ya, Char? And save a batch of Mind-Wipe for later, in case things get out of hand. We're behind on rent this month, and we could use the extra tips.*

Heard, he Taps back, mind preoccupied with the tantalizing curve of Indigo's figure.

Devil damn me, if those two don't fuck soon, I'll have to take matters into my own claws.

And then, there are the two tortured, silver-haired Nephilim boys tucked away in their private booth, sharing their woes and comparing war stories. I never expected to play house with not one, but two half-angels. Yet, here we are, keeping secrets dark enough to make a sinner blush.

The club's the liveliest it's been in months. The bachelorette party drew in more than a few curious patrons, and for the first time in ages, I'm getting a taste of a truly successful night of debauchery. I suck in a breath, shutting my eyes and imagining what life could be like under better circumstances—where my business thrived in the Hills, where I had endless money to decorate the place to my standards, where my new club boasted a revolving door of elite clientele and sinful wretches.

I glance over at Jeremy again, taking in his gray aura, which has stopped flickering ever since his excommunication. His gaze catches mine for a second, and he offers me a small smile. He's more vibrant now—the ailment that plagued him when he first turned up at my doorstep has seemingly passed, though the bags under his eyes tell me he still suffers through restless nights. He took quickly to Vincent, his fellow excommunicated demon hunter. In fact, he spends more time with him than with any of us. Oh, to be a fly on the wall during their private conversations...

The bride-to-be sets her sights on Vincent, the unassuming, disinterested silver fox who could charm the leaves off a tree if he flashed it a smile. She slips into their booth, hanging off him, a bottle of beer in one hand, playing with his gray hair with the other.

"You're way too handsome to be in a place like this," she slurs. "How much extra do I gotta pay to spend a night with you?"

"My lady," Silver Fox places his hands on her waist to remove her from his lap, "my company, regrettably, comes with a price you simply cannot afford."

My ears perk toward the entrance as the door swings open, revealing two new guests. Both Jeremy and Vincent's heads whip in the same direction, the younger's posture stiffening as they catch sight of the newcomers. Jeremy rises to his feet but pauses when Vincent places a hand over his, gesturing for him to sit back down.

Clad in expensive three-piece suits, drenched in over-priced cologne, and sporting freshly polished dress shoes, their auras and appearance say it all. A rush of disdain overcomes me as the two draw closer.

Demons. Specifically, Greed Underlings.

Wonderful.

"Who hired the traveling salesmen strippers?" the bride shouts, elated, rising to her feet as the demons approach the stage. The two reek of everything that defines Greed Underlings: impulsiveness, arrogance, and an unmistakable air of wealth that makes them the most insufferable across all the Broodlines. When they set their sights on Indigo as she twirls on the stage, my heart nearly plummets into my stomach.

"Well hey there, kitten." The demon's voice sends a wave of disgust through me. I instinctively take a step forward to shield Indigo from the goons, but her melodic voice stops me.

"Hiya, Dax. Fletcher." Her demeanor shifts instantly. She speaks with a kind of sweetness that could rot teeth, with a bubbling giggle lilting through every word. "I've missed you both."

Dax flashes her a grin so spine-chilling, I'm grateful I can't read his mind. "You takin' clients tonight, sweetheart?"

"I'm sure I can squeeze you in. Two minutes enough, or you think you got a full five?" Her voice drips with false innocence, but the insult lands like a slap.

He flashes her a predatory grin. "You better watch that smart mouth, kitten. I'd hate to have to rearrange it."

"You'd never hurt me, Daxxy," she practically sings, hopping off the stage and sauntering up to him with a pout on her lips. "You think I'm too pretty for that."

I fight the smirk tugging at my lips. I love watching Indigo play with her food—even more so when she toys with one of her own kind. I can tell from their beating hearts, distinct scents, and lack of fangs that these two are likely Siphoners—a breed of Greed demon that feeds off human sin. You've got to hand it to the Prime: he was wickedly creative when he fashioned his monsters, even more creative when he and Cherry conspired to weave the perfect lie about vampire lore through classic literature and cinema. Humans would never guess that all supernatural creatures are just different types of demons from varying Broodlines, hidden in plain sight.

"How can I help you two tonight?" I ask, stepping between the goons and the raised stage. "Indigo's on the clock for a couple more hours. Can I interest you in one of my other girls?"

"How much do you cost, Red?" Fletcher hisses, licking his lips.

"I'm off the menu."

"Shame." He shakes his head. "I'd kill to get lost in between those thighs."

Don't roll your eyes, I remind myself. *Smile at the clients. Play the game.*

"Greed sent us," Dax says. "Wants to make a little business arrangement."

"Let's speak in my office then."

I lead the demons through the party of hens dancing in my club, past the regulars indulging in Indigo's show, and usher them into my office. Jeremy stands close by, eyes searching mine as his instincts scream at him to follow—to protect me. He tells himself he's better equipped to handle demons than I am, that I should focus on the party while he disposes of the newcomers. But something holds him back, words whispered by a certain Silver Fox. "Leave it be, Jeremy. They're no longer your problem."

I shut the door behind me, offering my two empty chairs to the Greed goons. I move to stand behind my desk, arms folded over my chest and eyes narrowed in contempt. "Whatever this is, make it quick. I've got a bachelorette party to tend to."

Dax leans forward, folding his fingers over my desk. "We've come for Greed's share of the old man."

Confusion sweeps through me as my expression sours. "I beg your finest pardon?"

"The blue-eyed geezer you're babysitting," Fletcher adds.

"I know *who* you're talking about. I just don't know *what* you're talking about."

The goons share a knowing glance and a sickening chuckle. "Looks like Debauchery conveniently omitted the terms and conditions of your charge. Allow us to explain—"

I raise my hand, stopping Fletcher mid-sentence. "You can skip the sales pitch. I'm not interested. My instructions from Cherry were clear, and I'm not about to let either of you trick me into doing something stupid."

"Clearly, you don't know how this works—"

"Clearly, I don't give a damn."

"These two bothering you, Reagan?" Indigo's purple head peeks through as my office door groans open.

My jaw clenches as I raise an authoritative eyebrow at my vampire. "Get back on stage, Indy."

"I'm on break." She grins triumphantly. "Let me take care of my friends here. No one knows Greed demons better than a Greed demon." There's something in her stormy-gray eyes that tells me to read between the lines—a warning she desperately wishes she could Tap into my mind to convey, if only we belonged to the same Broodline.

"There are rules at stake here that are bigger than all of us, succubus. You should hear us out at the very least," Dax warns. "When Deception's snakes and the rest of our Brood come banging on your door to collect what their Primes are owed, you'll wish you did."

I meet their haughty gaze with one of pure malice,

my golden veins pulsing brighter with warning. "Then they'll join you in whatever comes next."

"Come on, baby." Indigo pats Dax on the chest. "Let's leave the big, bad succubus alone."

Dax and Fletcher begrudgingly rise from their chairs under my scrutinizing gaze. Indigo flips her purple locks over one shoulder, playfully rubbing each demon's shoulder before escorting them out of my office.

They're only feet from the exit when Fletcher shoves Indigo aside and sprints toward Silver Fox.

The entire club erupts in chaos.

The bachelorette party is too drunk and high off Charlie's influence to realize they're in danger. The other patrons scramble to their feet to get a glimpse of the action. Fletcher and Dax abandon all pretense and drag Vincent from his booth, forcing him to the ground while pressing fistfuls of silver rings into his chest. Within seconds, black and white swirls of mist escape his body, flowing into the black gemmed rings on their fingers.

Black tourmaline rings—energy absorbers, just like the necklaces in my safe.

I should have known. I should have seen it coming.

Indigo strikes like lightning, launching onto Fletcher's back and wrapping her arms around his chest. Fletcher screams, thrashing to throw her off, but her claws puncture his skin, digging into his ribs and anchoring her in place. The toe of her stiletto punches into Dax's stomach with supernatural force, launching him across the floor toward my feet. I smirk down at the goon and hoist him up, grasping his collar and groin. My tail wraps around his waist, spinning him toward a booth table, his chest cracking against the wood. I grab his wrist and shove down just above his elbow, pressing him into a painful hold. My tail pushes his other shoulder flush against the table, forcing him to still his writhing torso. "You shouldn't have taken your chances," I snarl into his ear.

From the corner of my eye, I see Jeremy lift Vincent from the floor, supporting his weight as he attempts to lead him to safety, but he doesn't go unnoticed.

Fletcher sees him, and realization dawns on his twisted features.

"You've got another one?" Fletcher hisses at me against Indigo's grip. "Dax, Debauchery's been holding out on us—wait till the boss hears about this."

Fletcher's blood-curdling shriek fills the club when Indigo roars and unhinges her jaw to sink multiple rows of razor-sharp teeth into him. He struggles against her iron grip, kicking desperately to escape, but the little vampire never relents. Instead, she tears into his flesh, black demon blood spurting from his jugular as she drains him dry. She's ravenous, a beast unleashed— horrific, deadly, and absolutely beautiful.

Dax screams as his shoulders pop and crunch, dislo- cating with sickening cracks as he wrenches himself free of my hold. His limbs snap back into place, and he lunges toward his partner, but my tail catches his neck first. Fletcher's body crumbles to dust once Indigo drains the last drop, and she rises to her feet. Her once-sparkly purple bra and panties are now covered in a black sheen, darker than the Hollywood night sky.

My tail coils around the demon's throat, squeezing tightly as Indigo approaches. Her face is a macabre canvas with splattered black ichor dribbling down her neck, a stark contrast against her pale-white skin. She flashes him one of her signature sweet smiles and bats her lashes, her monstrous teeth receding until only the two sharp canines that mark her vampirism remain.

"Blood traitor," Dax spits at Indigo. "Greed will skin your ass when your contract's up and you're back with us. Trust me."

"Like Hell he will," I growl at the demon. "The only creatures more untrustworthy than Deception's snakes are Greed's buffoons. Now, get the fuck out of my house."

Dax straightens his suit when I release him, dusting off his shoulders. He shoots Indigo a final warning glance and utters "This isn't over," before he makes his way out of the club, leaving us alone with nothing but a freshly-spelled bachelorette party, two high-strung Nephilim, and an unlikely pairing I've always been fond of.

I walk up to Indigo, the sweet, coquettish vampire who flipped a switch in an instant to protect me, to protect a charge she herself wasn't too fond of. A charge she warned *me* not to trust.

And she did so at great risk to her undead life and reputation within her own ranks.

Not because she had a stake in the game, but because her loyalty to me knows no bounds—not even ones forged in demonic Broodlines.

I wipe the dark blood dripping from her chin and tuck a piece of that beautiful purple-blue hair behind her ear with a smile.

I've learned to trust Indigo Moon implicitly over the few years I've known her. I've heeded her warnings, listened to her woes, and given in to her charming wiles. Despite being Sired by one of the Big Thirteen, a Prime whose very existence makes my skin crawl, her devotion to me is something I'll never take for granted.

And in this tangled web of darkness and sin, I know the most innocent faces often hide the sharpest fangs.

TRACK FIFTTEEN
Nothin' but a Good Time

TRACK FIFTEEN

NOTHIN' BUT A GOOD TIME

The night is far from over after the showdown. The bachelorette party still rages on, freshly poured glasses filled with Charlie's signature elixirs ready for consumption as soon as the bride demands another round. Honestly, I could use a fucking drink myself.

But Indigo's back on stage, completely cleaned up in a new outfit—this time in a bikini top made entirely of safety pins and a pair of purple thigh-high boots—twirling around the pole like she was born for it. She even has Jeremy up there with her, teaching him amateur dance moves and giggling at his complete lack of rhythm.

The bachelorette bimbos eat it up, as does Charlie.

Stop staring, sugar. He's no threat to our girl. I shoot my bartender a little mind blast, hiding my smirk by resting my hand under my nose.

Charlie, ever the silent brooder, raises a pierced

eyebrow and glances at me before refocusing on the stage. *It's not her I'm staring at. It's the old man.*

With knitted brows, I follow Charlie's gaze past the center stage to see Vincent Thane sinking into one of the leather booths, still recovering from his encounter with the goons, his dark aura flickering like a dying flame.

It occurs to me that, after all these weeks, I still don't know a single thing about him other than his lineage. I promised myself I'd do a little digging after my last conversation with Indigo, and it may be time to finally make good on my word.

After sauntering through my club and checking on the other patrons, I make my way to Silver Fox. He takes a swig from a nearly-empty beer bottle, and I clear my throat.

"Think it's time you and I had a little chat."

"By all means." He offers me a tired smile and gestures for me to take the seat across from him. "How can I help you, Miss Reagan?"

"You wanna tell me what happened back there?"

"Ah, the Greed Underlings?" He chuckles. "You were right to question their motives but a fool to dismiss them. There *is* a pact in place, though neither of the brothers likes to play by the rules."

"What's the pact?"

He hesitates then, searching my eyes, as if wondering whether he can trust me with his darkest secrets. Quite the change for a man who couldn't stop talking when we first met. Finally, with a defeated sigh, he speaks.

"Each brother has a right to some of my essence. Every year, they trade me off to the winner of their annual poker game. The winner keeps me hidden and safe from harm, free to have his way with me, and the losing brothers send their Underlings to collect their share in the interim. Greed hasn't won a game in eight years, so it doesn't surprise me that he was the first to send his riffraff."

I recall the night Cherry took a hit from my necklace, how a small taste brought him euphoria beyond imagination. *"I'd almost forgotten the taste of a young one,"* he'd said.

And suddenly, it all makes sense.

The Nephilim are a drug to the Primes. And Silver Fox is the Golden Trio's infernal doobie.

My hardened gaze softens as a newfound understanding washes over me. "What's your story, Silver Fox?"

"My story?" he drawls, an almost-pained smirk reaching his wrinkled eyes. Those icy blues glance over at Jeremy with a familiar gleam stinging at them. "It looks a lot like his, just 35 years and 3 Prime Evils later."

The sorrow in this voice, laced with regret and remorse, grips at the frayed remains of humanity left in me. It knots my stomach, sowing the seed of curiosity. For a moment, just a moment, I'm tempted to ask how? *Why?*

But curiosity is known to kill the cat, and demons aren't guaranteed resurrection.

My gaze narrows as I study the ex-demon hunter. The bags under his eyes mirror those of Jeremy's dearly departed mentor, hanging over cheekbones sharp enough to cut diamonds. His salt-and-pepper beard spreads across what I imagine is a perfectly sculpted jawline, and for that, I'm grateful—grateful he isn't clean shaven, that is. I'm a sucker for hard edges.

"You're playing a dangerous game with that boy, Miss Reagan. You might want to consider a plan B if things go south."

"Why, Silver Fox, you seem to be singing a different tune. Just a few weeks ago, you were giving me advice on how to corrupt the incorruptible in this very same room."

He offers me a small smile. "Couldn't resist the temptation of the game."

"Had I known you were interested in playing, I would have extended a formal invitation."

"No invitation necessary. I was dealt in the day Cherry dragged me into your club and asked you to babysit his—what was the word you used? *'Sex slave?'*"

"In our world, that kind of position is the highest form of praise. I'd be honored if I were you." I shrug nonchalantly, flashing him one of my signature smirks.

"Suppose I should be." His brow raises along with the curve in his lips. "Humor an old man. Have you ever asked yourself why Cherry made this deal with you? Why he left me under your watch while he and his brothers are off doing God knows what?"

"I don't question my master. I do what I'm told," I bite. It isn't a full lie, but it's enough to spare.

"And how has that worked for you?"

Irritation builds within, glowing in my pulsing, lava-like veins. "Whose side are you on?"

Thane lifts his hands in mock-surrender. "No sides, just an interested spectator."

"Or a backseat driver."

A throaty chuckle vibrates in his chest. "You're a clever woman, Miss Reagan. Cherry doesn't give you enough credit."

"Preaching to the choir, handsome."

The sound of the bride-to-be's boisterous laughter jolts me out of our bubble, and I'm reminded that, despite the mysteries of demonic politics, I am still running a business. The broad's onstage with Jeremy now, trying to pull him away from one of the dancers and have her way with him. "You're young enough to be my son, but you sure are a cute one, aren't ya?"

He chuckles nervously, afraid to offend the guest of honor but too inexperienced to indulge in her. He realizes he's a fish out of water, a creature on the wrong side of the tracks at the mercy of the monsters he was always warned about. But there's still something in him that slowly peeks through the cracks. It just isn't quite out yet.

"You should talk to him." Silver Fox nods at Jeremy, who indulges the drunken bride by dancing with her.

She wraps her feather boa around his neck, pulling him closer—putting on a little show for the hens.

"And say what?" My eyes never leave Jeremy.

"Get to know him a little. He's been through a lot."

I sigh. "I know what he's been through."

Vincent leans in closer, lowering his voice. "You're still in the game, Reagan. You've got him; now, you need to keep him."

My eyes meet his, hardened by frustration. "Is that how Cherry and the others got you? By making polite conversation?"

"You can learn a lot about someone by hearing their side of things. Things you can use to your advantage. Things you can manipulate."

My tone turns cold. "You're an enigma, Silver Fox. Flip-flopping like a pancake in bacon grease."

"I've found if you stay on one side for too long, you'll inevitably get burned."

"How'd you 'burn' your way out of the Order then?" I ask, lifting my chin in defiance. "You're an old man, probably older than you actually look. I'm sure you've sent many Underlings and Hellspawn to their fiery deaths and given a few Primes a swift kick in the ass in your heyday. So, what did you do? Why'd they cast you out?"

"The Order doesn't care about bloodlines or long lists of good deeds and hefty accomplishments. You could banish a Prime like our friend over here did and still be shunned for even associating with demons. It's a wonder his mentor lasted as long as he did."

The fucking old bastard's avoiding my question by pivoting elsewhere—something he's likely learned from Cherry. Something we've *both* learned from Cherry. I'd keep him around long term if he wasn't such a liability.

In a moment of weakness to prove this know-it-all wrong, a quip escapes me quicker than I can think. "His mentor didn't associate with demons. He associated with the Devil's Second."

"Ingenious, if you consider it. Treading the knife's edge of darkness, always a careful distance away and never fully immersed. His soul knew its fair share of corruption, but what Nephilim's hasn't? The Order simply chalks it up to collateral damage, forces ritualistic cleanses to wash it all away, and then sends them back into the field, good as new."

My lips part in shock before I whisper, "That's barbaric."

"Such is the path of the righteous."

I regard Vincent differently now; with tolerance, even respect. Unable to resist my curiosity, I press further. "Did you know him? Lovejoy."

"I did."

"So did I. His soul was just as tainted as Jeremy's, yet the Order never excommunicated him. Why?"

"His soul was marked by the Nightmare and Fear Primes early on in his career. As far as anyone else was concerned, he was a martyr. He knew it too and used that to his full advantage. But from what I understand, he met his end in the best possible way. Death is a blessing compared to what they would have done to him, had he survived. Had they known of his involvement with the witch."

I huff out a laugh. "Good riddance—he was dreadfully dull and far too sanctimonious. I hope that bombshell gave him what he deserved."

I expect him to lash out over my blatant disrespect for the dead, but instead, he laughs—a sound both unexpected and unsettling, almost as if he agrees with the sentiment.

"Anyone foolish enough to willingly crawl into bed with a monster deserves everything coming to them."

"Speaking from experience, Silver Fox?"

He cracks a smile. "35 years worth, succubus."

It's 1:45 AM when Charlie finally ushers the bachelorettes out of the club. He rolls his sleeves up higher, tying his luscious, long, dark blonde hair into a high ponytail, and begins cleaning up the mess they left. I'll always thank Cherry for siring this one—a silent but deadly Underling who's as loyal as he is efficient. The demon never complains about anything I throw his way.

Take a load off, sugar. Go dance with our girl.

The incubus hesitates for a moment, glancing down at his tray of empty glasses before setting it on one of the tables. He trudges over to the pole-laden stage in the center of the club and takes a seat on the edge. Indigo perks up, settles beside him, and tucks a lock of purple hair behind her ear before handing him a half-empty bottle of beer. They share a smile—two helpless demons so in love with each other, everyone but them knows it.

One day, they'll figure it out.

I'm so absorbed in their little Romeo and Juliet love affair, I almost miss how the club still pulses with laughter and energy, despite the party being over. The music is finally tuned back to my favorite '80s rock station, and center stage, my human dancers fawn over Jeremy like he's the best thing since sliced bread. He's looser now, cheeks flushed with embarrassment, though his grin couldn't be wider. He's learned their names, calling out to them as he shows off the moves Indigo taught him then bursts into laughter when he fails spectacularly.

It isn't until he takes a spin around the pole, nearly trips on his own feet, and falls into a fit of giggles alongside the dancers that it hits me: I see him. The *real* him. Not a Nephilim suppressed by the sanctimonious pressures of a higher power and calling, but a sweet young man who hasn't tasted the simple pleasures of life.

Laughter. Dancing. Friendship. Family.

I look around my club, the one place I begrudgingly call 'home.' It's never once felt like it, but rather, a failing project in need of constant upkeep and revival.

But then I look at how Indy lights up a room like the sun itself whenever she laughs. The irony isn't lost on me —a vampire as radiant as the sun. Then, there's reliable Charlie, his flannel sleeves rolled up to his elbows, a dish rag over his shoulder, and a helpless smile painted on his features as he watches her shine. Even the elusive Silver Fox, an excommunicated hunter with more secrets and skeletons than a sinner in church, sits across from me with a far-off look in his eye.

And then, there's me. The boss. The serious one. The one who's both within and without, never quite joining in on all the fun but relishing in the enjoyment of others.

We're a motley crew if I've ever known one.

Bad Decisions has never really felt like home.

But for the first time, here—with these damned creatures—I believe it could.

REAGAN... I REALLY WANT TO KISS YOU.
COME FIND ME WHEN YOUR HEAD'S A LITTLE CLEARER. IF YOUR FEELINGS HAVEN'T CHANGED.
MY FEELINGS HAVE CHANGED. JUST NOT THE WAY EITHER OF US EXPECTED.
TRACK SIXTEEN
Kashmir

TRACK SIXTEEN

KASHMIR

The analog clock on my desk flashes vibrant red as it strikes 2 AM. High-pitched beeps toll the end of another workday, and moments later, the music on the main floor dies into silence. By now, Charlie will be ushering out our last two or three patrons and locking up for the night.

Tonight was unlike any other at Bad Decisions. Despite the unfortunate mishap with the Greed Underlings, the place never felt more alive. If it were up to me, there would be no infernal deals, no demonic corporate ladders, no innocents to corrupt and deliver to my Prime. I'd be perfectly content among my dysfunctional family of misfits, caring for them as my own blood.

Even those two silver-haired ones. Insufferable as their righteousness could be, they possess a certain charm I could learn to live with.

The club is empty when I finally emerge from my

office. My human dancers have gone home, Indigo's likely out hunting with Charlie trailing behind, Silver Fox retired to his room at The Starlight, and Jeremy...

He exits one of the private VIP rooms, hair damp and curled against his forehead. His white t-shirt hangs loose, revealing a glint of silver underneath his collar—that protective amulet is useless to him now. The tattoo on his neck marking the Holy Order fades quicker by the hour, its intricate linework becoming less discernible with each passing moment.

"Well, well," I purr suggestively, leaning against a leather booth with a hand on my hip. "Looks like someone got a happy ending after all."

Jeremy's cheeks flush red. His hand finds the back of his neck, rubbing it in a bashful gesture as his gaze shifts from me to the ground. "Not really—I mean, kind of, but..." His words trail off as his shoulders rise and fall with exasperation.

Something twists inside me, a curiosity piqued by his jumbled words and the charming blush creeping from his cheeks to his neck. I approach him with languid steps, like a predator circling prey. His posture straightens—how can he look so captivating and so broken at the same time? His heartbeat pounds in my ears as I draw closer.

"Kind of?" I catch the hem of his shirt between my fingers, toying with the fabric. "I don't like unsatisfied customers."

"I-I'm not—I didn't ask—"

"It's so easy to get caught up in the fun, isn't it, Jeremy?" I let his name roll off my tongue with dark amusement. "To let go. To feel free. When no one's watching, where there are no consequences...it's all very intoxicating."

He swallows hard, and I can see the conflict in his eyes, those seafoam greens with golden flecks surrounding his irises. There's something compelling about him in this moment, about someone left wanting more.

"Which of my girls didn't meet your expectations?" I ask, my voice dropping to a husky whisper.

"Chardonnay," he manages to croak out.

"Ah, one of the humans." I chuckle softly. "Love 'em to death, but I've always found they lack a certain...flair. There's nothing like the touch of a succubus, wouldn't you agree?"

"Mm-hmm," he agrees, the sound barely conscious.

I peer up at him through my lashes, fingers finding his belt loops and tugging him an inch closer.

"I know what lurks in your heart, Jeremy. Despite every voice telling you it's wrong, your body betrays you, craves more. It's like an addiction. Once you've had a taste, the hunger never fades. Not forever. And even though you should hate how it happened, how it all came apart...part of you still wants to finish what we started."

The air between us thrums with unresolved desire. His shallow breaths, parted lips, and hooded eyes feed the hunger growing within me. For a moment, I consider throwing the deal out the window, consider keeping Jeremy all to myself and wasting away together in Hollywood's gutter, where I can feed off him until he withers away like Vincent. But I can't. He belongs to Cherry, and I deserve my end of the bargain.

Finally, I press my body against him, melting into the hard ridges of his abdomen and trailing my hands up his chest. My lips meet with his ear then, and I can't help but bite the soft skin of his earlobe. "Let me take care of you, Jeremy."

He shudders against me, releasing a soft moan as his hands find my hips instinctively. I pull back then, waiting for his confirmation. When he nods, I take his hand and lead him into the private room.

I haven't taken a client into the VIP rooms in ages. As a business owner, it simply wasn't done. As a succubus, I preferred more direct methods. But Jeremy wasn't just any client—he was my golden ticket.

The lights remain on from when he left. This circular room is no bigger than a small bedchamber: a dark gray polyester loveseat curves along the wall, red and pink lights dancing overhead to mask the room's imperfections and wear.

To Jeremy, this is an intimate sanctuary where his

fantasies become reality. To me, it's just another expense draining my budget with constant repairs and replacements.

I gently push him onto the seat and a light layer of dust swirls into the air. I nudge his knees apart to step between them then reach for the remote control and flick on the sound system. A slow, hypnotic groove pours from the tired speakers, setting my languid, sultry pace as I rock my hips to its rhythm. He watches me intently, a man bewitched, as I slowly unzip the front of my black dress, stopping just below my breasts. He leans forward instinctively, fingers itching to touch, mind begging for some sort of stimulation other than watching for a change.

The poor fool. The poor, innocent, *eager* fool.

Everyone knows the hands-off rule in the private rooms. Everyone except Jeremy Roache.

And so, I lift my foot to collide with his chest and push him back into his seat. It's a simple, dominant move, one that usually drives clients to the edge.

But something flashes in Jeremy's eyes the moment my heel connects with his chest. His breath catches, and he stares at my shoe with a mixture of terror and recognition. I slip into his mind, pushing past the static like an antenna hunting for signal. His thoughts fragment into violent snapshots—choppy blonde hair, a wicked, black-painted grin, maniacal laughter echoing off brick walls, a scorpion crawling up his chest, the crushing weight of a stiletto against his throat.

And then comes the feeling. Not a memory—something far worse. Something so recent, it pulses through him like fresh blood from an open wound.

The agony of having your soul ripped from your body.

The dread hits him like ice water, paralyzing and absolute. My gaze drops to that thin scar nestled between his clavicles, and understanding crashes over me.

October did this to him.

She pinned him down with her heel pressed to his throat and tore a piece of his soul away.

My own dread claws at my insides like a ravenous beast, my stomach churning at the visions from his memories. I step back immediately, and my first instinct is to ease his suffering—to pull him back from the edge of panic, to offer him peace when he's clearly known so little of it.

I kneel beside him, taking his trembling hands in mine. "Look at me, Jeremy," I whisper, guiding his focus to my eyes. "You're okay. You're with me. She's not here." His breathing gradually steadies as I speak in low, soothing tones. "She's not here."

I hesitate before doing what I know might help, remembering what happened the last time I used my abilities on him. My demonic nature is designed to influence emotions, to ease or manipulate what others feel. But using those powers on Jeremy before had consequences I hadn't anticipated.

Still, watching him trapped in October's torment, I can't allow this spiral to interfere with my plans. I have to try. I have to take his pain away.

"Close your eyes and breathe with me," I whisper, placing his hands against my chest. I start as any human would—guiding his rhythm, matching every inhale and exhale until we move as one. When his eyes finally close, I let my glamour dissolve.

Crimson tint and golden veins bloom across my flesh, replacing the pale, freckled façade. I channel my demonic essence, watching the molten patterns beneath my skin pulse brighter and release tendrils of golden mist. The pheromones spiral through the air in a hypnotic dance, seeking Jeremy with predatory grace before slipping past his lips with each breath.

My own breathing falters. What if he overdoses again? What if my magic consumes him, turning him into the monster I created before?

This time is different. This time, I'm not trying to break him.

I'm trying to put him back together.

To my surprise, his panic starts to melt away. The tension in his shoulders releases, his breathing steadies, and his hands fall from my chest to rest near my knees. I run my hands over my skin, triggering my human glamour and once again becoming the pale redheaded version of myself I've perfected over the years.

A soft sigh escapes Jeremy's lips as his head falls back against the booth, eyes fluttering open. The vibrant green returns to his irises, chasing away the darkness that had clouded them. He looks at me with a lazy, contented smile—tired but peaceful.

"You heard my thoughts, didn't you?" His question catches me off guard.

I stiffen. "Why do you ask?"

"Debauchery and Deception demons are mind-readers. Or so I've read."

"You're quite the little scholar, aren't you, Sparky?"

He nods slowly, his smile widening as if he's proud of himself. "Always got teased for that by my superiors: 'Roache hides behind his books,' they'd say. Declan was the only one who encouraged my love for reading. He said an educated mind is a powerful mind—that it would be my greatest weapon."

The urge to cringe crawls up my spine, but I mask it with a smirk. That helpless smile of his, so languid and dreamy, spreads to his gentle green eyes as his head lolls back to study my features. He watches me like I'm the most precious thing in existence, the center of his entire universe, and releases another sigh. His fingers inch toward mine, as if drawn by invisible strings, before hesitation dawns on him. They curl slowly into fists, remembering what I am, even if his Demon-Kissed mind yearns to forget.

Goodness. The pheromones really did their job this time. Thank the Devil for small favors.

Silence stretches between us, thick with yearning and heavy-lidded stares, until he finally speaks. His voice is so rough, so unlike his usual gentle tone, that it makes me tense. "I wish I knew what you were thinking."

"No, you don't." I playfully roll my eyes at him. "You wouldn't like hearing all the voices in my head."

"Yours can't possibly be as bad as mine were." The lights cast beautiful shadows upon his features, darkening under his brow and contouring the hollows of his cheeks. The stubble suits him and there are even little hints of white and gray among the golden hairs. "It's been a week—maybe longer?—since I heard the last voice. When Reili…when he…"

Poor thing can't even finish the sentence. The wound is still raw, still festering with pain from the betrayal, but my influence calms him within seconds. With a deep inhale, he continues.

"When it happened, it was almost like…like someone turned the dial down on a radio. They were still there, the voices, just…soft whispers as opposed to screams. Now, it's all static. It's never been this quiet before. But all I can think about is how badly I wish I could hear them again."

I try to follow his point, to piece together what he means, but none of it makes sense. It's all just the ramblings of a broken, pheromone-drunk man. There's a cold, familiar, *haunted* look in his eyes while he stares aimlessly into the depths of the room, his Adam's apple bobs as he swallows hard. I wish I could place that look, but it hangs loosely in my mind like a memory I try desperately to cling to.

"What were the voices?" I ask.

"Prayers. Human prayers. People begging for…whatever they typically beg for. Most of the time, it was for money and luck. Other times, it's for health, or for sick or dying loved ones. You know that movie that came out earlier this year? The one where the guy becomes God and gets a whole e-mail inbox of prayers?" He snorts out a laugh. "I *wish* that's what it was like. Would be easier to get through, so much better than trying to weed it all out in your head. Declan, he…he was *so* good at that. He always compared it to organizing a closet. Every prayer has a place—a box. You sort them as they come through. He was trying to teach me."

Empathy twists in my stomach, so gut-wrenching, it almost feels like my mind is betraying me. I hated that hunter, the mess he made of October. I may have only met him once or twice, but everything about him screamed 'self-righteous dickhead.' But the way Jeremy speaks of him, honors his memory with admiration and hope…it's all so devastatingly pure.

I'm glad he's gone. I hope October gave him what he deserved.

"How old are you?" Jeremy asks, that delicate flush creeping from his chest to his ears. I don't miss the twitch in his muscles as he rubs the back of his neck like he did earlier, an innocent attempt to calm his nerves.

But before I can muster some semblance of a response, he interjects. "Never mind. That was stupid of me. Never ask a lady her age."

A smirk tugs at my lips. "So I'm a lady now? Not a demon?"

His eyes widen like a child caught enjoying a meal they initially refused—satisfying, if you enjoy making men squirm. Which I do.

"I'll tell you mine if you tell me yours."

His hand drops to his lap, where he starts fidgeting with his nail beds. "21, I think. I don't actually know anymore."

"I'm going to need a little more context there, handsome."

"Well, I was born in '82, but…" He trails off, and a haunted look clouds his eyes, one that seems to hide shadows deeper than darkness itself. "Then that witch happened. The Devil's Second."

The color nearly drains from my face, and I imagine I almost turn as pale as the fluorescent lights in my office.

"She did this." He runs his fingers through his salt-and-pepper hair, fingertips toying with idle strands that fall above his brow. "Aged me up, I guess. I don't really know. I'm—ah—still figuring it all out. New surprise every day."

His fingers trail from his hair to his neck, settling beneath his Adam's apple, where a small scar lingers—so faint, you could miss it. You'd think it'd been there for decades, but I know better now, especially having witnessed his memories.

"'82 was a good year," I derail, desperate to change the subject. "One of my favorites."

"So you're definitely older than me."

"Why so interested in my age? You got a thing for older women?"

He chuckles, and the light returns to his eyes. "Call it a morbid curiosity."

A morbid curiosity. Oh, the audacity of this fella. I finally prop myself next to him on the stale gray loveseat and do some quick math. "I'll be 111 in a month."

"Fuck." It's the first time I've heard him curse, and I can't help but savor how easily the word slips from his lips. The corner of his mouth tugs upward, catching me off guard. I half expected him to recoil, maybe even flush with embarrassment, but he doesn't. Instead, that lopsided, shit-eating grin spreads across his features.

And then, he laughs. *Really* laughs. And I can't help but join him.

We settle into comfortable silence, two opposites who have no business enjoying each other's company. We each have our roles: mine to seduce, corrupt, and deliver, his to...what now, exactly? What is his purpose now that the Order has cast him out? What does an ostracized, destiny-less Nephilim do with the rest of his semi-immortal existence?

I think of Silver Fox holed up at The Starlight, drowning in his own misery...and my smile falters.

"What did you do to me earlier?" Jeremy asks within the silence.

Dread crashes over me. Lovely—he caught on to that. Smart boy. Do I tell him the truth? Do I admit to using my manipulation abilities on him? Is it worth breaking the trust I'm slowly beginning to build? "Just a little trick I've learned over the years."

"But why? Why have you been so nice to me when all I've done is try to kill you?"

Once again, I'm at a crossroads. Do I feed him a carefully crafted lie or tell him the truth and risk losing everything? I choose something in between. "Figured I owed you for, ya know, the whole manipulating-and-lying-to-you thing."

"A demon with a conscience." He chuckles. "Never read about those in the books."

"Have I earned a whole paragraph?"

"More like an entire chapter."

Moments like these feel stolen from movies, designed to make audiences lean forward, hearts invested in the unfolding romance. I've witnessed this turning point countless times in scripts, when walls crumble and something tender takes root. Is it admiration? Is it his lust and curiosity clouding his better judgement? I knew he felt something for me the night we met. What began as pure, burning hatred has softened into something I can't quite name. I'll call it mutual respect for now.

But the chains around my heart know better.

"You're an enigma, Jeremy Roache." I sink back into the couch, propping my arm along the backrest and resting my head against my palm as I prepare to take a leap of faith.

"How so?"

"Your entire world has been shattered. You're a lost soul in a sea of monsters that would swallow you whole. But there's something about you. A sweetness. An innocence. It's like you can't help it. Instead of letting your trauma break you, you're kind in spite of it. Deep down, beneath your crumbling exterior, faulty wiring, and flickering lights…you've got great bones." As the words leave my lips, I realize I'm not just talking about Jeremy anymore. I think of my club's damaged ceiling, the botched floors, the faded booths—all of it salvageable beneath the decay, just like him.

"And what about you? You're just as…mind-boggling."

"Mind-boggling?" I repeat with a chuckle.

"Yeah." He joins my laughter. "I've seen you with your employees. They're not just Underlings to you. They're like family. Even the vampire, Indigo—she's a Greed demon. You owe her nothing. And Vincent? It's clear you're protecting him from the demons who have been after him. You love them, in your own way. You'd do anything for them, even risk your life against your worst enemy. Demons don't do that."

His logic is so beautifully, tragically flawed.

He doesn't know Indigo was pawned off to me in a poker game. He doesn't know Charlie entered my service because I needed a master mixologist to manipulate patrons. He doesn't know Vincent Thane was forced on me against my will. He doesn't know that, despite these simpler truths lying between us, there's one that will never see light: I still intend to deliver him to Cherry.

I'm too lost in thought to offer a response.

"Reagan…" My name trails into the quiet of the space between us. "I really want to kiss you."

No, you don't, I think automatically. His confession shouldn't surprise me; I've been hearing it in his thoughts for days, but something about him finally speaking the words aloud catches me off guard. It's the first genuine piece of himself he's offered—something I didn't have to deliberately extract through seduction or manipulation. For once, he's making the move.

And so, I humor him.

I lean in and press a kiss to his cheek. Disappointment clouds his eyes for a fleeting moment, quickly replaced with another lopsided grin.

I offer him a gentle smile. "Come find me when your head's a little clearer, if your feelings haven't changed."

I leave him in the private room and slip back into the main floor when a scratching sound echoes from the back entrance. Odd, since I wasn't expecting anyone tonight. Probably just another group of drunks who missed the fact that our neon sign is dark, signaling we're closed.

With a raised eyebrow, I approach the door cautiously, reaching out with my demonic senses to see who's waiting outside. An outdoor security camera would do wonders—I make a mental note for later and reach for the doorknob.

But a hand on my shoulder stops me cold. I spin around to find Jeremy towering over me, his expression so determined, it sends a chill down my spine. He takes my face in his hands and captures my lips with his own.

And for a moment, I see stars.

It's a soft, tender kiss fueled by raw passion and yearning unlike anything I've ever experienced. But I can tell the pheromones have worn off. I search his mind for any hesitation, any sign this bold move stems from my manipulation.

And there's nothing. No lingering magic. No fear. Just a desperate need for connection.

It's hard not to want a succubus. It's only natural. But in this moment, all he can think about is how human I feel.

Jeremy pulls away slowly, lips still ghosting over mine, as if separating would cause him physical pain. His fingers tangle in my hair, thumbs brushing softly against my temples as he draws my forehead to his. My breath catches, trapped in this intimate cocoon where angel and demon exist alone, sharing something sacred.

My heart swells, and for a terrifying second, I hunger for more than just his essence.

When he finally speaks, his voice is like honey against the harsh silence of this empty, seedy strip club. "My feelings *have* changed, just not the way either of us expected."

Oh, Jeremy. Sweet, naive Jeremy. I expected this completely.

But what's really terrifying me is that mine are changing too.

I almost forget about the scratching at the back entrance. I grasp Jeremy's hands, freeing myself from his grip, and motion for him to wait.

I open the door to reveal a stocky black cat with a dense, rugged coat. In its mouth, a single red rose.

I've seen the creature before. Many years ago, back in Savannah. All at once, the memories return, and I know exactly who this feline belongs to, and I fight the bubbling lump in my throat with a gulp. In seconds, the cat transforms into a demon from my Broodline—a lesser incubus dressed in luxurious black fabric from head to toe. I survey his form with practiced scrutiny.

"Can I help you?" I ask flatly.

"I've come to deliver a message, Miss Valentine."

The demon presses the rose into my palm, its petals the exact shade of my demonic skin. A black velvet envelope clings to the stem, sealed with molten gold wax. The seal bears an intricate rose strangled by thorns.

Cold dread fills me. With trembling hands, I lift the envelope and breathe deep: Chanel No. 5. Her signature scent. My fingers fumble as I break the seal and withdraw blank charcoal card stock. Golden calligraphy bleeds across the surface, as if written by a ghostly pen, each letter burning into existence with slow, languid grace.

Finally, a kiss mark materializes at the bottom, shimmering like citrine jewels against the dark paper.

Dearest Reagan,
You are cordially invited to surrender to your darkest desires.
Enter The Fox Den, where predators become prey.
Sinfully yours,
Valentina Rose

Side B
CHERRYBOMB MIX
B

I'M RIGHT BEHIND YOU, PRETTY GIRL.
TRACK SEVENTEEN
One Way or Another

TRACK SEVENTEEN
ONE WAY OR ANOTHER

1912

Savannah, Georgia

My gran was a superstitious kind of woman. She was always spitting some malarky about medicinal masturbation or ludicrous rumors that lazy sex breeds ugly children. Oh, and that absolutely hysterical one where your child's traits depend on which parent has the most mind-blowing orgasm (and we all know who took the cake when making me—I am *nothing* like my mama and an exact copy of my daddy). God, what a woman. I often hoped I'd grow up to be just like her, too old and tired to hold up pretenses and conform to polite society, just spewing all the bullshit my withering mind could muster.

Unfortunately, everyone—including Daddy—blamed

her theatrics on hysteria. Medicinal masturbation would have done her wonders.

But Gran had an old saying, one that stuck with me since the days she'd tame my unruly auburn curls in her boudoir. Any time it rained—and boy, did it rain cats and dogs in Savannah—Gran would look out the window, sigh, and say, "I pity the man being buried on a rainy day. Their poor soul's goin' straight to Hell."

The concept eluded me as a child, but as an adult who savors delicious irony, I couldn't possibly be happier that today, of all days, the sky sent a downpour so torrential, it felt like God himself wept for the dearly departed.

My home swarms with high society's two-faced lick-spittles and clucking hens, all eager to shake my parents' hands and pay empty respects to the esteemed Mr. and Mrs. Baudelaire. I stand on the second floor landing overlooking the parlor, watching countless narrow-eyed mothers fan themselves as they run their fingers along my fireplace or eye the freshly fluffed pillows on the arm chairs. Their lips curl in disgust at my choice of décor, wincing at the shades of red adorning every rug and throw.

"Could she at least have put all this red away for the wake? So disrespectful."

"I always knew John Blythe's daughter got her wires crossed somethin' fierce. That girl's not right in the head, just like her gran."

"You know what I overheard a few months back at

book club? Jeanette Fairchild said the Blythe family name is bigger than their bank accounts these days. You *know* they married their girl off to the Baudelaires to save their assets. And now this? Such a shame. Wouldn't put it past John to have orchestrated the whole damn thing."

I could listen to these cackling magpies for days. Everyone's got a goddamn opinion in this town, with larger-than-life ideas and conspiracies. Still, they aren't *completely* off…

Despite the unfortunate downpour, the air is hot enough to wilt a preacher's collar. My guests fan themselves with their prayer books and wipe the sweat off their brows, all while gulping down my mother's famous sweet tea. I grip the banister of the staircase, pausing when I notice movement out of my peripheral vision; a dark, eight-legged creature crawls near my freshly painted red nails. I lay my palm upward, ushering the little thing onto my index finger and bringing it to my face to study it further: a small, red, hourglass-like shape adorns its bulbous body. I smile at the black widow spider, one of the most lethal arachnids in the world. I face it without an ounce of fear.

Just as I intend to face my guests.

My plan is simple: make a statement. Expose my family's skeletons. And *truly* destroy the Blythe name.

My very own flesh and blood, but only for a little while longer.

For in a few hours, once the dreadfully provincial

masses have had their fill of it all, I will deliver a cursed soul to the Demon of Debauchery.

With a small grin, I place the spider on the banister and watch it scurry off. She's free to weave her web wherever it pleases her, free to devour her quarry without a second thought.

"I'm right behind you, pretty girl," I whisper at the spider.

My freedom is just within reach, and I intend to savor every last drop.

Descending the staircase, I relax my shoulders, hold my head high, and face my demons.

Draped in head-to-toe red.

The parlor falls dead silent—not the respectful quiet of mourning, but the sheer breathless hush of scandal. My dress is a crimson gown of lace and silk, blazing like a single flame in a dark cave. Each gaze burns with the fear that my very presence would condemn their souls to Hell. The clucking hens huddled near the fireplace are stunned into stillness, and sharp gasps cut through the scene like a knife. The very air seems to recoil in my presence, and I revel in the theatrics with another one of my smirks.

The sharp click of my heels against the parquet fills the silence as I glide through the horde. I know these faces. I remember their fraudulent smiles as I walked down the church aisle in the white silk dress my mother chose. It was the day my father bartered me to the Baudelaires to salvage our family name.

Now, I walk down another aisle, this one carved by a parting crowd with their crocodile tears. My husband waits for me at the end once more—but this time, I'm in a dress of *my* choosing, on *my* terms, and him? He's stone-cold dead.

Before I can reach the open casket, a firm grip on my forearm drags me through the crowd and away from prying eyes.

"You foolish girl," comes the menacing drawl of Mr. John Blythe himself. "Have you misplaced your wits along with your utter lack of shame? How dare you step foot into this parlor in that...*color*. Lookin' like a...a..."

I pull my arm away and raise my chin in defiance. With added grit and unwavering confidence, I threaten, "Say it, Daddy."

His eyes, that same moss-green I so often see in my own reflection, narrow. "A whore."

I can only respond with a haughty laugh. "You'd know all about that now wouldn't you? After all, it was you who found me at that club, you preying on women less than half your age while Mama sat at home tending to your dying business."

"Listen here, you little trollop," his voice drops to an even deeper, unforgiving tone, "I damn near moved Heaven and Hell to find you a suitor who'd deem you proper, despite whatever demon has taken root inside you. Now that poor boy's lying dead in a casket while his whore of a widow makes a mockery of his life. I will not have it. I will *not* let you make us the laughingstock of Savannah. Now, get yourself changed into something more suitable for the wake of your dead husband."

"You care more about the Baudelaires than you do your own kin," I say as he starts to walk off. He pauses to face me once more.

"Of course I do. We needed that money. *His* family money."

"You mean my money. That's what it is now. *Mine*. And you won't see a goddamn cent of it."

"Don't you dare use the Lord's name in vain Mar—"

"Don't *you dare* call me by that name ever again. It's dead to me. And I'm leaving."

"And just where do you think you're going?"

"I'm taking my inheritance, soiling what's left of our family reputation, and catching the next train to California."

"California," he huffs in disgust. "I can assure you darling, California's nothing but a cesspool of desperate fools and the vultures smart enough to prey on them. There's no place for you there."

I flash him a smirk. "On the contrary. I think I'd fit right in."

As if on cue, the French doors connecting the sunroom to the parlor fling open to reveal two dashing guests—a fabulously-dressed gentleman clad in an intricate three-piece suit and his devastatingly beautiful escort.

Mr. Cherry and Valentina.

"You must be John Blythe," Mr. Cherry drawls, his

voice carrying that familiar Savannah honey. "Desmond Sheffield, of the Atlanta Sheffields. I am terribly sorry for your loss."

My body goes rigid with fear. Surely, Daddy would recognize them from the club? He must have seen Valentina's performances countless times…but the realization quickly hits me: the demonic glamour. They can wear any face they choose, present themselves as anyone they wish. What one mortal sees can be completely different to another. Such an advantageous gift…

My father straightens his posture at the mention of his name, clears his throat, and excuses himself to offer the alleged Desmond Sheffield a drink. Cherry shoots me a wink over his shoulder as he follows him, leaving me alone with the dark-haired goddess—no, demoness—I'd been itching to see.

"My deepest condolences, Mrs. Baudelaire," a voice purrs at my side. My skin prickles as excitement rushes through me in cool waves. Oh, how I love her voice. How it grounds me and gives me strength even when my insides are crumbling. Valentina stands by my side in a dress that rivals my own, one I know she spent hours tirelessly sewing to perfection. It mirrors mine in its silhouette, and one could almost mistake them for exact copies, if not for the stark contrast of my red fabric.

"Thank you, Miss Rose," I respond, maintaining the charade. It's part of the plan, of course; Mr. Cherry and Valentina would stroll into the wake, claiming to be long-time friends of the Baudelaires, weaving their influence throughout the crowd. Once the last guest leaves, I'll make good on my end of the deal.

And I'll be free.

"I can't wait to be rid of that last name," I mumble loud enough for the two of us to hear.

"Pretty thing like you won't stay on the market for long. You'll get snatched up by the next geezer in a matter of days. Seems your daddy's already laying the groundwork."

We glance at my incorrigible, pathetic excuse for a father. Knots form in my stomach as he stands beside Cherry, relentlessly schmoozing this so-called import and export mogul with deep pockets and even deeper proclivities—or so I've heard.

"Guess I'll just have to keep picking them off one by one then, like I did my last."

Valentina's lips curve into that heart-skipping smirk —the one that speaks of secrets shared between musical numbers and promises made against satin pillows. Is that pride glimmering in those mahogany eyes? Does she revel in my darkness, how seamlessly I succumbed to it? How easily I can mask the truth with quick-witted retorts?

Those lips, the candy-red smile that blesses every dream, is my salvation and damnation. I'd give every-thing I have just to bask in the warmth of her beautiful smile—my family name, the comfort and security of high society, even kill a man.

In fact, I already have.

In her eyes, I don't see my reflection as an obedient daughter bound to her father's will, but something more. Something wild and dangerous. Confident. Powerful.

"You could take my name," she says, her voice barely a whisper as she dares to step closer to me.

My eyes dart around the room as panic tickles my nerves. In Savannah, even shadows have eyes and ears. Women like us…we exist in stolen moments, in knowing glances across audiences, in gentle brushes against each other's skin. Demon or not, Valentina knows the rules as well as I do.

Still, I humor her. "Rose?"

"Valentine. Just imagine it: Ruby Valentine, the Dazzling Gem of Los Angeles."

The vision blooms before me in intoxicating waves, just as it has every night since I met the she-demon. My name in lights, the adoring fans, ink flowing across photos as I sign autograph after autograph. Oh, and the hundreds of silk gowns I'd wear, paired with perfect diamond earrings…

And through it all, her: Valentina Rose. This exquisite creature who saw something in me no one else dared to see.

It's so close now, so dangerously close. I could almost taste the champagne on her lips…

"Ruby," I repeat, noting the color of my nails and dress. "I've never felt like a Ruby."

There's that chuckle, the one that never fails to send a shiver up my spine. "There's power in a name, my beauty. You'll have the luxury of choosing whichever one you'd like once this life is behind you."

My attention turns to another woman who enters the parlor as the guests start to disperse. She's a short, dainty little thing wearing a skintight dress I'd only seen in the papers. Her blonde hair gathers in a delicate, twisted bun at the nape of her neck beneath an oversized mourning hat draped with mesh. A mysterious, intriguing specimen who feels just a little out of place— she's a vision.

I watch as she weaves through the crowd and stops right in front of my husband's casket. She clutches her black pearls, fighting sobs as she looks down at his pale face, and carefully places her gloved hand over his heart…

It's an intimate moment, one only I seem to notice. And for the first time, I realize there are repercussions to the selfishness of my actions, that I was the cause of a broken heart.

I shouldn't care. No one ever cared for mine.

In seconds, she's gone, leaving nothing but a trail of tears and emptiness in her wake. I take a deep breath and a sharp inhale; with the last guest gone, it's finally time.

Father and Mother disappear with the rest of the rabble, leaving me alone with Valentina, Mr. Cherry, and my husband's corpse. I step up to the casket, taking one last look at the man who bought me, who swore he'd 'set me right' and mend my reputation before my secrets got out.

I remember the night he accepted the dowry from my father—the measly remains of our family fortune—and the smarmy grin on his face when he said, "She won't even recognize herself when I'm through with her."

That's when I knew I had to kill him. I'd never let another man own me.

With Mr. Cherry's deal in place, I knew this was my moment; he was the soul I was meant to deliver to a demon. How I hoped he'd rot in Hell with the rest of the monsters just like him.

"I'm not entirely sure how this works," I say with a hint of shame. "Is there a ritual of some sort? An incantation? Some of the best witches in the South have the cleverest rhymes."

Ignoring me, Cherry glides over to the casket and pokes my husband's corpse with his cane. I truly do not know what to expect. Is it meant to be a smoke-and-mirrors magic show? Will I be able to see his soul leave his body? I wait with bated breath as Cherry continues to poke.

But a disappointed "Hmm…" is all that fills the air, and all at once, the color drains from my face.

Thump, thump. Thump, thump. My heart is in my throat as Cherry turns to face me. His lips move and words come out, but I can't hear them. I struggle to focus on that moment while the anxiety continues to claw at my insides and dread begins to take over.

"I'm afraid this body is void of a soul," he repeats—and that's when the panic sets in.

"I beg your finest pardon?"

"I do dislike repeating myself." Cherry primps his quaffed hair. "For the last time, this body appears to be soulless. Gone. An empty husk. Useless to me, and by extension, useless to you. I believe the deal is broken, darling."

"H-how can there be no soul? He was alive and I killed him. Did it pass into heaven?"

"What a complicated question. I'm not here to provide a demonic Sunday school lecture, but a deal is a deal. You give me a corrupted soul, and I make your wildest dreams come true. This body has no soul. Therefore, our deal is abrogated."

"What about my father? What if I gave you his soul?"

Cherry lifts his chin, looking down at me with narrowed, calculating eyes. "You'd kill your own father?"

"Yes." The words leave my mouth quicker than intended. "I'd kill anyone to leave this place—to have my freedom."

Cherry's sadistic smile deepens, making my insides twist. "Sweet girl. His soul is not yours to give away, nor is it mine to take. It belongs to one of my brothers."

"W-wha—what do you—"

"Your father is a greedy, greedy man, Mrs. Baudelaire. A proud, insatiable creature always in search of more and willing to do just about anything to get what he wants—even make a deal with a demon. It's almost… adorable, how alike you two are."

The sentiment leaves a bitter taste in my mouth, rendering me speechless. There isn't another human, dead or alive, whom I loathe more than John Blythe. Learning he made his own deal with another demon only deepens that hatred for him…and in turn, for myself.

I never wanted to be like him. Physical similarities were punishment enough. Nothing says self-loathing more than becoming the mirror image of the parent you despise.

"I believe you're out of options, love. You failed to deliver the soul we agreed upon, and therefore, yours must take its place."

Thunder booms beyond the walls then, and the sky seems to darken. Rainfall transforms into a growing tempest as the magnolia blossoms wilt and shrivel. Mossy tree branches bang against paneled windows, and the howling winds whistle from beyond creaking walls.

My heartbeat pounds in my ears. "I-I don't understand–"

"Did you think there would be no consequences if you failed?" Mr. Cherry's melodious, spine-tingling laughter fills the air as he sets down his cane. "I'm a demon, darling. You should have known what you were getting yourself into."

His hands clamp around my wrists like iron shackles. Every candle in the parlor dies at once, plunging us into darkness. I watch in horror as his fingernails blacken and stretch into curved talons that bite deep into my flesh. I swallow my scream while his thumb carves deliberate circles into my wrist, flaying skin from bone until each breath becomes agony.

Dozens of cracks spiderweb across my skin, racing from wrist to forearm, spreading like lightning across my entire body. A molten amber glow erupts from each fissure, turning me into a fractured constellation of pain and fire.

Then, darkness swallows everything.

And the transformation is excruciating.

Pressure meets my knees when I collapse onto the cold, wooden floor. My fingernails claw at the intricate laces of my dress, desperate to shred them as fire ignites in my skull and back. I continue to shriek, but the noise that escapes my throat is inhuman: a monstrous wail, like a wounded animal calling for help, but no one can hear me. Even if they did, no one would help me.

Another roar rumbles in my chest as my bones snap and realign beneath my muscles. Flesh tears with wet, violent sounds, and finally, I feel my skull and shoulder blades burst open as something unfurls from the wreckage. Then comes the agony in my lower back, where I feel something emerge. Is that…a tail?

Make. It. Stop.

I don't know how to end this nightmare. All I can do is endure the torture and pray for mercy.

When it finally does end, silence devours the room.

I blink once, twice, three times as my vision comes to. Blurred forms take shape, and I find myself seeing the world through different eyes—*powerful* eyes, with vision that can see more than just color, shapes, and movement.

I see…*everything.*

Emotions. Thoughts. Secrets.

And they're all pouring out of the only two creatures in the room.

I look up at Mr. Cherry, who stands with Valentina hanging off his frame. Dark tendrils spiral around them —not smoke, but something far more substantial. The very essence of their being made visible, twisting like serpents. But threading through that darkness is something else, something that hits me like the scent of jasmine after rain.

Satisfaction.

It pours off them in waves, and dear God above, I can taste it—*actually taste it.* How can I taste an emotion, much less one that isn't even mine? It fills my mouth like honey laced with poison, making my stomach clench with unholy hunger.

I struggle to find my limbs, to force myself upward and gain control of my body. My skull aches with the sharp pain of the small horns that press against bone. My gums burn with the fire of damnation itself. When I run my tongue across them, something sharp pierces the flesh. The coppery taste of blood and sulfur fills my mouth, dribbling from the side of my lips. I instinctively raise my hand to wipe the liquid away, and my heart stops dead in my chest.

Crimson red skin.

Glowing yellow veins.

Blood as black as a moonless night in the bayou.

And as I glance in the mirror above the fireplace, I see limbs so foreign, so fantastical, I cannot believe them real: a pair of wings and a tail.

I've become the very thing Daddy assumed possessed me.

I've become a demon.

My, my. Red really is your color. Mr. Cherry's voice rings through my mind in an eerie echo. He kneels before me, marveling at my features as if I'm a work of art. There's something in his eyes I can't place, but it's a look I suddenly find myself yearning for. The hurt and confusion melt away in his presence, if only for a moment, replaced with the insatiable urge to…earn his praise.

"You were right, Valentina," he says to the dark-haired beauty, his eyes never leaving mine. "She'll be of much better use to us as a demon than she ever would be as a human thrall. She'll fit right in with the rest of them."

The words sink in, pulling my heart into my stomach as my gaze darts between Valentina and her benefactor. Her gaze is void of the warmth it once had, now replaced with a treacherous, victorious grin. It's as if I see her for who she really is now, the rook protecting the king on this infernal chessboard. She never cared for me. She only wanted me for him.

That's when the most devastating revelation cuts through me: I've traded one cage for another, allowed yet another man to own me. I'm nothing but a deadly debutante who murdered a man in cold blood and sold her soul for a chance at freedom.

Only to be tricked by a woman who couldn't care less.

"Come on, darling." Mr. Cherry places his coat over my shoulders and runs his fingers delicately through my hair. "We've got a train to catch."

I look out the window with new eyes, watching as rain coats the wrought iron balconies, all while Spanish moss sways in the stormy winds.

And at that moment, I realize Gran had it all wrong— my husband's soul isn't going to Hell on this rainy day.

I am.

TRACK EIGHTEEN
Girls Girls Girls

TRACK EIGHTEEN

GIRLS GIRLS GIRLS

Two rival estates sit atop one of the highest points in Beverly Hills.

One is an opulent mansion owned by one of the most prolific businessmen in Southern California, a place where men flock to feel like kings, shoving their self-importance so high up the metaphorical food chain, they actually believe they have power over the models and waitresses serving at their beck and call.

The other mansion is the complete opposite.

It's a daunting, haunted behemoth straight out of a horror-lover's wet dream, a place where men come to fulfill their darkest desires, the ones that cater to degra-dation and humiliation. The women who occupy it aren't mere waitresses and models; they're full-blown succubi, hand-picked by Cherry's right-hand, Valentina Rose.

My very first love.

I haven't spoken to her in a while, longer than I care

to admit. We parted ways a decade after I moved to Los Angeles, where she eventually was granted a new business venture of her own and I was sent from brothel to brothel until I finally climbed the ranks enough to be assigned Bad Decisions and The Starlight.

A stretch-limo delivers us right at the entrance of the manor. The driver opens the door, escorting me safely onto the grounds, Jeremy and Vincent trailing behind me like two silver-haired, degenerate bodyguards.

"Where are we, Reagan?" Jeremy asks as the limo disappears down the hill.

I inhale sharply, taking in the acres of red rose bushes and brambles of thorns that twist into protective tunnels around this fortress of sin. "The Fox Den. The Debauchery demon safe haven of Los Angeles." My eyes cut to Jeremy's. "Also a glorified whorehouse, but you won't find that in the tabloids."

We wind up the endless pathway through rose tunnels to the main entrance, where two Watchers—bodyguards likely gifted to Cherry by the Demon of Domination—stand sentinel. Their eyes lock onto the silver-haired Nephilim, and both go rigid.

"They're with me. By invitation of Valentina," I mutter in Hellspeak. I drop my human glamour for a heartbeat, golden eyes flashing with demonic fire. Both Watchers incline their heads, pressing their palms to ornate double doors carved with an intricate fox head, and grant us passage.

The interior is exactly as I remember—dripping in

Gothic luxury, a monument to wealth and power. Dozens of oil portraits line the foyer walls, each depicting the same dark-haired beauty with luminous amber eyes and sun-kissed skin. Every gilded frame marks another decade of her immortal history.

The mansion brims with more revelers than a Gatsby soirée: demons and mortals alike flood the halls in pure euphoria, voices raised in song, bodies swaying to music that seems to pour from the very walls themselves. Every demon wears a human glamour, seamlessly blending with the crowd of mortals who somehow earned invitations to this otherworldly gathering. I motion for the Nephilim to follow me deeper into the manor, but I freeze in my tracks when a familiar, honeyed voice strikes my ears.

"Well, well, if this isn't a blast from the past. The Black Widow in the flesh."

I swallow hard, closing my eyes, fighting the tension building in my veins. I turn to face the voice and find a breathtaking woman perched atop a spiral staircase, gripping the black banisters; a vision of black lace, cinched leather, and pearls.

I don't smile. I don't even flinch.

"Valentina."

Her eyes linger on me, taking in the differences of my human glamour, comparing it to the one she knew. Then, those tawny eyes shift to Silver Fox, and a delightful smile spreads across her features. "And Vincent Thane, what a sight for sore eyes."

"Miss Rose." He bows his head and offers her one of those gentle smiles whose intent I've never understood.

"You want the usual, Vinny?" She nods at one of her incubi lingering behind us. He slinks up behind Silver Fox, clad in skin-tight leather pants and straps crossing his chest, trailing his fingers up the old man's arm. "Take him to floor three, Riot. Keep him nice and busy until my old *friend* Reagan here is ready to leave."

I don't miss the inflection in her tone when she says 'friend.' It stings, prickling at my nerves. Riot nods with a seductive smile, taking Silver Fox by the hand and leading him up the grand spiral staircase.

"You've been busy, haven't you?" Valentina says, nodding for us to follow her deeper into the mansion as she meets us at the foot of the stairs.

"Same could be said for you. How do you keep this place afloat with the competition right across the street?"

She flashes me a knowing grin, small wrinkles etching the corners of her lips. "Everyone knows foxes hunt bunnies."

The Fox Den is nothing short of a labyrinth, no doubt purposely designed as such. Its long hallways and countless intricately carved doors can easily land a wandering fool in the wrong bed. Valentina always loved her themes. From gem-themed names for the Follies to coining her employees at The Fox Den, The Vixens. Not much has changed since the early 1900s. She's still filthy rich, still preying on innocents, and still tucked safely under Cherry's demonic wing.

At least he made her dreams come true; she finally got the Gothic mansion she always dreamed of, where she tortures and feeds off the damned and depraved.

We enter deeper into the labyrinth of the mansion, rubbing shoulders with countless Debauchery Underlings, a mixed bag of Sired and Turned. Deep rust-orange and emerald-green hues cover the space, decorated in brass finishings, velvet, and candelabras. When we finally reach the main lounge, we're met with the heady scent of fruit, florals, and lust. A giant runway splits the room in half—probably where her Vixens do their nightly performances. Debauchery Underlings and their victims drape over the plush couches, drinking their fill of sexual essence and liquor.

"Are you going to introduce me to your friend, Reagan?" Valentina purrs, eyeing Jeremy hungrily.

"This is Jeremy," I say warily, taking his hand in mine. Her tawny eyes watch as our fingers intertwine, then narrow.

"Didn't know you liked them underage."

"I'm 21," Jeremy blurts out.

"I'm sure you are, baby." Valentina chuckles. "Make yourselves right at home. One of my girls will be with you shortly. Oh, and Reagan." She lifts a perfectly manicured finger, beckoning me closer. I lean in, breathing in that familiar scent of Chanel No. 5, nearly stumbling at the flood of memories. "I'd love for you to take the stage at eight. You know, for old time's sake. Would you?" Her smile doesn't reach her eyes.

The words hit like a carefully aimed dart. That habitual urge to please her, to obey, claws at my chest before I can stop it. I nod—too quickly, too eagerly—and she wiggles her fingers in dismissal as she melts back into the sea of patrons.

Jeremy and I slide into an ornate booth beneath a golden candelabra that bathes us in wavering light. I watch tension coil through his body as he absorbs his surroundings—muscle by muscle, his frame goes taut. His eyes dart frantically from corner to corner, jaw clenching as a thin sheen of sweat breaks across his brow despite his white-knuckled attempt at composure. Under the table, my fingers find the hard line of his thigh, pressing into the rigid muscle.

"You okay, Sparky?"

He nods, swallowing hard. "I've never been around so many demons before. They're all staring at us."

Jeremy's right—every demon in the lounge is staring at us with equal parts intrigue and worry. I scan the area, nodding at notable Underlings I've crossed paths with over the years.

"Of course they are." I lean closer, my voice dropping to a murmur. "A high-level Debauchery demon just walked in with a Nephilim on her arm. They can't decide if they should be impressed or start running."

"Won't you get in trouble for bringing Vincent and me here?"

"No, handsome. And if anyone tries to lay a hand on either of us, they'll leave this house missing a limb."

He huffs out a laugh. "Didn't realize you were so violent."

"I'm not." I meet his eyes. "But you are."

Then, I hear it: a familiar, spine-tingling laugh from the farthest corner of the lounge. Jeremy and I both freeze.

There he is. Debauchery incarnate himself.

Cherry holds court amidst a circle of adoring demons and pets, regaling them with his newest theatrical anecdote. He gestures wildly, his cane cutting dramatic arcs through the air as his haughty voice and lilting accent commands every eye in his corner.

"Reagan, is that..." Jeremy trails off as his eyes widen at the Prime, memories of our tryst visibly flooding back to him.

"The Demon of Debauchery," I finish, crossing my arms and leaning into my seat with a smirk directed at my boss. "Cherry."

Jeremy's brow furrows. "Cherry? That can't possibly be his name."

"It's the name he prefers."

"Primes don't give their names freely. Knowing their true name grants power over them."

I arch an eyebrow. "And that is precisely why he uses an alias, just like the rest of us."

"Us?" Realization dawns across his face as he pieces it all together. "Reagan isn't your real name, is it?"

"It's the name I claimed when I became a demon." I hold his gaze, unflinching. "Did you think I'd freely give you my name the night you asked me to take you in?"

"I…" His voice trails again.

I pat his thigh. "My human name means nothing now —not to you, not to me, not to anyone."

The Nephilim drops the subject faster than it started, his eyes fixing on Cherry again like a cat on a canary. That same hunger that filled him the night of the church rave burns in him now, but this time, there isn't a lick of hesitation. I truly take in the sight of him, and, Devil have mercy, how the man has changed in just a few short weeks.

He's still all long legs and arms, but there's something wild about him now—hair tousled like he's been running through a storm, clothes just as ruffled. Those beautiful green eyes have shadows dancing within them, pulling me in like a moth to a flame. That once-stiff spine has *finally* learned to bend since his walls came crumbling down. He's almost…aloof, with just a dash of confidence I never expected from such a pious young thing. The vision of him sitting so close to me, firelight painting his harsh features with the most delicious strokes, sends a thrill straight through my core, filling me with a hunger all my own.

Now, whether it's the intoxicating atmosphere of the Den or the Vixens working their influence, I can't say. But there's something about this newer, ever-changing Jeremy that keeps reeling me in…

It's almost as if the darkness I've so carefully sown

has become my very own addiction—one I'm simply powerless to resist.

And Devil damn it, that is what truly terrifies me.

Cherry catches sight of us instantly and makes his way toward us. We both rise to our feet instinctively, ready to receive the Demon of Debauchery.

"My sweet cherry pie," he sings. I force a grin, ignoring the nickname. "And your lovely scoop of vanilla cream. What a delectable little trifle you both make. All that's missing is a cherry on top."

Though Jeremy doesn't stiffen further, the air thickens with his desire. The memories flood his mind and eat away at the noise until all we both can see are flashes. Red, blue, green. Bodies, lips, hands…

It's enough to convince us to finish what we started that night at the church.

"I don't believe we were properly introduced," Cherry purrs, stepping closer to the Nephilim. He's a few inches shorter than both of us but stands taller than anyone else in the room. "Cherry Morningstar, the Demon of Debauchery—bad to the boner and always dressed for the occasion."

My gaze flits to Jeremy's neck, to the fading tattoo that once burned any time a Prime was near. It's barely there now, a mere shadow of the dark ink that once seeped into his veins. It no longer warns him of the evil that stands before him. It's just a part of his past that continues to wash away with every passing day. Relief never tasted so sweet.

"I'm…" The Nephilim is at a loss for words as he stands practically sandwiched between Cherry and me. His thoughts flick back and forth between memory and fantasy, wishing he truly *could* be between us, with his cock buried inside me while Cherry's is buried inside him. The idea certainly sends a shiver up my spine, and for a moment, I, too, salivate over the reverie.

"Jeremy." The name escapes my lips without a moment's hesitation, causing him to break his gaze and turn to me. "This is Jeremy."

"A lovely name." Cherry grins, all teeth and mischief. "One I hope to hear you scream over and over tonight, Reagan."

"We'll see about that," I tease. "Valentina asked me to dance for the eight o'clock crowd. For old time's sake."

"My beautiful girls together on stage again? Splendid, darling—absolutely sublime." He claps his hands together as his grin grows. "It'll be like 1911 all over again, without a messy scandal attached. It's been far too long since I've seen you dance."

"I've danced plenty of times, boss," I drawl, cocking my hip just so. "You're just never around to enjoy it."

"Consider this making up for lost time, then." He winks at me then trails his long, painted fingers up Jeremy's arm. "Come, Jeremy. Why don't you grab us a seat to enjoy the show? I'll catch up in a moment."

Jeremy searches my eyes, worry creasing his features, but I nod toward the crowd gathering for the show.

Cherry links his arm through mine, his voice dropping to a silken whisper.

"Where is my Thane?"

"In one of the Vixen rooms." I nod skyward. "Getting nice and ripe for you to feed off later. He's safe, don't worry; Valentina gave him to one of her best."

"That's a good girl," he purrs, twirling a lock of my hair around his finger. "Truly, Reagan. You're doing *so* very well. The boy's almost completely turned. One step closer to our endgame."

My lips form a hard line. "'Our endgame', Cherry?"

"Of course—another angel turned to darkness and a fancy little promotion for you. You remember the deal."

"The deal," I remind myself. "Right."

"I've already discussed it with Valentina. She's more than happy to take you under her wing at the Den—that is, of course, if you're comfortable doing so, what with your…history and all."

My brows knit with a mixture of confusion and building anger. "I don't want to be taken under anyone's wing, Cherry. That wasn't part of the deal. You promised me relocation to Beverly Hills."

"That I did, and oh, look—The Fox Den is right in the heart of it."

"As a *new business* owner," I hiss.

"Let's not get ourselves wound up with the semantics, love. You're due for the stage. Your little Nephilim and I will be watching from the audience."

"Don't hurt him, Cherry," I warn, my voice harsher than I anticipated. "I need him in one piece for tonight."

A mischievous grin crosses his features. "You've grown rather fond of this boy, haven't you, love?"

"He's been a tough cookie to crack." I shrug. "I've enjoyed the challenge."

In fact, Jeremy has been less of a challenge than initially anticipated. What *has* been a challenge, however, are all the little monkey wrenches being thrown my way.

Asshole Nephilim.

Vincent Thane.

Demonic politics.

The list never ends.

But Cherry was right—I'm due for the stage, and I'm about to give my Brood the show of a lifetime.

A ruby-laden bodice, crimson-feathered skirt, and red rhinestone heels wait for me in the changing room, laid out at an empty vanity mirror. A black envelope and a single red rose rest on top of the ensemble. I suck in a breath as I lift the envelope, her signature scent still clinging to the paper. Her handwriting. Her best laid plans, all unfolding exactly as she intended.

I look forward to your performance tonight, Miss Reagan. Now, go out there and kill it.

Tears prick my eyes as I crumple the note, hurling it and the rose into the nearest waste basket. The memories surge back—the night I sold my soul to Cherry, then the year after, when I was deceived into demonhood.

I never discovered who orchestrated it all. No proof, no trail, no crumbs left behind. I could only suspect the worst—that Valentina played me, marked me as her fool, wanting me bound to her for eternity. Not as a mere mortal she could dazzle with fame and fortune, but as a damned creature like herself.

One she could torment forever.

But I never gave her that satisfaction, and I won't start tonight.

With unexpected familiarity, I begin to pin up my hair away from my face, the curls easily securing in perfect rolls. I slip into the outfit she so carefully selected —an exact replica of my costume from my Ruby days. She's trying to recreate that night, the night my father discovered his daughter was a hellion harlot who'd fallen in love with a woman.

She wants to give me the chance to rewrite history, to reclaim that stage as a powerful succubus who can prove to her entire Brood she's superior to them all.

Maybe this is her twisted version of an apology.

But I doubt it.

When I finally take the stage, it's as if the purest air floods my lungs for the first time in years. I block out the crowd lurking in the shadows and surrender to the music, to the way the feathers whisper against my skin, the way the bodice molds me into a deadly hourglass of beauty and blood-red rubies.

I don't just dance on this stage—I conquer it. My body moves like liquid fire, each move a deliberate promise and threat. My hips roll to the rhythm of the music, forming figure eights as my muscles ripple below my ruby-crested bodice. It becomes second nature after a while, and I lose myself in the music.

I find Jeremy in the crowd, seated terribly close to Cherry, whose arm drapes over him in an assertive, possessive hold. I watch as my Prime's nose trails up Jeremy's neck, lips parting ever so slightly to plant open-mouthed kisses on his neck while hooking the pommel of his cane on the younger's knee, pulling his legs apart. Jeremy's lost in a trance, eyes glued to me, watching every tantalizing turn, every effortless curve.

His thoughts scream at me—begging me to peel away the bodice, to give him a glimpse of what lies beneath. I ache to grant his wish, to unravel myself like a crimson rose and devour every ounce of his innocence.

But then, I catch sight of Cherry's cane.

The black tourmaline crystal embedded in the pommel pulses amber—it's activated. Fury coils in my chest, my jaw clenching tight.

No. Absolutely fucking not.

I will not let him steal what's meant to earn me the respect of my kin.

Jeremy is not his pet to feed from. Not yet.

Possessiveness floods through me, and I spin languid

pirouettes toward the runway's edge. Jeremy leans forward as I draw closer, green eyes blazing with such raw desire, my pulse stutters. I lean down and cradle the Nephilim's face in my hands, crashing his lips to mine. It's a declaration of dominance, marking my territory. I'm showing them—all of them—exactly what they're dealing with, that a human-turned-demon who clawed her way from the bottom could outshine them all.

And every demon in the room—Sired, Turned, even Prime—holds their breath.

Finally, they see me for who I really am: a demon who corrupted the incorruptible.

TRACK NINETEEN
Black Velvet
WHY DID YOU INVITE ME TO THE DEN, VALENTINA?
I MISSED YOU.
CORRUPTION IS EASY, MY BEAUTY, AS EASY AS BREATHING FOR CREATURES LIKE US.

TRACK NINETEEN
BLACK VELVET

THE VANITY LIGHTS CATCH THE DELICATE CRYSTALS embedded in my red bodice as I slip into the dressing room. Half a dozen Vixens immediately flock around me, bursting with praise over my performance—some with their makeup half-finished, others already undressed after their own acts. I offer small smiles and murmured thanks as I weave through the little crowd toward an empty dressing table.

Settling into the chair, I begin the familiar ritual of undoing my hair, releasing each perfectly coiffed curl from its pins. They hit the table with tiny metallic chimes as the girls drift back to their own stations, their chatter filling the space around me. They're already planning my return, babbling about how cabaret is making a comeback, how I should make this a regular thing, how the audience was completely enthralled.

Everything about this moment pulls me back to

where I started nearly a century ago, and, despite myself, my heart swells with the weight of those memories. The controlled chaos backstage, the easy camaraderie between performers, the nostalgic blend of stale makeup and cheap perfume hanging in the air—it feels like coming home.

I unclasp my garter straps with practiced precision then begin working the hooks along the front of my corset. As the stays loosen, air rushes back into my lungs. The familiar ritual of undressing after a show feels like second nature, and tonight, it's especially welcome after years of being suffocated by latex in the trenches of Hollywood.

Beverly Hills is a place I've coveted since it exploded in the 20s, where I knew I belonged; among the rich and opulent, just like the society I was born into. It was so close now, I could almost taste it.

But the weight of Cherry's little curveball does not go unnoticed.

As I brush my curls into loose waves, I wonder if my Prime ever intended to grant me the seat I'd demanded. Did he think I wouldn't make good on our deal? Did he think I'd fizzle out and fail, that I'd sooner die than successfully corrupt a demon hunter?

The invitation to The Fox Den was an enigma of its own. Why now? And for what purpose?

Questions linger in my mind as loud as the amplified riffs of an electric guitar, so loud, I almost miss the room falling into a quiet hush. Through my vanity mirror, I notice the Vixens' attention dart toward the double mahogany doors, now wide open, revealing none other than the black diamond herself, Valentina Rose.

"Make yourselves scarce, Vixens," she says in that ever-so-slight Italian accent of hers. "There are guests who need tending to in the salon."

The girls disappear one by one, some teleporting out in a huff of smoke while others scurry off through the doors. I remain perched on my stool, rolling the black stockings down my knees after kicking off my heels. I pretend not to notice her, the Italian beauty who has haunted my dreams for the better part of a century. The double doors close with a soft click, leaving the two of us alone under harsh yellow lights and heaps of costumes, masks, and accessories.

It really does feel like coming home.

"You were magnificent up there, Reagan. Such a natural… Hell, you always were."

I bow my head in thanks, hiding my smile by removing my lipstick with a handkerchief. "Been a while since I took the stage."

"I couldn't tell." Valentina glides across the floor, her heeled steps a quiet thud against the expensive carpet covering the floor. She leans against my vanity table, crossing her arms over her chest and watching me with those deep, intense brown eyes. So incredibly beautiful…

"Why did you invite me to the Den, Valentina? Why now, after all these years?"

"I missed you." Her candy-painted smile sends

butterflies spiraling through my stomach, their wings beating as frantically as my pulse. But my eyes narrow at the deflection. I can sense there's something more, something she isn't telling me. Our bond won't let her hide it for long.

I follow the delicate curve of her silhouette, longing to trace my fingers along her sides, to feel her soft skin beneath mine again. Even her hair—much shorter than I remember, falling in thick black waves just to her shoulders—suits this new persona she's adopted. Valentina had always been a timeless beauty, her style like a relic preserved from another era. But this modern transformation, the polished look of a powerful businesswoman thriving in a male-dominated industry? It makes my mouth water.

She crosses one ankle over the other as she watches me change back into my previous outfit. "I'd been planning this little soirée for a few weeks now, a gathering of Hollywood nobility and Debauchery Underlings. Thought you'd make a lovely addition to the guest list."

I nod once, unconvinced. She's never once invited me here before, even after everything we've been through. "Cherry got to you, didn't he?"

Her lips press into a tight line. "He did."

Sighing, I remove the heavy crystal collar, replacing it with my usual black leather one before I turn on my stool to face her.

"Well?"

"He mentioned your little deal. Mentioned how close

you are to fulfilling it. I wanted to give you an opportunity to prove yourself among the elite."

I scoff. "The elite. You mean his Sired."

Her brown eyes search mine. "You've done well, Reagan. *Really* well."

I lower my gaze, the weight behind her message hitting me like a brick. Valentina's a master at deflection, a skill she passed on to me. Finally, I look up at her again, chin lifting with defiance and purpose. "It's not enough, though, is it? It's not enough that I lured a Nephilim into my bed, spread the seed of corruption through him. There's still something missing. He's not... fully there yet. What more can I do?"

She takes my hands in hers and pulls me up to stand. We're nearly the same height—her in heels, me barefoot. She tucks a single red curl behind my ear and caresses my cheek with her thumb.

"Corruption is easy, my beauty. As easy as breathing for creatures like us. Once you plant the seed, it's only a matter of time before it takes root and grows into a gift that keeps on giving. But the fruits of our labor won't blossom without a little help. They need structure, guidance, and a whole lot of water."

The implication hits me like a big, sloppy kiss— lingering, tingling, leaving a memory sure to stick. After all these years, after every effort to shed the skin of my former life, Valentina still manages to make me feel like the Southern belle whose innocence she stole. I should hate her for what she did, for the life she pulled me into.

Instead, admiration tickles my insides, warmth spreading up my chest to my cheeks.

"How did you do it with me?"

She's got that same sultry laugh, the one I fell for hook, line, and sinker a century ago. Her scarlet-painted fingers toy with the ends of my hair as she leans in to whisper, "There was darkness in you, darkness only demons know how to pull, but you wanted it. Whether you knew it or not, you always wanted it. And that, my sweet, is the key to corruption. They give you an inch, and you take the whole fucking mile. Feed their beast, and it'll feed you for the rest of your life."

Her candy-red lips curl into a smirk while her amber eyes glimmer through thick, dark lashes. It's a look of reverence, I hope, a look I'd do anything to see again and again until one of us meets the Devil for our final end.

"Our prey are not as complex as we make them out to be, Reagan. They're fueled by one thing—survival. You've been sitting pretty in Hollywood's gutter year after year, playing fetch at Cherry's every beck and call. You're doing exactly what humans do—surviving. But you know better. I taught you better. It's time to stop thinking like a human and start acting like what you *really* are."

There it is again: the reminder of my eternal struggle. Demon versus human. Despite every effort to abandon it, my humanity refuses to let go.

My shoulders slump as reality seeps into my molten veins. It's as apparent as the opulence of this mansion or the jewels dripping over my bodice. Cherry has always favored his Sired demons over those of us who were Turned. It's a battle I'll keep fighting for the rest of my cursed life.

"He'll never give me what I truly want."

Valentina's devilish grin only grows. "So take it, Reagan. Take what you want and never apologize for it."

I lean into her touch as her fingers caress my cheek again, melting into the impossibly soft warmth of her hand. Her thumb brushes just beneath my lower lip, as if wiping away excess lipstick from my chin. I'm transported to a time when a love like ours—no, a *lust* like ours—had no choice but to hide in the shadows. Back then, my father's reputation and family name kept the beast caged inside me, that darkness desperately yearning for freedom.

Valentina gave me that freedom.

But as I've always said, I traded one prison for another the day I became a demon.

At least now, I don't have to apologize for who I really am.

In the heat of the moment, I grab the pearl collar around Valentina's neck and pull her closer, crashing my lips to hers. All at once, the memories of my former life flood back. The sweet taste of Moscato on her lips, the delicate scent of Chanel No. 5 on her neck, even the soft, barely-there whimpers she masks with sultry purrs. Her fingers meet my jaw, squeezing tightly, as if to remind me who's in charge, but I fight back. Locking her wrists behind her, I guide her to the nearest chaise and push her onto the supple velvet. I drape a leg over her thigh to straddle her and press my body impossibly close to hers. I yearn for friction, to feel her skin against mine as we had countless times during my human days, even during the days of my early demonhood. I writhe into her as my tongue snakes into her mouth, and fuck—*fuck*—she tastes like Heaven, Hell, and every realm in between. Sweet, spicy, hot, and delicious.

"Missed me too, have you?" She chuckles against my kiss.

"Just need to blow off some steam."

"You don't need to lie to me, beauty. You know I can read you like an open book." She runs one of her long nails down my spine, setting my nerves ablaze. Instinctively, I grind into her hips, desperate for friction, desperate for her touch, desperate to fuck like only demons do.

Raw. Passionate. Unafraid of inflicting or receiving pain.

I want her to ruin me like she always did.

The soft click of a door handle turning catches both our attention. For a moment, the old fears resurface again, when being caught in an intimate moment with a woman meant more than shame—it could cost you your life. But this isn't the 1910s, I remind myself. This is the turn of a new century, where no one—not even demons—is bound by societal norms.

And there's no John Blythe around to shame me anymore.

I twist my head to peer at our intruder. Jeremy rests against the doorframe, hands shoved into his pockets, looking effortlessly handsome. Maybe it's the suspenders, or the way his salt-and-pepper hair falls over those green eyes, or the charming stubble that's overtaken his features. Or perhaps it's his overall demeanor: the calm, the curious, the quiet hunger.

"Want to join us, handsome?" Valentina croons, pulling me closer by the thigh possessively, as if marking her territory.

"He likes to watch," I chuckle into her ear as I run my nose from her earlobe to cartilage.

"Oh, I know. This one's very easy to read."

Valentina could unveil the Pope's proclivities if given the chance. She's a natural as a succubus—intuitive, seductive, and far too deadly.

Jeremy's eyes never leave my body. He marvels at my thick, strong thighs wrapped around Valentina's waist, how my outfit cinches me to perfection and accentuates my breasts. The hunger within him grows, and his thoughts and voice are suddenly loud and clear.

"I'd rather have her for myself."

Valentina cocks an eyebrow—not in disappointment, but in surprise laced with intrigue.

"Very well then. By all means."

She plants one last, lingering kiss on my lips and bites

down—hard. Blood wells instantly. She licks at the dark ichor with deliberate slowness, savoring each drop as a throaty moan escapes her. When we finally pull apart, she pushes me off her lap in a casual dismissal and rises.

My pulse hammers with anticipation as she stalks toward my Nephilim. Each step is predatory, calculated. She lingers near him, drinking in every detail before positioning herself inches from his face. Her breath ghosts across his ear as she leans in.

"A word to the wise," my dark-haired beauty whispers. "If you fail to make her come, I will tear this door down, tie you to that chaise, and force you to watch how it's done. Over. And over. And over again. Until your balls are empty and my name is all you can hear on her lips for an eternity. Understand?"

Jeremy's expression shifts between pained and defiant as he gives a single, slow nod. It only makes Valentina purr that low, sultry sound that's seduced me through 92 years of surrender.

The laugh that promises exquisite ruin.

"Good boy. Now, take care of my girl."

TRACK TWENTY
I Want to Know what Love is

TRACK TWENTY

DOWN A SHORT, NARROW CORRIDOR HIDDEN WITHIN THE labyrinth, connected to the Vixens' dressing rooms, lies a library straight out of my Southern Gothic fantasies. Floor-to-ceiling black wood paneling lines the walls, accented by sumptuous curtains embroidered with red and black roses. As I lead Jeremy inside, we both pause to absorb the sheer magnificence of the space.

The ceiling soars three stories high, every wall lined with thousands upon thousands of volumes—classic literature, philosophy, history, the complete works of centuries. For a moment, I expect Jeremy to drop to his knees in scholarly reverence.

Then, I remember: his reading consists entirely of Nephilim histories and demonology texts. This secular paradise might as well be forbidden fruit.

But Jeremy isn't captivated by Gothic architecture or leather-bound classics.

He stands before the grand fireplace, hands tucked in his pockets, the top buttons of his shirt undone, watching me with something close to worship.

"You kissed me in front of all those demons. In front of a Prime Evil." His voice carries no resentment, no anger or disappointment—only wonder, disbelief, and something startlingly close to pride. I feel it building inside him, threatening to spill over in waves my succubus nature hungers to consume.

With practiced indifference, I saunter the length of the library, trailing my fingers along the spines of hundreds of books on black shelves. "You seemed to enjoy it."

"They all know what I am, that I'm their enemy. But you kissed me anyway. You risked your rank within the hierarchy by bringing a hunter into their den." His voice grows quieter, more intimate. "You marked your territory."

"Are you my territory now, Jeremy?" My voice drops to a low, velvety purr—the same tone I'd learned from Valentina.

His gaze settles on the collar around my neck, the one that marks an ownership I'll never escape. He ignores my question entirely. "Will your Prime punish you?"

At this moment, I'm grateful beyond measure that he can't hear my thoughts. He'll never know about the schemes plotted against him, how every tender moment has been part of an elaborate trap designed to shatter his soul while my Prime feeds on the pieces. I flash him a small smile and sit on a large mahogany desk in the middle of the room.

"If he does, it's a punishment I'll probably enjoy. Cherry acts very differently from his brothers. He embraces all sinners—especially ones like you."

Jeremy's gaze shifts away from mine as he rubs his chin, staring into the dancing flames. I can see the battle raging in his mind as clearly as if it were written across his face—the pull between craving this attention from any demon, even Cherry, and his terrorizing fear of completely surrendering. He's terrified of becoming another Vincent Thane, outcast and broken. As his thoughts spiral toward darker, more self-destructive places, I act quickly to pull him back.

"There's nothing wrong with wanting Cherry, you know. Everyone wants him."

"Do you?" His eyes snap back to mine, searching for something he's afraid to find.

"I've had my fill of him over the years." I shrug with calculated indifference. Ironically, it's not even a lie. I perch myself on the edge of the mahogany desk right next to the fireplace, just feet away from him, and cross my legs slowly. My skirt rides up just enough to draw his attention.

"I see."

"Jealous?" I lean forward slightly, my voice a teasing whisper.

"N-no," he stammers, running a hand through his hair. "I...I liked seeing you two together when we were at the church. *Really* liked it. But…" His voice trails off as he struggles with the admission.

"But you want me all to yourself."

The confession tears from his throat like a prayer. "I do."

"Then take me," I whisper, slowly unbuttoning my blazer. It's an invitation. Permission. A line we're both ready to cross. This is different from the church, where I manipulated him through a false identity. This is me— the succubus, the creature he's sworn to destroy.

"Wait," he breathes. "Not this way."

My head tilts in question. He moves closer, shoulders squared and hips swaying with newfound confidence even as his heart hammers against his ribs. "I want to see you. The real you."

My brow arches impossibly high. "You mean…"

"Yes." He nods, bracing his hands on the desk on either side of my thighs. "Every inch."

I never expected to hesitate at a request like this. This isn't some desperate patron with twisted fantasies about his ex-wife or some young woman who'd never look twice at him. This is a man asking to see my demonic form—not despite what I am, but because of it.

Most of my existence has been spent crafting the perfect glamour for victims, hiding my true nature from human eyes. Only during Halloween week have I been able to let my guard down and blend in openly, but now…

I place my hands over my arms as I have countless

times before, but this time, I falter, hesitation flickering through me. Channeling my magic, I let the glamour dissolve. Cracks of molten gold spread across my skin as my pale complexion deepens to crimson. I run my fingers through my hair, allowing my horns to emerge while carefully tucking my tail away.

Within moments, I'm revealed in my true form. Despite the clothes still covering my body, I've never felt more exposed, more vulnerable.

I meet his gaze cautiously, bracing for disgust or fear, even anger.

Instead, his lips part in wonder.

"You're…" His voice trails off like dust in the wind, so small, you could miss it. I expect the usual song and dance, that familiar look of shock and disgust. I know he's seen far uglier creatures than me. No one faces Nightmares and Fear without a permanent scar on their psyche. But there's something other than disgust in his eyes. There's…curiosity. Hunger.

His eyes trail up the path of twisted veins glowing against my crimson skin before they finally settle on my face. The amber glow of my demonic orbs reflects in his stare, and I swear, he takes a step closer.

"You're so incredibly beautiful."

My breath catches in my throat, nearly choking me. I've lost count of how many times I've been called beautiful. They usually come in instances not unlike this one, when my prey falls for the perfectly-crafted guise of my human glamour. The notion's a complete fallacy, of course. I design my glamours to represent my victim's preferences.

But right here? Right now? Jeremy sees me as a demon.

Not a heartbroken punk haunted by death. Not a Southern belle caged by society. No, I'm a full-fledged succubus, horns and all.

And he finds me beautiful.

"You sure know how to make a gal feel good." I deflect my bashfulness with a suggestive smile, grateful my crimson skin hides the deeper flush spreading across my chest.

"What if I wanted to really make you feel good?" His voice drops to a husky whisper, experimenting with tones he'd never dared use before. His aura has shifted to dark gray now, the white flickering weaker with each passing moment. I can see exactly where this is heading, the precise moment he'll cross the line of no return. I know what breaking this final boundary will cost him—and I've never craved anything more.

"I'm tired of watching, Reagan," he whispers as he bumps my knees apart to settle between my legs, lifting my dress up my thighs.

I hum in response, running my fingers through his hair while the tip of my tail caresses his cheek. His lips part, trembling on a silent plea, and those eyes…those beautiful seafoam green eyes. How precious they look in the dim light, blinking slowly and burning with anticipation.

My tail trails along his jaw until it finds his bottom lip, and he instinctively opens wider.

"Please, Reagan." My name is a prayer in this moment of intimacy. "I want you to teach me."

His eyes flit to my lips and back up before he leans in for a kiss…but comes to a halt when I firmly press my hand against his chest. Worry etches delicate lines into his features as he's jolted back by my touch, but it quickly melts away as he watches my knees part even further, inviting him in for a taste.

"On your knees."

With a hard gulp, he does as he's told. He looks beautiful between my legs, his gray hair a stark contrast against my crimson skin. My glowing veins reflect a beautiful gold in his eyes, and before I can command him again, his lips hover over my knee. He seeks permission through his innocent stare, and I grant it to him by running a claw down his cheek to his chin, pulling him closer.

"I can't believe you're real," he speaks in soft, hushed tones against my skin. "Just so beautiful." The ever-growing stubble on his chiseled jaw rubs against my knee as he trails his nose upward. He moves slowly, planting sweet kisses along my thigh, tracing the map of my glowing veins.

Though every caress is laced with threads of uncertainty and naivety, there is a hint of confidence there. Desire and curiosity seep from his pores in a beautiful, tantalizing mist; I can't help but take a whiff.

Sublime.

That's the word Cherry used when he took the tiniest hit from the black tourmaline crystal, but sublime doesn't even touch the surface of what it feels like coming from the source.

It's…transcendent. Euphoric. *Divine.*

The inner workings of my demonic magic coil within me. The pheromones build instinctually, threatening to release through the cracks, but I fight to keep them down. I won't risk it again, not when my lover is so eager to please. I remove my blazer and pull the dress over my head to reveal strappy lingerie. His eyes rake over my body, studying every inch now that we're in the safety of a locked room, but he lingers at my hip, right where my spider tattoo is—where his holy blade slashed me weeks ago.

Worry clouds his gaze for a moment, brows knitting as his lips part and close. His mind repeats the same words: *I'm sorry. I'm sorry I hurt you.*

I tangle my fingers in his thick hair to redirect his attention. "The best way to learn is to dive headfirst. You're a smart boy. Your instincts will take over."

"You'll tell me if it feels good?" he asks, kissing my scarred hip gently.

"Mmhmm." My legs spread wider for him as I lean back, resting my weight on my elbows. I drag my hand from my breasts to my pussy, pulling my panties aside and spreading my lips to reveal my pierced clit. Finally, I find myself whispering the words I thought to myself the first night I met him, this time under *far* better circumstances.

"Eat your heart out, Mr. Nephilim."

The poor darling is so unsure at first, so determined to please me that he's shaking with anticipation. His tongue darts out to lick my hole and straight up to my clit, where he ultimately settles to play with the silver ring and ball nestled between my nerves. He's a natural, I'll give him that. A nervous one, but I imagine with his voyeuristic streak and curiosity for sex, he's learned a thing or two from watching. He experiments at first, alternating between licking and sucking my clit then running his tongue down and back up again. When he finally looks up at me, I see ravenous hunger darkening those once sweet eyes.

"Very good," I praise him, grinding myself against his tongue. "*So* very good."

The words set him off in a way I'd never expect.

Eager to please, his tongue moves quickly. Licking. Sucking. Slurping. Like a man starved, he moans against me, circling my clit as the heat builds quickly within me. My body erupts in goosebumps as my pleasure builds, and despite how badly I need to release, I grip his hair to control his speed.

"Easy there, Sparky," I breathe out, something between a chuckle and a moan. "I'm not going anywhere. Take your time."

"You just taste so fucking good," he moans against my clit, sending ripples of pleasure through my body. He circles his tongue around my hole again, lapping at the sweetness pooling between my thighs. Then, he pulls away to nip at my inner thigh, alternating left to right with varying aggression.

I hiss as the pleasure and pain ebbs and flows, and I grasp his head to shove it back between my thighs. I crave his exploration, to discover which parts of me he enjoys the most, to inhale the sexual energy trapped inside him. I need it like I need air, need *him* more than I ever expected. Finally, an idea strikes, and I reach down to grip his chin.

When he looks up at me, he leans his head against my thigh, eyes searching mine with helpless vulnerability. What I see there blindsides me—tenderness, reverence, something achingly genuine.

Something unexpected crashes over me. This connection we've forged, two beings from opposite worlds finding solace in each other's touch…it's so raw, so *real*, that everything else fades away. The games, the manipulation, the carefully laid plans.

I don't want to think about Cherry's deal or my mission anymore.

I just want this, want him. All of him.

And I know without a shadow of a doubt that he wants me too.

I lean down while pulling him up towards me. It starts slowly at first, lips brushing softly, tongues dancing hesitantly, delicately, with nothing but a crackling fire and shallow breaths filling the room. My fingers grip his hair, pulling back gently, and I capture his lips in a slow, firm kiss, practically inhaling his very essence. He whimpers against me, melting into my touch and leaning upward ever so slightly to deepen the kiss.

"Do you want to fuck me?" I murmur against his lips as he presses his length against my thigh.

He nods quickly. "So fucking bad."

I reach between us to unzip his slacks and slip my hand into his boxers, eliciting the most delicious, virginal groan in his chest. I grasp his cock, stroking the length of it and memorizing every inch, every vein, every sensitive spot. He's hard, *so incredibly hard*, and Heaven, Hell, Purgatory, I want to feel every inch of him inside me.

I press his head against my entrance with one hand and wrap my fingers lightly around his neck with the other, claws digging into his jaw. "Fuck me, Jeremy."

With a shuttering moan, the Nephilim pushes himself into me. For a moment, I'm afraid he'll come right here and now, before we even get the chance to enjoy each other.

He struggles to find his rhythm at first, thrusting into me with no particular cadence, like he's desperate to feel closer. My hands settle on the bulbous curve of his ass, guiding him in and out, encouraging a sinfully slow pattern.

His hands trail up my sides slowly, reaching the swell of my breasts before thumbing my nipples. He takes one into his mouth, and once more, his rhythm falters. The sweet thing, struggling to multitask while his body and mind desperately want to try it all.

My hands continue to guide him while his tongue rolls over my pierced bud, tugging lightly against the metal and eliciting a delicious moan from me, encouraging him to continue.

And continue, he does.

Eventually, Jeremy drives into my cunt with a passionate, relaxed pace. He pulls out fully and sheathes himself with a staggering moan, his lips capturing mine in feverish kisses.

For a virgin, he's divine.

So divine.

And with every touch, every kiss, I drink deeper from his essence.

The golden veins beneath my skin pulse brighter with each taste, warm currents of electricity surging through me like liquid lightning. I feel revitalized, reborn —as if I'm drinking from the Fountain of Youth itself. It's unlike anything I've ever experienced with previous conquests. Pure. Motherfucking sublime.

In this moment, a Nephilim has surrendered himself to a demon, forsaking every vow and rule ever drilled into him.

A demoness has opened herself to her enemy—one she should despise.

But I can't hate him, not when he sees exactly what I am and reaches for me anyway. Not when acceptance shines in his eyes instead of revulsion.

We shouldn't work, shouldn't fit. But we do.

And for this stolen moment, there is no game.

No Cherry. No mission. Just us: angel and demon, creatures bound to powers greater than ourselves, enslaved to entities who see us as tools, connected despite every law of Heaven and Hell.

I'm about to pay the Devil his due, and I'm dragging Jeremy down with me.

I reach for one of his wrists, bringing it between us. Guiding his thumb to my clit, I move our fingers in a circular motion. He drives into me faster now, watching as his body pulls pleasure from mine. A rush of heat surges through me, both our moans filling the air. I've never felt more alive, more in tune with my demonic nature, than in this moment, in the arms of a Nephilim buried deep inside me.

And just as my body shatters with release, bloodcurdling screams tear through the mansion, turning my ecstasy into ice-cold dread.

TRACK TWENTY ONE
Heaven and Hell
REAGAN, NO! DON'T!
YOU'RE ALRIGHT, MY BEAUTY. LOOK AT ME.

TRACK TWENTY-ONE

HEAVEN AND HELL

It's always the same motherfucking story. The setting changes, but the ending never does—demonic blood spilled and another one of Cherry's businesses torn apart from the inside out.

My instincts kick in as the screams beyond the walls grow louder. Countless Vixens scramble through the hallways, just like my girls did every time attackers hit Bad Decisions—searching for safety that might already be out of reach. All at once, a dozen succubi voices crash into my mind like alarm bells:

Demon hunters!

Nephilim have invaded the Den!

Those who can port out, take as many as you can with you.

Protect Cherry at all costs.

My heart lurches as I sit up. Jeremy springs to his feet, eyes wild with panic, thoughts scattered as he hears the screams too.

"Jeremy—it's the Order," I rasp, pulling my bra straps over my shoulders. "I need to find Valentina and Cherry. Get out of here before they catch you."

"I won't leave you." He grabs my wrist. "There's only one reason they're here, and it's me. Please, let me protect you."

"Don't be ridiculous," I chide, yanking my arm away. "They're here to do what they do best—slay demons. Question is, how the fuck did they get in? The Fox Den is one of the most protected safe havens in Los Angeles. There must be a leak—" My eyes snap to his and narrow. "You…you can't still hear them, can you? Can they hear *you*?"

He shakes his head frantically. "N-no. I told you—I stopped being able to hear them the night we…"

Panic radiates from him in waves, and despite my own growing anxiety, I can tell he's being honest. Still, it doesn't make sense. How in the Thirteen Realms of Hell did the Order breach our defenses?

"I can hold them off with my pheromones," I say as I pull on whatever articles of clothing I can find. "But my priority is Cherry. If you plan on stopping me, this is where I thank you for the fuck and we go our separate ways."

"Fuck that," he spits, the curse still foreign coming from his lips. I watch as he searches the drawers scattered throughout the library. "I told you: I'll protect you. I know them better than anyone here. I know how they work—how they kill."

"What are you looking for?"

"Ah-ha," he exclaims when he finds a drawer filled with knives.

"Don't touch those!" I reach for him. "Those are demonic-kissed relics. They'll burn you alive."

"Nice to know both sides had the same idea," he says, staring down at the assortment of blades. His hands reach for mine again, this time tenderly. His eyes, once bright and vibrant, now appear darker, stripped of their verdant luster. Even the laugh lines carved around his eyes seem weighed down with concern. "I can still teleport, Reagan. Let me get you out of here. I can handle them all, I promise."

"Not without—"

"Valentina and Cherry, I know. I'll go with you. C'mon; we need to move before we lose anyone else."

I stop in my tracks, tilting my head. "'We?'"

He bites his bottom lip and winces, as if he just caught himself breaking his own rule. "Never mind. Let's go."

I don't have time to ponder his subconscious blunders. We dress quickly and flee the study, racing through the labyrinth of hallways and rooms. My heart hammers in my ears, drowning out the death cries of my Broodkin, the horrified screams of the human clientele, and those two cursed Latin words that mark a successful kill.

We reach the foyer, where Watchers and succubi once stood in all their Hellish glory, but now, we face a scene that sends acid carving a path up my throat.

A bloodbath unlike anything Bad Decisions had ever seen.

Bodies litter the floor—some human, most demon, none Nephilim. The foyer is slick with black blood, evidence of my demonic siblings cut down. I try to push away the familiar pain twisting in my chest, the same ache that cripples me whenever I find one of my own slaughtered. These aren't my girls—but they *are* Valentina's. Part of my Broodline.

I'd rather die than stand by and watch another demonic massacre.

"Jeremy, we need to split up," I whisper under my breath. "Find Vincent; he's with that incubus upstairs. Go find him, and I'll find Valentina."

Jeremy begrudgingly agrees and darts up the spiral mahogany stairs in search of the Silver Fox.

Scanning the salon, I catch sight of a majestic creature facing off with a demon huntress.

Valentina stands in all her demonic glory before the ornate fireplace, flames casting her shadow long across the room. Her bat-like wings span the entire wall—at least eight feet of lethal beauty. Her spade-tipped tail coils like a serpent ready to strike while her twisted horns curve delicately above her dark hair. Under any other circumstances, I'd fall for her all over again.

But there's only one reason a succubus would ever reveal her true form to a demon hunter—when she's ready to kill.

Rage coils within me, hot and unforgiving. Valentina's glowing yellow eyes catch mine in a warning stare. *I've got this, Reagan,* her thoughts ring loud and clear alongside mine. Her threatening claws curl like a lioness ready to strike, and an eerie growl spills from her snarling lips. We couldn't be more alike in this moment: two strong, determined demonesses hell-bent on protecting their own. I know what lurks behind that unrelenting fury. It's a poison we share, one that twists like vines through every muscle and vein until it renders us useless.

The demon huntress is named Keller, if memory serves, the very same who had a hand in Jeremy's excommunication. She's a ferocious creature, muscles thick and taut from days of training, reflexes as swift as a serpent's. She hurls balls of light at Valentina, who, in true dancer's fashion, dodges them with perfect precision. Valentina flaps her wings, fanning embers and soot from the grand fireplace toward the huntress, then pulls a heart-shaped velvet chaise in front of her to form a barrier. Keller's Holy Light bounces off the gold clawed feet of the chaise, shooting to the ceiling and ricocheting into the fireplace. It creates an explosion so cataclysmic, it knocks Valentina over the furniture and onto the floor with a heart-wrenching shriek.

I screech her name then, practically feeling the searing pain flowing through her veins as the remnants of holy magic sting her skin. Keller turns to face me, her hard features twisting into something even darker, more sadistic.

Despite my better judgment, something builds within me—a force that, up until recently, felt so foreign, a creature, one ancient and famished, dying to escape the cage I've fashioned for it.

My demon within.

The primitive force surges through me, granting me unnatural strength, a physical boost of power I never thought imaginable. I lunge for the demon huntress, running at a speed I've only witnessed in vampires, and launch into the air, claws bared and razor-sharp teeth elongating. I feel the skin at my shoulder blades tear as my bones protrude and contort out of my back, unfurling into limbs I often keep locked away through demonic glamours. My wings—not as long as my ex-lover's but just as menacing—extend from behind me. The glow of my golden-cracked veins erupts in rhythmic bursts, and a monstrous screech escapes my throat as I grab Keller. We topple to the floor, my legs straddling her hips in a tight hold as my claws reach for her neck. She struggles beneath me, limbs flailing as she desperately reaches for her blessed weapon just inches away.

"You will never hunt another demon ever again," I snarl, the words scraping raw from my throat in Hellspeak. My voice has shed all humanity and transformed into something beyond supernatural, ungodly. Deadly. *"I will enjoy devouring your sanctimonious flesh."*

"Reagan—no! Don't!" Valentina's weary voice rasps.

But it's too late.

I plunge my hand into her chest and watch the

huntress' eyes widen in absolute terror. My fingers close around her heart, claws piercing each chamber, severing every ventricle that keeps her alive. Her ragged gasps and gurgles fill my ears and I twist the organ in my grasp, relishing in the sparkling scarlet flowing out of her chest cavity. With one, swift motion, I tear my fist from her ribcage, and the demon huntress falls limp beneath me in a lifeless heap.

The heart of a Nephilim beats its final rhythm in my palm. Blood like liquid starlight trickles down my arm, pooling in the golden cracks etched in my skin. This heart is nothing like the human ones I've seen; it's breathtaking and fragile, wreathed in wisps of white light that fade with each passing second. I'm too mesmerized to fear what Nephilim blood might do to me, too entranced to heed the sirens shrieking in my mind, warning that mere contact could kill me in a poisonous fury.

I don't care.

I burn with the need to taste this holy lifeblood we demons are taught to fear above all else. Its beauty, the way it flows like silk against my skin, that intoxicating scent…

I have to know.

My tongue snakes out from behind razor-sharp teeth to lap at the dying heart. It teases my taste buds, numbing at first, offering just a hint of euphoria—but the pleasure is temporary. It's brutally replaced by waves of insurmountable agony.

Within seconds, my insides erupt in flames. The blood seeping into me attacks every nerve, burning like the purest alcohol. Except instead of dulling my senses, it heightens them. In this moment, I understand the agony Jeremy must have felt when my pheromones first consumed him.

Nephilim blood is a drug, but not the kind that helps you forget—the kind that destroys you from the inside out.

My throat seizes, and my claws rake at the collar around my neck as it suddenly feels like it's strangling me. Valentina's voice fades to a muffled scream, and I realize it's not the collar choking me at all.

It's the hands of another demon hunter.

I recognize him even through my rapidly blurring vision—the middle-aged ginger who snubbed Jeremy the night he discovered what I am: Reili, the short, stocky bastard who reeks of corned beef and disdain. Despite his stature, his grip is unforgiving as he forces me to my knees in front of Valentina. She backs against the fireplace grate, unafraid of the flames but terrified of the Nephilim who will likely kill her the moment he's finished with me.

My vision continues to slip until everything goes black. That's when I hear it: the words that haunt every demon—Prime, Sired, or Turned.

"Malum interfice."

Kill the evil.

This is it. 111 years on this Earth, 92 years walking

among the damned and debauched. A century of corruption and consumption, of jumping from one cage to another...all for it to end here, at the hand of a demon hunter.

What lies beyond death for demons? It's one of our greatest mysteries. Only rumors, never facts. Do we meet the Devil? Or does everything simply end?

I suppose I'll find out the moment his holy blade takes my head.

"Get your fucking hands off her."

The words shatter my resignation like glass. My vision swims back into focus as Reili's grip falters, and there stands Jeremy Roache—shirt torn and crimson-stained, suspenders hanging like broken wings. He's a vision of pure, unforgiving rage, chest heaving as if he's crawled his way out of Hell itself to reach me. One of Valentina's cursed blades gleams in his grip.

Impossible. My former lover's soft, velvety voice echoes in my mind as she Taps into my thoughts. *He shouldn't be able to touch it. It should kill him.*

But he *is* holding it, just as he held me in his arms not an hour before. There's no sizzle of burning flesh, no smoke rising from his skin, just a cursed relic settling into his grasp as naturally as his holy blade once did.

He quickly wraps his arm around Reili, yanking his former colleague flush against his chest. The demon hunter's grip loosens slightly as Jeremy swings the blade out in front of his neck, the edge kissing Reili's throat, but Jeremy's gaze never leaves mine. He watches me with fury blazing in his once sweet, kind eyes, like he'd destroy the world—betray the life he's always known—just to protect me.

Valentina and I suck in a breath.

"You'd protect a monster over one of your own?" Reili rasps against Jeremy's hold, frantic and desperate.

Jeremy's lips curl back in a snarl as he whispers in the hunter's ear, "You abandoned me when I needed you the most. You *all* did."

Reili lets out an incredulous laugh. "You're a stain on your father's legacy and a disgrace to Declan's honor, blood traitor. You remember the sacred texts, don't you? If you go through with this, there's no turning back—your soul will be lost forever."

Jeremy's voice is a low, dangerous growl as he yanks Reili's head back by a fistful of hair. "'*He who taketh the life of a Brother shall damn his soul to the depths of Hell, there to be devoured by the King of Demons.*' I've already lost everything that's ever mattered. The Devil can have what's left."

A gut-wrenching squelch echoes as Jeremy slices Reili's throat open. My eyes widen in horror as glittering scarlet spills from the demon hunter—a mesmerizing, kaleidoscopic marvel that reminds me of my primal trance just moments before. My left wing shields my head while the other covers Valentina, whose bat-like wings also wrap protectively around her body. The holy blood splatters across my back, searing into my skin. I squeeze my eyes shut and hiss softly, pushing through the pain. It isn't as agonizing as the initial burn of the Nephilim blood seeping through my arms, but *fuck*, does it sting.

Valentina's fingers find my cheek, and I look down at her instinctively. Glowing yellow eyes cast beautiful shadows in the darkness of our winged cocoon. The cracks mapped along her gray skin give her a stone-like quality, and I remember the first time I saw her in demon form. She was breathtaking, a work of art carved by Michelangelo himself. Sometimes, I wonder if that was Cherry's intention all along: to create his Underlings in the perfect image of a Renaissance statue, cracks and all.

For a moment, in the wake of another demonic slaughter, there is only us, two damned pieces of art barely held together by cracking marble.

"You're alright, my beauty," she whispers, her lips mere inches from mine.

I nod quickly, wincing as the blood splatters cool against my skin. Whether or not I believe her remains to be seen.

"Look at me," she says—no, demands—and I do. Her lipstick has faded, revealing naturally ink-black lips that contrast sharply against her razor-white teeth. She kisses me then, soft and tender, a promise we will endure, that the righteous and holy will never tear us down.

After all, the world cannot exist without evil. But evil is relative, and all we're doing is fighting to survive.

My vision blurs again, this time coupled with my heart hammering against my ribcage. A dull ache spreads from my stomach through my limbs, and no matter how desperately my brain commands them, my legs won't respond. All I can think about is the hunger awakened by the Nephilim blood—the *need*, the urge to *devour*. It clouds my judgment and pulls at every aching desire coiled within my core.

I *need* to stand.

I *need* to get Valentina and Jeremy out of here.

I *need* to make sure Cherry made it out alive.

But I can't.

My wings fall limp against my back as I struggle to twist my neck toward the scene behind me. Weary muscles betray me, and soon, I'm collapsing into Valentina's arms, unable to move, unable to speak, a prisoner in my own failing body.

But one image sears itself into my mind before darkness claims me: Jeremy Roache, standing among a sea of corpses—holy and unholy alike—clutching a severed Nephilim head, his face twisted with deranged triumph.

I'VE KILLED FOR HER. BECAUSE I CAN'T IMAGINE EXISTING IN A WORLD WHERE SHE DOESN'T.
TRACK TWENTY TWO
Breaking the Law
REAGAN... YOU'RE OKAY.
OF COURSE I'M OKAY. IF I SURVIVED THE '90S, I CAN SURVIVE ANYTHING.
I KNOW WHAT WILL HEAL YOU. FEED ON ME. YOU'LL GET YOUR STRENGTH BACK.

TRACK TWENTY-TWO
BREAKING THE LAW

I drift in and out of consciousness for what feels like hours. When I finally awaken, I find myself in the safety of my dungeon boudoir, surrounded by the black-painted concrete walls I'd grown to tolerate for forty years. I'm in the same ensemble I wore to The Fox Den, dried Nephilim blood crusting my skin. I rise from my bed, my head pounding like it's been banged against a brick.

I don't feel aches like this, haven't for almost a hundred years.

Whoever lied and said Nephilim fluids were a drug needs a swift kick in the peach, twenty times over.

The sound of two tortured souls lamenting over drinks catches my attention. My heightened senses pick up their voices with crystalline clarity, every whispered word magnified as my awareness sharpens the longer I remain conscious.

The voices drift down from upstairs. I slowly climb toward the main floor of Bad Decisions, each step sending sharp pain through my joints, their words growing clearer with every labored movement.

"They're going to find me and kill me." Jeremy's voice reaches me first, eerily calm despite the strain threading through each word.

Silver Fox is next. "They can't find you, not anymore. Not after..."

"What I did." Jeremy's muffled words escape as if he's rubbing his hands over his face. "I killed a brother."

"He stopped being a brother the moment you stopped being able to hear the voices, Jeremy. It was the same for me."

"Then how did they find me at The Fox Den? How?" Something pulls at my insides as his voice cracks. "They almost killed her. If they killed her...I would have gone after every single one of them."

My breath catches in my chest. I stand frozen, a foot on one step of the stairs, the other planted on the step below.

"You've grown far too attached to that succubus, Jeremy," Vincent muses. I could slap the old man for toying with his emotions like he tries to toy with mine. "Devil knows why you came here in the first place. She lied to you, betrayed you. Why did you stay?"

Silence befalls them for a moment. I imagine Jeremy sheepishly rubbing the back of his neck, that crooked smile of his on full display, running his fingers through his prematurely gray hair.

"When she found me at the cemetery the morning after Declan died, I was desperate for companionship, for someone to know how I felt. I was just so *lonely*. My powers were already on the fritz; I couldn't control any aspect of my life. Declan thought I was an amateur, and that evil witch tormented me everywhere I went, even when she wasn't around. But Reagan, she…even in her lies, I felt something real. And then, when the Order cast me out, she told me I had a place at Bad Decisions, even after I tried to kill her. And then, I started to get sick. I didn't know where else to go, so I came here. The truth is, my soul was damned well before I met her. She just gave me the chance to accept it."

There's silence again, and I picture him lost in thought, trying to find the words.

"She's just…beautiful. And *so strong*. We shouldn't be together—we're creatures from opposite ends of creation. But she makes me question everything I thought I knew, makes me want more from life than duty and righteousness. She brings out the darkest parts of me, accepted me when the Order cast me out for it, and what's worse? I love it. Every damned second of it. She makes me feel alive when everything else feels dead inside. I've killed for her because I can't imagine existing in a world where she doesn't."

I lick my lips and swallow hard, blinking back tears. Whether it's the lingering effects of the Nephilim blood overdose or the stubborn humanity still clinging to my soul, I can't tell. I press my back against the cool stone of the stairwell, fighting the dread and guilt churning in my stomach. His confession—so raw, so beautiful—shatters something inside me.

Because he has no idea what's coming.

I can't handle any more of this. I rush to the top of the stairs as quickly as my healing body allows and slowly slip past the doors onto the main floor.

And there they are, two silver-haired Nephilim slumped at the bar, nursing twin glasses of amber liquid, looking utterly broken. Their heads whip in my direction, both expressions softening with relief.

"Reagan," Jeremy breathes, pushing himself up from his stool and rushing over to sweep me into his arms. His embrace catches me off guard—it's warm and safe, different from before. He buries his face in the crook of my neck, one hand cradling the back of my head. When he finally pulls away, it's with a shuddering exhale. "You're okay."

"Of course I'm okay." I shrug, trying to sound casual. "If I survived the '90s, I can survive anything."

He huffs out a bitter laugh and meets my gaze, searching it desperately. There's something fundamentally wrong with him now. His once-vibrant green eyes have gone dull and sunken, dark shadows carved beneath them, crimson veins threading through the whites like cracks in porcelain.

And his aura…

It's black as night.

I expected to be thrilled at the sight. I expected to be overjoyed, ready to pack my bags, to wave goodbye to this sordid club and that seedy motel and never look back.

But I can't bring myself to feel the relief, the triumph I've waited for.

All I can think about is Jeremy's confession.

Silver Fox clears his throat, and I meet his piercing blue stare. "You good, Thane?"

"Clean as a whistle, Miss Reagan." He lifts his hands in surrender. "How's your head?"

"Throbbing." I could have chosen a better word—Jeremy goes rigid at the sound of it. I glance at him and watch something dark and ravenous flicker across his features.

"No surprise," Vincent muses. "Pure Nephilim blood is lethal to demons. The tainted variety is a little more… palatable. You're lucky you survived."

"Very lucky," Jeremy murmurs, pulling me deeper into his embrace. My demonic instincts warm to his touch, sensing the hunger growing in him with every second he remains close. "I know what can heal you," he whispers against my ear, his breath hot on my skin. "Feed from me. You'll get your strength back."

I jerk away, searching his rapidly darkening eyes with mounting alarm.

But his stare is unwavering, deadly serious, and the

relentless ache in my bones whispers I should consider his offer.

"Guess I should thank the Devil for small favors." I flash Silver Fox a brittle smile. "Well, if you two don't mind, I'm going to get out of these clothes and wash the dead Nephilim off me."

Jeremy doesn't even flinch at my callous words. It's as if he's forgotten what he did—what blackened his soul beyond recognition.

When I head back down the stairs, I feel the weight of my young Nephilim's stare burning into my spine. I smile grimly as his footsteps echo behind me, closer than they should be.

The game is over.

And I've won.

WHY CAN'T I STOP THINKING ABOUT YOU?
TRACK TWENTY THREE
Heat of the Moment
I'M AFRAID I HAVEN'T A CLUE.

TRACK TWENTY-THREE

HEAT OF THE MOMENT

WE ENTER MY DUNGEON BOUDOIR IN HEAVY SILENCE, EYES never meeting, no pleasantries exchanged. There's so much both of us want to say, so much hanging in the balance—his confession to Silver Fox, my ulterior motives.

But we don't need to share it right now.

Not when we have unfinished business.

There's a hunger inside me growing with every step, with the rising confidence in his powerful stare, the tensing of his lithe muscles. His white shirt hangs loose and untucked from his slacks, suspenders fallen off his shoulders.

I don't need to read him to know there's only one thing on his mind right now: *me*.

The old Jeremy would be agonizing over the consequences of his actions—pacing around my club, panicking, calculating the most convenient escape route back to

Devil knows where—but he isn't. He's here, in my den, body and soul dripping with darkness for me to devour.

But I want to play with my food first.

I turn away to face my vanity, studying my features as I brush my hair, deliberately ignoring him. I avoid his predatory gaze through the mirror as he presses against me, hands gripping my waist before traveling to clutch my hips. He pulls them backward, desperate to feel me against his hardening cock, and for a moment—a tempting moment—I almost oblige. But instead, I pull forward. In a twisted game of tug of war, he grips my hips tighter and slams back against me. There's an ever-so-slight rhythm to the rocking of his hips, like he's testing the waters, trying to find the perfect cadence. One of his hands trails up my spine, sending a rush of goose-bumps over my skin before it finally pulls my thick, wavy locks over one shoulder.

"I can't stop thinking about you," he groans against my ear, teeth grazing the lobe. "Why can't I stop thinking about you?"

"I'm afraid I haven't a clue," I purr and finally spin around to meet him. My fingers trail up the rigid muscles of his abdomen up to his chest to toy with the collar, the demon hunter's dried blood crusting the white cotton. There's something about him like this, the almost effortless, charming dip in his head as it hangs low to stare into my soul. His hand finds the back of my neck, thumb trailing my jawline so tenderly, it takes my breath away.

"You know, handsome, killing someone to protect a gal is the quickest way to her heart. You sweet on me or something?"

He exhales a laugh. "Something like that."

"I didn't think you had it in you." I lean in dangerously close, our lips ghosting over each other in barely-there kisses.

I can see the glow of my amber eyes reflected in his, holding a spark of mischief and a hint of that morally gray line I love to tread. He towers over me, clinging to me like a beast would its meal, and whispers, "Neither did I."

I lick his bottom lip, teasing, tasting the delicious dregs of his arousal seeping from him. I want to taste him again, to inhale every last ounce of his divinity and let it fuel the raw power dormant within me. Now that I've known the pleasure, I need more. More of his lips. More of his body. More of his darkness.

His innocence is a fleeting luxury, like gold dust disappearing on the wind. His aura consumes me, darker than some of the most damned creatures in Hell. It occurs to me I've done it: I corrupted the incorruptible.

Which means our time together is nearing its end.

But before it does, I need one last fill.

The room blurs when he spins me around again and digs his hips into my ass, pinning me against the vanity. There's a forcefulness in him now, a strength he'd never dare unleash before. He presses a hand onto my back, sending my chest down to collide with the cool wooden tabletop. His other hand grips my wrists to pin them behind me and hold me down, and soon, the familiar sound of unzipping pants echoes in the air. I wriggle my ass into him, eager for my own pleasure and friction, eliciting a delicious groan from his chest. He finally lifts the pencil-thin skirt up to my hips and sighs as he marvels at the curves he so desperately craves.

My ears perk as I hear him rustling around the table. In seconds, the rush of cool metal collides with my skin as he slowly, teasingly, drags it from the small of my back, down the crack of my ass, and down to my soaking cunt.

It takes seconds to realize he has my eyeliner dagger in his hand. I mewl at the touch, instantly craving more relief from the heat radiating off us both. The blade never draws blood, never gets close to hurting me, as he twists the hilt to hook it under my fishnet stockings and tears them open in one swift motion.

He hums behind me, all too pleased with himself when he curls a finger inward to pull my torn stockings and thong to the side, teasing my entrance. Every inch of my skin is set ablaze, writing beneath his grasp.

"Now, where did you learn that?" My words come as a raspy, strained purr.

"From watching," he mutters, the blade clattering to the table. He runs his fingers from my clit to my entrance again and dives two fingers into me, releasing my wrists to snake around my neck. I push back into him, craving more out of his touch.

I lift my torso off the vanity, pressing my back against his chest and watching our reflection as his fingers dig into my neck. There's something in his eyes I've never seen before—something that has me wondering if I'm imagining it.

Dozens of black veins spider-web beneath his eyes, seeping into his eyeballs until they turn dark, nearly swallowing the whites. His green eyes are grayer than usual, void of their verdant luster but blown wide with pure lust. The corruption grows as his fingers thrust in and out of me with quickened vigor, and I can't get enough.

"Come for me, Reagan." His voice is as deep and raw as sin, eyes never leaving mine. "Come for me, and I'll fuck you."

His command would be encouragement for any other woman, but to me, they're a challenge. After all, *I'm* the demon here, and *I'm* going to fuck *him*.

"Is that so?" I tease, finally mustering the strength to shrug him off me. Channeling my inner succubus, I press my hands against his chest, sending him back first onto my king-sized mattress, and unlock my true demonic form.

My wings sprout from my back, unfurling in primal glory as my golden veins pulse with raw power. His eyes rake over me hungrily, still dark and demented—his corruption made manifest. I tear the last bits of my clothing off me with my claws, keeping my thigh-high boots on when I straddle the Nephilim and wrap my own hand around his neck.

"Don't forget who taught you what true pleasure is," I growl as I use my other hand to free his rigid cock from his slacks. He hisses, eyes shutting tightly as I fully sheath him inside me.

I ride him slowly at first, rolling my hips to a tormentingly languid pace, my clit rubbing against the silver-gray hairs twisting down his lower abdomen. His hands find my hips, guiding my movements faster and harder.

I bend over to capture his lips, drawing his essence into me, feeding on the raw sexual energy he so willingly offers. Instead of my feeding depleting him, he's invigorated; with a strangled growl, he flips me onto my stomach and settles behind me. I watch in the vanity mirror as he drives himself forward, pushing into my waiting cunt, lifting my ass high for maximum entry.

His thrusts are sloppy at first, out of tempo with his heaving chest. I can taste his end nearing; it builds tightly against me while we fight for dominance, fight for the first orgasm, fight for the win.

"Is that the best you got, angel?" I twist my head to look at him, controlling the rhythm of our dance, circling my hips as I fuck him back hard. The sound of slapping skin, ragged breaths, and uncontrollable moans fills the air, along with the thick, almost suffocating weight of our shared lust.

"I'd do anything for you, Reagan," he moans as his

thrusts grow faster, harder. "Anything. My soul is yours."

That's when things take an unexpected turn.

I see it happen through the mirror, a climax so strong, the Nephilim screams in absolute agony. I pull off him with lightning speed; I remember what happened to me the last time he came—there's no telling what could happen now.

He crashes onto his back, that strained, animalistic growl rumbling deeper from his chest. His eyes are pure black now—not demon black, no, something *far* worse— and ice-cold dread slams up my spine like one of his holy blades.

Jeremy stares at me with those agonized eyes, chest heaving as something spherical writhes beneath his skin, traveling from his abdomen to his chest like a creature trying to claw its way out. He clutches his sternum and doubles over, shimmering scarlet blood erupting from his mouth in ruby droplets across my black sheets.

"Jeremy..." My voice breaks.

"Reagan." He chokes on the word, blood speckling his lips. "Get...Vincent."

DESTINY IS A FASCINATING CONCEPT, ISN'T IT?
TRACK TWENTY FOUR
Holy Diver

TRACK TWENTY-FOUR

HOLY DIVER

I scream for Vincent Thane, the only creature close enough to hear me, the only one who will know what to do—how to fix this. He appears in my dungeon boudoir within seconds, but his expression remains eerily calm.

"I don't know what's happening," I shout, adjusting Jeremy's clothing to preserve his dignity.

"Let's get him upstairs," Vincent says, reaching for him. "Help me."

Jeremy is 165 pounds of deadweight, leaning heavily on both of us while groaning in agony. We drag him up the stairs to the main floor, where fluorescent lights flicker overhead, casting an eerie glow that makes the horrifying scene even more unsettling.

Vincent and I carefully lower Jeremy onto the center stage. Frozen, I watch as my Nephilim claws at his skin just like he did the first night we met, when my pheromones sent him into toxic shock. But it doesn't make sense—they haven't affected him this way in weeks. Why now? Why is his body betraying him?

"Reagan, make it stop," Jeremy groans in agony.

"I don't know how," I whisper as icy talons of dread sink deeper into my chest. "Vincent, what's happening to him?"

"The same thing that happened to him the night he came to Bad Decisions. It's the corruption attempting to eat him alive," the older man states almost nonchalantly. "Can't you see his aura? There's barely a trace of gray left. His divinity is desperately fighting to survive and failing. The soul never recovers from killing one of your own. Such a shame about what happened with Reili…"

Something in Silver Fox's cold voice makes my blood freeze.

"He's never mentioned Reili's name to you."

My stomach twists more when a knowing smirk cracks Silver Fox's calm exterior. "Destiny is…a fascinating concept, isn't it? To be born with a blade already placed in your hands, told to wield it in the name of righteousness and good. Imagine being raised to believe that every decision, every action you make, carries divine consequences. Imagine being given books riddled with rules, warned that breaking them means suffering a fate worse than death. Now imagine being so close to fulfilling your life's purpose, you'd do just about *anything* to succeed…even answer a call from an old friend. An old friend you're forbidden to see, all with the hope that it will bring you one step closer."

His lyrical confession is like a knife in my chest, searing hot like one of their blessed blades. "It was you." My words are low enough for only us to hear. "You tipped off the Order. You lead them straight to The Fox Den. *Why?* They excommunicated you!"

Vincent steps closer, invading my personal space as his voice slides to a deep, guttural tone. "Excommunicated or not, you never stop being a Nephilim, Miss Valentine. They can strip away my wings, my title, my divine purpose—but the blood? The soul, no matter how corrupted? That's eternal, and so is that burning need for justice, for vengeance," he says in a dangerous whisper. "The angels bred us into weapons of mass destruction then sent us to fight in a holy war we can never win. We're forever locked in battle—good and evil, light and dark, each side convinced they'll be the victor. But here's the truth they don't want you to see: we're just tipped scales pretending there can be balance. One cannot exist without the other—it never has and it never will. Yet, despite that, by the grace of our *beloved Creator*, we will keep fighting. Keep trying. Even after He's abandoned us all."

He watches as the young Nephilim writhes in agony, clawing at his skin as if to rip it off, sweat streaming from his pores. If Jeremy can hear him, I can't tell. His chest heaves like a revving engine, and something pulls at me —the urge to take his pain away, to make it all stop.

"The Order turned their backs on me, just like they did to Jeremy, all because we dared to show an ounce of weakness. But I'll tell you another secret, Reagan. Even the holiest of souls have darkness within them. They're every bit as twisted as the humans they've sworn to protect. That hypocrisy isn't just their weakness—it's their poison."

"You wanted to teach them a lesson. You *wanted* Jeremy to kill them."

Vincent chuckles, glancing down at Jeremy with pity. "I hoped that would be the case, yes. I knew he'd tear through Heaven and Hell to protect you. The poor boy loves you, for Christ's sake, in his own broken, desperate way."

"He doesn't love me. He can't. I've done nothing but manipulate him, use him for my twisted agenda. I'm a *demon*, Vincent. I'm not capable of love—or being loved."

"No? Then what do you call a demon who showed mercy to a broken angel when his own kindred abandoned him?"

"It was all calculated," I insist, though my voice wavers. "Every touch, every kiss, every moment—it was just part of the game. When Cherry gets his hands on him, Jeremy will see me for what I am."

Vincent's eyes still. "You will not be handing him over to Cherry, Reagan. Not like this."

His words are heavy with implication and laced with threat. No matter what sordid reality Vincent lives in, Jeremy is *mine*. Mine to betray. Mine to deliver. But in this torturous state, on the precipice of life, death, or eternal damnation, the old man is right.

I couldn't deliver him to Cherry like this.

I climb onto the stage and crawl to the Nephilim. He heaves again, coughing up shimmering, scarlet blood.

"Jeremy," I call to him. He lifts his head to meet my gaze, pure agony etched across his features as dark veins surface beneath his skin, his tanned complexion drained to a sickly pale. I cradle his head in my hands.

He clings to me like cellophane, unbearably close, fingers tangling in my crimson locks. Every touch sends the power trip straight to my head.

"Heal me." His voice trembles over my skin, the soft breath of every syllable caressing me like the touch of a lover. "Reagan, *please.*"

Reagan, please.

There's power in a name, even if it isn't my true one. It's…intimate. The words, every syllable, every choked-out plea. He needs me. He needs *me.*

I look to Vincent once more.

His nod is all the permission I need.

I cradle Jeremy's head in my hands again, forcing him to meet my gaze. I whisper words of encouragement—soothing lies that it'll all be okay, that the pain will end soon, but I have no idea if it will. I don't even know if what I'm about to do will save him or kill him. All I know is that I have to try.

Because if he survives this…I will finally win.

With a deep breath, I channel every ounce of demonic magic within me, the strongest dose of euphoria I can muster from deep within my infernal core. It flows from my body through the cracked veins in my skin, a glowing gold mist Jeremy absorbs. My claws circle the tense muscles in his back, soothing him through his tears.

The words slip from me without realizing, spoken in a radioactive, distorted voice, in a language I know well but seldom use.

"Turn."

Within seconds, his shaking stops. His labored breathing slows to the gentle rise and fall of his chest. For one precious moment, I have my Nephilim back.

But the moment vanishes faster than I can blink.

There's a wild card in this infernal game I foolishly overlooked, one that strikes when you think you're safe, a vicious reminder that Hell never plays fair.

Some call it the plot twist.

I like to call it *'the reckoning.'*

It all happens in a blur yet somehow in slow motion. No sound effects, no script, like a perfect Hollywood picture crafted by the latest award-winning director.

I'm hurled across the stage with primal force, my skull cracking against a metal dance pole. The world around me begins to collapse—light bulbs exploding in erratic flashes, rock posters peeling away and crumbling to ash, the ground trembling beneath us. Jeremy's inhuman shriek sends fractures racing through the wooden stage, as if Hell itself has torn open to claim him.

Instead, deadly skeletal hands reach upward through smoky tendrils.

The scene unlocks a memory I've buried for decades.

His skin and hair bleach stark white. Something beneath his flesh pulses like captured sunlight, spreading through hundreds of veins before splitting his skin apart to reveal blinding radiance. He claws at his back, screaming as his bones contort with squelching pops and wet snaps. Two bone-like horns erupt from his skull, twisting and ribbed like spinal columns. Finally, a pair of white feathered wings burst from his shoulders...

Only for every feather to fall away, revealing pristine bone.

The scene is straight out of one of Indy's favorite horror films, enough to force the bile into my throat, enough for me to question every move, every bad decision I've ever made.

But I can't look away.

"Vincent." His name escapes as something between a whisper and a cry. My chest tightens as I stumble backward, ankles weak and knees wobbling. I stare at my claws dripping with glittering scarlet, fearful of what will happen once it seeps into my skin. But the scarlet transforms to black before my eyes, sparkling like diamonds. "What did you just make me do?"

Vincent's voice caresses me like a deceitful lover. "What was necessary."

Jeremy's transformation continues, and, hidden in the moment of horror and consequence, a revelation hits me like a brick to the face.

"You manipulated this whole thing. From the day

Cherry won that poker game and dropped you on my doorstep, you knew this was coming. You saw an opportunity and took it. You *wanted* Jeremy to become a demon."

Silver Fox smiles down at me. "You forget, Miss Valentine—I've spent 35 years under the thrall of the three worst Primes. Greed made me insatiable. Debauchery unleashed my darkest impulses. And Deception taught me how to pull all the right strings. I couldn't sit and watch another Nephilim fall victim to one of their games. My life's at its end. His doesn't have to be."

"His life *is* over, Vincent!" I sob. "How is this better? How is *any of this* better?"

He crosses the space as he speaks, confidently striding past Jeremy's writhing body. "Because they need a corrupted Nephilim to stay on this plane. I asked you weeks ago why you think Cherry asked you to watch over me, why he planted the seed in your head to corrupt Jeremy. You never answered, so I will ask you once more." He bends at the knees, squatting in front of me, his face mere inches away. "Why did Cherry make you play the game?"

It was all connected.

Fucking Hell, it was *all* connected. The black tourmaline necklace. The poker game. *Everything.*

"He needed a new demon hunter to stay on the human plane. You're no spring chicken. They just use you for a little hit. You're not the full meal anymore."

The Silver Fox flashes me one final, gentle smile. "Turning Jeremy into a demon is the best thing we could do for him. It saves him from himself, from wasting away while these monsters continue to thrive, from becoming a sick, pathetic creature like me."

In that moment, the chaos stops. The lights cease their frantic flickering and the ground stills beneath us. Everything returns to as it was—except for one devastating development.

Jeremy Roache lies before us, a divine creature with a bloodline thick enough to trace back to God's first angels. He cowers, clawed fingers raking through white hair, clutching the monstrous, spiraling white horns that now jut from his skull.

Heaven and Hell fused into one being. Angel. Demon. Beautiful. Terrifying.

And absolutely enraged.

TRACK TWENTY FIVE
Cold as Ice

TRACK TWENTY-FIVE

COLD AS ICE

Jeremy Roache is a demon. Jeremy Roache *is a fucking* *demon.*

The entire scene plays through my head like a broken record, skipping and scratching until it's burned into my brain. It triggers a memory buried deep in my psyche—one that's now just a distant whisper among the voices I constantly sift through. I see in him what I imagine Valentina saw in me the day I turned: a cowering, monstrous creature hungry for vengeance and thirsting for blood.

But this creature isn't just any demon. He's something new, mixed with the blood of an angel. The very first of his kind.

This wasn't part of the plan. It was *never* part of the plan.

Through all my years of calculated precision and deductive reasoning, even I couldn't have anticipated this. Vincent's influence had been there all along, hidden in plain sight. It was woven into his Shakespearean prose, into that reserved-yet-aristocratic flair masking his true deception. He truly was a product of the Golden Trio who'd clung to him like parasites—a debauched, greedy deceiver, a masterpiece of corruption.

Was it worth it, I wonder? Would his holy crusade against those he'd willingly surrendered to finally grant him the outcome he so desperately craved? Would denying the Primes their conduit truly destroy their plans?

It seems that despite the corruption, despite the darkness that devoured him as easily as it devoured Jeremy, and despite his Order's rejection, a Nephilim's work is never truly finished.

Vincent Thane sought to destroy his demons from within, driven by nothing more than the need for absolution from his own damned choices.

And he succeeded. Without even lifting a finger, he became more demon than the broken creature trembling before us.

"Reagan." A pained, dissonant voice shatters our silence. My name falls from his lips like a heartbreaking plea, just as it had hours before—begging for salvation, yearning for deliverance—but this voice is unrecognizable now, hollow and echoing like demons in their truest form. I know what he's feeling; it's the same barrage of emotions that hit me the moment I opened my eyes after my own transformation all those years ago.

"Reagan, what have you done to me?"

What have you done to me?

It's the first question a Turned asks when their transformation is complete, in that brief limbo of confusion and disarray right before reality sets in.

I can't find the words; not even *I* know what I've done. There's never been a demon-Nephilim before, and there's probably a good reason for that. Whether the transformation kills them or their power is so unfathomable, they're executed before they can truly exist, I don't know. I simply don't know.

What I do know is that this is it. This is the moment I've been waiting for since 1912, when I was made a fool of in Savannah.

I finally have the upper hand.

Jeremy cowers at my feet like a newborn fawn clinging to its mother. His glowing white eyes—so similar yet impossibly different from mine—bore into me with such desperation, it brings me to my knees. I take his face, his beautifully cracked, luminous face, into my hands and brush the damp silver hair from his forehead.

There's beauty within the macabre, Valentina once said to me, and I made little effort to understand them. But here and now, with a creature of my own unintentional design, the sentiment weighs heavier than ever. Jeremy *is* beautiful. My thumb runs gently over a crack that splits his brow, traveling down his left eye and cheek—the same way he'd trace his fingers over my own. The gesture, though intimate, causes him to jolt back, baring his razor-sharp teeth. He looks menacing; I'm certain he'd tear my limbs from my body if given the chance. When I scramble to my feet and back away, my spider-webbed wings spreading in defense, he recoils.

Then, glistening tears begin to fall from his eyes, following the cracks that map his beautiful, broken face.

"You're afraid of me, aren't you?" he whimpers.

I flash him a small, pitiful smile. "No, I'm not. What I *am* afraid of is that I might actually prefer you this way."

The words tear from my throat, raw, unfiltered, and without second thought. Not calculated. Not strategized. Just the pure, bleeding truth. Whether I believe them becomes irrelevant as my tempest of conflicting emotions spirals beyond control. I'm quickly reminded of my deal, of harsh truths revealed by Vincent, of the convenient circumstances that lead to Cherry's treachery.

And in this moment—this pivotal turn of events so masterfully orchestrated against my better judgment—I find myself faced with an impossible question: what do I do now?

Cherry's deal is null and void; he saw to that when he went against his word and offered me a fraction of what I demanded. He twisted the contract, as most demons do, and I was a fool to miss the fine print. It's clear he never intended to grant me a true spot at the top. I'd be pacified with false acceptance, Valentina's empire would continue to flourish, and Cherry would gain a new plaything to feed off to his heart's content.

But none of that matters now, not with Jeremy's damned soul caught between Heaven and Hell.

I fight the smile threatening to break across my face. I *do* have the upper hand now. The answer to my impossible question becomes crystal clear.

I carry on as if nothing has changed.

I allow Cherry to believe he's won.

And I deliver Jeremy to the Demon of Debauchery.

YOU CAN'T PROTECT US FOREVER, REAGAN.
THEN I'LL DIE TRYING.
DARLING! YOU RANG?
TRACK TWENTY SIX
I Hate Myself for Loving You

TRACK TWENTY-SIX

I HATE MYSELF
FOR LOVING YOU

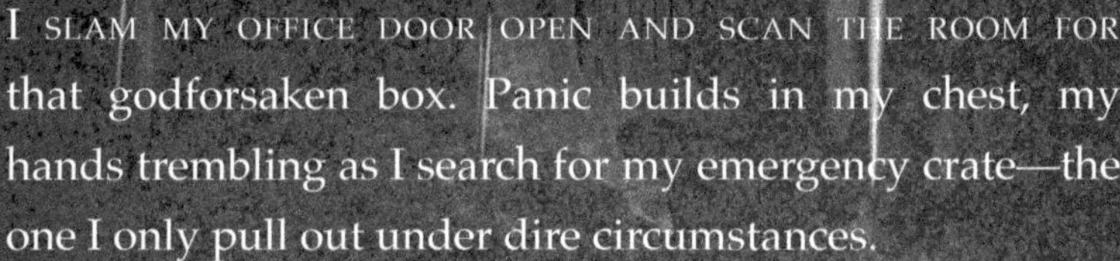

I slam my office door open and scan the room for that godforsaken box. Panic builds in my chest, my hands trembling as I search for my emergency crate—the one I only pull out under dire circumstances.

Where did I leave the damn thing? There are only so many places it could be in a room this small.

Beyond these walls, Jeremy lies where I left him: in a pool of his own blood and shredded angel feathers. The scene is straight out of a nightmare—not an atypical occurrence these days in my poor, unfortunate club—and I can't help but wonder if it's the last mess I'll ever have to clean up. Once Cherry's here, once I've delivered Jeremy to him, it'll all be over. I'll never have to touch a single mop or broom again, never have to take late-night trips to the hardware store to stock up on tarps or bleach. The days of running this club and motel will soon be behind me.

But I'll never get there without the fucking box.

My search is interrupted when a voice invades my head.

Reagan. What the fuck did you do?

It's Charlie. His rich, slightly-raspy baritone echoes loud and clear in my mind. My head shoots up toward the door where my trusted ally stands, mouth agape as he takes in the sight of my bloody, disheveled state.

Char, I'm going to need you to take Indy and get out of here. Now. Head to the Valley, drive up north—I don't care. Just get the fuck out of Hollywood.

He shakes his head furiously. *I'm not leaving you alone with whatever the fuck is in there.*

He's my problem. I can handle it.

Charlie's mouth hardens into a stubborn line. *What are you going to do?*

Don't worry about it. Just get yourselves out. Keep your cell on you. I'll contact you when it's safe.

The demon twists his neck with gritted teeth to look back at the wreckage. *You can't protect us forever, Reagan.*

Then I'll die trying. Now—out. No one can know about Jeremy, not until I'm through with Cherry. You never saw us tonight.

Charlie's broad shoulders slump in a way I'd never expect, dejected and helpless, like a man—a demon— finally at his wits' end. I try not to notice how he unclenches his jaw, swallows hard, and nods in a way that's almost heartbreaking. I turn away because I can't bear to watch him go, to utter what might be our last goodbye…

Because, truth be told, it very well might be. Not even I know how all this is going to go.

I've dedicated my entire demonhood to ensuring the safety of those under my employment. They're the closest thing to family I've ever had, and now, with my fate hanging in the balance, with that monstrous creature cowering on the dance floor, their safety has never been more important. All at once, the dream I had of thriving in Beverly Hills with the little family I've curated turns to ash in my hands. I have to let them go. I have to give them their best chance.

I look at Charlie one last time and flash him a smile, one of those rare, knowing smiles. It's one that says, "Thank you for everything."

And it takes every ounce of self-control to hold back tears as he mirrors the gesture.

I shoot him one more little message before he disappears. *Wait—Char. Where's the goddamn summoning boombox and mixtape?*

He shakes his head with an incredulous smile, and for the first time in what feels like ages, he opens his mouth to speak.

"Where you always leave it, boss. In your dungeon."

Thud. Vincent and Jeremy's heads snap toward me as I drop the emergency crate beside the main stage. Clapping my hands, I dust off the filth and release a sigh. The old box groans under the weight of its contents—handcuffs, silk rope, leather restraints, and every other accessory my girls need to keep their clients satisfied. A crude cherry drawn in black marker adorns one side, faded but still recognizable. Some traditions never die.

I nod toward Vincent. "Hey, Silver Fox—make yourself useful and grab one of those protection potions Charlie snagged off Jeremy the night he came to us."

"W-what?" Jeremy's voice cracks with panic.

Vincent moves without question, and I use his distraction to dig through the crate. My fingers find what I'm looking for beneath the usual collection of silk and leather—a cherry-red boombox that's far more than it appears. The demonic relic hums with dormant power, exactly what I need for the next phase of this diabolical scheme.

"Wait, what are you—" Jeremy attempts to scramble to his feet, but I'm faster. In one fluid motion, I guide his hands behind the nearest dancer pole and secure them with furry handcuffs, adding rope for good measure. He strains against me, those gigantic white and black wings beating frantically, his voice trembling with fear.

"What are you doing? Stop—Reagan, stop!"

"Hush up, Sparky." I tighten the rope around his wrists. "It's for your own good."

"You're going to kill me, aren't you? You should kill me—I can't live like this. I-I can't be a monster."

"Jeremy." I speak his name in warning, but my voice carries a haunting echo that seems to shake the walls. His struggles come to a screeching halt, and his head whips around to face mine with wide, terrified eyes.

That's when I remember the one fatal flaw in our demonic makeup, the weakness not even the Primes can escape. It's why we all choose new names, why most of us pick aliases both outrageous and unrealistic, the reason I chose Reagan Valentine over the pitiful name John and Margaret Blythe assigned to me at birth.

Knowing a demon's true name grants power over them.

"Jeremy," I repeat again. "I'm going to need you to stay put. Like I said, this is for your own good—just until we can figure out more about what's happened to you."

"Isn't it obvious?" His voice drips with venom as he grunts against the pole. "You made me into a fucking demon."

I suck in my bottom lip, fangs grazing the supple skin as his words cut deep. "I didn't mean to."

"But you did. And I don't want to live like this. Just get Vincent to stab me in the heart with my blade—"

"This what you're looking for, Miss Reagan?" Vincent appears at my shoulder, protection potion in hand.

I nod. "I can't touch it. I need you to pour it on the rope and cuffs."

Vincent obeys without hesitation. The moment the

holy liquid hits Jeremy's restraints, his composure shatters. He writhes against the pole as the potion sears his skin, glowing veins of magic spreading until his struggles slow then stop entirely.

"Vincent," Jeremy mutters, his voice breaking on the name. "I trusted you...with *everything*. How could you..."

Silver Fox's shoulders tense, and he can't even bear to meet Jeremy's burning stare. When he finally speaks, his voice is barely above a whisper. "Better get a move on, Reagan. You've got a Prime to summon."

The room grows heavy with shared conviction. Vincent carries a decades-old vendetta against the Primes who enslaved him at the expense of an innocent man cursed to walk the same path. As for me? My reasons span an entire century, and it is time to earn what I rightfully deserve.

"Reagan." Jeremy's voice drops to a whisper—one last desperate plea. "Reagan, I need you."

My eyes slam shut as I fight the tears threatening to spill. *Don't fall for it. Don't let him break you now.*

"I can feel you fighting this, Reagan. Whatever the Primes are making you do—"

I swallow the lump in my throat and force myself to dig through the crate, searching for the mixtapes feeding the demonic boombox. "That's just Vincent's emotions bleeding through, Sparky. Don't worry—you'll learn to filter them out."

The change is instant. Jeremy's voice hardens to steel.

"I *hate* you, Reagan. I *hate* you for what you've done to me. I *hate* that you made me fall for you."

Each word lands like a physical blow, cutting deeper than any blessed weapon ever could. But I can't let them shatter me, not when I have a deal to honor.

Scanning my fingers through the wooden crate for the infernal mixtape, I finally come across the one I need —the barely-touched, dust-collected clear plastic case labeled 'Cherry Bomb' in gaudy red glitter pen.

Only a creature as narcissistic and egomaniacal as the Demon of Debauchery would force his own Underlings to jump through hoops just to summon him. Where boomboxes and mixtapes were declarations of love to most mortals, this was Cherry's twisted way of inconveniencing those who faithfully served him. The ritual, while terribly unnecessary, was as theatrical as him. Insert the tape, skip to track six, then manually force the cassette to play backwards until it finally summons him —usually in a huff of red smoke with all his bombastic glory.

It was only fitting that he'd make us work for his attention. Figures.

With arms folded over my chest, I stand before the red boombox and listen as the backward track slows to a low, guttural melody laced with otherworldly static. The box begins to tremble, its milky-green screen flashing erratically like something possessed. The analog numbers jump frantically—3:33 to 6:66 to 0:00—until they transform into a completely different alphabet alto-gether, one I recognize as Hellspeak.

The entire boombox pulses a glowing red, living up to the namesake of the mixtape itself: a perfect cherry bomb primed to detonate. Tendrils of crimson vapor pour from the miniature speakers, pooling across the dance floor like some ethereal fog machine. The back-ward melody reaches its crescendo, and then—

Silence.

Deafening silence.

Followed by a dramatic explosion of red smoke as the Demon of Debauchery materializes center stage, spin-ning gracefully with arms outstretched, like he's accepting applause from an invisible audience.

"Darling! You rang?"

TRACK TWENTY SEVEN
Back in Black

TRACK TWENTY-SEVEN

BACK IN BLACK

The Demon of Debauchery drops from the stage to the blood-soaked carpet with fluid grace. "Whatever this is about, Reagan, I'm going to need you to make it quick. I've got a nine o'clock I simply can't miss." His head tilts in wonder as he scans the empty club, taking in the carnage of angelic proportions. "Saggy tits on a sacrificial lamb, this place is a bloody mess. What the fuck happened?"

My wings flex against my shoulder blades as I flash Cherry a razor-sharp smile. "Just making good on our little game. I'd like to introduce you to someone special." I step aside with theatrical flair, mirroring the verve my sire so often exudes, and fold my wings back to reveal the world's first-and-only Nephilim-demon hybrid. "You remember Jeremy, don't you?"

Cherry's practiced charm evaporates instantly. Worry lines carve themselves into his ageless features as his red-tinted glasses slide down his nose. Those ancient, demonic eyes widen as they take in what Jeremy has become.

"Reagan..." His voice drops to a horrified whisper. "Darling girl, what have you done?"

I can't keep the satisfaction from my voice. "Exactly what you asked: I corrupted a Nephilim in ways no demon has ever dared."

Cherry begins to circle, his movements gaining confidence with each step. His demonic eyes trace the impossible sight before him: a being whose existence defies every law between Heaven and Hell.

Wonder replaces the terror on his perfect features, lips curving into a smile that promises nothing good. "Extraordinary. Absolutely extraordinary." I glance down at Jeremy while Cherry circles him, pushing away the echo of hateful words that still cut deep.

"He is, isn't he? And completely worthless to you now."

Cherry's smile dies. "I beg your finest pardon?"

The words pour out with decades of suppressed frustration. "I know exactly why you wanted him, why you and Greed and Deception pass Vincent Thane around like some sort of sacred blunt. It has nothing to do with demonic pissing contests and everything to do with cold, hard survival. A Nephilim's life force is the only thing keeping you tethered to this plane, and Vincent's expiration date is on the horizon. He's damaged goods on borrowed time. That's why you sent me on this wild goose chase: to secure you a fresh supply all to yourself. It was never about fun and games, never about those empty promises of the promotion I've been chasing for decades. This was always just another way for you to get ahead without lifting a finger."

I expect to see the fear return to his eyes, to watch him fold like a house of cards. But instead, Cherry lifts his hands in mock surrender, a playful smirk tugging at his lips. "Fine, you caught me—you figured out my deep, dark secret. The Nephilim are conduits for the Primes, and frankly, the lot of us have grown bored of sending our Underlings to do our dirty work on the human plane while we collect dust in our respective realms. Some of us want to get our own hands dirty for a change. So what if a few human-angel bastards are all it takes to keep us topside? Did you really think robbing me of one would stop me from finding another?"

"I don't doubt it would complicate your plans, but there's more at stake here." I keep my voice level, calculating. "You've told me about your turf wars, how crucial it is to protect your assets. I understand power struggles —your Sired made sure of that. But forget planes and conduits for a moment. Consider the ultimate prize: the first demon-angel hybrid ever created. That's the kind of leverage that rewires the entire demonic hierarchy."

My master mulls over my words, sauntering languidly through the expanse of my club, twirling his bejeweled cane and nodding thoughtfully. He pauses to study Jeremy's bound form, marveling at the bone protrusions twisting from his skull into ungodly horns.

"I have to say, I'm quite proud of you, darling. This little quest seems to have helped you embrace those darker impulses you've always been so reluctant to grasp."

"I can't take all the credit." My eyes flash toward the bar, toward Vincent lurking in his shadows. "But I have one final request before I hand the Nephilim over for good."

"Always a catch." Cherry punctuates his words by jabbing his cane at Jeremy's withered wings, who recoils and snarls at the Prime. *Our* Prime…

Before he can strike again, I take one fluid step, putting myself between Cherry and my progeny. My wings unfurl in a protective arch as my tail whips out, batting his cane aside with enough force to send vibrations up his arm.

"I want what I'm owed, and you're going to do everything in your power to grant it to me."

He waves his hand dismissively with a roll of his eyes. "I already told you, The Fox Den will be 50% yours once the rebuild is done—"

"This goes way past Beverly Hills, Cherry. I'm aiming higher." I take a final, sharp breath and release the tension building in my shoulders. With my head held high and resolve held higher, I name my price. "You're going to make me a Prime."

Silence falls between the three of us. Jeremy's heavy

breath catches in his chest, and his head turns in reptilian fashion, eyes narrowing as he stares at me. His thoughts —once loud and clear in my head—are nothing but static now. Erratic. Incoherent. Just like his aura the night I met him. The weight of my betrayal tugs at his features, brows knotting and jaw clenched as a slew of curses repeats within the static of his mind. I force myself to look away, maintaining the façade of confidence I've grown so accustomed to, and stare straight into the shaded eyes of my master.

I expect him to shoot me down as he always does, to burst into a rhapsody of insult and anger, flailing his arms and cane around before kicking both Jeremy and me to the curb. But if there's anything I've learned about the Demon of Debauchery over the last hundred years I've spent by his side, it's to always expect the unexpected.

That said, I didn't expect this.

Laughter claps throughout the club like thunder. Cherry's cackle snakes up my spine like ice water. Pure elation transforms his face, bringing him to the edge of tears. He collapses into one of the stained velvet booths, slaps his knee, and even removes his red-tinted sunglasses to wipe at his eyes. My irritation no longer simmers—it boils, erupts, and shatters the cage of manners and submission that has imprisoned me since childhood.

But before I can take a step forward and assert my dominance, he finally speaks.

"You want me to make you a Prime?" A wheezing laugh hisses through his teeth.

I shift my weight from one leg to the other—a small betrayal of my wavering resolve—but keep my chin lifted in defiance. "Yes."

"You're not very well-versed in demonology, are you, darling?" He slaps his sunglasses on, prowling around Jeremy again like a predator scenting blood. "Why don't we ask your little monster here—after all, he's devoted his pathetic existence to studying our kind. Probably knows our history better than we do ourselves." Cherry stops directly in front of the Nephilim, seizing his chin between thumb and forefinger with deliberate cruelty. "Tell me, love, how did the Thirteen Prime Evils come to be?"

Jeremy's growl is as monstrous as his appearance, and he leans forward, as if to chomp at Cherry's silver-ringed fingers. Cherry jolts back in another fit of giggles, patronizing Jeremy with a wagging finger and condescending coos.

"Come on, now, Je—rem—y." Cherry drags out every syllable until it's painstakingly deliberate on his lips. "Give us a little history lesson."

His growling ceases, but anger, loathing, and confusion still pour off him in waves. He rises from his hunched position, craning his neck to watch us both with predatory precision. From the corner of my eye, I catch Vincent Thane stepping out from the shadows. I wonder if he's proud of his handiwork, of the role he played in this twisted game that was never his to orchestrate. He gives Jeremy a subtle nod, as if granting permission to reveal secrets known only to the Nephilim and their Order. And so, the younger one recites the passage as though it's been engraved in his mind since birth, never missing a beat, despite the saliva pooling in his mouth, the heaving of his chest, the demonic rasp that has replaced his once sweet, angelic voice.

"'And it came to pass that when Lucifer was cast down from the Heavens, his soul shattered into thirteen pieces. And in his great wrath against the Judgment of The Creator, he did take unto himself the fragments of his soul and forged them into thirteen Prime Evils; sons born of his very essence, that they might hold dominion over the Children of God and corrupt all that is Good and Pure, and sow Chaos and Disorder throughout the Earth, and seek evermore vengeance against The Creator.

And lo, when Lucifer Morningstar had raised up this Legion of Evil, the Heavenly Father looked down upon the Earth and sent forth His most Holy Ones, that they might establish their own host—an Army of the Nephilim—to stand against the Darkness.'"

The words flow like biblical verses from archaic texts lost to humanity, revealing secrets of a world so vast and brimming with insurmountable power, it could bend the very fabric of reality. It's a world humans could never comprehend, yet one they live alongside daily, carefully hidden and protected by those of us who dwell in the shadows. It's the one thing Heaven and Hell have always agreed upon: keep the humans ignorant. Keep our worlds separate.

Cherry breaks the silence with another one of those spine-curling laughs, followed by applause. "Bravo, bravo. An excellent performance. Of course, Daddy tells the story a little differently, but the gist is there. You see, Reagan," —his attention flits to me again—"there can't be *two* Debauchery Primes. I simply can't wave my wand and make you one. Such matters transcend my humble station, you see."

"Then I suggest we take a little trip Downstairs and demand it of him. Ask him to make me a Prime. Your partner. Your equal. Take the Nephilim with us, show him what I've done, and *demand it.*"

There's forceful dominance in my tone, not unlike the kind I've used on my victims over the years. But instead of bringing a man to his knees as a dominant, degrading him and forcing him to do as I say under the tantalizing glow of filtered red light, I stand as an equal, one who accomplished what others never dreamed of.

"Even if it were that easy, why should I? I gave you a job to do, and you failed. Why should I reward you for your insolence?"

A sardonic laugh escapes me. "Insolence? Is that what you call this? I did exactly what you asked. Hell, I've done what no other demon could ever do. I found the purest soul, turned it black, tore it to shreds, and rebuilt it in our vision. Not even you or your brothers could do it. I'd say I'm just as good—if not *better*—than a Prime."

"You're absolutely darling, Reagan. Do you know that? And completely, utterly clueless, just as you were when Valentina and I lured you into our web of darkness all those years ago." Cherry's eyes soften behind his lenses as he tilts his head to study me intently. "Don't you see, love? None of this would have been possible without me, without my influence, without the teensy-weensy little seeds I planted along the way. You forget we Primes inherited one of Daddy's most key abilities: the power of omniscience. All-seeing. All-knowing. All-encompassing. Everywhere. Nowhere. And right under your sweet little nose."

Cherry has the audacity to tap my nose with his fingertip, a gesture so condescending, it makes my skin crawl. Jeremy immediately struggles against his restraints, and a snarl builds in his throat.

Is this what it means to own a lesser demon? To have a creature of my own making spring to my defense at the first sign of threat? A hellhound bound by a loyalty forged through damnation, even if he hates me?

I try to ease his suffering by reaching into his mind as I've done countless times with Charlie, offering solace, attempting to quiet whatever torment plagues him. But his mind resists me, slamming shut like an iron door barred against invasion. How can someone so newly turned possess such control?

My thoughts are interrupted by Cherry, who once more continues to triumph over me with his bravado.

"Why do you think this one was so easy to corrupt,

Reagan? Hm? Surely you didn't think he fell for your pretty smile and wicked tits, or the promise of late nights full of pleasure beyond his wildest dreams? He fell for you because I made it so. Because October Winters just happened to involve herself with the right Nephilim at the right time. It was no accident that she happened upon your little club six days before Halloween. It wasn't a coincidence I showed up at the demon den when she and her little plaything infiltrated it. And it certainly wasn't by chance I came to her with a little deal of my own, to collect the essence of a demon hunter. You wouldn't have been able to find *or* corrupt him without that crystal. In fact, you wouldn't have been able to do it at all if not for our little blonde bombshell tainting his soul to begin with. If anything, you should thank her."

I've fallen for this song and dance more times than I care to count. Fell for it first at eighteen as a starry-eyed debutante who dared to dream of her name in lights. Fell for it again when a dark-haired beauty offered me the world. Fell for it every single time my master wielded his authority like a weapon against me.

I'd been forced to memorize the perfectly choreographed routine of heartbreak and betrayal, courtesy of the Demon of Debauchery himself.

Now, Cherry aims to shatter what's left of my humanity, the very thing he's spent decades tormenting. But I don't flinch. Don't gasp. Don't grant him the satisfaction of watching me crumble under the weight of his revelation. I simply stare at him with the kind of stillness that precedes violence. Primal fury builds behind the quiet, but when my voice comes, it's as cold as ice.

"Some omniscience. Perhaps there's a flaw in the grand design; we both know you never expected me to turn him into a demon."

I'm met with one of his mischievous grins. "A glitch in the matrix, if you will. One I didn't see coming, no, but it works beautifully in my favor." His cane taps against the floor in a slow rhythm. "Though it's just as I told you—*I* can't make you a Prime. Only Daddy holds that power. And getting an audience with him in this climate?" He lets out a theatrical sigh. "Why, that could take ages, darling. If only we knew someone who could expedite the process—someone closer to him, someone he favors far above me and my brothers, someone who has him wrapped around their little finger…"

The screech of tires against asphalt cuts through his words, echoing from beyond the club walls. A car door slams. My ears twitch at the sound, already knowing what comes next.

Seconds later, sunlight floods Bad Decisions as the front entrance flies open, revealing a silhouette I'd recognize anywhere—leather jacket, skin-tight jeans, and thigh-high boots cutting a familiar figure against the daylight.

"Ah, there's my nine o'clock right now!" Cherry exclaims, glancing at his watch with theatrical delight. "Only ten minutes late—that's a record."

"Give me a fucking break, Cherry—you know time

works differently Downstairs." The voice cuts through my stupor like a blade through silk. Cool. Melodic. I've only known it for a few months, experienced it in stolen moments that burned themselves into my memory, but it's already carved into my very soul. The scent that follows—cigarettes and leather and that cheap toner—culminates into something so distinctly *her*.

And when she finally reaches me, the prickling of my nerves dissipates, replaced with warm relief that triggers the smallest of smiles.

"October fucking Winters."

DEMONHOOD SUITS YOU, JIGGORY.
TRACK TWENTY EIGHT
Dead End Justice

TRACK TWENTY-EIGHT
DEAD END JUSTICE

The bombshell Devil's advocate steps into the light looking a little less glorious than the last time I saw her, shaggy blonde locks an inch or two longer, in desperate need of a root touch-up. But she's still got that same devious smirk, the one that reminds me that no matter what mess she gets herself into, she'll emerge from the flames unscathed. There's something missing, though—where's that nifty little earring of hers?

October's thick-heeled boots clunk heavily against the linoleum. Her dark eyebrows raise impossibly high at the sight of Jeremy, whose attention has now turned to her. There's a ravenous look in his glowing white eyes, saliva and shimmering black blood running down his chin as he heaves and snarls at her.

"Well, well, well. If it isn't the little roach himself. Demonhood suits you, Jiggory."

"For the last time, you evil fucking bitch," Jeremy's

growl reverberates along with the flickering lights, "my name is *Jeremy*."

October's gut-wrenching chuckle fills the air. "I wouldn't be announcing that all over town if I were you. Knowing the name of a demon comes with plenty of perks for me, but it absolutely *sucks* for you." Jeremy snarls at the witch, saliva continuing to drip from his lips. "Down, boy."

Oh, how I missed her. October finds the bar, rummages through Charlie's stash of beer, muttering something about avoiding the Demon-Kissed batch, and pops the cap with her teeth. After one deep swig, she surveys my club and sighs.

"Place looks less like shit than the last time I saw it." She hops on the bar top, crossing her legs and lighting a cigarette with a snap of her fingers. "You clean up recently?"

Shaking my head, I shoot her a smirk. "Thought you were done with us after torching the cemetery. What brings you back to our little slice of Hell?"

She takes a drag before continuing. "Came to have a little chitchat with Cherry, but it seems like this science experiment is worth a look-see. How the fuck did you manage…whatever this is?" She gestures at Jeremy, fingers wriggling with indifference.

"Marvelous, isn't it?" Cherry chimes in, leaning in to give October a two-cheeked kiss while muttering pleasantries. "A demon-Nephilim hybrid, first of its kind. And from my Broodline, no less."

"You must be so proud." October's voice flatlines. "I can see it now: 'World's first Dephilim, straight from the infernal loins of the Demon of Debauchery.' Oh, how your brothers will cower at the thought of a super-beast who can fuck them to death—"

Jeremy's deranged voice cracks through the room and cuts the conversation short. "Where's Declan's body? Whatever you did, you had no right. He didn't deserve it!"

October tilts her head with mock admiration as she places a hand over her chest. "Aww, how cute—it has opinions. Looks like you finally grew not just one spine, but two." She gestures at the vertebrae-like horns jutting from his skull.

Something stirs within me as Jeremy continues to snarl like a wild animal, a primal need to soothe him, to pull his metaphorical leash and force him to heel. The entire situation is uncharted territory. I've never sired anyone, and I'm navigating these new instincts as they surface. We're connected on levels that didn't exist before, both privy to each other's thoughts and emotions, bound by something far deeper than mere attraction.

Despite my imposing demonic form—wings spread wide, horns spiraling like an infernal crown—I've never felt more powerless. Fear devours me from within, manifesting in the rigid ache spreading from my shoulders to my spine, the tension locked in my jaw, the way my knuckles flush pink against crimson skin.

I fear losing control.

I fear what Jeremy might become if he breaks free.

And October's harsh judgment of my progeny only feeds the terror flooding my veins.

"How'd you do it, Cherry? How did you even manage to get close to a Nephilim, let alone turn one?" October asks my Prime.

"Oh, darling, I wish I could take credit, but this little science experiment isn't my handiwork. Not all of it, anyway." Cherry slides his sunglasses down his nose and raises his eyebrows at me. October catches on quickly, shock and amusement flickering across her dark-rimmed eyes.

"No fucking way." She chuckles to contain her mirth. "Reagan? *You* did this? How in the actual fuck?"

I step from the shadows into the light, positioning myself both above Jeremy and as his shield. He looks to me like a wounded animal—eyes fearful, hatred still lingering in their depths. Despite the anguish flooding his heart and the weight of my betrayal tearing through his fractured thoughts, something else flickers there: hope. The last remnants of his humanity cling to the belief that I'll protect him, that I'll defy October and Cherry in some final act of redemption.

It's a foolish hope born from an innocent, shattered soul who dared fall in love with a demon.

"Cherry and I made a deal a few weeks ago." I fold my wings, crossing my arms over my chest as I lean against the pole Jeremy's bound to. "Corrupt a demon hunter, earn advancement through the Broodline ranks. Mr. Nephilim here fell into my lap like a gift from the Big Guy himself. I planned to spend months breaking him the way you broke his mentor—one righteous piece at a time—but something was already shattered inside him. And I have you to thank for that, October."

She flicks her pale blonde hair over her shoulder effortlessly. "All in a day's work."

I continue weaving the tale: Jeremy's swift excommunication from the Order, how he came to live under my roof, how he slowly unraveled from something radiant into something lethal. October's expression balances perfectly between amusement and fascination, leaning closer with each revelation as I build toward the final blow: how his overheard confession, his love for me, became his complete undoing.

"You Nephilim are so quick to fall in love," she says with a sadistic grin. "But who could blame you? Succubi are hard to resist."

"You're forgetting the crucial part of this fairytale, darling," Cherry says, spinning his staff between his fingers. "Tell her, Reagan. Tell her what you demanded of me."

My throat tightens as I force down my pride. I shift my weight and mask my unease with a sultry smile. "I demanded Cherry make me a Prime for accomplishing what no other demon ever could. And I need your help to make it happen. I need you to arrange an audience with your master."

October jolts back, eyebrows raised in surprise. The gears turn visibly in her head. Her thoughts, usually difficult but still readable to me, fall completely silent. She's working hard to shield both Cherry and me from whatever she's planning.

"So, what—you want me to call up Lucifer and ask him to make you a Prime? Because you think you deserve it?"

I avoid everyone else in the room and stare directly into the hazel-gold eyes of the Devil's Second. "Yes."

Silence stretches between the four of us as October Winters contemplates my fate.

She could laugh in my face, deny my request, and abandon me to Cherry's wrath. And Cherry...Devil knows how he'll punish my insolence.

I can only hope the impression I've made will be enough to tip the balance in my favor.

Finally, a proud grin splits across October's features. "Now that's what I'm fucking talking about."

An invisible weight lifts from my shoulders, quickly replaced by relief. Cherry interjects faster than lightning, hooking his cane over my shoulder to turn me toward him, his voice low but frantic. "But it's never been done, darling." There's a deceptive, sing-song quality to his words, and I can taste the panic radiating from him.

"Yeah, and it's a damn shame," October cuts in. "I've gotten bored of this sausage fest for the past thousand years. Would be nice to have another hot bitch at the top...or close to it."

That's when the Prime's composure visibly wavers. It starts with him pinching the bridge of his nose then massaging his temples as he begins pacing along the main stage. He mutters obscenities under his breath like a desperate, manic man whose reign is suddenly in jeopardy. And then, he snaps.

"And where would that leave me, hm? You lot can sit around and talk about big, Earth-shattering moves all you want, but you fail to recognize the logistics. Very out of character, Reagan. I would have thought you'd have this all planned out." There's that hint of feigned disappointment in his voice, theatrical as ever.

I move to stand next to my favorite witch, and both of us stare him down with unwavering resolve. "Oh, I've considered the logistics perfectly. There are a few options, starting with you giving up your seat."

"You could just retire to your realm. Take up gardening or knitting or something," October adds with a triumphant, sadistic grin.

"But it's boring down there." He stomps his foot like a petulant child, his voice growing more dramatic by the second. "Hellspawn are no fun. Everyone just does what I ask them to. It's *horrible*."

He's truly lost it, regressing from one of the most dangerous Primes to a sniveling coward making one last desperate plea to save himself. He understands October's hold over his father better than anyone—how, even when she's angered him, the Devil still favors her above his own sons. A few weeks ago, Cherry dangled me before his brothers like prized meat, all because of my connection to the wicked witch. He never suspected his greatest bargaining chip would soon become the key to his demise.

He should have never underestimated the power of a witch and a demon, both scorned by men who believe themselves superior.

"Then there's the second option," I state flatly, studying my nails with calculated nonchalance. "We can work together. As partners."

Cherry's pacing stops. A silver-ringed hand flies to his chest as he gasps audibly. "*Partners*?"

"It wouldn't be the first instance. Lucifer fused Nightmares and Fear into one entity—what's to say he couldn't arrange something special for us?"

"*Us*? Share a *body*? I'm the Demon of fucking Debauchery—sex incarnate, humanity's deepest desires. I'm not about to become some horrific amalgamation just because you're on a power trip, Reagan."

"Don't be ridiculous. My body is the only thing I control in this infernal existence, and I won't surrender it for anything. Not after being traded around for a century by you and your Sired. No, my proposition is simpler." I pause, letting the word hang between us. "Corruption comes naturally to creatures like us, *darling*," I drawl, wielding his pet name like a blade. "But unlike your brothers, your particular brand of sin benefits from partnership. Two to seduce, two to corrupt, and two to destroy. Male, female, and everything in between. The

Devil could grant us equal authority. Just imagine it, Cherry—imagine how much territory we could claim *together*. We could even run your brother out of Vegas and take back what was rightfully yours from the beginning."

For a moment, there's a glimmer, the tiniest twitch in his brow, his grip tightening on the pommel, deafening silence hanging between us like a blade. *I have him*, I think triumphantly. *I fucking have him.*

But then, Cherry's demeanor shifts back to his usual theatrical indifference, all traces of his earlier panic erased.

"You don't want this job, love. It's all sex, drugs, and rock and roll—you'd grow tired of it."

"I wouldn't," October replies with practiced indifference.

I flash her a conspiratorial grin. "Perhaps you and I should be the next Debauchery Primes then."

Cherry's scoff echoes throughout the room, his voice dripping with venom. "Look at you. Two peas in a bloody pod. And to think, your paths would have never crossed all those years ago if not for me."

Something shifts in me then. I look to October, whose expression has darkened. "All those years ago?" I ask.

That's when the shit-eating grin spreads across Cherry's face. "Oh, did I leave out that little detail? Silly me. I thought you knew." He begins to pace again, this time with confidence and a head held high. His cane and heeled shoes tap against the rotting wood dance floor.

"Savannah's lovely in the summertime, isn't it, Toby? Before all this global warming nonsense. And the hurricanes were such an easy place to reap souls, with all the dead bodies lying around, especially during the dawn of a new decade."

The blood drains from my face as my Prime turns to the blonde witch beside me. Her expression remains stiff, collected, so unlike the quick-witted spitfire I know her to be.

Cherry continues his revelation. "Why, it was almost serendipitous that you happened to be in town when one of my Sired and I were attending a funeral. You remember, don't you, Winties? That behemoth of a mansion with Gothic interiors and lovely red accents?"

October's voice drops to something almost sinister. "I've been around for a thousand years and reaped millions of souls. You think I remember every house I've visited or every soul I've collected?"

"Ah, but you remember this one, don't you? Remember the little arrangement we made between reapings?"

My stomach plummets in a sickening free fall, leaving me hollow as the truth crashes over me: my entire demonic existence has been orchestrated by someone I considered a friend.

"That was you?" I ask, my voice cracking. "The woman crying over my husband's casket? You took his soul?"

For the first time since I've known her, October Winters falls completely silent.

Cherry wastes no time twisting the knife deeper. "Right under your nose too. If she hadn't taken his soul, you would have completed our original deal and lived out your days as Tinsel Town royalty. A sparkling actress with fame and fortune beyond your wildest dreams, just like I promised. Instead, you're trapped working at a seedy strip club and motel, bound to me for eternity." His smile grows wicked. "You'd probably be resting peacefully at Hollywood Forever right now rather than existing as my eternal servant. And what a shame that would have been. Mortality is terribly overrated, my love. You got the better end of the deal."

I search for the words to fight back, but nothing comes to mind. I can't process the agony tearing through my chest, gripping my pounding heart and crushing it. The air thickens, suffocating me as the weight of my stolen life drags me deeper into despair.

"Reagan." Jeremy's pained, demonic growl cuts through the silence, and I flinch at the raw anguish in his voice. I look down at my progeny through blurred vision. Tears streak his face too, and I understand why: through our bond, he feels everything I'm feeling. My suffering has become his own.

But it's short-lived.

I watch the shift happen in real time—devastation morphing into pure, unfiltered rage as he remembers that, beneath everything else, he still hates me. I'd hate me too after everything I've put him through.

Jeremy's attention snaps to October, who's already making a quiet beeline for the exit. I should have fucking known. When push comes to shove, the bitch has only ever had her own back.

"October!" he bellows, but the witch ignores him, quickening her pace toward the front door. Jeremy springs to his feet with savage force, hands still bound behind him by the protective potion. A sickening crack of bones fills the air, making me flinch as he begins brutally contorting his arms with an agonized roar. Within seconds, his bound hands are in front of him, dislocated shoulders snapping back into place with sickening pops.

And then, there's a flash of light. Not the holy radiance I've grown used to, but searing, fire-like brilliance that illuminates everything in its path. Hellfire, straight from the depths of the Underworld, but it's more than that. So much more.

Light erupts from Jeremy's feet, fracturing across the dance floor in jagged lines. It races through the carpet beneath the leather booths, spreads across the linoleum around the bar, and finally reaches the exit. It cracks into the steel door, nearly melting the handle as October reaches for it.

"Fuck!" She jerks her hand back, shaking it. Fire could never hurt a pyromancer; but Hellfire infused with Holy Light is an entirely different beast.

"What the fuck did you do with Declan's body?" Jeremy growls.

October takes a deep breath, her jaw clenching so hard, I worry it'll fuse shut. Those deadly golden eyes flit to the monstrous Nephilim still tied to the dancer's pole and darken with renewed fervor.

October Winters doesn't do confessions. She isn't the type of villain who reveals her schemes in theatrical monologues, complete with maniacal laughter as flames consume her victims. No, she's far too indifferent for such dramatics. The world is her playground, and she answers to no one except her master—certainly not a Nephilim.

She's impulsive, ruthless, and utterly selfish. A woman who delights in watching her enemies writhe beneath her heel.

And that's exactly what she intends to do now.

"It's killing you, isn't it, Jimbo?" Her voice drops to something eerily calm. "Not knowing what I did, where his body ended up? I bet you're dying to know every gory detail—how he begged for his life, how he screamed my name. I know you'd just *love* to wrap those grubby little hands around my throat and torture it all out of me."

"October, don't," I warn, watching Jeremy's fury build as the light beneath his cracked veins pulses like molten lava.

The witch ignores me, sauntering closer to the stage. "You know what the best part is? I'll never tell you any of it. You'll spend an eternity wondering where it all went wrong, what you could have done differently. Why poor Declan Lovejoy's legacy was crushed before it could begin. And here's what's truly delicious: you'll never see him again. Not in Heaven, that's for sure. Because that's not where I sent his soul, and that's certainly not where yours is headed."

The Nephilim's chest heaves with something beyond rage, lightyears past frustration. He yanks against the iron pole, shrieking as electric jolts course through him. October stands only feet away now, tilting her head at the monster he's become.

That's when Jeremy gets a clear view of her. His eyes search frantically—neck, ear, finally settling on her face. I slip into his mind for a moment, and my body turns rigid as I sense his realization.

He knows.

He knows what she did.

And I'm beginning to piece it together too.

Through gritted teeth, he snarls, "Where's. Your. Familiar?"

She brings one delicate hand to her cheek, resting her elbow on her other arm, batting her lashes with a smile both playful and deadly. Only then do I notice the obsidian scorpion ring adorning her left ring finger.

"Let's just say I traded my earring in for something more... *symbolic*."

A sonic boom reverberates through Bad Decisions as Jeremy's fury reaches its breaking point. His bonds explode into fragments, freeing his hands as twin blasts of Holy Hellfire erupt from his palms and slam into the club's walls. Within moments, the entire space is engulfed in flames.

Cherry tumbles off the stage onto the floor, his black tourmaline-crested cane rolling to the opposite side of the room. October is blasted against the wall, flames searing her skin as the wallpaper begins to curl and disintegrate. The shockwave hurls me from the stage into the bar, where my head collides with the wood.

Everything becomes hazy, an obscure medley of shapes and colors as my sanctuary transforms into a hellish battlefield.

The flames devour my withered dance floor and reduce my leather seats to ash. The acrid mixture of burning wood, metal, and fabric claws at my lungs, choking me with toxic fumes that make every breath a struggle.

At my feet lies Cherry's staff. I reach for it, channeling the Nephilim essence trapped within the crystal pommel to heal my wounds and grant me strength to stand. Vincent's essence illuminates the crystal with amber light as I draw it into my palm and devour it through my cracked veins. Within seconds, my vision clears, and my wings surge with renewed power.

I race over to Jeremy, whose demonic form now rivals the terrifying Underlings of Nightmares and Fear. His head hangs low, back hunched as his claws gouge the floor, sending fresh cracks through the quaking structure.

I drop to my knees before him, my wings instinctively spreading to shield us from debris as the ceiling threatens to collapse. "Jeremy, stop it—stop this." I invoke his name like a spell, praying our sire bond and the ancient Power of Naming will end this madness. I grab his face, forcing him to meet my eyes, but it's too late. Power ripples beneath his skin, the walls and floor trembling as veins of Holy Hellfire split the club open. But he isn't stopping. My authority over him crumbles to nothing.

I have no control.

I. Have. No. Control.

When his eyes finally meet with mine, it's like we're the only two creatures in the world. Damned to serve an archaic evil against our better judgement. Damned to forfeit our humanity. And for a moment, I see him again—the *real* him. The sweet, innocent angel who saw beauty beneath the cracks and dared to love a demon.

It's quickly replaced with pure, utter loathing. When he finally speaks, the words tear through my already-broken heart.

"To Hell with you and to Hell with Bad Decisions."

Jeremy's monstrous roar echoes through the club as Holy Hellfire erupts from the floor's cracks, surging like geysers of destruction. Despite my fury, despite the anguish buried deep in my heart, I still search for Cherry.

It seems even betrayal won't break the bond between

Prime and Underling. I wish the same could be said for the monster I've made.

My Prime struggles to his feet, gripping the last piece of furniture still standing amid Jeremy's inferno. I watch his hands curl as he summons his teleportation power; I instantly sprint toward him, weaving through the flames.

"Don't you fucking dare, you coward," October snarls as she notices the crimson clouds of Cherry's demonic teleportation swirling around him. She lunges for his ankle before he can vanish. I take one last look at Jeremy before seizing October's leather sleeve.

There's no saving him now.

Leaving him to die is the last bad decision I'll ever make.

In seconds, we vanish.

Away from the neon-lit purgatory I called home for forty years.

Away from Bad Decisions.

My body hits cold asphalt as the California sun sears my skin. I lift my head to survey our location, noting we're just across the street from the wreckage. I quickly duck behind the nearest dumpster, shielding myself from human eyes as I channel my glamour to conceal my horns, wings, and tail. My reflection in a storefront window shows an ordinary redhead with singed clothing and soot-streaked skin.

Behind my reflection, an inferno rages, and a gasp catches in my throat. No sight of Jeremy, not a single trace. Just a Hollywood strip club and motel burning to the ground and collapsing into a heap of smoldering rubble.

I'll never forgive myself for what I've done to him. In the end, embracing my selfish, demonic nature destroyed everything. My businesses, my relationships, my reputation. Decades of fighting my humanity—all for nothing but a burning pile of broken dreams.

Cherry coughs as he brushes debris and cinders off his once-immaculate ensemble.

"Congratulations, darling. You single-handedly created the deadliest weapon known to demonkind. Daddy will sooner rip that lovely head from your body before he *ever* considers making you a Prime."

Cherry's words cut deeper than any blade could reach, piercing the armor I've worn for decades. As if the universe needed to twist the knife further, my eyes find October backing away slowly, her body already poised for flight, just as she's done for millennia. Our gazes lock, and I realize we've reached a pivotal moment, the crossroads where we part ways forever. It finally hits me: I've lost it all.

I've lost my chance. My club. My motel. My friends. *My* Jeremy.

And now, I'm about to lose October Winters.

I open my mouth to speak to her—the Hellion harlot Hell-Bound to the most powerful entity in existence.

But she's gone before I can get a word out, hopping into that cursed red Camaro that appears at her command. Its engine revs, making the ground shake, and she takes one last look at me before driving off. In her eyes, I see something that makes my heart stutter. It's the same thing lurking behind Cherry's bravado, the very same thing that's been haunting me since I hopped on that train to California over a century ago.

Fear.

Cherry's right. Damn it all to Hell, he's *always* right.

The future of demonkind hangs in the balance, the scales tipping toward oblivion with each passing moment. Thousands of years of hiding in plain sight, decades of building sanctuary on this mortal plane—all of it on the precipice of annihilation.

And I have no one to blame but myself.

EPILOGUE

Live and Let Die

EPILOGUE
LIVE AND LET DIE

JEREMY ROACHE

Our Father, who art in Heaven, hallowed be Thy name—*ah, fuck it.* Who am I kidding? God isn't listening to me. Not anymore.

A puddle of rainwater soaks my feet as I back away from the explosion I caused. Bad Decisions and The Starlight are gone now—metal beams tear into asphalt, termite-eaten wood have long crumbled to nothing. That neon sign—the girl with the pitchfork—lies shattered against the rubble, split in half like everything else I touch. Hordes of people swarm the corner of La Brea and Hollywood in broad daylight, news vans screeching to a halt as some beautiful reporter clutches her coat and microphone, demanding the perfect shot from her cameraman.

That's all this is to them—a perfect Hollywood scene.

The strip club on one of the most famous boulevards burns with no hope for survivors.

Because of me.

I slink into the shadows like the coward I am, retreating to the alley where I first met *her*. That memory will rot in my brain until I die. The night I failed Declan. The night I proved what a worthless piece of shit I really am.

But this? This massacre I've caused?

This makes that night look like a fucking joke.

I shouldn't care about Charlie and Indigo. I shouldn't think about the human girls under *her* employment, the ones who were probably coerced, trapped, believing they have no choice. Monsters like me don't get to feel empathy, not anymore. Not after I allowed myself to fall for a demon.

I've got no destiny left to fulfill, no higher purpose. Just this rotten life to live.

Cursed. Monstrous. Alone.

Completely fucking alone.

Declan's as good as dead—eternally bound to that evil witch. Did she even survive the blast? Is her body crushed somewhere beneath the rubble I created along with the mentor I failed to save?

I can't think about it. I won't.

I press my back against the cold concrete wall, dragging my clawed hands over my face, feeling the veins spider-webbed into my cheeks. I trace each crack with my fingertip, just like I did the night she and I…

No. Don't think about her.

My hands are something straight out of a nightmare —*my* nightmare made flesh. Boney and grotesque, with white, razor-sharp nails curving like crescents. The veins crawling up my limbs look like fractured earth bleeding hellfire, and the wings? The tail? I can't even recognize the parts of me that made me…me.

How do I turn this shit off?

How can I glamour myself like other demons when I'm barely even that? When I'm just some failed experiment?

I can't turn to her—the redheaded monster who saw right through me, who knew exactly how weak and lost I was. I should have seen her for what she really is: a lying, self-serving woman who saw an opportunity and took every advantage.

I can't help but wonder if this was all worth it to her.

Who am I kidding? Of course it was. Destroying me was worth the chance at becoming a Prime.

And then there's Cherry. The sire of my…what? Broodline? I can't even stomach using the terminology I've spent my entire life studying. Primes sired Underlings and Underlings their own. Is that what I am now? Some bastard creation—an Underling of an Underling? Where in the demonic hierarchy does a freak like me even belong?

Probably at the very fucking bottom, next to Hellspawn and dirt.

I can't turn to him. He's just as diabolical as the rest of them.

That only leaves…

"Jeremy," a voice calls to me. The name strangles me like a pronged collar, yanking me back when all I want is to disappear, to crawl away somewhere. The world needs to be safe from the monster I've become, but I can't escape it. I hear him loud and clear.

"Jeremy, help me," he calls again, this time more strained. My ears perk in the direction of my caller as my body involuntarily moves. I desperately try to take control of my legs, to stop and survey the damage before diving headfirst into an electric hazard and human exposure nightmare, but I know why I can't stop. It's one of the oldest rules in the book.

My name is a weapon to be used against me.

I reach for a giant concrete slab, one of the exterior walls of Bad Decisions plastered with crass posters of half-naked women. My new strength allows me to hurl the slab away as I frantically dig through debris, unhinged doors, and broken glass, my hands bleeding black from the sharp edges.

I keep digging until I finally find him.

Vincent Thane.

The excommunicated demon hunter who gave me a chance when no one else would. The only person who believed I was worth saving.

Buried under the rubble of my bad decisions.

"Vincent," I choke out his name, my voice cracking and unfamiliar. He's paler than death itself, his once-vivid blue eyes now glassy and gray, life slipping away with each shallow breath. I see him for what he is now—what I imagine all demons see: a flickering aura of black and white, growing dimmer with every passing second. Broken glass crunches beneath my knees as I pull his head into my lap with trembling hands. "I'm so sorry. I didn't mean for this to happen—not to you."

"I've overstayed my welcome, Sparky." He uses *her* nickname for me now—not out of mockery, but because he knows the consequences of my real one. "My time was up long ago. I just needed one last shot at atonement before crossing over."

Tears bite at the corners of my eyes. There's nothing I can do. I've failed him just like I failed Declan. "Do you know where you're going?"

Vincent coughs up a familiar shimmer of Nephilim blood. "Haven't a clue. Most of my life was spent fighting for the greater good, fulfilling my destiny. The rest of my life? Tied to the three darkest creatures of all. And you want to know something?"

I nod quickly, gripping his hand as it turns cold.

"I enjoyed that darkness for a time. There was...freedom in it, however fleeting but so very flawed. It seems my whole life has just been an endless succession of bad decisions." A hint of a smile creeps across his lips, reaching those piercing eyes. "I don't know where I'm going, don't know if what I did will undo decades of wrong, or if the Creator will even grant me forgiveness. But whether I'm going upstairs or down, I'll go in peace knowing you didn't end up just like me."

The words hit like a blade, and I finally release the sob I've been choking back. "But Vincent, I'm a demon. That's worse than death."

"You're not *just* a demon, though. You're the first Nephilim demon. There is still angel in you yet. Don't let go of that. Don't let the darkness win."

"You're the only person I've got left. After you go, I'm…*completely* alone."

"No, you're not." He lifts his hand to cup my cheek, fingers tracing the fresh cracks mapping my skin. "Our family tree is a strong one. It dates back millennia, to the Creator's first angels. Most of the Order's holy lineage has diluted over the years as it expanded farther from the source. But ours? Ours is the most potent and the most susceptible to corruption."

My heart lurches to a crawl as heaviness fills my chest. I search his eyes, swallowing the acid creeping up my throat. "O-ours?"

"Ours. We share a father. The Archangel of Innocence."

"Why didn't you tell me sooner?"

He winces a smile again. "Would it have changed anything?"

"We could have gotten out of Los Angeles—could have found our own way. Away from the demons, the Order—I could have taken care of you. We could have been free. Together."

"Free," he repeats with another cough. "You know better than anyone that none of us are ever truly free, brother."

I can't find any words of comfort, nothing to soothe the pain he feels or right the wrongs I've done. All I can do is huff a laugh through my tears and bring his cold knuckles to my lips. "Some family strength we've got. Both of us fell for the darkness so easily."

"Nothing's as black and white as they make it seem. We Nephilim are built for failure as much as we are for glory—just another failed experiment. But your story isn't over. You're going to change the world."

"C-change the world?" I stumble over my words. "How the fuck am I supposed to do that? There's a target on my back—Cherry and Reagan want to deliver me to the Devil."

Her name stings like poison on my tongue.

"Beat them to it. That vampire girl—the one with the purple hair." Vincent's voice grows weaker.

"Indigo?" I ask, my brows knitting.

"She belongs to Greed. Not right now, of course—she's still under the thrall of Cherry. But she and the bartender got away. You need to find her and let her take you to her Prime." His eyes bore into mine with desperate urgency.

"I don't understand. Why go from one Prime to another? What can Greed do for me?" My voice cracks with confusion.

"Don't underestimate him. He's an impulsive, hungry beast. He will stop at nothing to destroy his brothers—and he'll destroy himself in the process. You're a powerful commodity right now, brother. The Primes will be fighting over you like dogs over scraps of meat. Align yourself with the highest bidder and destroy them from the inside out." Vincent grips my arm with surprising strength for someone so close to death. "Find the vampire and make a deal with Greed. Trust me, Jeremy."

A dull ache tugs at me again at the mention of my name. All I can muster is a slow, deliberate nod.

Vincent fades faster now, his eyes rolling back with every blink, glittering blood trailing down his chin in scarlet ribbons. Suddenly, he chuckles—a broken, breathless sound that only deepens my confusion. "What was that silly rule in the book? 'Be killed by a demon and ascend to the Heavens to carry on the work of the Creator from above?'"

The passage spills from my lips without a second thought. "'*He who is struck down by the forces of darkness shall rise to the Heavens above, there to serve the Creator from the celestial throne.*'"

"That's it. So, what do you say, brother? Will you do me the honor?"

"Y-you want me to kill you?"

"Consider it a mercy. Or payback for all I've done. However you see fit."

I can't do it. I can't kill him—not when I've just found him again. Dread claws at my chest as the impossible choice tears me apart, but cold logic cuts through every desperate thought.

He's dying anyway. At least this way, he has a chance to Ascend.

We can only hope it's enough.

I pull my brother into one final embrace, sobbing tears into his salt-and-pepper hair, whispering one last apology before I place my trembling hand over his chest.

And then, he looks at me one last time…and smiles. "Give them Hell, Jeremy."

I nod once, tears still streaming. *This is mercy*, I remind myself. *Soon, he will be free.*

With viperine swiftness, I drive my claws into my brother's chest and crush his heart until it crumbles to ash in my grasp. I fight back tears as his body dissolves into silvery sand, scattering on the wind and leaving me alone with nothing but a promise and a new destiny.

On unsteady legs, I finally rise to survey the devastation I've caused. No sign of Reagan. No Cherry. No October Winters. All that remains is my shattered heart and a burning need for vengeance.

I owe Declan Lovejoy that much. I owe Vincent Thane everything.

The Thirteen Prime Evils *will* know death. One by

one, I will make them suffer as they've made me, and I will savor every second.

And when the last of them falls, I will destroy the one who made them.

I will destroy the Devil…and that fucking witch.

READY FOR MORE?

The Hellion Harlot Collection (or Hellion-verse) is a multiple-book collection centered around October Winters and the badass ladies she meets along the way. Buckle up for thrilling, fast-paced novels, comics, and novellas welcoming you to the darker side of storytelling.

Indigo Moon and **Charlie Maynard** will return in the riveting third installment of the Hellion Harlot series. Running for their lives and haunted by their pasts, two demonic hearts bound by tragedy must survive an ancient evil—and each other.

From the mystical land of Los Angeles, California, Nikkita Bell is an author-illustrator who has carved out a distinctive niche where literature meets visual story-telling. Specializing in adult dark paranormal and urban fantasy with horror and romantic elements and a gothic neo-noir flair, each of Bell's novels become an immersive experience where readers encounter dangerous, high-stakes, and fast-paced narratives through captivating illustrations and music-inspired themes.

Through her groundbreaking hybrid graphic novel format, Bell welcomes you to the gothic side of story-telling filled with morally complex anti-heroines who embrace their darker natures and never apologize for it. She has built her brand on a simple but powerful premise: villainous books about villainous women doing villainous things.

When she isn't crafting the next femme fatale to follow to Hell and back, Nikkita enjoys orchestral music, pretending to sing opera, and snuggling with her husband and two cats, Ciri and Yennefer.

Looking for more bookish updates, adventures, and kitty escapades? Follow Nikkita on Instagram, Tiktok, and Threads @nikkitabell, and don't forget to sign up for *The Hellion Harlot Club*, the Nikkita Bell newsletter, at nikkitabell.com!

DEMONIC GLOSSARY
THE THIRTEEN PRIME EVILS

Also referred to as 'The Big Thirteen' or 'The Primes,' the Thirteen Prime Evils are the head demons and sons of the Devil who have dominion over specific vices. Each Prime has Underlings that consist of High-Level, Mid-Level, Lesser, and Hellspawn (imps) minions that do their bidding throughout the human plane. Most demons live in their own level or realm in Hell, but a select few have a permanent foot on the human plane, where they may reign in a city or cities of their choosing.

DEMON OF CHAOS

This Prime is the embodiment of disorder, often manipulating and feeding off of human emotions and sowing confusion and disarray. Often appears as an unsettling, tumultuous, disjointed figure often compared to a swarm of bees. Chaos typically feeds on the aftermath of the events caused by majority of the demons, specifically Violence and Destruction.

DEMON OF DEBAUCHERY

Currently inhabiting Los Angeles, CA. Also known as Cherry (ala Debau*chery*). The master of excess, forbidden pleasures, desires, temptations, and indulgences. Occupies the seat of Hollywood, CA and the entertainment industry. Often appears in human form as an avant-garde, handsome young man in flashy clothing and accessories. Very colorful personality. Part of the Golden Trio (Deception, Debauchery, Greed).

DEMON OF DECEPTION

Currently inhabiting Las Vegas, NV, Deception is known as the 'cover up' or the 'cleaner' demon, Deception is typically in charge of protecting the exposure of the Underworld and supernatural creatures. He, along with Debauchery and Greed, have a permanent spot on the human plane and does not typically inhabit his realm of Hell. Deception is often associated with law enforcement (dirty cops), ponzy schemes, con-artists, thieves, etc. Underlings can take form of snakes, and primarily shapeshift and teleport in order to deceive. Typically causes unsolved murders. Part of the Golden Trio (Deception, Debauchery, Greed).

DEMON OF DESTRUCTION

One of the two oldest, most archaic demons on the list that isn't physically related to the Devil, and instead was an entity created by the forces nature and then given a corporeal and magical host through the Devil's power. The Demon of Destruction holds dominion over natural disasters (e.g. volcanic eruptions, tsunamis, hurricanes, earthquakes etc.) and is commonly worshipped by shamans and druids. Unlike Pestilence, this demon does take corporeal form and visits the human realm in the event of a large disaster occurrence and his form changes depending on the type of disaster. He specifically enjoys being in the thick of the disaster rather than sending Underlings to do it for him.

DEMON OF DOMINATION

Domination has played a bigger role in historical events and has manipulated the rise and fall of empires, monarchs, and kingdoms. Responsible for acts of slavery, brutal dictatorships, the implementation of caste systems, and royalty. While some believe that they were hand-chosen by God to lead nations, they were actually chosen by demonic intervention and manipulated through the power of this Prime. Rumor has it that he physically possessed history's most infamous humans.

DEMON OF DOUBT

Doubt is a shadowy presence that is not often seen in a corporeal form but is often seen on the human plane by other supernaturals (invisible to humans). He often invades human minds to sow paranoia, inadequacy, lack of faith, trust, and confidence. This demon is typically the cause of crippling anxiety and indecision, and often causes humans to be paralyzed by their own doubts. Often works hand-in-hand with Deception and the Fear and Nightmare twins.

DEMON OF ENVY

Similar to Debauchery, Envy is one of the more flamboyant and avant-garde Primes. Often the cause of one of the greatest sins of all, he is also depicted as immature and takes the form of a petulant child. He feeds on jealousy and resentment and turns admiration into hatred. He manipulates spite, covetousness, and his Underlings have the ability to steal the happiness from their victims.

DEMON OF GREED

Currently inhabiting Manhattan, NY, Greed is the typical money-grubbing Prime, Greed is the most intelligent and strategic of the 13. Often depicted as having dominion over politicians, financial institutions, and feeds on the desires of a human's pursuit of wealth. Greed acts as if he is better than the other Primes, and often pushes them around. He currently has a seat in Manhattan, NY and oversees major corporations and influences people of power. Part of the Golden Trio (Deception, Debauchery, Greed).

DEMON OF MISFORTUNE

Often referred to as the 'unlucky' demon or the 'bad luck charm,' Misfortune is the most recluse of the Primes, often keeping to his realm in Hell and using his Underlings to do his bidding on the human plane. He is the reason 'things randomly go wrong.' His Underlings take form of physical objects that act as bad luck charms and tethers him to the human plane without physically being on it. Typically worshipped by practicers of voodoo and hoodoo.

DEMONS OF NIGHTMARES AND FEAR

Also known as 'The Twins,' this demon is two in one body (therefore considered one solid entity despite their dominion over two evils). They often appear on the human plane in the form of the viewer's worst fear, but two headed. Their Underlings are best known for possessing children, and using them to do their bidding. When humans are asleep and being fed on by Nightmare Demons, they enter the Nightmare Realm in which they are vulnerable to soul consumption. Nightmare and Fear

Feedings are usually what cause exhaustion, fatigue, and phobias in humans.

DEMON OF PESTILENCE

One of the two oldest, most archaic demons on the list that isn't physically related to the Devil, and instead was an entity created by the forces nature and then given a corporeal and magical host through the Devil's power. Responsible for sickness, diseases, and pandemics. Has not been seen on the human plane in centuries, but operates through his own realm in Hell and uses Underlings to spread maladies.

DEMON OF VENGEANCE

Manifests as a man who appears battle-weary with scars. He typically feeds off of humans' desire for revenge and turning justice into cruelty. He manipulates grudges, feuds, and retaliations. Often seen on the human realm working hand-in-hand with Violence, Envy, and Greed. He, himself, has a few feuds with his own brothers, and it is rumored that he does not favor Destruction and Pestilence due to their natural ties to the world rather than their sinful or emotional dominion.

DEMON OF VIOLENCE

The most powerful of the demons, Violence is known as the most ruthless of all the Primes. He is the cause of war, anger/rage, and physical and psychological harm. Of all the Primes, he has the largest army of Underlings at his disposal and he primarily operates from his realm in Hell. He is rarely seen on the human plane unless there is a mass world-wide event that he prefers to feed off of (WWI, WWII).

ACKNOWLEDGEMENTS

I still can't believe that I'm here again, 10 months after the release of my debut novel, writing a brand new acknowledgement section again. The person I was when I wrote the first one is vastly different from the one I am right now, and it's all thanks to the incredible people who held my hand during this journey. I didn't know what to expect when embarking on this journey for a second time. I didn't expect to fall in love with my craft so much, and in turn, forge relationships with readers who turned into friends and family in such a short time. Here's my love letter to each of you:

NIKITA:

I've spent months trying to curate the perfect message of acknowledgement to you, but I don't think I'll ever be able to properly articulate how much you mean to me.

So, the only way I can do so is by gifting this book to you on your birthday. You're the friend I never knew I needed, a mere carbon copy of me in all the ways that matter, the light at the end of a dark tunnel, my voice of reason, and the Reagan to my October. I wrote this book to immortalize you, to remind you that you are seen, respected, and loved. Thank you for being my muse, for holding my hand through the scariest moments, and for reminding me why I do what I do. I can't imagine existing in a world where you don't.

KRISTA A:

To my beautiful birthday twin, the kindred spirit who has talked me out of one too many boughts of imposter syndrome, the long-lost sister who championed me on the days I couldn't champion myself... Thank you. Thank you for listening, for showing up for both of us every single day, and for kindling the flame of my creativity. You're one of the reasons I saw this book through, and on days where I didn't believe in myself, you always did. A friendship like yours is hard to find, and I thank my lucky stars every single day that this little Hellion world brought us together. I'd be lost without you, and I love you forever. Buckle up for book 3, because she's all yours.

STEPHANIE S:

If I ever need a reminder of what true strength and unrelenting friendship looks like, it will always be you. We survived a grueling season together this year, and it grew us closer as sisters. You've been with me since day one, always there to talk me out of my bad ideas, reminding me to put myself first and never apologize for it. Reagan lives in you, my darling Stephanie, through her wit, loyalty, and pure strength. You inspire me every single day, and I am incredibly proud to call you my friend. I couldn't have written this book without you, nor could I have ever mustered the courage to see my crazy ideas through. Thank you for being my sounding board, my conscience, and my guide. I love you forever, thank you for always seeing me.

MARY CATHERINE S:

Who would have thought that holding a door open for a stranger would lead to such a beautiful, spiritual friendship that was written in the stars? My MC, you've shown up for me in the last year in ways others haven't. Your quiet strength, wisdom beyond your years, and unwavering friendship have kept me steadfast and true to myself, and for that, I will always be grateful. You're the adorable bunny to my snuggly kitty, and I love you very much!

EMILIE S:

To my real life October Winters, thank you for standing by my side during this whole year and process! Thank you for bringing my dreams to life, for showing me what kindness and compassion is, and for coming through for me when I needed it the most. You've given me motivation, strength, and never fail to put a smile on my face, and I am so honored to have met you and hugged you in real life! Your friendship is a gift, and I'll treasure it always.

SAM & MAGGIE

To the girls who came into my life when I least expected it and left the largest mark… What would I do without you both? You've sacrificed hours for me, spent time in my home, and never failed to check in on me and lift me up on the days that feel a little too low. Sam, thank you for dreaming with me. Maggie, thank you for being my cheerleader. I love you both so much, and can't wait to make beautiful memories together in the months to come!

CHARLIE P:

To the real life Bartender Charlie, the brother I wish I always had and finally do have, thank you for coming into my life when you did. Meeting you in person and having you join the Hellion family has been one of the greatest treasures in my life, and you've inspired me so much with this world! Thank you for being by my side, for driving 10 hours to see me this year, and for being the greatest friend I could possibly ask for.

CHERISH G:

Will there ever be enough words to accurately describe how much you mean to me? How it felt to cry together at the airport? How that moment felt when we realized we couldn't bear to be apart now that we've met in real life? Never. They will always be these unforgettable memories, the little moments that remind us that true magic exists through friendship. Thank you for being my constant, and I am so so so incredibly proud of the author you are. I can't wait to give back to you what you've given to me when it's your turn to shine in the sun!

JAYLA M:

I'll never forget the day I met you, sitting front row at my first ever bookish panel in Arizona, smiling as I talked about villainous women doing villainous shit. I never imagined that you'd become like a sister to me, who would spend hours and hours voice messaging back and forth with me, who would explore a Sleepy Hollow cemetery with me, and dream big with me. Jayla, I am so proud of the woman you are, and even prouder to call you my friend. Thank you for cheering me on, giving me the strength to keep going, and being the greatest mamacita in the world! I adore you!

ALI L:

To one of the biggest Reagan fans out there, to the girl who gave me the inspiration for Cherry's appearance, and the girl who always has inspiration ready for me whenever I need it… I hope you absolutely adore this book! You've been such a bright, shining star for me during the journey of writing this book, and I love you!

THE HOUSE OF BELL (MY EDITING TEAM)

This book would not be what it is without my incredible editing team. To **Megan**, who shows up every single day for her clients and gives 300% of herself into her work, thank you for making this story the best it can be. To **Alexa**, who's been on this journey with me since book 1 and believed in me when I didn't believe in myself, thank you for giving me a chance and being as excited about my work as I am. To **Slasher**, the compassionate soul who fell into my lap when I needed her most, thank you for giving me the strength and motivation to keep on keeping on. And to my beautiful **Sarah**, a pillar of strength during the most dangerous storm, thank you for never, ever faltering, and for seeing me through yet another Hellion. I love you!

THE MARVELOUS MR. BELL:

To the king of my world, my one true love and partner in crime… Here we are again, buggy. In many ways, this book was the amalgamation of both of us, a true example of what happens when two minds come together to create something beautiful. Thank you for inspiring every chapter, for walking me through every detail, for fact-checking, researching, brainstorming, and spending many-a car ride agonizing over the details of this story with me. You are not just my husband, you're an extension of me, and I hope you can see that through the words I write. In many ways, Jeremy and Reagan are you and me. You're the sweet, innocent, kind soul who saw something in a girl who may smile on the outside but feel broken on the inside. Thank you for healing me through this process, for being a business partner, confidant, and greatest soulmate a girl could ask for. I couldn't live this life without you, nor would I ever want to. Thank you for following me to the moon and back.